DUKE OF RATH
SEVEN DUKES OF SIN
BOOK ONE

MARIAH STONE

Stone Publishing

This is a work of fiction. Names, characters, places, and incidents either are the products of the author's imagination or are used fictitiously. Any resemblance to actual persons, living or dead, businesses, companies, events, or locales is entirely coincidental.

© 2024 Mariah Stone. All rights reserved.

Cover design by Qamber Designs and Media

Editing by Beth Attwood

Proofreading by Leigh Teetzel

All rights reserved. This book or parts thereof may not be reproduced in any form, stored in any retrieval system, or transmitted in any form by any means—electronic, mechanical, photocopy, recording, or otherwise—without prior written permission of the publisher. For permission requests, contact the publisher at http:\\mariahstone.com

GET A FREE MARIAH STONE BOOK!

Join Mariah's mailing list to be the first to know of new releases, free books, special prices, and other author giveaways.

freehistoricalromancebooks.com

ALSO BY MARIAH STONE

MARIAH'S TIME TRAVEL ROMANCE SERIES

- Called by a Highlander
- Called by a Viking
- Called by a Pirate
- Fated

MARIAH'S REGENCY ROMANCE SERIES

- Dukes and Secrets
- Seven Dukes of Sin

VIEW ALL OF MARIAH'S BOOKS IN READING ORDER

Scan the QR code for all ebooks, paperbacks, and audiobooks.

"I loved her against reason, against promise, against peace, against hope, against happiness, against all discouragement that could be."
—Charles Dickens, *Great Expectations*

"But for all these misdeeds, I am responsible to God and God alone."
—Fyodor Dostoevsky, *Crime and Punishment*

The Seven Dukes of Sin Credo

One:

All desires are natural...no matter how wicked.

1

Rath Hall, March 1814

Blood dripped onto the gravel path, leaving a trail as Dorian Perrin, the Duke of Rath, strode out into another day of torment. His Irish wolfhound, Titan, trotted by his side, their steps rustling in the silence of his ancestral estate. The black outlines of barren trees stretched their thin branches through the mist like claws as cool, damp air sliced through his shirt to his hot, sweaty skin.

Good. He deserved every pain.

Dorian's torn knuckles on his left hand bled freely, while his right remained gloved, concealing scars that served as a constant reminder of the duel that haunted him—evidence of the most horrific thing he had ever done. He removed the glove only for his boxing sessions, as he had this morning. Twelve years encased in a glove hadn't done his scarred skin any good.

Titan kept trying to lick the blood off Dorian's exposed knuckles with his pink tongue. The dog's wiry gray hair was springy under Dorian's palm as he absently stroked the wolfhound. One of Titan's eyes was milky white, the other black and shiny. He reached Dorian's waist, and his long, sharp teeth made even the footmen wary.

On the cut lawn, a groom held Erebus, Dorian's massive black Thoroughbred, in place, the stallion snorting and pawing the grass as they waited. Dorian laid his gloved right hand on Erebus's neck, feeling blood ooze beneath the leather.

"Dorian, dearest," came a high, feminine voice from behind him, and Dorian turned, swiftly putting his hands behind his back.

Lady Buchanan, his deceased mama's sister, stood before him with his sister, Chastity.

The dark walls of Rath Hall emerged from the mist behind them—three stories of weathered stone, covered in lichen and moss. Tall pointed paned windows pierced the façade with their leaded glass. Turrets flanked the structure, their spires dissolving into the fog above.

"Aunt," he said in greeting. "Sister."

The morning chill stuck needles into his skin, and his forehead felt cold and clammy as his hair, misted from exercise, stuck to it. But that was not nearly enough pain and discomfort to distract the beast within him.

His aunt's eyes, gray, kind, and intelligent, took him in with concern. "Will you not break your fast with us? I'm only here for the day."

A lady in her sixties who still preferred dresses with fitted bodices and full skirts—the fashion of the previous era—his aunt had arrived yesterday to stay overnight on her way to London for the opening of the season in a few weeks. Rath Hall was only one hour away from London, an exclusive location that was close enough to enjoy both the country and the city.

Titan sat down by Dorian's boots and gave an impatient whine.

His sister, Chastity—shockingly brilliant and happily unmarried—was twenty-eight, four years younger than Dorian. She was as dark haired as he, with striking blue eyes shining behind spectacles. Unlike what most ducal sisters would wear, she was dressed in a simple gray gown, her hair in a tight and functional chignon.

"I assumed you would want to take breakfast in your chamber," he lied. "And Chastity knows I go for a ride every morning."

He felt blood drip from his hands to fall on the grass behind his feet. Chastity's gaze slid over his bod, stopped on the crimson drops, then followed their trail from the grass to the gravel path on which she stood.

Her face paled. "Dorian, you're hurt!" she exclaimed, moving towards him.

He stepped back, bumping into the horse's side, but Chastity didn't stop. She flew past the groom, and grasped Dorian's left hand before he could stop her. She gasped, looking at the bloody splits on his knuckles.

His aunt gasped as well, and he winced. He should have bandaged them. Or ridden away faster.

"What did you do?" Chastity demanded.

He felt his teeth gnashing against each other. "I overdid it with boxing, that's all. There's no need to cluck."

Earlier this morning, he'd driven his fists into the well-worn leather of the punching bag in his training room for hours. Each punch hurt to the bone, the taste of sweat on his upper lip salty, the coppery scent of blood satisfying. The constant pain of his right hand was replaced with a sharper agony, which felt sweet.

His aunt hurried towards him, skirts rustling. "I'm here for only one night, and you're doing this? Beating yourself into a bloody pulp?"

His hand inside his glove was slippery and hot, pulsating with pain. He was breathing hard, struggling to take enough air into his lungs.

"I did not know you did this," she continued. "Chastity, were you aware?"

Chastity shook her head. "Only that he trained in the mornings. Not what he did... Dorian, why haven't you at least bandaged these?"

He swallowed. The wretched truth was he wanted to feel more pain. Every drop could bring him closer to his atonement. "I'm fine." He tore his hand away from Chastity.

"Let me get the nearest medicine basket," she said, all business. "My antiseptic... The wounds need to be treated right away, to avoid rot."

Rot...

Oh yes. He knew how dangerous rot was and what the sight of his blood did to his sister. She'd almost lost him once. That was the reason she had become so invested in medical research.

Lady Buchanan's eyes filled with tears. "Look at yourself—hiding from your family, punishing your body, isolating yourself. Why are you doing this?"

Dorian met her gaze, his jaw clenched. How could he explain the demons that haunted him? The guilt that gnawed at his soul? "I am content as I am, Aunt," he ground out. "I have no need for society's frivolities or familial obligations."

She shook her head. "My dear boy. You should be embracing the joys of life—finding a loving wife, starting a family, living out your happiest years."

Dorian turned away, his shoulders tensing. The weight of her words settled heavily upon him. A wife? A family? Happiness? Such things seemed distant and unattainable. How could he, with hands stained by blood and a heart blackened by rage, ever hope to deserve such blessings?

"You know not of what you speak," he muttered, his tone harsh even to his own ears.

Chastity's gaze dropped to his gloved hand. "I know you can barely write with your right hand, and yet you keep beating it into bloody pulp? It's as though you're punishing yourself for something, brother!"

Dorian's head snapped up. "Mind your own business, Chastity."

Tears welled in Chastity's eyes as she squared her shoulders. No, he was too harsh with her. She didn't deserve this. His anger melted into a gnawing guilt.

"Do not snap at your sister," his aunt commanded. "I meant what I said. What you must do is marry. You must father an heir. It's not just your duty as a duke. It will also be good for you. Love can heal you, nephew. If not your wife's, then your love for your child."

He let out a low growl.

"Do not growl," said his aunt. "You're not a lion. And you know I'm right."

"Aunt, I swear—"

"I know I've been talking about this for years, but who else would, with both your parents being gone? You know your mama, my dear sister, would say the same were she alive. She would! And your babies will be like my grandbabies."

He let out a long sigh, making a conscious effort to not growl. "Aunt, I have told you many times, I do not want a wife. I do not want children."

His aunt stepped forward, making her eyes big and teary like those of an abandoned kitten, and leaned towards him, laying her hand on his shoulder. "A grandniece or -nephew would make me so very happy, dearest. Who knows how many more years I have on this Earth? I'd like to spend them rocking and playing with a grandbaby."

Goddamn it…

The only way to get to him was to make him feel pity for the woman who was like a mother to him. His own mama had passed away when he was twelve, and he hadn't seen her for several years before that—his papa had sent her away to "make a man of the future duke and not a soppy, misbehaving brat."

He owed his humanity—what there was of it—to his aunt.

He would move mountains for these two women.

"I'll give it my consideration," he muttered.

His aunt beamed at him. "That's all I ask. Now, we won't stop your exercise. Go and ride your hellish steed."

"What about your hands?" asked Chastity.

"His name is Erebus," he mumbled, still somewhat speechless at his weakness in the face of his aunt's emotional manipulation and the irritating feeling of joy at seeing her happiness. "And my hands are fine."

He hated the look of helpless anguish on his sister's face as she and his aunt turned and retreated into the house. But he didn't care about his wounds. If he died of rot, even better. His misery would finally end.

He mounted Erebus, and the groom stepped away. He was grateful to finally be alone, with just his horse and his loyal hound. Dorian clicked his tongue and spurred Erebus, and they flew, with Titan a little behind, his strong legs pumping.

He galloped through the foggy countryside, his muscles burning, rising slightly from the saddle as his hips moved in sync with the horse's gait, absorbing the motion. Dark silhouettes of gnarled trees loomed through the fog overhead, old and lifeless, just like he felt inside. He relished the sensation of the wind cutting through him. The speed. The freedom. A wild flight.

Dorian's fury burned within him as he rode, seeking solace in the intensity of his physical exertion. Yet no matter how far or fast he rode, he could not escape what was in his head... what never left him.

The vivid memory of the day when his wrath had led him to take Mr. John Rose's life in a duel...

His suspicion of John sabotaging his pistol.

The assurance of both his and John's seconds that nothing was untoward.

And then the explosion of the gun in his hand.

Wrath consuming him, taking over him in an unimaginable force.

The fight... John's gun firing... His body slackening against Dorian.

Dead.

When Dorian finally returned to Rath Hall and dismounted next to the pond at the back of the garden, his clothing was drenched with sweat. His breath pumped out of him, blending into the cold, foggy air. Titan was breathing hard, too, as he walked around the pond's shore sniffing at the overgrown grass.

Dorian's muscles ached, which was exactly what he wanted. Yet his mind remained restless, haunted by memories of that fateful morning twelve years ago when he became a murderer. Though it was March, and the water was bitterly cold, Dorian took off his boots, ran a few steps, and plunged into the pond's murky depths.

The shock pierced through his very soul, but he welcomed it. The icy embrace of the pond enveloped him, its numbing touch creeping through his veins. Each stroke felt like a battle against the relentless grip of the past. Dark, silty water clouded his vision. He continued swimming, his limbs growing heavier with each passing moment, his chest tightening. Could he ever escape this darkness? Could he ever be free? he wondered, his heart heavy with sorrow and regret.

The icy water clung to Dorian's skin like a shroud, chilling him to the bone as he dragged himself up the muddy bank. He collapsed, gasping for breath, his chest heaving.

As he blinked the water out of his eyes, a movement caught his attention in the distance—two riders he recognized at once, even through the fog. These dukes were his closest allies, bound together by their shared sins and secrets. As he stood up, water running off him to puddle on the ground, they rode closer and stopped before him.

"There you are, Dorian," Lucien, the Duke of Luhst, called out as he descended from his horse, his voice amused as he surveyed his friend's drenched form. His golden hair was accentuated by the yellow patterns on his coat, his family crest bearing an elegant stag. "Engaging in your customary pursuits, I see. Enough. We've come to fetch you back to the city. Your absence has been noted."

Next to Lucien, Constantine Buccleigh, the Duke of Pryde, dismounted as well, standing tall and proud. He was clad in indigo, the wolf on his crest a testament to his fierce loyalty and honor. He hadn't changed much in the past twelve years, apart from growing colder, wearing his pride like suit of armor. However, since that terrible morning, he had become a friend, Dorian's closest after Lucien.

"Where are the rest of the seven?" asked Dorian.

He meant the rest of their brotherhood—the Seven Dukes of Sin, as they playfully called themselves, since they seemed to embody the seven deadly sins. Even their names fit: Rath, Luhst, Pryde, Enveigh, Irevrence, Eccess, and Fortyne.

"Waiting in Elysium, of course," replied Pryde.

Emitting playful whines, Titan trotted towards them. The fearful beast was gone, and Dorian's hound of hell wagged his wiry, broom-like tail as he licked the hands of the dukes, whining and whimpering. Pryde's face split in a grin, and the prideful duke was replaced by a boy happy to finally be able to play with a puppy. He dropped to his knees and scratched Titan's long belly as the dog lolled on his back in bliss.

"Let us depart for the city, and may the demons within us be appeased," said Lucien.

They left their horses at the stables and strode into Rath Hall through the grand but dim hallways where portraits of Dorian's ancestors stared at them from dark oil paintings. Tall Greek statues, sideboards with statuettes, vases, and relics from all over the world filled the halls—treasures his father had been so proud to acquire.

The dukes followed Dorian to his bedchamber where his valet, Howe, threw a glance at his hand. The flesh was still raw, although it had stopped bleeding. "I'll clean them myself," Dorian said.

He didn't even let his valet see the scars on his right hand. He went into the changing chamber alone and removed the glove, absorbing every bit of the excruciating pain. He cleaned the blood in the washbasin, dried his skin, and put a fresh leather glove on his right hand.

As he returned to the room, the butler, Popwell, was pouring drinks for Luhst and Pryde, the clink of fine crystal and the rich aroma of aged brandy filling the room.

"Is Chastity at home?" asked Lucien as he looked out the window.

Dorian, Chastity, and Lucien had grown up together, and Lucien always asked about Chastity. Dorian knew he could trust Lucien like a brother, after everything they went through, but Lucien was a rake, a man who could seduce almost anyone he set his sights on.

"She is, probably still breaking her fast with my aunt."

"Lucien, you know you can literally have any woman in the world but Lady Chastity Perrin?" asked Pryde.

"He knows." Dorian threw a somber warning look at Lucien, who, uncharacteristically for him, looked sheepish.

"That must be killing you," Pryde said.

"What of your aunt?" Lucien asked, clearly changing the subject. "Did she speak to you of marriage again?"

Dorian sighed, his thoughts momentarily pulled away from the past by the mention of his beloved aunt. "Yes, she remains ever hopeful. I would do much to make her happy, if only I could reconcile it with my own desires."

He paused, meeting the silent, understanding gazes of his friends. They all knew well the weight of familial duty and societal expectations that accompanied their titles. And the constant struggle of rebelling against all that.

"Speaking of desires," said Lucien. "I hear the city is positively teeming with lovely young ladies this upcoming season. Perhaps one of them might yet thaw Rath's icy heart?"

Pryde chuckled at Lucien's jest, but Dorian remained silent while Howe pulled a fresh shirt over his head. He couldn't get his aunt's request out of his mind. He wished he could make her happy, yet he couldn't fathom the idea of having a wife. Or looking for one…

Good Lord, he could only imagine the dreadful nights of attending balls where eager debutantes and their mamas would hover around him. A physical shudder ran through him. This caused Howe to stop tying the collar of Dorian's shirt and murmur an excuse.

"It's not you, Howe," muttered Dorian. "No need for an apology."

"Do you know whom I saw in the city last night?" said Pryde, and relief flooded Dorian at the change of topic. "Mr. George Rose."

Rose...

Dorian froze, his knuckles whitening where they gripped the edge of the table. He felt as though a cold hand had reached into his chest and seized his heart, squeezing mercilessly.

"Indeed?" he managed to force out, his voice tight.

His valet fastened the last button on his waistcoat, seemingly oblivious of the storm brewing within his master.

"Ah, yes," Pryde continued, seemingly oblivious to Dorian's discomfort. "Poor man was attempting to sell whatever he could to pay off his family's mounting debts. It appears that John's education at Oxford drained them dry, and now they're left with nothing."

Dorian clenched his jaw, struggling to maintain his composure as guilt gnawed at his insides like a ravenous beast.

"Why are they left with nothing?" he asked through parched lips.

"Well," Pryde said, clearing his throat, "because everyone believes John ended his own life, rumors started circulating around the Roses. You know what happens to families in those situations. Their old acquaintances, especially the good ones, stopped seeing them, afraid to be associated with a tarnished family. The six daughters became unmarriageable, so they're left with the expenses of a large household but dwindling income. Since John was their last hope to change their financial situation, they've been scarcely able to provide for themselves."

"Six daughters..." Dorian echoed.

As the faces of his two friends swam before him, his mind reeled.

"How unfortunate…" mumbled Luhst, his eyes still on Dorian.

"It is. I tried to help," said Pryde. "I gave the Duke of Fortyne's card to Mr. Rose, and they're meeting later today."

Dorian scowled at Pryde while Howe fiddled with his cravat at his neck. "You know Fortyne. No doubt he'll pick up the estate for pennies and then turn it profitable."

"Well," said Pryde, "Mr. Rose is desperate to sell today to avoid landing in debtor's prison. Anything he can get quickly is better than nothing."

Debtor's prison? And what would happen to the six young women and their mother? Without money or connections, would they all end up in a workhouse? Dorian's hand ached again, the scars, the torn sinews, the new splits on his knuckles… Fury burst through him like the blast of a gun, followed by remorse for the life he had destroyed.

Not just one, as it turned out, but eight more. Six sisters and two parents.

Could he have eight more lives on his conscience? Goddamn it. His aunt's pleading expression came to mind, the hope and the tears in her eyes as she spoke of grandbabies.

Goddamn it again.

Mr. Rose had six unmarriageable daughters and a large debt he was desperate to pay off.

"Perhaps…there is another way," Dorian said, and he couldn't believe the words had actually left his mouth.

"Another way?" Pryde raised an eyebrow.

Dorian let out a curse. The solution swirled in his mind. He must be mad thinking about this, but he'd have to endure one of John's sisters for only a year if her family agreed. He'd pay off the family's debts. He'd pretend it would be a real marriage for his aunt's sake. He wouldn't touch the girl, would never claim his rights as a husband. When no child would come in one year, they'd just say the woman was barren and there was nothing to be done. Then his aunt would, with luck, leave him alone and concentrate her efforts on her next victim who could still bring her grandbabies—Chastity.

Was he mad, or did this plan make sense?

"Yes," Dorian said, locking eyes with each of his friends in turn.

His mind reeled. Was he truly considering it? To marry his victim's sister was to bind himself to the family he had so grievously wronged. Doubt and hesitation clawed at him. Was he being a fool? Was he that desperate to relieve this plague on his soul?

And yet he knew this was the closest he could ever come to atoning for his sins.

His knuckles hurt, pain pounding with the beating of his pulse. He would do this, not for his own sake, but for honor, for penance, for the chance to right even a fraction of the wrongs he had done.

He took in a lungful of air. "I will marry one of the Rose daughters. I will pay off Mr. Rose's debts."

"You've never even met any of the daughters!" exclaimed Pryde. "Will you propose without laying eyes on your betrothed? And how will you decide which of the six to choose?"

"Why not? It doesn't matter who she is. I will choose the youngest if she's of age—she will likely be the most pliable and amenable and unencumbered by romantic attachments. How old is she?"

"Eighteen, as far as I know," Luhst answered.

He always seemed to have the relevant information on every unattached female in London.

"Then she will do."

"Are you certain, Dorian?" Lucien asked quietly. "This is a

monumental decision. It'll change the course of your life forever."

"I know," Dorian replied. "It is the only way I can appease my aunt while helping the family of the man I murdered."

"You must think again!" Pryde said. "There are so many things to consider. Think of your reputation. The Roses have been surrounded by scandal for years."

"Because of me," said Dorian.

"And what about us—me and Lucien? We helped you cover up the murder."

"I'll never betray you two. No matter what. You know that—loyalty till death."

"And how in the world are you ever going to look her in the eye and be yourself?" Pryde asked. "What if you fall in love with her—or she with you? Have you considered that? And what about getting closer to the family of your victim?"

"No, Constantine. I won't have an issue with her ever wanting to get close to me. I must be the least lovable person in the entire world."

Howe helped him put his arms through the sleeves of his black coat bearing the Rath coat of arms: a lion in flames. As Dorian looked at himself in the mirror, Howe took a brush and swept away any dust from his shoulders and from the crimson waistcoat.

"But—" began Pryde.

Dorian stood straight, squared his shoulders, and tilted his chin up. His gaze was stern on himself. He would accept this challenge, even if it led to his destruction.

"You were there," he said. "You know what I did. You know I must atone. Take me to Mr. Rose."

2

"Who are they?" came the whisper of one of the congregation. The woman covertly looked over her shoulder as the vicar droned the Sunday sermon.

A shiver ran through Miss Patience Rose, despite the morning sunlight spilling through the small windows of Harringer's church hall. The whole congregation sat in front of her, with two empty pews left between them and her family.

"The notorious Roses," came the loud whisper of another woman. "Their son took his own life."

Mama must have heard it, too, based on her sudden pallor. Patience squeezed her mama's hand. Her five sisters sat on the same pew, squeezed together like pickles in a jar, trying to occupy as little space in the church as they could.

Their habitual spot for twelve years now.

"Ohhh," the first woman whispered back and stole a curious and worried glance at the Roses. "How awful. What a scandal!"

"Oh yes," said the second woman. "Bad business. He was their last hope to improve their fortune. Now Mr. Rose is at the of complete ruin, in London trying to sell their estate. worth much anyway."

Mama fidgeted, her eyes reddened with tears, her mouth in a straight line. Patience laid her head on Mama's shoulder and stroked her hand.

Thankfully, the mass was over in a few minutes, and the Roses were the first to shoot to their feet and leave. As Patience walked after her sisters and mama, the voices, the rustling of clothes and shuffling of feet against polished stone of the church echoed loudly. Mama seemed more agitated than usual, covering one gloved hand with the other to hide a patch and a large seam Patience's sister Anne had repaired so well. She was the embroiderer and the seamstress in the family.

When they stepped out of the church and into the fresh March air, Patience sighed with relief, and was just about to start down the packed dirt path back home to Rose Cottage when, to her surprise, Mama called, "Let us stay awhile."

This was so unlike her, the fidgeting, the strained smile that didn't reach her big, worried eyes.

"Are you certain, Mama?" asked Patience.

"Everyone's going to come out now, Mama," said Anne, glancing at the rough stone church surrounded by well-kept bushes and a cut lawn.

Mama's eyes darted towards the doors, where the voices of the congregation could be heard growing closer and closer. "Indeed," said Mama, and they stepped to the side of the gravel path. "I have an idea that might help Papa. Positive thoughts, right, girls? While he's in London, I'm going to try and do my own bidding here. It won't hurt, right?"

"That depends," said Patience's oldest sister, Emily, who was twenty-eight.

"You will see," Mama said and put on a smile that was so

false it set Patience's teeth on edge. Just like Mama, all of the sisters put on a smile, as well.

One after another, the congregation exited the church. The more affluent parishioners, draped in their Sunday finest of silks and velvets, walked out with a leisurely grace, and the village's simpler folk followed them. The tenants and local farmers wore sturdy clothes, their fabrics coarse yet clean. The village bakers, tailors, and craftsmen in slightly better, practical garments, mingled among them.

As they passed by the Rose family, their conversations faltered momentarily; their steps hesitated. With subtle shifts in their paths and quick, evasive glances, each deliberately widened the gap, ensuring a clear distance of at least five steps between them and the Roses, as if the air around them was tainted with the shadow of scandal.

Finally, Lady Justina Fitzroy, the Marchioness of Virtoux, came out with her son.

Patience fiddled with the edges of her dress. The marchioness was a beautiful woman, tall and quite broad-shouldered; she had the air of a queen, unapproachable and proud. She was dressed in a modern, high-waisted gown with an imperial silhouette, which was quite unusual for women her age, who generally preferred the styles they had worn when they were younger, with fitted waists and full skirts. Lady Virtoux was the patroness of the Harringer parish and owned one of the estates nearby where she sometimes spent the winter before heading to London for the season, which would start soon.

Her son carried the honorable title of Viscount of Mique, inherited from his father. He was a man in his forties, well-built and with handsome, sharp features, a strong nose, and a square jaw. He had narrowly set green eyes and a generous mane of wavy dark hair.

Lady Virtoux threw a puzzled and disgusted look at Mama, Patience, and her sisters. Then she averted her eyes, walking in the other direction and whispering something to the viscount. Patience bit her lip and wished they would have left as they had every Sunday for years now, hurrying out before their presence would offend everyone else, none of whom had exposed family secrets or scandals surrounding their name.

Mama's hands trembled as she clasped them together. She drew in a deep breath, as though steeling herself for something, and walked straight towards the marchioness.

"Mama!" Patience hissed, and Anne threw her hand out as though to stop her.

It was like watching an accident about to occur and having no power to stop it.

"Lady Virtoux," Mama said as she approached the lady and curtsied. "Lord Mique." She curtsied to the gentleman.

Both stared at Mama with expressions of utter horror and stepped back.

"I beg your pardon," said Lady Virtoux as she turned her back to Mama, about to walk away.

"Please!" exclaimed Mama. "I wouldn't have approached you were I not so desperate. Just a moment of your time."

Patience and her sisters exchanged glances. Anne's eyes were tearing up, her cheeks ablaze.

"What is she doing?" whispered Emily. "Clearly, her presence is not desired."

"Keep your tears away, Anne," whispered Beatrice, the second oldest. "Pull yourself together. We do not need another humiliation. Smile, everyone. Like always."

Patience watched in horror as they stretched their lips, but they looked like a child's drawings, with sad eyes, their thin mouths wide and crooked.

At that moment, the parish vicar, Mr. Menon, came out. A

short man in his fifties with a round, egg-like head and a large stomach, he had a big smile on his face...but as his eyes fell on Mama and Lady Virtoux, it vanished.

He frowned, and Lady Virtoux sighed heavily. "I suppose one must be virtuous and charitable, especially after Sunday mass. What can I do for you, Mrs. Rose?"

Mama licked her dry, pale lips, her hands shaking. "Thank you. You're very kind, Lady Virtoux."

The Viscount of Mique stood with his nose high and clutched at a handkerchief, as though ready to use it to stop a bad smell, which none of them had.

"It's my husband's estate. Our home. Rose Cottage and the five farms that belong to it. I wouldn't have asked, but the situation is very dire indeed. My husband is in London now, trying to sell everything to pay off our debts. Most of them to your family, of course. You're a lady of great mercy. Please ask your husband to recall his writ of ca. sa. against mine."

A writ of ca. sa., or capias ad satisfaciendum, was a complaint made by a creditor against the debtor in a court of law.

Lady Virtoux's upper lip rose in an expression of appalled displeasure. "The court has given Mr. Rose time to sort out the payment, and it's more than fair."

"Indeed. However, if he fails to find a buyer or fails to gather enough money to pay off the whole debt, he will be put in the debtor's prison. Please, Lady Virtoux, we are about to lose our home. Please do not take our children's father from them... We already lost our son..."

To the utter horror of everyone present, standing around the lawn before the church, Mama gave out a small sob. She didn't have a handkerchief, and clearly Lord Mique wasn't going to offer his, and so Mama wiped her tears with her gloved fingers.

The mention of John's suicide made everyone present stand rigid, frozen in place. Then whispers rippled through the crowd, their hushed voices carrying a mix of pity and contempt. Eyes darted between Mama and the grand lady, eager to witness the unfolding drama. Some turned away, their disapproval evident in the set of their shoulders and the tight press of their lips.

Anne grasped Patience's hand and held it tightly.

The grand lady's expression turned into a full sneer as she looked down her nose at Mama. "You dare to approach me with such an impertinent request? Your family's financial disgrace is well-known, and you have the audacity to seek my assistance?" Her voice dripped with disdain.

Mama's face paled. "Please, Lady Virtoux, I am begging... Mr. Rose might die in debtor's prison, and my girls and I, we might be pleading for alms on the streets in just two weeks' time."

"You should have thought of that before borrowing money left and right," Lady Virtoux proclaimed. "Besides, as a woman you ought to know your place, and it is not to intervene with the business of men. Do not dare to come to me again, I do not wish to be associated with such disgrace."

Patience stepped forward, placing a gentle hand on her mother's arm. She met the grand lady's icy gaze without flinching. She would not let this woman's cruelty crush her family's spirit. They would find a way; that was what Mama and Papa had taught them.

"Please forgive Mama, Lady Virtoux," she said as she pulled poor, sobbing Mama away. "We will not bother you again. And rest assured, we will manage."

Under heavy gazes and whispers, they walked away, down the dirt-packed road towards Rose Cottage. It would take them at least one hour to reach home on foot, but the exercise would be welcome to distract Mama from the horrible scene that had unfolded, to absorb sunshine, and to think positive thoughts.

Besides, Patience couldn't wait to get back to her roses.

Indeed, during the walk, Mama calmed down and even managed to put on her usual smile.

"Mama," Patience said as she was struck with a sudden idea about halfway home, "what if we used the lavender and rose petals from my garden to make sachets? We could sell them at the market and earn a little extra coin to tide us over until Papa returns."

"Marvelous idea, darling!" said Mama. "At last your roses might come in handy. Do you still have some dried flowers left over from last year?"

"I'm sure I do."

"I know where they are, sister," said Anne. "I'll look."

Anne was Patience's best friend, and not just because she was closest in age. They both harbored a secret liking of science. Anne was a mathematician, while Patience was a botanist, though they could not share their passions and achievements with anyone but each other.

"But Patience," said Emily, "who would buy anything from us?"

The question hung over the seven women in silence. Who, indeed, especially after the scene at the church?

"Someone might," said Patience, although with little conviction. "It's worth a try."

And half an hour later, while Anne went to look for the rose petals and lavender, Patience went to the garden to prune her hybrid roses. She knelt beside a bush, inhaling the air that carried the promise of spring.

She wore a light green gown that had seen better days, its hem dirtied by soil, and a yellow apron with at least five patches. She used the side of her wrist to push away strands of blond hair that fell from under her battered straw bonnet. She preferred to work with bare hands, despite the toll it took on her skin—she had calluses, scratches, and dirt under her fingernails she could not remove no matter how long she scrubbed.

With no servants, her and each of her five sisters was responsible for their own domain in the household, and hers was the vegetable garden that stretched behind her. Though it was too early in the season to grow much besides peas and radishes. They still had a few wizened root vegetables and potatoes in the cellar from the previous year, but they wouldn't last much longer.

Indulging in botanical projects such as hybridizing roses was not practical. So she had to be quick before Mama or one of the sisters other than Anne discovered her.

With her fingers, Patience inspected the bush, seeking out deadwood and diseased stems after winter. It was mostly bare, still in its dormant phase. However, small reddish leaf buds were starting to swell, showing the first signs of new growth. The hybrid's form was upright and vigorous, with fewer thorns than the typical gallica, making it easier to handle. Though the plant had no flowers yet, Patience could already imagine the blooms to come.

The rest of the garden flourished. Truly, she loved taking care of plants—seeing carrots and cabbage and parsnips grow, fighting pests with natural means, improving fertilizer, coming up with ways to increase crop production. Plants thrived under her touch, and she could feel them respond to her.

Her vegetable garden and the apple and pear orchard behind it were in perfect order, ready for the main crops to be planted, fertilized, tended, and harvested.

Twenty or so feet away from her stood tiny Rose Cottage. Unlike the orchard and the vegetable garden, it was not at all perfect, nor was it a place where she felt happy. For years, it had stood sad and crumbling. The white paint on the window frames and the shutters had peeled to the point where most of it was gone, and the shutters hung askew. Bricks crumbled. The roof had caved in on one corner and leaked terribly so that mold grew on the walls and ceiling. Some windowpanes had been long broken and replaced with pieces of wood.

If only John had been alive. He would have finished his education in Oxford, would have been a lawyer in London, and would help Papa—with his connections, with money. Perhaps he would have even been able to help some of her sisters marry well...

"Patience, there you are!" Anne exclaimed as she approached. Her golden locks, so typical of the Rose family, bounced as she hurried towards her. "Papa is back from London! He's crying his throat out looking for you."

"Oh, you didn't tell them I was here, did you?" Patience winced. "I don't want him to know I'm with the roses."

"Always the diligent gardener," Anne teased, sitting on the ground beside her. "I do not think it's about roses."

"He came back early," said Patience, brushing the soil from her hands. "Did he say if he managed to sell the estate?" The question made her chest ache. It would be hard to leave here, the only home she'd known in her eighteen years of life. Her roses. Her vegetables. Her orchard.

"No," said Anne as she helped Patience stand. "He's just crying for you like someone's chasing him."

Patience raised her eyebrows. "What could he want with me?" She was grateful to be the youngest, with no prospects or expectations. She could garden, do her studies, and research. "Do you think he might have found a way to improve our situation and avoid debtor's prison?"

Anne chuckled softly. "You're an eternal optimist, dear sister."

Patience smiled. "Aren't all of us Roses?"

The sudden sound of many quick, heavy steps crunching on the gravel pathway shattered the peaceful atmosphere in the garden. Patience looked up, her heart skipping a beat as she recognized her papa's and mama's voices.

"Patience! Patience!" cried Mama as she ran behind Papa, holding her skirts up, frantically looking around. "Where are you, you dreamy girl?"

"I have returned with news that will change our lives forever!" Papa cried, his voice carrying across the grounds.

Patience exchanged a startled glance with Anne before they both scrambled to their feet, curiosity and apprehension battling within Patience. As she and Anne hurried towards the house, Patience could see her four other sisters following her parents.

Papa, a short man with shoulder-length wavy gray hair, breathed hard. He had a round face with big blue eyes and was dressed in a worn, dirty beige coat and breeches.

"There you are!" Her mama pointed at Patience. She was breathing hard, her corset under her dress's fitted waist probably tightening her chest way too much. "There she is, Mr. Rose!" she said.

"Ah, Patience, come here!" Papa cried as he, breathing hard as well, stopped, clutching at his round stomach, his face flushed with excitement. "Girls, gather around."

The sisters exchanged uneasy glances, their mother's excited expression wavering as the weight of their circumstances pressed down upon them all.

"I've told you," their father continued, raising his hands for emphasis, "always keep your hopes up. Even in the darkest hour, like we went through."

"*Went* through, Papa?" asked Emily. "Did you find a buyer?"

"No, better!"

His pale blue eyes landed on Patience, and he grinned a little madly. Patience didn't like that at all.

"Patience, my dear," Papa proclaimed, "you are to marry a duke!"

A stunned silence fell over the assembled family, and Patience felt as if the air had been punched from her lungs. Her sisters stared at her in disbelief, their expressions varying from shock to envy.

"Me? A duke?" Patience managed to choke out, her voice barely above a whisper.

"Indeed," Papa confirmed, his eyes shining with pride. "The Duke of Rath has offered for your hand, and I have accepted on your behalf. This union will save our family from destitution."

Patience's dirty hand clutched at the apron on her stomach. The world careened from under her feet. She could hear the words, but they didn't really register. How could a duke want her? She'd never been out; no one in high society even knew she existed.

"Why me?" Patience asked. "I have five older and more accomplished sisters!"

She glanced at Anne, who offered her a supportive smile.

"The duke asked for the youngest," Papa explained, "because he felt it would be less likely that you would be involved in any romantic entanglements or have suitors vying for your attention. The duke seemed quite taken with what he's heard of your pleasant and amiable nature."

Her father's words hung in the air, the garden spinning slightly around her. She blinked rapidly, her hand reaching out to grip something for support and finding Anne's arm, which felt solid and reassuring. Her voice faltered as she attempted to speak, and only a whisper came out. "A…a duke?"

"How is that fair?" exclaimed Beatrice, who was now twenty-seven. "Emily and I were both out! The oldest sisters should marry before the youngest!"

"I quite agree," said Patience. "Perhaps the duke would like to see Emily paint…or hear Beatrice sing. He'd change his mind!"

Clarice, the third oldest, scoffed. "Is it not enough that we have suffered the loss of our brother?"

Patience flinched at the mention of her late brother, her heart aching with the familiar pain of his absence.

Frances, the fourth oldest, added, "And now we must endure the indignity of being passed over for marriage?"

"Dearest ones," said Mama, "do not succumb to your dark emotions. Envy…this is not how we raised you. Remember the basket. Lock it all in."

"Well said, darling," said Papa. "Indeed, the duke was quite adamant. I was as surprised as you are. He did want the youngest… He'll pay my debts right after the wedding so that I won't go to debtor's prison, we won't have to sell our house, and we will not need to leave. But he also had conditions."

Patience swallowed hard. She could see her roses drying here, the peas and the radishes wilting without her care. Her paper never being written. Her hybrid rose she still hadn't named forever dead.

Like her dreams.

"Once you are married to the duke for a year, he will grant us an estate that will provide us with a steady income," said Papa. "However, you must remain with him, or the arrangement will be nullified."

A wave of despair washed over Patience as she realized the full extent of the sacrifice she was being asked to make. Her dreams of continuing her botanical research and completing her paper slipped through her fingers.

She didn't want this. She never wanted to marry anyone, let alone a duke. What if he was old, lustful, and cruel, just looking for young flesh?

Her mama laid her hand on Patience's shoulder and looked pleadingly at her with her big brown eyes. "This is what a woman does, darling," she said. "This is why you were born a girl. To secure an advantageous match for your own sake and for the sake of your family. With John gone, there are very, very few things that can help us. This is it. Our only chance, darling."

As the weight of her family's expectations bore down on her, Patience knew she could not succumb to the sadness and darkness within her. She had always been an optimist, and now more than ever, she needed to hold on to that part of herself.

"Very well," she said, tears pricking at the corners of her eyes. "I will marry the Duke of Rath."

With a heavy heart, Patience succumbed to Mama's squeals and Papa's happy exclamations. Her sisters resumed a squabble, and Anne looked at her with concern.

Her life, as she knew it, had come to an end—and there was no turning back.

3

The day of the wedding... three days later.

Dorian's gaze kept darting down the aisle between pews towards the great oak doors his bride would soon enter through.

He kept clenching and unclenching his wounded hand to relieve the pressure of the leather glove against his scars. The old dean of the St. Benedict's Cathedral of Rathford cast side-eyes at it.

The cathedral was particularly pretty today, with candles lit all around, little bouquets of snowdrops, crocuses, and primroses decorating the intricately carved columns, the pews and the altar behind the dean, which was covered with a fine white linen cloth. Ornate tapestries adorned the walls.

The air was thick with the scents of beeswax, incense, and the perfumes of his esteemed guests. Yet, to Dorian, it smelled of a prison.

The wooden pews were filled with guests. There was his

aunt sitting next to one of her best friends, the Dowager Duchess of Grandhampton, and to Chastity. His sister couldn't believe her ears when she heard of his sudden engagement. Behind them sat Lord Spencer Seaton and his wife, Joanna, and Spencer's brothers, Richard and Preston, with their spouses. Spencer's sister, Calliope, who was a duchess now, sat with her husband, Nathaniel, the Duke of Kelford.

Their whispers filled the air, and Spencer kept throwing Dorian sympathetic but puzzled looks. Like everyone, he was shocked to get an invitation to the sudden wedding of his friend who had been a sworn bachelor.

Behind the Seatons, Pryde, Enveigh, Eccess, Irevrence, and Fortyne sat with different expressions on their faces. Pryde was scowling at Dorian. His lectures had not ended for the past week. What was he thinking, marrying the sister of his murder victim? Did he not think the truth would come out? What about honesty? They had sworn to stay silent, sworn to forget, sworn the deed was done, and he could now be putting himself in danger of criminal repercussions if she found out.

Lucien had been more focused on the idea that Dorian could release his dark energy every night in one woman's arms.

Eccess was ecstatic as he laughed drunkenly, saying how marriage to a stranger was a very amusing jest.

Irevrence, through his rebellious nature, noted it wouldn't work out anyway.

Enveigh only glared at him from under his dark locks, his steely gaze hiding an ache. "You're doing something the rest of us are too cowardly to do," he'd said.

And Fortyne noted only that he was making a mistake because if he was going to marry, he should have found a wife with a dowry and connections. Marriage should be a lucrative transaction, not an act of charity.

All of them, however, were dying to see Dorian's bride, just as he was.

He knew only that she was eighteen, and her name was Miss Patience Rose.

Her family was on the other side of the aisle, all of them rosy-cheeked and blond with blue eyes. And they were all fidgeting with excitement. If she was anything like them and like John, who had looked quite angelic, she would be very pleasing to the eyes.

Finally, the organ began playing solemnly, the notes echoing against the walls, and a nervous shiver passed through Dorian. Something cracked in him. He was not one to run away from danger. He'd saved Joanna, Spencer's wife, from death. He regularly won boxing matches. He had called at least a dozen duels, for God's sake.

But something about seeing the woman he'd be tying himself to forever was unbearable.

He turned away from the door, moments ticking by in the violent beats of his heart. His chest felt too tight, his stomach a knot, and his pulse beat like a war drum in his injured hand.

He heard the creak of the doors and the rustle of clothes as the guests turned around to see her, murmuring excitedly. His glove-free left palm was slick with perspiration, and he wiped it, quite unduke-like, against his black pantaloons. As time stretched thin, he heard her slow and light steps. *Lord, could this please be over?*

This torture would be the penance for his greatest sin. This marriage, a small step towards redeeming the unforgivable.

There was no way back now. He had to face his fate. See his jailor, his executioner in a bridal dress.

He turned around.

His gaze fell on her.

Time stopped.

No, it didn't just stop.

It stopped existing.

Everything vanished except a small, sweetly rounded, blond figure with large blue eyes and a perfect, angelic face. The sunlight that fell through the stained-glass windows of the church seemed to make her glow with a soft golden light, her hair a halo around her head. Her big eyes sparkled. She had high cheekbones in a soft, full face. A straight, pretty nose. Plush lips the color of a pink rose, with a defined Cupid's bow, and a lower lip fuller than the upper one. She had generous breasts, a distinct crease between them visible above her collar line. She had rounded shoulders and was all curves and softness—a young woman full of life. Even the old muslin dress that, he guessed, had been white in its early days but had become grayish-yellow, didn't change the strange, exuberant sensation of freefalling that had spread through his stomach.

Dorian had seen much beauty in his life. The glamorous women of the ton, his own elegant home with the magnificent art that his father and ducal ancestors had collected. He had traveled to the Mediterranean and the Alps and Scotland. Every month, he frequented the most beautiful sex workers London had to offer in Elysium. He'd seen breathtaking sunsets, landscapes, the magnificence of the sea.

But with that angelic face, that innocent smile, that look of genuine kindness, she held a kind of inner light—one that couldn't have been any more different from the darkness that he carried within him.

With a terrifying awe he knew it.

Never in his thirty-two years had he seen anything as beautiful as Miss Patience Rose.

His bride.

4

Patience walked down the aisle, unable to feel her own body.

The nave stretched out before her with its gorgeous, clean mosaic floor, and to her left and right were the pews filled with people, every one of them staring at her. Because of the blinding light, she couldn't see the most important person… the man who stood waiting for her at the end of the aisle.

The man who would own her, command her, do with her as he pleased. A shiver ran through her. She was going to marry a complete stranger who had enough power and wealth to arrange this marriage without ever seeing her.

Why did he want her so?

To her left, her family wore their best clothes, her mama and sisters in oft-repaired bonnets decorated with snowdrops, their cloaks with visible patches and seams closing the holes. Her papa, in his usual beige coat and breeches, had washed his mane of curly white hair, and his balding forehead and red cheeks shone. His bright blue eyes held an air of adoration and love because she was going to marry the duke and save them.

Somehow she was moving her feet, though every step felt

like she was crawling through a swamp. She felt so small and insignificant under those high vaulted ceilings, walking this grand, endless nave.

The people on the other side of the aisle were the duke's guests, no doubt. Beautiful, proud men and women so breathtaking every one of them could be a painting or a piece of art. Their clothing had no holes, no patches, no stains. They wore jewelry, artfully created silk and satin flowers, high cravats, and coats of arms. Their backs were straight, their hands free of dirt and callouses, their skin smelling like expensive perfume.

They were grand and tall and important.

And this was what she was going to marry into? She, who had to sit at the back of the church every Sunday because not a single respected family in their parish wanted to come near them. She, who shared a bed with two of her sisters. She, whose fingernails had never been clean in her entire life.

A duchess…

What a jest!

A jest…and a loss. She'd never finish her paper now, never see the fruition of years of work on her hybrid rose. She didn't know much about being a duchess, but she was pretty sure she wasn't supposed to crawl in the dirt all day.

Well, she'd make the best of it. The main thing was that her family would be safe. John was supposed to have improved their situation after he graduated from Oxford and became a solicitor. But he never would, of course.

She would.

Papa wouldn't land in debtor's prison, and her sisters and mama wouldn't go to a workhouse or land on the streets. Sacrificing her rose project and her scientific ambitions was worth it.

All she had to do was to turn away from this sadness and

swallow her tears and put a smile on her face like she'd done her entire life since John's death. She needed to look at the good side of things and forget what she was losing.

Look straight ahead, at her husband-to-be.

Then the blinding sunlight was blocked by the wall, and she could finally see the man next to the vicar.

And the very little composure she had managed to gather vaporized.

He was tall. Standing on the platform by the altar, he seemed to tower above her, high into the vaulted, Gothic ceilings. How old was he? Much older than her, but not as old as she'd feared. Closer to his forties, she thought. Like the carved statues in the church, he seemed eternal. A lock of white against dark, almost inky hair made his striking sky-blue eyes even more breathtaking.

She was almost at the platform now, and she couldn't pull her eyes away from him.

Good God, he was built like a Greek statue, with thick, muscular thighs bulging under black pantaloons. He had narrow hips and a trim waist; a broad chest and shoulders were clearly visible even under the layers of an immaculate tailored black coat. Beneath it, he wore a red waistcoat and an elegantly tied, crisp white cravat.

His hair was in a fashionable windswept style arranged around an angular, perfectly shaven face. He had high cheekbones, and the otherwise straight bridge of his regal nose had a little bump... Perhaps from a break? In fact, he had a few imperfections. There was a tiny patch of skin a third of the way along one of his thick black eyebrows and a white mark to the left of his full lower lip. Were these scars? From what?

He looked at her with such piercing intensity, a shiver ran down her spine. It was as though he was peering right through the mask of her smile and straight into her fear, into her sadness, into her loss. How completely out of place she felt, hung in the air, uprooted, drifting.

Her legs felt soft and wobbly, and her stomach seemed filled with buzzing bees. She couldn't feel her hands holding the bouquet of snow drops, though with the edge of her vision she saw the white petals shaking. She felt clammy and flushed, burning all over. The closer she drew to him, the smaller she felt under the cold and penetrating gaze of this great man.

Her husband. The most important person for the rest of her life. She'd belong to him, be his...

Oh God, what did this gorgeous man think of her? He must be looking at the yellowed fabric of her dress with disdain, seeing every patch and every seam.

But no. What did she learn was the best thing to do when one was afraid or uncertain?

Smile. Look at the positive. And never, ever show them or yourself those dark, unhealthy feelings.

So that was what she did.

She spread her lips wide, smiled as she kept looking at him.

And then she flew.

Her foot caught at the edge of the platform, of course, and the wooden floor rose towards her face.

The impact against her face would be devastating. She could already anticipate the hard slap, the pain exploding through her cheek and eye and her nose, through her skull. How utterly embarrassing, the first thing she'd do before her husband the duke, his aristocratic guests, and the vicar would be fall right onto her face!

A collective gasp echoed through the cathedral.

But the floor never touched her.

The sensation of falling stopped, and she was simply suspended in the air as two strong hands grasped her by her shoulders. It was like a guardian angel had come to save her, the force so much stronger than anything she was capable of.

She felt warm, safe, and protected. A little out of breath, too. His touch sent wonderfully prickly sensations, like tiny bubbles, rushing through her.

The next moment, she was yanked upright. He let go of her, and once again she stood empty and alone, with her heart slamming her ribs, staring into the icy eyes of the duke.

The vicar cleared his throat, and the rush of voices around the church silenced, as well as the organ.

"May I begin, Your Grace?" asked the vicar.

"You may," said the Duke of Rath.

Oh, that voice... Deep and velvety, buttery and smooth.

The rest of the ceremony passed quickly, as if in a haze. The vicar droned blessings and prayers, and then the duke said I do, and so, blasted, did she.

When it was time for him to put the ring on her finger, her cold, clammy hand shook as she stretched it out for him. When he took it in his hand, she realized something odd...his right hand was encased in a glove. A thick leather glove, black like the rest of his clothes, and his hair. The leather was smooth, except for a few patches where it was rubbed raw from use.

Why was he wearing a glove? Was his hand injured? That must be it, perhaps a cut or a riding accident; it must be healing.

With his ungloved left hand, he placed the golden band on her fourth finger, the one that connected to the heart, they said. The touch of his warm, dry fingers sent a shudder through her body. His fingers were long, his hand large and utterly masculine, slightly bronzed by the sun, with scabs on his knuckles... Had he hit something recently? What must the other hand look like if this one was ungloved?

Then they signed the parish marriage register, and it was done.

Under cheers and murmurs, they walked back down the aisle without touching each other and climbed into the carriage waiting outside. Someone showered them with petals.

But there was no joy in her heart at all. It was the hardest day of her life to keep her positive thoughts afloat. Her papa would be safe. Her sisters and her mama would be safe.

But would she?

5

The carriage was rocking under her, and stunning countryside passed by the window, with its rolling hills and hedgerows under a sky the color of her husband's eyes...

The air was fresh, but Patience was breathless.

The duke and she were alone.

It must have been the first time in her life she was alone with a grown man who wasn't her papa or brother. It was most definitely the first time she had sat in a carriage drawn by four horses, with a driver and two footmen standing at the back. The first time she was in a vehicle draped in black and red silks embroidered with golden lions in flames.

The cost of the curtains and the silky material covering the walls must have been more than all of her sisters' gowns combined. Goodness, she could have asked Anne to make a ball gown out of this fabric.

Out of the window, she could now see fluffy white clouds passing overhead, tenants working the fields, clusters of trees dotting the landscape interspersed with bushes and undergrowth.

All this belonged to him. As did she.

She fingered the crease of her gown in her old lace gloves, her whole body clammy, the straps of her bonnet digging in too tight under her chin. He sat, handsome and intimidating, with eyes that were dark blue now, the color of the endless ocean, under long, thick, elegantly arched eyebrows. She could smell him over the rich scents of leather, wood, and clean fabric—musk, bergamot, and pepper. Good Lord, he even looked a little like a lion. With close-set eyes, high cheekbones, and a nose that looked broad and long while still being regal and attractive. His sharp, angular jaw worked under his perfectly smooth skin, the full lips of his broad mouth stretched into a flat line. His shoulders under the exquisite coat were tense, his large hands fisting the edges of the bench so tight, the leather glove on his right hand was stretched to the limit. His dilated pupils flickered left and right as he tracked the passing trees, bushes, and fields. He was breathing hard, the edges of his crimson waistcoat rising and falling quickly.

Definitely displeased. Or was he simply as uncomfortable as she was, having just married a stranger?

The need to smooth the situation, to lighten the mood, to make him feel at ease scratched at her stomach. That was what she did best.

But what did one ask their own husband when one knew nothing about him?

Could she ask why he was so vexed?

What did he have for breakfast today?

What was his favorite color?

What did he like to read?

Could she make a jest? Lord in heaven, send her an idea for a jest…

Nothing. All she could think about was how big he was in

the enclosed compartment of the carriage...which wasn't actually small at all. It was bigger than the larder at Rose Cottage.

Silence stretched between them so thick and long, it felt like a high-pitched note. She didn't know where to put her legs so that she wouldn't touch his. It was impossible. His long, muscular legs were open, surrounding her knees, and she did her best not to stare at the lines of muscles bulging against the fabric. After a while, he crossed his big arms over his chest, and even through layers of his clothing, she could see how his flesh rippled.

Finally the pitch reached a breaking point, and she couldn't be silent a moment longer.

For God's sake just say something positive! she managed to command herself before she opened her mouth.

"I suppose congratulations are in order," she said in a croaky voice.

His sharp gaze landed on her like a slap. A lion, indeed, cold and watching his prey. His gaze penetrated her, digging deep into her face, and she felt naked and vulnerable even though she was fully clothed in gloves and a bonnet and a long coat.

"Congratulations on what?" he snapped.

Oh, his voice. Even tinged with irritation, it remained the most resonant male timbre she had ever heard.

"Our nuptials."

"I don't believe it's customary to congratulate each other."

She chuckled. "I suppose."

Silence fell once again, and she scratched the soft upholstery of the seat with her gloved fingertips. She felt a thread inside her glove catch on a snag in her nail and itched to free her hand and smooth it, but she couldn't.

She couldn't imagine feeling more vulnerable.

He returned to staring out of the window. The edge of his jaw moved so fast, she thought there might be a creature trying to break out of there. Her rib cage felt constricted and tight in her corset—*oh, damned corset*—and she kept sucking in air in an attempt to calm herself. Good God, how long could the ride from the village church to Rath Hall take?

Someone needed to say something. Anything.

This was undoubtedly the tensest, most awkward situation she had ever experienced. She couldn't endure the silence any longer. The discomfort hung in the air like an acrid smell she desperately wanted to dispel.

"What did you have for breakfast?" she blurted out, and he looked at her in confusion.

No smile, not even a shadow of one, but at least the angry, jaw-working look was wiped off his face. His mouth relaxed from the scowl, eyes brightening to the shade of a sky just before dusk. Something lightened inside her.

"Toast," he said, looking a little struck. "And coffee."

Coffee... Right away her mind went to the botanical plant, called *Coffea arabica*. It came from inland East African regions and had red berries that could be roasted and were beloved by many. The plant grew in subtropical highlands and loved warm temperatures and humid conditions. She longed for an opportunity to see the real coffee plant and study it.

But that was not what a duchess would talk about.

"I've never tried coffee," she said. In fact, they didn't even have money for proper tea, so the tea they drank was mint, lavender, rose hips, and other herbs and plants Patience could grow or forage in the nearby woods. "Is it good?"

He kept staring at her with his penetrating glare. "Yes."

"How does it taste?"

"Intense. One can say a little bitter, but pleasantly so. Roasted."

"Oh. Is it true one feels alive and energetic after drinking it?"

He nodded. "I suppose so, yes."

She chuckled. "Did you know that according to a legend, coffee was discovered when some goats ate coffee berries and began running around as if possessed?"

"No. I didn't."

"And they're quite pretty plants. That's at least from what I can say from botanical illustrations I've seen. Very pretty, glossy leaves. White flowers. Red berries."

He narrowed his eyes. "Botanical illustrations?"

"Yes. My brother brought a book of botanical illustrations the only time he visited us from Oxford."

His face changed, and she didn't know what she'd said. From showing surprised interest, to paling suddenly as though he'd seen a ghost.

Then it all changed again in a second. Creases formed between his eyebrows. His eyes became dark, with large black pupils, the irises the color of a stormy ocean.

"Madam, perhaps you would do yourself and me a favor by not talking for the rest of the trip."

She opened and closed her mouth. What could have upset him so much?

Mama was right. She should have never been so interested in botany. He was a duke—of course he'd disapprove of her scientific interest. Good Lord, she was already spoiling this marriage in the first minutes of it.

Perhaps she should return to the topic of breakfast but stay away from talking about plants, no matter how much she enjoyed thinking about what a coffee plant looked like, what root system it had, and how to get it to flower and then to produce berries.

"Do you like strawberry jam?" she asked.

Do not think about strawberries! That they grew well in a

well-drained, loamy soil and could be harvested in late spring to early summer, especially if there was much sun.

He scowled at her. "I asked you not to talk."

"I thought strawberry jam was a safe topic. Do you like strawberry jam?"

He cleared his throat. "I don't mind it."

So preserves was a safe topic. "Neither do I. How about raspberry jam?"

He pinched his nose between his fingers. "Please. I am begging of you. You do not need to fill silence with questions about my jam preferences."

"Forgive me. Um... Would you like to ask me a question?"

"No."

She blinked. "Oh. Is that how ducal marriages work? No one talks to each other?"

"That is certainly how I would like it."

"I must admit, I've never been very good at silence. My mother always said I was born under a chattering star," she offered with a small, hopeful smile.

The duke's gaze, icy and unforgiving, swept back to her. "And I was born under a star that appreciates peace and quiet."

"But surely, Duke, there must be something you enjoy discussing. Politics, perhaps? Or maybe you have a passion for horses? Men usually do... At least that's what I read."

His eyes flickered with an unreadable emotion. "What you *read*?"

Oh, it was better when he was silent. "Yes. I don't know many men. Many people, I should say. Most of what I know is from what Mama and Papa told me and from reading."

He looked her over, and a hot blush crept to her cheeks.

Good God, he was so worldly, so experienced. For a moment, she was envious. She knew what he must be thinking. She was young, naive, and sheltered. What business did she have being the wife of this self-assured, confident man? He needed someone strong by his side. It must feel so calming to know exactly what one wanted to say and not to try to please anyone at all.

"Don't you have some country friends? Daughters of a local vicar must pity you and offer you some company."

Embarrassment hit her whole body in a hot wave. "Indeed, the vicar and his wife and daughters have been the only neighbors to keep company with my family. But only out of obligation, not genuine interest. Still, it was nice to have someone else to talk to than my sisters and parents."

He wore an expression of shock and a strangely intense guilt that slumped his shoulders and darkened his gaze. He turned away from her, the veins on his neck bulging rhythmically.

He was walking on some sort of an edge, like a furious lion, not that she'd ever seen one alive. She should leave him alone. And yet, she couldn't stop poking the predator.

His gloved hand twitched again, leather stretching over the knuckles. And if she was right, a fleeting expression of pain ran through his face.

"May I inquire, what happened to your hand?" she asked. "I noticed the glove."

For a moment, it seemed as though he might relent, his posture relaxing ever so slightly. But his body tensed again, and when he spoke, his voice was colder than the winter winds in Siberia.

"Miss Rose, is it your intention to torment me with your questions? Or do you hold such small intellectual capacities that you find my explicit request for silence difficult to understand?"

Patience recoiled as if struck, her cheeks flushing with

embarrassment and something akin to anger. She had been nothing but cordial, making an effort to ease the uncomfortable situation, but he repaid her kindness with disdain. Her voice, when she finally spoke, was quieter but carried a steeliness that surprised even her.

"I was merely trying to make our journey less...oppressive. Not an easy task, as I'm learning."

Patience thought she saw a flicker of regret in his eyes. But as quickly as it appeared, it was gone, replaced once more by the icy façade.

The rest of the journey passed in a heavy, uncomfortable silence that felt like a third being sitting in the carriage. Patience sat, her hands folded neatly in her lap, her mind racing with questions.

Papa had said the duke wanted to marry quickly and that he chose her because he was looking for someone amenable, and that was what she was trying to be. Pleasant. Companionable. But if he was so eager to be left alone, why did he marry at all? He could have had his pick of better-bred young ladies who knew how to be a duchess and were ready to be what he needed. Patience's family name was slathered in scandal. She had no idea about anything but her garden, her roses, and how to keep her head high and be positive.

So that was what she would do. Stay positive. Smile.

But through her determination, a horrible thought scratched at the back of her psyche.

He was cold, and possibly cruel, by the looks of the blood on the knuckles of his hand, and God knew what hid under his glove... He didn't care about her. He didn't want to talk to her or be in her presence.

He was still a stranger who had a plan for her...of that, she had no doubt.

Based on his cold demeanor and cruel words, that plan may be quite terrible.

And she was utterly under his control.

6

Patience stood next to her husband—what a strange notion—in the ballroom of Rath Hall and did her best to remember the names of the guests to whom she'd been introduced. They came one after another to congratulate her and the duke.

There was the duke's aunt, Lady Eleanor Buchanan, a warm woman with very kind eyes. Patience wondered if the whisper she'd heard during the ceremony—*I like her!*—had come from her. The duke's sister, Lady Chastity, had the same coloring as her brother, but with lovely feminine features. Though her manner was as cold and aloof as his.

Her new sister...

Then there were two Lord Seatons and their wives. Two duchesses of Grandhampton, one of whom was a dowager in her older years, and the other a young, pretty lady. There was the Duke of Grandhampton, the Duchess and Duke of Kelford. He had three sisters, one of whom was around her age. The other two were very charming twins a couple of years younger.

All of them were striking and beautiful and extremely polite.

And all of them made her head spin as she tried and failed to imagine how she could ever fit into this regal room. It had dark blue paneled walls, detailed moldings on the ceiling, and multiple crystal chandeliers. Heavy velvet drapes of a deep burgundy flanked the long, arched windows, pulled back just enough to let in the sunshine. The intricately carved dark mahogany furniture with red upholstery was arresting. And rich scents of perfume, champagne, and decadent food filled the air.

It was strange to have several footmen and a stately butler walk around the room, serving everyone drinks, when for most of her life her family couldn't afford a single servant. She felt like she needed to join them, to take one of the trays out of their hands and offer the guests refreshments. They'd had a housekeeper and cook before John went to Oxford, but they had to let her go after they spent all their money on John's tuition.

Patience kept nodding politely and smiling with all the warmth in her heart to these kind people who seemed to welcome her to her new life and didn't remark on her near fall at the wedding. They didn't show any sign they noticed the poor state of her dress or that she had no idea what to talk to them about. She kept asking them questions about themselves just so that no one would suspect how utterly out of place she felt.

And since leaving the carriage, she hadn't exchanged a single word with her husband.

"Finally I get a chance at an introduction," said a tall, handsome man with golden hair and violet eyes. He had a perfectly fitted coat, a light yellow waistcoat, and wore a golden signet ring with a stag. He gave a bow, and his eyes ran over her with male appreciation. "Dorian, will you introduce your best man and best friend to your wife?"

Dorian…her husband's name was Dorian. The vicar had said it during the ceremony, but her head had been swimming, and it was only now that she registered it. What a beautiful, dark name…just like him.

As Patience glanced up at her husband, the muscles of his jaw moved, and he glared at his supposed best friend. An unease shifted in Patience.

"Duchess, allow me to introduce Lucien, the Duke of Luhst."

"Pleasure," Luhst murmured and stretched his hand out towards her, bowing once again.

What was she supposed to—

"Your hand, Duchess," said Lucien with a soft smile and a cunning glint in his eyes.

Did he want to kiss her hand? Was that allowed? Her husband didn't even kiss her hand! She glanced at Rath, whose face was twitching with barely contained rage.

"Lucien—" growled her husband, just like an angry dog.

"Oh, go on, Duchess," murmured Luhst like a devil, "you don't want to leave me rejected like this. It's merely a gesture of high respect and appreciation from a man to a woman of high class."

She felt everyone's eyes on her. She had no idea about these things. But her husband was positively scaring her. She shoved her hand into Luhst's; he bowed his head even more and lightly touched his lips to her skin.

She burst into flames. That was what it felt like, her whole body hit by fiery wall of embarrassment. When the Duke of Luhst let go of her hand, she wanted to disappear.

"See, not so scary?" he said with a devious smile.

"You are despicable!" barked the Duke of Rath at Luhst, making everyone's heads turn to him. "You've seduced every woman in London and now are trying for my *wife*?"

He was making a scene. And Patience didn't understand why. This fury she saw in him, the clenched fists, the quickly rising and falling chest, the sinews on his neck bulging beneath his red skin.

Was he going to throw himself on his best friend for kissing her hand? No, surely not because of her!

"Please forgive me," she muttered. "I am in urgent need of fresh air."

As Patience hurried away from the tense scene in the ballroom, she navigated through the unfamiliar corridors of Rath Hall, her heart pounding in her chest. She passed through an arched doorway, finding herself in a long, elegantly decorated gallery. The walls were adorned with portraits of the duke's ancestors with dark, almost black backgrounds. The polished marble floor echoed with the click of her heels, and the afternoon sunlight streamed through the tall leaded-glass windows, casting intricate patterns on the plush rugs.

At the end of the gallery, Patience reached a set of French doors that opened onto a stone terrace and closed her eyes, gulping in the cool, fresh air full of scents of decomposing vegetation and nature. Taking in breaths of air was soothing.

It was only when she opened her eyes that she noticed what spread before her, just a few steps down from the terrace. A garden.

It was as vast her eyes could see—although she couldn't see much at all because of the dead and dried-out trees, bushes, underbrush, and grass.

The overgrown expanse sprawled before Patience, wild and untamed. What must have once been manicured lawns were now a tangle of weeds and grass, the blades reaching towards the sky in defiant spikes. Dandelions, their yellow heads bobbing in the breeze, dotted the greenery.

She thought she could almost distinguish what must have

been flower beds in a jumble of foliage. She saw old, desiccated rosebushes in the chaos of brambles and thorny vines that had crept in from the edges, snaking across the soil like grasping fingers. The trees, ancient and gnarled, loomed over the garden like beasts frozen in time. Heavy with age and neglect, their branches drooped low to the ground, creating shade that swallowed the light.

She walked what must have once been a path, barely discernible amid the overgrowth.

She gasped, mesmerized. What a huge space, and yet so abandoned, so lonely. Such a stark contrast with the rest of the house, which was refined and opulent.

She craved to touch and to see her rosebushes so much, her fingers tingled. She walked through the garden, lightly brushing her fingers over the leaves and stems. She relished even the dandelions, nettles, and coltsfoot. With some work and planning, this garden could be beautiful.

Her own personal heaven. She could see it in its full glory in her inner eye.

She must have walked for a few minutes when she turned a corner and stopped.

There was a glasshouse.

A glasshouse!

She'd only read about them in one book. She'd thought they were a myth! They were very expensive and difficult to build. She knew this could be a haven for plants.

It was a large rectangular building with a vaulted ceiling high enough to accommodate trees. The iron frame, once painted a deep black, now bore the marks of time, with green rust-resistant paint flaking away to reveal the weathered metal beneath. The neglected state of the structure made it clear that no one had set foot inside for an extended period. Grime and dirt obscured the glass panes, making it difficult to discern the interior, though Patience could make out the silhouettes of dry grasses and twisted branches pressing against the clouded windows.

Oh, what plants used to grow there? Her curiosity was piqued, and for the first time in four days, she felt a ping of happiness, a true joy her heart could sing. Could she possibly be allowed to use this?

She approached the building and laid her hand on the glass door, which was covered in a layer of dirt so thick she could barely see what was inside. Would the duke really mind if she brought it to order and restored it? Could she use it for botanical experiments? Oh, what if she could get her hands on some exotic plants that were difficult to grow in this climate…like tomatoes, lemons, oranges, figs, and perhaps even a *coffee arabica*?

As Patience reached out to open the door of the glasshouse, she hesitated. A thick bush obscured part of the view, revealing shards of broken glass. Frowning, she noticed the glass to the right of the door was shattered. Dirty glass shards littered the ground, some hidden by the bush. It appeared as if the break had originated from within. How? What happened? Yet another mystery to add to this house and her new husband.

"Stop," said a cold, velvety voice behind her, and a wave of dread washed over her.

She turned. Among the overgrown bushes and trees, stood the Duke of Rath. He was breathtakingly, heartbreakingly gorgeous, a dark lord among dead vegetation and rampant weeds.

"Um…" Her fingers clenched at the skirt of her dress. She suddenly felt like she'd stepped into someone's private space without permission.

"What are you doing here?" he asked.

It was the first thing he'd ever asked her, she realized

distantly. And it sounded like an accusation. She felt like she needed to justify herself.

"Am I not supposed to be here?" she asked, fumbling with her dress.

His eyes darted to the glasshouse behind her, and a haunted expression flitted over his face. "No."

"Why not?" she asked as she took a few tentative steps away from the glasshouse and towards him. "This is just a garden, and one that needs attention."

His jaw twitched as he followed her every step. "Because I said so."

She stopped a few steps from him. He appeared quite as furious as he had back in the ballroom. But right now, he wasn't scary. He looked...lost.

He was the master of her and her husband, and as her mama taught her, she was his to command. But she couldn't accept the premise of this explanation.

Because I said so? No. She had questions.

"What is your reason for a 'no'?" she asked.

His face straightened in surprise. "My reason?"

"Because while 'no,' without a doubt, does mean 'no,' the reasoning 'because I said so' is not well-grounded. Or defensible. Or very adult, to be frank."

Slowly, he stalked towards her, a storm brewing in his eyes. His upper lip curved upward, as he was about to bare his teeth.

Her stomach dropped in real fear.

Take it back, take it back, take it back!

Distantly, she registered herself backing away from him. He was so much larger and taller than her—she had to crane her neck to look at him, for God's sake! And those muscles, Lord, he could snap her in half if he wished to!

"Are you calling me *a child*?" he rumbled.

"No," she said as she kept backing up down the gravel path,

her hands searching for something big and sturdy to put between herself and the furious, advancing duke. "I merely require more explanation than 'because I said so.'"

Oh, no, she'd made it worse. She could actually see his white teeth as his lips thinned and curled inwards.

"Do you think you're so smart, arguing with me, asking imprudent questions? Your queries are dangerous. You are the one behaving like a child, sweet girl. You just stepped into an unfamiliar world. There will be no one to pour your soul out to here. No one to let you cry on their bosom. You just married a duke. You need to learn to compose yourself, think about what you say and ask. Safe is the last thing you should feel."

Every accusation was a blast straight to her core. Naive. Young. Desperately trying to please. All true. How did he see her through like that? It must be because he was so much older, so much more experienced. Never in her life had she been near such a confident, powerful, intelligent man.

She didn't know what to do. Should she shut up? Keep talking? Reason with him? He must see his behavior had no logical ground.

"But isn't it safe when there are dozens of footmen on the property?" The words blurted out of her like hail as she kept backing up and he kept slowly advancing on her, his fists clenched. "The concern for my safety being a woman alone outside can with all likelihood be overlooked. Unless there are wild bears living somewhere in the overgrowth, which I highly doubt since bears do not like the company of people, and there aren't many left on the British Isles. Therefore, I'd argue that the reasoning about wild animals is also void. So I'm perfectly safe here. Are you perhaps concerned I'll use the garden to run away—that I will hide among the brambles and scramble over the wall? I'm very interested in staying, as the contract with my father stipulates that you will pay off all of my family's debts and save my papa from debtor's prison and my family from being on the streets. So I won't run away. And this garden does need lots of work...which I'm happy to provide. I'd love to, in fact. I can see a stunning chestnut tree here. And a lovely ash tree there. And just pruning some branches, removing these dry bushes, and putting in some fresh boxwood shrubs could bring in plenty of light and new life."

She turned to the glasshouse and sighed. "And this..." she said with her voice ringing in awe. "Oh heavens...please allow me to restore this to its original glory."

When she looked at him, his lips were pulled into a fierce snarl. His gloved hand was twitching, clenching and unclenching.

"You are forbidden to lay a single finger on the garden!" he roared, and she startled, taking a step back. Just a few more and she'd be pressed against the panes. "And especially do not ever dare to step anywhere near the glasshouse!"

"But, Your Grace—"

"In fact," he growled as he began pacing in a semicircle around her, looking as though he was going to devour her. "You will have to follow certain rules. Do you understand?"

She felt her shoulders tense and her neck shrink into her frame. She nodded.

"Number one, you will have your own part of the house, and I will have mine. You will not be allowed into any of my chambers."

She swallowed, blinking. What in the world had caused this outrage?

"No sneaking around in my part of the house. You will only come by invitation! Number two, there will be no wifely duties. Do not expect me to come to you. Do not appear in my bed to tempt me."

Wifely duties? Tempt him? Good God, was she so repulsive to him? It must be the dress!

"Why?" she asked, her voice trembling as though she was hurt.

She wasn't hurt. Why should she be hurt by the unpleasant attitude of someone who didn't even know her?

He threw her a glare of such magnitude she felt as if he'd scorched her like dry grass.

"Do not pretend like you are not relieved. You will be busy enough with duties as my duchess. You must perform certain obligations and organize entertainments I've long neglected. And there will be social obligations and events for the London ton."

She licked her dry lips and took a step closer to him, which made him flinch and step back. "I understand."

"If you fail to keep to the rules, I will be forced to punish you."

Punish her? She blinked, her cheeks heating. "Punish me how?" she asked.

He mumbled something under his breath that could only have been a curse. "You do not want to find out, Duchess," he growled.

Duchess...it was as though he was addressing someone else. *Smile. No matter what, look at the positive. He hasn't thrown you out yet. He mustn't throw you out. You must please him and adhere to his rules so that your family is safe and provided for.*

"I'll do my best to adhere to your rules, Duke," she said and smiled. "But may I ask you one thing? Why did you marry me?"

Color drained from his face, and his eyes darted nervously as his jaw clenched. "What?"

Patience's eyebrows rose. Was she seeing this right? Such a fearsome man as the duke looked hesitant...cornered...

"Well," she said as she approached him, feeling brave,

"since Papa returned from London with the news of our betrothal, I've been puzzled. You'd never met me. You didn't know my family. I have no dowry, yet you're willing to pay Papa's debts. I'm just a simple landowner's daughter with no titles and a scandal surrounding my name. Why choose me over a respectable young lady from a noble family?"

Shoulders squaring, he drew himself up. His eyes narrowed, brows lowered, and upper lip curled into a snarl, baring his teeth. A flutter rippled through Patience's stomach as she realized her moment of triumph had evaporated.

"Rule number three," he growled. "Do not ask questions!"

7

"Welcome, gentlemen." Thorne Blackmore, the owner of the most exclusive underground club in London, spread his arms wide.

Dorian and the six other dukes entered the long three-story brick building situated in the bowels of Whitechapel. It was beautifully maintained and had a large back mews with household buildings to sustain all of Elysium's operations and whatever other shady business Thorne Blackmore undertook to acquire such riches. The entrance was marked by a semicircle of six sharp, sunray-like triangles above the door, a symbol known to all members.

The large, semidark room welcomed Dorian with indulgent scents of expensive alcohol and tobacco, exotic perfume, and coffee. Dark teal walls with exquisite, sensual art surrounded him in candlelight. A string quartet in the corner played "Stabat Mater" by Pergolesi, and a pair of superb opera singers —one male, one female—sang the slow, emotional piece, their voices interplaying so expertly, the high notes stabbed straight into Dorian's heart.

Thorne Blackmore certainly knew how to please his clients.

"Good evening, Mr. Blackmore," said Dorian as he strode in and looked around the room.

There were several tables with chairs, where members could usually eat, drink, and gamble, but which now stood empty. The panther in the cage at the far end lay on his stomach and raised his head, his eyes on Dorian and his friends while a python slithered very slowly around the branches of a marula tree behind a glass wall.

"I hear congratulations are in order," said Blackmore.

Dorian's jaw worked. "Thank you. Your sister was at my wedding with Lord Richard."

Thorne cocked his head, his cold, dark eyes warming momentarily at the mention of Jane. "I'm sure she enjoyed herself."

Dorian nodded. "I hope so."

Silence hung in the air, with the unspoken question: Why was Dorian spending his wedding night here, and not with his wife? But Blackmore was paid very well to keep his mouth shut and satisfy the deepest, secret cravings of the dukes.

"I apologize for having canceled our reservation a few days ago," said Dorian. "I had urgent matters to attend."

He had, of course, needed to meet with Mr. George Rose in London and arrange many things for the wedding, including the special license.

"Of course," said Thorne Blackmore. "I hope you understand the irreversible fee and the extra payment for an urgent booking for this night. I had to close the club for regular visitors."

"Most certainly," said Fortyne as he was already putting down his violet coat and hanging it on the back of the chair. "Do put the bill in my name. This exuberant night is my wedding present to one of my best friends. It seems Rath urgently needs his...ahem...usual distraction."

Blackmore raised one dark eyebrow and cocked his head in understanding.

Pryde clenched his fists. "Clearly, if the groom abandoned his bride mere hours after their vows, the marriage was a mistake." His chestnut eyes met Dorian's directly and accusingly. "This is just the beginning of a complete disaster. And you know why."

The beast within Dorian lashed like a fiery, burning whip against raw skin. "You know nothing, Constantine."

Dorian was furious with himself. With Miss Rose—nay, with his duchess—for asking all the right questions, for not being afraid of him, for not keeping her distance.

He'd come here because he wanted her.

Truth was, the moment he'd seen her in the church, he had been completely smitten with her. And that terrified him. He'd never felt anything like that in his entire life—awe and a sense of wonder that she had miraculously stepped into his miserable, lonely life.

He wanted her. Badly.

And yet, she was so innocent. So pure. So young.

With that smile that warmed the icy depths of his heart.

He needed to appease the raging beast inside, which loved nothing more than to destroy beautiful things. Vases. Paintings. Art.

If he took her to his bed, he'd destroy her, too.

He couldn't do that to an innocent, beautiful thing like his wife.

He needed someone who knew what they were doing. Who knew what he needed.

Lilith.

"This is going to end badly," said Pryde, standing at Dorian's right shoulder. "She's *his* sister!"

"It's going to be fine!" Lucien stood next to Dorian and clapped him on his shoulder with all his might. "She's so pretty, friend. You did the right thing. Well, not yet. The aforementioned *right thing* is waiting to be done by you back in Rath Hall."

"Shut your mouths, both of you. You two are driving me insane!" Dorian roared and marched away from them, deeper into the club. "Where's Lilith, Mr. Blackmore?"

Blackmore, who watched them with an amused look, nodded. "All of the ladies are on their way to you, gentlemen."

And then they appeared. Lilith was a tall, willowy woman in her late twenties, with a mane of shiny black hair. Her big dark eyes were catlike—the hooded eyes of a true seductress—and they were trained on him. She was dressed in a crimson gown, which dipped low and left little to imagination. Her lips were painted red, too, and he wondered if she had dressed just for him, to match his colors.

The rest of the sex workers followed her. Blonds, brunettes, redheads. Thin, curvy, tall and short, from all kinds of backgrounds. All of them were beautiful and carefully selected by Blackmore—and fiercely protected by him.

They spilled through the room, each already knowing their roles and what each duke required.

Lucien wanted three ladies tonight. Pryde had one woman he'd always met with, although he'd always hid with her in a separate room, and Dorian never knew what he did in there exactly. If Constantine simply talked to her, spilling his deepest insecurities and secrets, Dorian wouldn't be surprised.

The Duke of Enveigh lounged against the plush velvet settee, his silky green waistcoat shining under the dark coat embroidered with the serpent of his crest. His gray eyes glinted as he watched the male courtesan slowly undress the blushing female sex worker, her gown slipping from her shoulders.

The Duke of Eccess threw his head back in ecstasy, his auburn coat adorned with the boar of his lineage lying discarded on the floor. The women, draped in silks of blush and gold, drizzled the finest Parisian chocolate over their bountiful curves, the rich hues of their silks a contrast to his honey-blond locks. Their fingers tangled in his hair as he feasted upon their skin, the dark brown depths of his eyes glinting with mischief.

Irevrence and Fortyne were led into separate chambers, and Dorian knew the rest of his friends would take their own chambers, too.

Lilith's gaze stayed fixed on him as she moved towards him and he moved towards her, but instead of desire stirring in his loins as it had every time he saw her, he couldn't stop seeing the golden curls and the innocent big blue eyes framed by long, curly eyelashes. Not the dark eyes of the woman before him, glistening with sin. Where Lilith was tall and willowy, Dorian suddenly craved lush breasts and curves.

"Your Grace," she murmured seductively into his ear as she laid her thin, perfect hand on his chest. "I was wondering where you were last week."

Her hands were clean and smooth, short nails manicured to perfect ovals. He had noticed how weathered, scratched, and reddened his wife's hands were. Faint traces of dirt remained under her short fingernails despite having obviously been scrubbed with vigor.

Almost as tall as he, Lilith leaned closer to his ear and whispered in a low, throaty voice that sounded like pure sex, "Come."

She took him by the hand and led him to the usual chamber where she accepted visitors. Every step as he followed her felt wrong. But the beast needed its relief, needed to be sated. He couldn't imagine going through twelve months constantly tempted by his wife but without sexual satisfaction.

Through the grand walnut doors, she led him into a corridor with several doors to the left and right. Passing by an open door, he saw the Duke of Irevrence, dressed in pristine white, reclining upon a bed with silk sheets like a fallen angel amid temptation. With his ash-blond hair tied back, Irevrence lazily looked over the several sex workers moving around him, ready to please him, to indulge in whatever whim or fancy struck his mercurial mind.

And there, in the most opulent chamber of Elysium, was where the Duke of Fortyne, in a rich violet coat, played a game of chance and seduction. Fortyne always requested the most exclusive sex worker. Dorian was not sure what it involved, but he was certain the bastard always won. As he did in business.

Dorian and Lilith arrived at a large and luxurious chamber with heavy brocaded curtains that completely covered the windows. An exquisitely carved large bed with silky rose-patterned sheets and a white mink throw stood at the far side. Golden candelabras lit each corner of the room, and a small round table for two with wine and refreshments stood by the fireplace, in which a real fire played.

On the sideboard was a box with an array of the instruments of pleasure Dorian liked to use with Lilith: ties, gags, thin silver handcuffs and fetters, blindfolds, a soft cat-o'-nine-tails, and others. He had bought them all and they were not allowed to be used by anyone but him.

The room was set for his pleasure with a knowing partner.

And yet the ache in his chest was a constant reminder of his wife.

Lilith undressed herself and stood before him naked. He

looked her over, waiting for his arousal to make an appearance, for the beast inside him to make its first hungry roar.

But there was nothing. Not even the memory of every time he'd had her pinned under him, with his hand on her throat, pounding into her like an animal, with no regard for her pleasure or comfort, only hearing the rhythmical, greedy slap of skin against skin.

And yet, she loved it. She had her climax before he did, every time. She could take all his brutishness, all his savagery.

Lilith and he...they fit. They were the same.

His wife, on the other hand, was everything he was not: light, innocent, open, young, naive, sheltered, curious, and she wore her heart on her sleeve.

Everything he craved. And everything he could never have.

Lilith came to him and kissed him, her lips tender and soft, and expert. He inhaled her scent.

Now. He would start to want her now. Now his beast would awaken and roar and he'd throw her on the bed. He'd spank her firm buttocks...and feel her wet arousal against his hand.

But he'd imagine his wife's luxurious behind.

He couldn't kiss Lilith back. He waited for her to do something. She wrapped both her hands around his neck, pressing her naked body into his clothes. He could feel her warmth, her silky skin, her familiar scent—a heady mix of flowers and musk that once would have ignited a fire in his veins. But now, even as her skilled hands worked to undress him, he found himself yearning for the delicate fragrance of roses that clung to his wife's skin. Lilith's touch, once electrifying, now felt hollow compared to the gentle brush of his wife's fingertips against his hand when he put his ring on her.

He wrapped his arms around Lilith and brought her to him. As her hands roamed over his body, Dorian's mind drifted to his wife. It was more than just her beauty that drew him in; it was her innocent spirit, her curiosity, and her bravery as she didn't back down from him even when he was so furious and no doubt terrifying, and the way she kept trying to break through his façade.

Forget Miss Rose! Forget Miss Rose!

She wasn't Miss Rose anymore. She was the Duchess of Rath. His to take as he pleased. His to bed. To kiss. To spank. To bring to pleasure.

"Is everything all right, Your Grace?" asked Lilith as she leaned back slightly, her half-lidded eyes watching him.

He let go of her and stepped back. The beast woke up and roared, angry at him now for starving it of its pleasures.

But he couldn't do it. For better or worse, he gave a vow to one woman before God, and he simply couldn't lay his hands on another.

"I can't," he growled, then turned around and strode out of Lilith's room, his heart pounding and his mind reeling.

He had never walked away from pleasure before, never denied himself the satisfaction of his darkest desires.

And as he navigated the dimly lit corridors of Elysium, he still felt the need pulsating in his body. Unsatisfied.

As he stepped out into the cool night air, he promised himself he'd keep strong however difficult it might be. He'd ride harder. He'd swim longer. He'd hire a boxing partner.

Anything to alleviate this tension rising inside him like steam in a cauldron.

All he needed was to maintain his self-control. And not imagine his sweet, virginal wife moaning with pleasure as he thrust into her...

8

"*Bonjour, Your Grace!*" exclaimed a female voice with a strong French accent the next morning, and Patience jumped in her bed, tugging the edge of her blanket all the way to her chin.

She blinked through the semidarkness at the female figure who marched through her bedchamber towards the windows. Right, her French lady's maid who'd come to help her undress last night.

"*Bonjour,*" Patience mumbled in response, "Mademoiselle Antoinette."

She was a petite woman with delicate features, chestnut hair styled in the latest French fashion, and warm brown eyes. Mademoiselle Antoinette pulled the heavy curtains open to let the morning light in, and Patience squinted her eyes.

"*Avez-vous bien dormi?*" asked Mademoiselle Antoinette as she hurried energetically towards the next window. "*Il ne faisait pas trop froid? Je me demande comment vous aimeriez être habillée aujourd'hui?*"

Despite Patience's limited French, she managed to understand that the woman asked if she slept well, if it was not too cold, and how Patience would like to be dressed today.

Yesterday afternoon, after the wedding guests left, the housekeeper, Mrs. Knight, had introduced the servants to her, but Patience felt so overwhelmed that all of the faces and names had blurred together. And when Mademoiselle Antoinette had come to help her to undress last night, Patience had sent her away as she was ashamed that a duchess's lady's maid would see the poor state of her clothes.

"Things could be better," said Patience as she forced out a chuckle.

She was still tired, her body heavy and aching with insomnia. In Rose Cottage, she slept in the same bed as Anne and Frances. In Rath Hall, her bed felt enormous and cold.

"Oh, forgive me," said Mademoiselle Antoinette with a heavy French accent as she marched back towards the door. "Do you prefer to speak in English?"

Mademoiselle Antoinette opened the door to pick up something and a small breeze rushed inside, bringing the faintest whiff of musk, bergamot, and pepper...

Her husband. Patience's nipples hardened of their own accord. Surely due to the breeze, not because she thought of him.

"I would, yes," said Patience. "I'm afraid my French is limited."

"Oh," said Mademoiselle Antoinette as she returned to the room with a large pitcher of steaming water. She approached the washstand, which held an ornate empty basin and a mirror. "Of course. If that's what you prefer. Most ladies I've served preferred French."

While she poured the warm water into the basin, Patience licked her lips nervously. It felt strange to have someone else prepare her wash water. Typically, at home, Emily would put the cauldron on the fire, and Patience was usually the one who'd bring jugs of warm water upstairs for each of the three bedrooms and pour it in the washbasins. Now, her hands felt empty, her stomach in knots with guilt and discomfort. What was she supposed to do with herself?

"Well, I did learn it when I was little. When Mama had more time and was able to tutor my oldest sisters, Emily and Beatrice. Some of it must have stuck in my memory. After that, someone would read out loud from the single French book we had in the house in the evenings when we all sat together after supper."

Mademoiselle Antoinette nodded and smiled. *"Bien sur!* Whatever you'd like, Your Grace. Perhaps you'd like to wash now?"

Still in her night chemise, Patience washed up, feeling on edge from the presence of a stranger in such intimate vicinity.

After she dried her face with the softest of fabrics, she looked helplessly at Mademoiselle Antoinette.

"Voulez-vous vous asseoir ici?" she asked as she gestured towards the padded oval dressing stool standing by a vanity table with a large mirror.

"Right," said Patience. "Of course."

She sat and Mademoiselle kept chatting away, gesturing animatedly, switching into French, and interrupting herself with an apology in English. She combed Patience's hair, and Patience couldn't shake the sensation of needles pricking her skin. A stranger, a servant, was tending to her, when all her life the only touch she'd known was that of her sisters or her parents.

She mumbled something at Mademoiselle Antoinette's suggestions for a hairstyle and accessories for today and sat for what must have been one hour while Mademoiselle created the most elegant chignon at the nape of her neck with soft little curls around her face. The updo was then adorned with jeweled hairpins and a small delicate hairnet made of gold thread.

This was the most beautiful hairstyle Patience had ever had in her life. The feeling of being completely out of her element was like walking on a shaking ground. She couldn't have felt more out of place.

Then Mademoiselle Antoinette laid out three gowns to choose from.

"*Celle-ci*," she said, "the pale blue muslin is light and airy, perfect for a morning walk if you please. This blue brings out your eyes, *non*? This soft lavender one is elegant yet practical. The mint green linen is fresh and will bring out your youthful skin. It is *très chic*, very fashionable this season in Paris. All the ladies are wearing this shade."

Patience looked them over. No seams, no holes, they were pristine. Newly made. All of her previous dresses had been worn by each of her sisters before her. "Where did they come from?"

"Oh, *je pense* it was Madame Eleanor Buchanan who wanted to give these to you as her wedding present. These were quite cleverly designed to fit most figures since they are sewn without specific measurements, but I'll adjust them once you try them on."

Oh, Dorian's aunt... How thoughtful yet practical of her. She must have foreseen Patience wouldn't own any gowns suitable for a duchess.

"*Alors*, which do you prefer, Your Grace?"

"I...I think the blue, perhaps?"

Mademoiselle Antoinette nodded and placed the lavender and the green dress back in the armoire. "Ah, *oui*, a safe choice! *Et vous savez*, at the last ball at the Tuileries, everyone was ablaze in such colors. *Les robes étaient absolument magnifiques!*"

Patience was struggling to keep up. The extent of her French was coming to an end. "I'm sure they were lovely."

Mademoiselle Antoinette gestured for Patience to raise her arms and when she did that, she pulled her chemise up and over her head. "And the hats! Plumes that touched the sky! *Vous devez voir ça*—you must try one sometime. Imagine, a feather soaring from a bonnet like a bird in flight!"

Patience could imagine nothing stranger than having a giant feather like a bird on her hat, especially when she stood naked before a woman she had met only yesterday. She wanted to cover herself while Mademoiselle, seemingly unaware of her discomfort, retrieved a fresh chemise. "The...the feathers sound...quite something," mumbled Patience.

As Mademoiselle Antoinette was about to put the new chemise over her head, Patience stopped her, one arm covering her breasts, the other stretched out for the chemise. "Please, I can do it myself."

Mademoiselle Antoinette chuckled. "*S'il vous plaît*, Your Grace! I am here to do this for you. Please, stretch out your arms."

Patience didn't have the courage or energy to contradict and simply did as Mademoiselle said.

"Oh, and the gossip, *mon Dieu!*" she continued as though there was no other care in the world. "Did you hear about Miss Beige and Lord Smist? *Scandaleux!*"

At least the chemise was on now, soft and white as a cloud and smelling like lavender and soap. Mademoiselle put a corset over Patience's head and pulled it down to her waist. Patience shook her head. "No, I haven't heard..."

Mademoiselle Antoinette waved her hand dismissively. "Ah, it is just as well. Better to stay above such things, *n'est-ce pas?*"

As Mademoiselle laced the corset and then pulled the

gown over top of everything, chirping about gossip and events of the London ton, Patience stood tensely wondering how this could be her life.

Several times she was about to open her mouth and say she'd do it herself, but she gave in to the inevitable, knowing Mademoiselle would just say it was her task to dress her.

It was one of the most uncomfortable things she'd ever experienced, having a servant dress her like a doll!

Her mind, completely disinterested in gossip, drifted to her roses. How had the bushes survived the travel? She had dug the best ones out, tied the root system along with some soil in pieces of canvas, and transported them here with her meager sack of clothes and her botanical journals. Now they stood somewhere in the household buildings, and the duke wouldn't even allow her to use the garden. What would become of them?

"*Voilà!*" exclaimed Mademoiselle Antoinette as she stepped away from Patience, looking her over.

And when Patience looked into the mirror for the first time, she didn't recognize herself. Never in her life had she worn such a beautiful gown or such an elaborate hairstyle. This was how she was supposed to look yesterday for her wedding to a duke. This Patience, in a gown that made her eyes shimmer and her hair shine like spun gold, looked like she belonged to the right of the nave, with her husband's guests, the dukes and the duchesses and lords and ladies.

But inside, she couldn't feel any less like one.

Patience had never felt so alone in her entire life as she felt in Rath Hall over the next few days.

Confined to her quarters by the first of her husband's rules, she had looked through every corner of her part of the house. Her quarters consisted of her bedroom, a dressing room directly adjacent to it, two additional bedrooms for guests, a sitting room downstairs where she could receive visitors, her own dining room, and a drawing room where she could write her correspondence, draw, embroider, read, or play a pianoforte.

The combined area was at least three times larger than Rose Cottage. She had shared that tiny house with seven other people, and now she was all alone in this vast space.

Everything was immaculate. Clean. Rich. Antiques and family heirlooms decorated fireplace mantels, sideboards, and walls. She was afraid to move the wrong way and bump against something, smashing it to pieces.

Rose Cottage was full of constant chatter, laughter, and the bustling activity of her family. In contrast, the calm silence at Rath Hall was eerie, punctuated only by the ticking of a clock or the echo of her own footsteps in the vast, empty corridors and rooms.

Her family had left the day of the wedding. So had the duke's sister, Chastity, and his aunt, who had both moved to Rath's London house to give the newlyweds privacy.

They truly didn't have to. These newlyweds weren't spending any time together to need privacy.

She hadn't talked to her husband since the day of their wedding, and yet, she could sense his presence in every little thing. He was in the dark stone walls, in the exquisite ancient furniture, in the portraits of his ancestors and the priceless art. He was even in the feminine style of her own quarters, silently pointing out how little she belonged there.

Her bedroom was an opulent prison with high ceilings and heavy antique furnishings. The air was still, holding the faintest scent of lavender and wood polish. A massive four-poster bed, draped with silky sheets, stood against the wall. The fireplace loomed, tall and cold. She was sure she could ask Mrs. Knight to have one of the maids light it, but she didn't dare. How could she command anyone?

In the mornings, Patience stood at the window, her breath hitching as she watched the duke spar with his trainer. Watching his hard, shirtless body move was the highlight of her day. Even from her window, she could see the rippling muscles of his chest and back play under his glistening skin. The jabs of his bulging arms were fast and unexpected, the powerful grace of his movements obvious. Like Ares, the god of war, he didn't hold back, wasn't afraid, just kept moving, concentrating on every step and maneuver. From time to time he massaged his gloved hand; it must have still pained him. But he never removed the glove.

It wasn't just his physique that drew her in. As he moved with lethal grace, she felt a pang of longing. Not just for his touch, but for the ease with which he inhabited his world. He was the master here, powerful and direct, while she was a prisoner, trapped by an obligation to her family and overwhelmed by a life she barely understood.

The emptiness of her bed, the silence of the rooms, the constant reminder that she was alone. It was too much and not enough. Seeing him, so vibrant and alive, only intensified her yearning. She wanted to be part of his world, to share his strength, to feel as free and confident as he did.

But all she could do was watch and wish, something within acutely interested in the cold man who seemed so far out of reach.

Then he'd pull a shirt over his sweaty torso, mount a black horse that looked massive and intimidating, and with an Irish wolfhound at his heels, he'd gallop away as though the devil chased him. After a while, she saw him dive into the pond near the house, and stay under the water for a long time, emerging all wet and exhausted, before walking back into the house.

Patience was in the sitting room, staring out of the window, when the housekeeper came in. Mrs. Knight was a woman in her late fifties, with a spare figure, a long, thin face, and gray hair in an immaculate knot at the back of her head.

She began shooting out questions, and Patience stood with her mouth gaping open while Mrs. Knight waited for her answers.

Patience smiled because she had no idea what the difference was between a velouté sauce and a hollandaise sauce, or which her husband preferred.

Whether she'd like Canard à l'Orange or Tournedos Rossini for dinner. And for soups, would she prefer Bouillabaisse or Potage à la Reine?

And for the next week's menu, would she like to include the duke's favorite dish?

Favorite dish? Goodness, Patience didn't know a single thing he liked, just what he didn't like.

Her.

Anywhere near him or the garden.

She threw a longing glance outside.

"Whatever you think best, Mrs. Knight."

The housekeeper's response was a barely noticeable pursing of her lips. Patience had just opened her mouth to ask what the duke's favourite dish was but closed it. Perhaps that was something a wife of five days was supposed to know, and this would be yet another way to show Mrs. Knight how unfit Patience was for the role of duchess.

"Perhaps Your Grace would like some new clothes?" asked Mrs. Knight as her gaze dropped very slightly down Patience's blue dress, which she was wearing again after cycling through the other two gowns. "I took the liberty to ask Lady Buchanan's modiste from London to come and take your measurements tomorrow. Would that be fitting?"

A blush hit Patience's face. Even the housekeeper knew better than she what should be done.

She smiled, her only shield against judgment. "Um. Of course. Thank you for being so considerate, Mrs. Knight."

Mrs. Knight made a little surprised jerk with her body as though something small had hit her. Was she not used to compliments? "You're quite welcome, Your Grace."

Patience grinned. "Oh, and my bed is so soft and has been exquisitely made every morning."

The only problem was, Patience couldn't sleep in it because she felt so alone and so small in that huge bed. At home, there were always noises around the house, someone talking, or laughing, singing, cleaning, floorboards creaking under someone's feet. But in Rath Hall, it was so quiet at night, she started imagining noises. Little scratches in the dark corners, distant heavy footsteps, an uneven, soft knocking against the windowpanes. She lay tense and on edge, her skin crawling despite the soft, clean sheets that smelled like lavender and soap.

But that was certainly not Mrs. Knight's fault.

Mrs. Knight cocked her head, little nets of wrinkles crinkling around her eyes. "I'm pleased to hear that."

Feeling like Mrs. Knight and she had started to turn a corner, Patience suddenly felt brave.

"The garden," she blurted out, unable to contain her dismay. "It pains me to see it so neglected. And I have these rosebushes from home..."

All traces of pleasantness disappeared from Mrs. Knight's face. "The garden is strictly forbidden, Your Grace."

"But why?"

Mrs. Knight's mouth twitched. "It's not for me to tell. You will have to ask His Grace."

"Oh," said Patience, the mention of her husband wiping

the smile off her face. "Right. Will he be dining with me tonight?"

"No, I'm afraid he wishes to dine alone."

So this was how things were going to go? This whole year? They'd be living separate lives, never seeing each other, never talking to each other. What was the point? And what about her? Her rosebushes would dry out and die like the garden outside Rath Hall, and she'd keep wandering empty rooms trying to decide between a Canard à l'Orange and a Canard Farci, or whatever those dishes were, until she'd wither and die herself.

"May I ask one more thing… Do you know why he always wears that glove?" asked Patience.

Mrs. Knight's gaze softened as she cocked her head very slightly. "I'm afraid it is not up to me to say. Shall we continue?" she pressed. "I need your decision on staff changes, guest room refurbishing, and the rearrangement of the family portraits. An artist will come next month to paint you."

The next day, just as Mrs. Knight had predicted, the modiste, Mrs. Newman, arrived with her entourage and swaths of fabric and lace. And for the first time, Patience's quarters didn't feel lonely.

"Your Grace, what do you think of this silk for a ballgown?" the modiste inquired, her eyes expectant.

"Um, it's lovely," Patience murmured, touching the fabric tentatively. "I will need it in seven days… My husband's aunt has kindly invited us for a soirée in her London home. But I—I'm not sure…"

"And this decoration here, will it please you?" another assistant chimed in, holding up a pretty drawing of a gown with an elaborate cascade of silk and taffeta flowers on one shoulder.

"Perhaps…" Patience said. All she could think of was how

much she missed her very real flowers back at Rose Cottage. They would be blooming in abundance once the weather warmed. And she would be here, looking out the window at a dead garden.

"You must choose, Your Grace. Different occasions require different garments, after all," the modiste reminded her, her tone both instructive and impatient.

"I just wish for something simple," Patience confessed, yearning for the familiarity of the dresses that Mama had laid out for her, the warmth of her family, the security of pen and paper in her hands, and the comforting snip of her gardening shears.

"Simple, Your Grace?" The modiste looked almost scandalized. "Your wardrobe must reflect your station."

Patience nodded, resignation settling over her like the heavy fabrics they paraded before her. Her thoughts wandered to the life she had left, where complexities were fewer and happiness seemed within reach. Here, in the shadow of Rath Hall's splendor, she felt more a specter than a duchess, wandering in expensive dresses and dreaming of sunlight and roses amid the gloom.

9

Dorian's chest tightened as he watched Patience descend the stairs, his eyes transfixed on her. Time seemed to slow, and the world around him faded away, leaving only the vision of his wife before him.

Gone was the plain, mousy gown that had hidden her true radiance. In its place, Patience wore a stunning blush-colored silk gown that hugged her curves and accentuated her delicate features. The color gave her a youthful, healthy glow. The high waist and low neckline drew his gaze to her ample bosom, the sight of which made desire stir in him. The puffed sleeves of her gown were embellished with crystals that glittered in the candlelight.

Her golden locks were carefully arranged, with a few curled tendrils framing her face and a delicate pink rose adorning her elegant chignon. A single curled lock of hair cascaded over her shoulder, and he wondered how it would feel wrapped around his fist.

As she moved, the silky fabric of her skirt flowed like a waterfall around her legs. Long, seductive gloves encased her arms, and Dorian stared at the tantalizing strip of skin between the edge of her glove and the hem of her sleeve.

And her face... Dear God in heaven, he could walk the entire Earth and not find a more beautiful woman. Her large, expressive eyes sparkled as they met his gaze, her long lashes casting delicate shadows on her flushed cheeks. She smiled at him shyly, but with so much joy, hope, and excitement.

He wasn't just in awe. He was in hell.

He had successfully avoided her for twelve days after the wedding, even though he'd been acutely aware of her presence in Rath Hall, as though he could sense her with his skin. He could hear her walking; he heard her voice through walls; he could smell her if she had been in the room.

She was an invader, this pretty little thing with her innocent eyes and her plush lips and body. She took over his thoughts—not one minute had passed that he hadn't thought of her.

And not just of her, but of John.

Without knowing it, she was his jailor.

How in the world was he supposed to go to his aunt's soirée with her looking like that? Every man would want her just like he wanted her.

He had been wondering if his inability to perform with Lilith was a sign of a long-term problem. But looking at Patience now, he very, very distinctly knew that he did not have a physical problem—apart from the discomfort in his breeches.

Say something, he commanded himself.

"Good evening." He cleared his throat as she came to stand by his side, so small and enticing he ached to touch her. "Duchess."

"Do you like my dress?" she asked. "Will you be glad to introduce me to the ton? Am I pleasing you?"

Dear God, did she want to please him?

He regretted avoiding her in the past couple of weeks, and yet it was necessary. Just hearing those words out of her plush, pink mouth had his blood boiling.

He nodded, unable to look away from her lips. "Indeed," he rasped. "You're pleasing me very much."

His mind was wiped clean. It must be her lips. Lips like that had no right to exist in the world. Plush and round, and with that Cupid's bow that fit right into a slight dip in the middle of her lower lip. How would that mouth feel against his tongue? Would she taste like strawberries, as he imagined? Or cherries? Or the roses, the scent of which always lingered around her? Would she sigh if he traced her lips with his own?

The next moment, his arms wrapped around her and he pulled her to his chest and covered her lips with his own. He had to bow to reach her face, so small she was.

Soft.

Her lips were the softest thing. Sweet nectar that set his body aflame. He dipped his tongue into her depths, and shyly, she welcomed him. He wanted her; the beast was raging against his senses. He had to make a conscious effort not to tear that delicate lace and silk, not to let the crystals sewn onto her sleeves scatter over the floor, and then take her like he ached to take her.

She moaned into his mouth and softened against him. The feel of her body, the smell of roses in his nostrils, was like an invigorating elixir coursing through his bloodstream. He didn't feel like a man anymore. He felt like fire itself. And she was his fuel, his air, his embers, and his heat. God, he had to have her.

She was his wife. This could be a real marriage. He could feel she wanted him like he did her. He could let her in, talk to her, have dinners with her, get to know her…

He wanted to.

What was he even doing?

He stepped back and let her go.

He'd just wanted one drink from her innocence, her purity. Like a balm to his jaded soul, being near her, hearing her voice—even her naive questions—soothed something within him.

She was breathing as hard as he, those delicious hemispheres of her breasts rising and falling. She was flushed, her lips red from his kisses, and he liked her that way. Her eyes were big and dark, staring at him with questions.

She was shaking.

Distantly, he realized so was he.

"Pray," she murmured, "what was that?"

"Your kiss," he replied.

"My *first* kiss..." she echoed, touching her lips with her fingers.

He wanted everything he did to her to be her first.

Her only.

"Good."

He wanted to corrupt her to his wicked ways and drink from her innocence and teach her all about the body and about pleasure. But he could not.

"Let us go, Duchess," he said, putting much-needed distance between them. "My aunt must be waiting for us."

As they walked out and got into the carriage, his whole being kept reeling from the kiss, from the power of desire that had consumed him. Goddamn it. He realized a simple truth. He was never going to stop at one kiss. No matter the consequences.

When they were driving through the woods leading to London in the carriage, she looked so small and innocent huddling in the corner opposite him, he ached to sit next to her and take her into his arms. Damn him, he shouldn't do it. He'd already given her security, safety, and riches. He couldn't—

shouldn't—give his victim's sister his empathy or his heart. It would be like tricking her.

And yet...

"What's wrong? Are you cold?" he asked, already unhooking his coat.

"A little..." she said as she watched him undress with big eyes, which were darkening as her gaze swept over his arms.

He watched her wrap his coat around herself and wished it were his arms. She leaned her face closer to the fabric. Did she take a sniff of it? Satisfaction spilled through his veins to see his coat cover her and protect her. The Rath crest of a red lion in flames on the coat was like a sign to the entire world that she was his.

"I'm mostly, er...nervous," she said.

"Nervous?" he asked. "You?"

"Yes, me! I've never been to a Mayfair soirée... I've never been to any soirée! What do I say? How do I behave? What am I allowed to ask...? What if I say something that would embarrass you?"

"Embarrass *me*?"

He understood her nervousness as a provincial girl being presented to high society for the first time. What surprised him was that even now she was worried about making *him* look bad.

He'd underestimated her. And the effect she'd have on him.

"Yes, you," she said. "You've been raised in this world. Everyone looks up to you. The grand, rich, powerful duke. I, on the other hand, know what it's like when everyone looks down on you. I don't want that to happen to you, too, by association with me."

Something in his heart melted. The need to take her into his arms pulled at his chest.

"Sweet girl," he said as he slid onto the seat of the carriage next to her. "I couldn't care less what others think of me. However, if anybody dares to look down on you, they will know the power of my wrath."

His chest cracked as the radiant, ice-melting smile lit up her face, the one he already knew so well even in the short time he'd known her.

"I suppose your temper has its positive sides," she said with a sigh of relief. "Confidence. I wish I had more of it."

His *confidence*? If only she knew...

He wished he could experience the world like she did, as a simple, wonderful place. He wished he had her inquisitive nature and curiosity about others, her wish to connect and her enthusiasm.

All he wished from others was that they would leave him alone.

"Do not think about confidence," he murmured.

Good God, listen to him, trying to comfort her. Since when had he become such a nurturing type?

And yet he continued, unable to leave her in distress, wishing to lift her spirits.

"You do not need confidence to get through today. I'll have confidence for you. If I had a drop of your natural charm and genuineness, I wouldn't need to scare people."

Her smile lit up the dark carriage like the sun.

"You do not scare me," she murmured, her eyes sparkling as she gazed at him.

Oh...Lucifer.

One hour later, they reached Mayfair, and his aunt met them with an air of excitement.

"My darling," she exclaimed as she looked Patience over

and grabbed his wife's hands in both of hers. "You are transformed!"

Patience beamed, and Dorian's heart swelled as true joy lit up his dear aunt's face. She was the only person who had shown him and Chastity compassion and human kindness after their mama was sent away, and he only wished he'd married sooner if it made her so happy. Then he felt a stab of guilt at the thought that this would be for only one year and with none of the grandbabies his aunt longed for.

"Never in my life could I have dreamed of such pretty gowns," Patience said. "The ones you gave me were magnificent!"

"It was my pleasure," said Lady Buchanan as she let go of Patience's hands and threw a cunning glance at Dorian. "And, clearly, you've outdone yourself with this ball gown! Do you quite agree your wife looks stunning, dearest?"

Patience's big eyes were on him, shining with hope. It seemed her chest stopped moving as she held her breath. Dorian nodded, sinking into their blue depths. "Quite breathtaking, indeed." He lifted her hand and put it through his bent arm.

For a few moments, they stood like that, gazes locked, and he felt a familiar urge to pull her closer and kiss her.

His aunt interrupted his wicked thoughts by leaning close to his ear, whispering, "You did so well, darling. My grandbabies will be beautiful! I implore you, take care that your marriage proceeds without fault."

His stomach sank. If only she knew that this marriage was doomed before it began.

"Patience—may I call you Patience? I know I must call you Duchess, but I thought you wouldn't mind? And you must call me Aunt, not Lady Buchanan."

Patience nodded. "I think that is a marvelous idea! I would most definitely prefer it."

"Capital. Now, tell me, Patience, how has Dorian been treating you?" she asked as she unwrapped Patience's hand from around Dorian's arm and put it around her own elbow, and led her towards the table with a punch bowl and glasses.

Dorian followed them, close enough to hear.

"Very well," Patience said and stole a glance at Dorian. "You have a wonderful nephew."

"Oh, I know I do," said Dorian's aunt as she smiled at him with a content smile. "If he appears grumpy or starts growling do not take it seriously. He's truly a sweet boy inside."

Dorian wanted to growl in response but restrained himself. As his aunt led him and Patience around the ballroom, introducing them to different important figures of the ton, all he could think about was how he could protect his beautiful wife from the predatory gazes of other men.

She was naive, and they'd crush her. Some of them would want to laugh at her expense, because she came from a simple gentry family. And perhaps they would even know the scandal surrounding her name. Others, predators just like him, would want to use her innocence to seduce her.

Dorian could feel himself bristle up as they navigated through the ballroom filled with two or three dozen guests. Everyone threw curious glances at his wife. Some were judgmental. Some were, like he'd predicted, full of male admiration and appreciation. Whispers came from all around them.

His aunt stopped before a group of people with Patience proudly at her side. A large circle of new acquaintances formed around them, his wife at the center of everyone's attention.

Lord Bentley, a gentleman his aunt's age, asked, "Your Grace, you're bearing yourself so well, you must be a quick learner. A useful quality for a duchess with such a steep climb in society."

Dorian tensed, already opening his mouth to protect his wife. But to his surprise, Patience didn't cower, didn't hunch, and didn't mumble something polite in response.

She chuckled and beamed that bright, glittering smile at Lord Bentley, the one that seemed to lighten up the whole room. "You're so right, Lord Bentley, it was some journey. Just the other day, I found myself in quite a predicament. You see, I was so accustomed to doing things for myself that I completely forgot about the army of servants at my disposal. I had spent a good half hour searching high and low for a broom to sweep up a small spill in my chambers, only to remember that I could simply ring for a maid!"

He stared at her in awe as ladies and gentlemen standing in the circle around them chuckled. The tension in Dorian's chest released. She didn't need to worry about confidence, for she wasn't just fearless with him, asking questions and making requests.

She was simply...herself.

He couldn't tear his eyes off her as she continued with a charming grin. "And then there was the time I nearly had my lady's maid in a fit. With my sister Anne not present, I absent-mindedly began darning a small hole in my stocking, much to my maid's horror! She insisted that such tasks were beneath a duchess and whisked the offending item away, leaving me to ponder the mysterious ways of the aristocracy."

As everyone around them chuckled again, Dorian could just imagine the shock of the French lady's maid he'd had Mrs. Knight hire. That also made humor spread through his chest like sunlight. His hand was right near Patience's arm. He could feel charges of energy running between them like tiny lightning bolts of pleasure.

During the conversation, the Dowager Duchess of Grandhampton had approached the group with Lady Hazel Fitzgerald, the eldest of the Duke of Kelford's younger sisters, who looked very nervous. He had greeted the older woman quietly, as he knew her grandson Spencer Seaton very well. The dowager was one of his aunt's closest friends, and the ladies greeted each other warmly. In her seventies, the dowager had striking blue eyes and perfectly coiffed gray hair.

"I must say," the dowager declared, "it is refreshing, to have such a new perspective and to meet a duchess with such a down-to-earth nature."

He agreed. Just like his aunt and everyone else around them, he was charmed by his own wife. He found himself conflicted, being proud of having this woman for his duchess and yet wanting to keep her all to himself and not let the predators of the ton try to dim her light or take her away from him.

Who knew a young and innocent girl like she would be the perfect wife and companion for him?

Who knew he'd like it so very much?

While his aunt led Patience to another group, and Patience continued to charm everyone, Dorian saw Spencer with Joanna and excused himself to go and talk to his old friend and his wife.

After that, Lucien and Constantine found him. Could he ever trust either of them with Patience like Spencer had recently trusted him with protecting Joanna?

Lord Spencer Seaton had returned to London last year, after having been press-ganged into a war. He had lost his title of duke, and everything else, since he'd been presumed dead. He'd had difficulty adjusting, and it was Miss Joanna Digby who had brought him back to life as they faced a common enemy. Spencer had asked Dorian to watch over her, and he had defended her against the powerful man who was trying to kill them.

Before he could ponder the question for any length of time, his friends pulled him aside, into an empty room adjacent to the ballroom.

"How are you doing after Elysium?" asked Lucien. "You left early. Did you feel well?"

"Fine. I—um..." He looked over his shoulder to make sure no one heard him. "I didn't partake of Lilith's services."

His friends looked at each other.

"Whyever not?" asked Lucien.

Pryde sighed deeply with understanding in his chestnut eyes. "Because deep down, he's a loyal man. He has a wife and wouldn't betray her honor with another woman."

Dorian felt his jaw working and nodded. Pryde understood matters of honor like no one else would.

Pryde shook his head. "I told you you're walking a dangerous line, friend. I warned you this was a disastrous match."

"If he wants to fuck his wife, what's wrong with that?" asked Lucien. "Look at her. I'd never leave her bed if she were mine."

A sharp slice of jealousy made him grind his teeth. The three of them turned to look at Patience, whom they could see through the open door. She stood twenty feet away, sparkling, laughing like a little bell, and making everyone around her laugh, too. Her gaze quickly darted to his and locked on, and the same euphoria as he felt when he kissed her filled him.

"I will pretend you didn't just refer to my wife and your bed in one sentence," said Dorian through gritted teeth as he turned back to Lucien. "Next time you imply anything similar, you're a dead man."

Pryde bit his lower lip, his chin jutting forward. "Rath,

listen to yourself. You're snapping at your best friend. You refuse to sleep with anyone but your wife. Clearly, you want her."

Dorian's jaws clenched so hard he thought they'd snap.

"He's right," said Lucien.

"You must think about what you are going to do," insisted Pryde. "You want intimacy with your wife, but clearly you can't tell her *everything*. It's not just about you. The two of us are at fault, too. We helped you cover it up. We orchestrated the suicide. We have lied to everyone for twelve years."

Lucien sighed. "I'm sorry. Just teasing you, friend. I'd never do anything to seduce your wife."

Dorian nodded. "I know. I know. I can't look at her without remembering the incident in Oxford with her brother."

"Your Grace," came a strangled-sounding female voice... one he recognized all too well.

He turned around to find Patience in the doorway.

"What is this incident that had to do with my brother?" she asked.

Dorian froze, his heart dropping like a stone.

Good God, how in the world had she come so close when he'd just seen her chatting with a group of people twenty feet away?

Her eyes were wide, the light he'd seen just a few minutes ago gone from them. The sparkling connection between them had also disappeared.

What had he even been thinking? Kissing her...being proud of her...imagining the life they would never have anyway?

This was the life written for him. Keeping his terrible secret. Being miserable. Being alone.

He searched for the right words, but all that came forth was a strangled "Patience, I—"

"Did you know him?" she demanded.

His heart pounded in his chest, shame and fear threatening to drown out all reason. Walls were closing in around him, the secret he had so carefully guarded now in danger of being exposed like an open wound. He could not bear it, especially not after he had allowed himself to believe, if only for a fleeting moment, that there might be something real between him and Patience.

"Enough!" he roared, his voice echoing through the chamber as he slammed his fist onto a nearby table, sending an ornate vase crashing to the floor.

Shattered pieces of porcelain rocketed around the room. The chatter of the people in the other room quieted. Several people rushed to the doorway to look in at him.

"Dorian—" Lucien said quietly, but with his usual warning. "This is a little too far."

"Your Grace, please—" Patience whispered, taking a tentative step towards him, her eyes wide with fear and concern.

A footman hurried over, gathering the broken pieces of the vase.

"Stay back!" Dorian snapped at Patience, unable to control the fury that coursed through him. "You do not understand the forces at play here, nor the danger you place yourself in by seeking answers!"

Patience hesitated, her brow furrowed. "But why? What did I ask?"

"I will not be questioned by a naive, sheltered girl who knows nothing of the real world!"

As the words left his lips, Dorian could see the hurt they inflicted upon Patience, her face paling as if she had been struck. And in that moment, he knew that the tiny glimpse of happiness he'd just allowed himself to experience earlier today was gone.

"Very well, Your Grace," she whispered, her voice brittle

with heartache. "If that is how you truly feel, then I shall trouble you no further."

With a final, anguished look, Patience turned and fled from the room, leaving Dorian with ladies and gentlemen staring at him in the wreckage of his rage.

"Pryde, you've never been so right. There are no two people as wrong for one another as she and I."

10

Patience hugged her knees under the silky sheets and hid her face in them. Her room was dark, the outlines of gorgeously carved furniture and the shadows behind paintings on the walls were like silent sentinels, guarding her desolation.

A scratch at the window made her shiver. A branch of the ash tree, perhaps? It must be.

The night behind the closed curtains and windows was quiet but felt menacing. She shivered, listening, but there was nothing but the wind rustling the branches and the grass.

She blinked her heavy eyes. They felt like they were full of sand, and her body ached and felt overheated, as though she was running a fever.

Since her wedding, she had been unable to sleep properly, lying awake most of the night. She missed her sisters' warmth, the sound of breathing, occasional snoring, and the dipping of the mattress as they moved. The sheets at Rose Cottage were scratchy and had holes, the sheep wool of the mattresses gathered in clumps at places. But it felt familiar.

Here... She lay on silky sheets on an inviting mattress, in

her big, beautiful room, surrounded by exquisite furniture. There was no one snoring or kicking her in their sleep, and yet she lay awake, miserable.

There were no carrots to scrub, no caterpillars to pick from cabbage leaves, no wasp nests to fight. Every day, she could eat meat that melted on her tongue and fish so fresh it still smelled of the sea in sauces with names that sounded like myths and tasted like something straight from heaven.

She had servants who sprinted to fulfill her every need at a single word.

She wore beautiful gowns that were every girl's dream and had a lady's maid who knew how to make her look like a goddess.

She could take multiple baths every single day.

And yet, she had never felt as alone and as abandoned as she felt now.

All of this felt false, like a golden cage where her eyes burned with insomnia and her body was so exhausted she felt as though she was slowly dying.

But your family will be free from debt and your father will avoid debtor's prison.

That was what she told herself every night when she performed her family's special ritual of putting bad emotions into a box. That did make her feel a little better. But she still couldn't sleep.

If only she had a warm body next to her to help her feel less alone... Even if it was a cat!

One year like this. That was the agreement.

Then he'd ship her out to another estate, where perhaps she'd finally be able to do her gardening and botanical work. Perhaps she'd even be able to invite Anne to live with her, if Mama could spare her. Once the duke would give them an estate to bring in income, they would be able to hire a servant or two, and her sisters wouldn't need to do all of the housework.

She and Anne would spend their days dedicated to science with no one watching over them. Anne would write another treatise. The first one had been published quite unexpectedly, given a woman's work on mathematics has never been published before. Her poor sister had a wounded heart that would not heal. She had secretly confided in Patience four years ago that Justin, now the Earl of Chans, had proposed and then left her. Yet another man playing with a woman's emotions, Patience thought.

But it did no good to dwell on that. For now, all she needed was to know if Rath really had paid off her papa's debts. If all this loneliness and isolation she felt was not in vain.

Yesterday, at Lady Buchanan's soirée, he had snapped at her, called her naive and silly. Her cheeks burned from embarrassment as she remembered the astonished faces.

Except... What exactly did she do wrong? He had talked about an incident with her brother at Oxford.

The incident...she'd thought it must be John's suicide at first. But Dorian's tone of voice, the complete dread and devastation on his face made her doubt it.

And he thought about that every time he looked at her? No wonder he'd locked her in her own part of the manor and avoided her like a plague, she thought with a twinge of pain. But then why had he married her?

The man was an enigma. Rich, powerful, angry, hurt, and damaged.

That was her husband.

She ached to know all his secrets, that mysterious connection between him, John...and, apparently...her.

She knew that despite her weariness, despite her gritty eyes, there wouldn't be any rest for her tonight.

Maybe knowing her papa's debts were paid would help her sleep.

That was something her husband could tell her. He had to.

She swung her legs over the edge of the mattress and put on her slippers. He'd told her his quarters were forbidden, but what would he do, really?

A chill ran through her as she put on a dressing gown.

Quite a lot, actually. That was what he could do. Those massive, muscular arms, the sheer strength in those jabs she'd seen him make every morning. The powerful thighs. The chest so hard it could have been made of stone.

He could do a lot to her if he wanted. And there was nothing she could do in response.

And yet, she couldn't just sit here and hide.

Anything was better than this loneliness.

She lit a candle, put it in a holder, and walked into the hallway.

She knew where his quarters were—Mrs. Knight had showed her so she'd know what part of the house to avoid.

She walked down the corridor of her own quarters and past the landing of the large central stairway that divided the house into two parts. With her heart drumming very hard, she crossed the invisible border that separated his territory from hers.

A wooden floor plank creaked, as though announcing to the whole house she was doing something forbidden. She froze, her own breathing loud in her ears, her pulse beating hard.

She listened for the sound of someone hurrying to stop her, for some kind of a guard, like the duke's valet or a footman, or even Mrs. Knight. Someone to block her way and demand what her business was here.

But no one came. The corridors were dark, with the night

inky and moonless outside, she could only see with the light coming from her candle.

She swallowed hard, trying to eliminate the dryness in her mouth. With her feet heavy, she kept walking into forbidden territory.

She guessed the duke's bedroom must be in the mirrored location of her own. She walked into his corridor, and noted the paintings here were all of maritime scenes, seascapes, male portraits, perhaps of his ancestors, and battles, while hers were much more feminine—flowers, female portraits, gentle rolling hills, and lush gardens.

She felt the scorn of the duke's ancestors on her. How dare she disobey her husband's rule?

But she was so desperately lonely she craved any human company, even that of the man she was quite terrified of deep down. He still intimidated her, with his godlike appearance and his demeanor like he knew, and kept, all the world's secrets while she was so young and knew nothing.

She stood before the door she supposed was his, and breathed deeply in and out, feeling like nothing would be the same again after she opened this door.

She turned the handle and entered.

A growl and barking exploded in her ears and a heap of rough, wiry fur reeking of dog knocked all the air out of her as it jumped on her and pressed her against the wall. The candle fell on the floor and darkness descended. In the very dim light coming from three large windows, she could see the gnashing of giant teeth as the dog barked, deafening her. She screamed, terror clutching her like never before.

This was going to be how she died. She'd stepped into the forbidden, and this was her punishment.

A hell beast was going to tear her throat out.

Flecks of saliva landed on her face and neck, dog breath gagging her.

"Titan, sit!" barked a powerful male voice.

One moment she was going to be the beast's dinner, the next, it let her go, backed away, and sat down by the feet of the very tall, very muscular, and very angry owner of the room.

"What on Earth are you doing here?" he roared.

Without waiting for a reply, he picked up her candle and walked to the nearby sideboard.

She was shaking, prickly fear still coursing through her in icy cold surges as she watched him try to light the candle.

He struck the flint and steel together awkwardly, his movements hindered by the glove. The sparks fell short, dying before they could ignite the tinder.

Patience bit her lip, a pang of pity striking her heart. What was hiding under that thick leather glove that he wore even now? Did he sleep in it, or had he swiftly put it on before he rose?

On the third attempt, he struck the steel, and a spark leapt forth and lingered on the tinder, catching slowly. Patience remained frozen as the tinder began to smolder. With a careful breath, Dorian coaxed the tiny flame to life, then brought a thin piece of wood to the flame, lit it, and brought it to the wick of the candle.

As he lifted the candle before him, golden light illuminated his bare, hard, muscular chest, which she could see through the opening of his dark crimson dressing gown. Did he not sleep in a nightgown?

What an odd thing to wonder, she chastised herself, when his Irish wolfhound had almost just eaten her.

She stared at Titan. She'd never become acquainted with the dog, but she'd seen him by Dorian's side every morning from her window.

How could this creature have been a hell beast one moment and the next, sit like a happy puppy, wagging its long tail, as it looked at his master very satisfied with itself. *Yes*, said Titan's fierce, toothy face, *I protected you, I'm a good dog.*

She straightened her shoulders and met her husband's furious yet sleepy face.

"What are you doing here?" he demanded again, calmer this time, accentuating every word. "I forbade you to come here."

She raised her chin and called upon the power of positivity and her smile. No fear. No negative emotions. She was fine. "I apologize for the commotion," she said, and Dorian cocked one brow.

"You're apologizing?" He shook his head, irritation in his tone. "Do state your reason for being here before I send you back to your room!"

"Perhaps if you hadn't restricted me to the point where I feel like I live in a prison, I might not have needed to barge into your room!" she exclaimed.

He raised both brows now. "Prison?"

"Yes. Prison."

"You have everything you could ever want."

"Not everything." She crossed her arms over her chest, feeling like she had his attention now, and walked deeper into his room, observing her surroundings. "First, I'd like to know if you did pay my father's debts."

This room was the exact reflection of hers, except it was all in dark blues with some red accents. The bedsheets were crimson and the curtains on the windows were navy blue with thin red stripes. The masculine space fitted him well. There were old swords and shields, and even a mace, hanging on the wall.

Oh, Good Lord, was he going to use any of them for her punishment?

"Yes, I paid your father's debts, Madam," he declared. "I did it the very day of our wedding."

Relief flooded her. "Good. At least I know my family won't be on the streets and my father won't be in debtor's prison."

His predator gaze narrowed on her. "Anything else?"

"Thank you," she said and smiled at him.

He looked quite disarmed for a moment, then swallowed and scowled again.

"Besides that," she said, "I must demand that I sleep in your bed."

His jaw dropped. He blinked. For that moment, he looked like a boy, carefree and surprised, perhaps even full of wonder. It made him look so young, despite the lock of white hair at his temple.

"Pardon me?" he demanded.

"I can't sleep. I haven't been able to sleep since I arrived here."

"Why not?"

"My whole life, I slept with my sisters. It seems I'm incapable of sleeping alone."

He licked his lower lip and bit it.

"And in addition," she said, "I'd like you to have dinner with me. It's been very, very lonely."

"Dinner?" he barked, his eyes widening now.

"Yes," she said and smiled despite his roaring and the anger she could see in him. "Dinner. That is what a family does. They share meals together."

"We are not a family," he growled.

"Clearly not," she scoffed. "I'm so very lonely here! I have no friends, no one to talk to. I'm not allowed to leave my quarters. I'm not allowed to have contact with my own husband!

And you won't even let me go to the garden! I brought some of my roses from home, and now they're slowly dying in the mews. They're still bundled up when they should be planted in their new soil, growing in their new home."

He gently placed the candle upon the sideboard and became unnervingly calm, and a chill ran through her. Very slowly, step by step, he walked towards her, holding her in his dark sapphire gaze.

Perhaps she had made a mistake after all. A much bigger mistake than barging into the room of a man who had a beast guarding him who was ready to devour even his wife.

The duke appeared far more lethal than any hellhound, older and dangerously enigmatic, with secrets lurking behind his eyes—secrets she was certain she wouldn't like at all.

He advanced towards her until he stood so close she could smell the clean, masculine scent of his skin. A warm sensation grew at the bottom of her stomach, and she ached for him to stand even closer.

"My dear girl," he murmured, distant thunder crackling in his voice. "You're in no position to make demands. You disobeyed me. You broke the rules. I warned you there would be consequences. You leave me no choice but to punish you."

11

"Punish?" she whispered, and by God even that whisper on her lips sounded so delicious he ached to kiss it away.

Dorian stared at his beautiful, fragile wife, the candle illuminating her curves, which even a dressing gown and a night shirt could not hide. Never in his life had he imagined he'd wake up to his dog barking his head off, going mad at an intruder...

Who turned out to be a creature of curves and golden locks and perfect skin and wide, innocent eyes, and pink lips... Lips the taste of which he'd never forget as long as he lived.

And yet, this gorgeous little thing was unhappy?

He'd never considered she might be unhappy. Wouldn't anyone coming from her poor circumstances be grateful for a home where she no longer had to worry about food, a place where she would be safe and protected? He had rescued her family, done them a favor, and improved her station in life, her fortune, and those of her sisters.

He hadn't imagined that he had actually made her less

happy—by the sound of it, quite miserable, in truth. She couldn't sleep, for God's sake.

And what were these demands about the garden? Why was it so important to her to go to that terrible place he'd contemplated burning to the ground?

But as he stared at her now, he could see that she did have dark circles under her eyes, and that the blush he'd seen at the soirée was much less prominent.

"Punish," he said when he could feel her lush body against his own, smell her rose scent tickling his nostrils.

Having a female here at all was new and strange. He'd never brought his lovers to the manor. The only females who entered his bedchamber were the maids and Mrs. Knight.

And now, his wife.

He swallowed hard, imagining her bent over his knee, her behind stuck in the air, bare flesh firm and rosy against his light slaps as she squirmed in pleasure.

Then his imagination shifted to a punishing coupling, where he'd pound into her relentlessly as she moaned and pleaded for more.

He nearly groaned, overwhelmed by his intense desire for this youthful goddess of beauty and light. He couldn't recall ever wanting anyone as much as he did her. Yet, he knew he couldn't simply impose his desires upon her.

Or could he?

What could he possibly do that would be a punishment to her when she already was lonely and miserable? When she already had nothing that she enjoyed here? So much so that she couldn't even fall asleep.

What could he do to discipline her but...be himself with her?

And what if, by some miracle, she would not be broken by

his wrathful ways, whispered a voice in his head, sounding annoyingly like Lucien. What if, instead, she'd bloom?

Open up...?

Be pleased...?

No, of course that wasn't possible. He'd only hurt her and scare her. And perhaps then she'd leave him alone.

It would have to be her decision. He would never force himself or his ways on her, nor on any woman.

"But you have a choice," he murmured as he had to physically restrain his left hand not to go up and brush his knuckles against the side of her shoulder. "For the punishment, that is. Choice number one," he said as he marveled at the slight tremble in her eyelashes at that, "is you have to organize my library."

He thought that would be the easiest, and no doubt she'd choose it. Organizing the library was not really a punishment, just a bit of work. Definitely much better than the second option.

"Choice number two is a spanking."

She gasped, her cheeks flaming so red his cock twitched in reaction. "You would s-spank me?"

"Yes."

She swallowed, her eyelashes trembling, and the pink tip of her tongue briefly licked her lower lip. "W-would it hurt?"

He blinked. "Are you seriously asking me that?"

"I am."

"Why?"

"Well, because I was never spanked. I need to know if it would hurt."

Good God, what had he done? What if she would enjoy his particular tastes? Had he just opened Pandora's box?

"It might. Would you like it to?"

She was so innocent; how could he corrupt her with his ways?

"No," she said, and laid her hand, very unexpectedly, on his chest, her thumb brushing his skin.

He sucked in his breath as the most delicious wave of pleasant tingles ran through him at her touch.

"No, I wouldn't like it to hurt," she said. "But then it wouldn't be a punishment, would it?"

He swallowed. She needed to be taught a lesson. He needed to show her how horrible a man he really was, so that she wouldn't want to be in his company, in his bed, or anywhere near him. So that she would leave him alone and wouldn't be a constant reminder of the sin he'd committed all those years ago.

He needed to scare her away, for her own good.

"Exactly. So, is it the library, then?" he asked.

"No," she said, "it's not the library."

She swallowed, and the blush that crept to her face was even stronger.

"I'll take the spanking, Duke."

12

Patience couldn't believe what she'd just agreed to. What on Earth was she thinking?

She didn't mind the idea of organizing his library; in fact, it didn't seem like a punishment at all. To her, it sounded like an adventure, a chance to discover new books and perhaps even unearth some botanical treasures.

No, she was going mad from loneliness, she thought. Was it that she craved human touch so much she'd take a spanking? Or was it that she couldn't tear her gaze from this powerful, wounded man, so haunted, with secrets lurking behind his eyes, that she was ready to accept anything he offered her?

Like that kiss before the soirée.

That kiss was magical.

"But I have conditions of my own," she said, her head high. "If I take the spanking, you will let me sleep here in your bed tonight."

His head snapped back. "What?"

"I came here for a night of sleep. And that is what I shall have."

"I do not let anyone sleep in my bed," he said. "No one ever has."

She frowned. "No one?"

"No one. Not even Titan is allowed."

She squared her shoulders. "Well, Your Grace, too bad. You took away my freedom, my life, and my family. I demand that you at least give me back some sleep."

He was like a cornered animal. It was quite a strange sight... He felt cornered—by her? He, who had all the power?

"It seems this will hardly suffice as a solution."

"We will try. If it doesn't, it doesn't. Then, I suppose, I'm doomed to suffer from insomnia for the rest of my days. You owe it to me to try."

He scowled, his fists clenching.

"Well?" she asked. "What do you say?"

He swallowed. "But you will never come here again. That is the lesson. You must learn to obey."

"All right. I'll stay away from here after tonight, if that's still your wish. But if you reconsider, if you decide you would like me to come to your room again after all, then you must let me sleep here."

He was silent for a moment, looking her over, his dark eyes like shining pieces of onyx. "Very well, dear girl, we agree so." He chuckled softly with self-depreciation. "But that will likely never come to pass, for after tonight, you will want nothing to do with me. You'll flee from this room as if possessed."

"We shall see."

He went and sat down at the edge of the bed, his knees wide apart. The sides of his crimson dressing gown fell away, exposing his powerful, well-defined thighs, strong knees, and sculpted, muscular calves, covered with soft-looking dark hair. A thrilling, hot shiver pulsed through her. For the first time in her life, she was seeing naked male legs.

"Come here, Duchess," he said softly, his gaze holding her like a physical touch on her skin.

She obeyed, not feeling the rug under her feet.

The warm simmer started to feel like an ache in the lower part of her stomach. Her sex felt hot and swollen. What was happening to her? She felt heavy and pliable, like she was made of warm wax, and he was the fire warming her.

She approached him as if on cotton legs. "Aren't you going to remove your glove?" she asked.

His gaze grew more tortured. "No."

"Do you ever remove it?"

"Do not talk of my hand or my glove."

She licked her lips. Yet another thing she was not supposed to do. But was she right that it pained him? "Do you like to do this to a lot of women?" she asked, and a pinch of pain in her heart told her she really wanted him to say no.

"No," he said. "I don't. I haven't done anything to any woman since I married you."

She nodded, somehow reassured. "I don't know what to do," she said. "You need to tell me."

"Just come here." He stretched out his hand.

It was his left hand, with long, beautiful fingers. Not the gloved one, which rested on his thigh. Which one would spank her? she wondered. Another pleasant shimmer of sensation went through her at the thought of that strong, bare hand on her body.

"Something must be wrong with me," she said as she took his warm and dry hand, so large it enveloped her small, cold one.

"Why?" he purred as he pulled her to him.

All she could hear was the strong beat of her heart in her ears and his velvety, buttery voice.

"I should be afraid, shouldn't I?" she asked.

"Are you?"

"Well, yes. And no... I trust you."

"Oh," he said, and there was a sudden change in his face, like he was puzzled, like he didn't know what to do with this information.

She was surprised, too.

They were still holding hands, and his warm touch was comforting and reassuring, the rightest thing she could ever do was to hold his hand like this and tell him about her feelings.

"My parents never punished me," she said. "They never punished anyone. Especially not John..."

She regretted talking about John the moment she said his name. Had she just spoiled the fragile trust, the tenuous connection they had?

She remembered John fondly. She was six when he brought her the book on botany from Oxford that would change her life and define her passion. He was someone who loved having fun, had sense of humor. Whenever he was there, she remembered laughter, even though some of her sisters didn't join in.

But Dorian's eyes only darkened and glimmered with interest.

"Did you ever do something you weren't allowed?" he asked. "Something you were supposed to be punished for?"

"Yes." She chuckled. "I secretly worked on my roses while I was supposed to be plucking weeds in the kitchen garden. Mama and Papa still don't know."

While they thought she spent many hours caring for carrots and parsnips, she sketched, artificially fertilized roses, experimented with grafting on fruit trees, recorded observations, and corresponded with two members of the Linnean Society of London—Mr. Jay Essop and the society's president, Sir James Edward Smith.

"Hm. Naughty girl," he murmured with satisfaction and pulled her closer to him.

He had her lie across his lap, with her elbows supporting her against the bed. She stared at the silky cover of his bed, and felt her cheeks and neck grow red-hot with embarrassment.

She felt him pull up her dressing gown and chemise, and cool air kissed first her ankles, then the backs of her thighs, and finally, her buttocks—which now felt quite as hot as her face.

He sucked in air and made a strange, guttural growl. Was that good?

A wave of fear mingled with exhilaration washed over her. It was like standing on a cliff's edge before a tumultuous sea for the first time, knowing that diving in could be thrilling, yet potentially deadly.

He exhaled slowly, then fell utterly still, leaving her uncertain whether he would act or remain motionless.

"Good God," he murmured. "You're the most beautiful thing I've ever seen."

"That can't be true," she said. "You're staring at my behind!"

She couldn't believe it. How could a man like him truly consider a country girl like her—who had never attended a ball, never had a finishing governess...or any governess at all—as the most beautiful thing he'd ever seen?

Surely not.

Then she felt his hand on her skin—his left hand, touching her directly. His caress was feather-light, yet it made her jerk as if scalded. A myriad of sensations, like starlight, shot through her. He began kneading and massaging her behind, murmuring things she never imagined a man would whisper to her.

"Beautiful."

"Soft."

"Sweet."

So far, everything had been delightfully pleasant, sparking a warm, simmering sensation in her core that tightened with a growing need. She wriggled in desire for more, craving his fingers and hands all over her.

She moaned.

He cursed. "Make more sounds like that and I won't be able to resist."

"Resist what?" she asked.

"What I've wanted to do since the moment I saw you in the church."

"And what is that?"

He growled and gave her a smack on the bottom, and she whimpered as an intense stinging shot through her. It was almost painful but also exquisitely pleasurable—a sensation she'd never felt before. Her sex grew even tighter and hotter.

"More, Duchess?" he asked.

"Uh..." She swallowed, trying to understand what just happened.

On the one hand, someone had hit her. And only her sisters had hit her when they were children and didn't know better.

But this didn't feel like violence.

It felt playful, like she was the center of his focused attention.

And it sent so much pleasure through her core, she couldn't even say what was happening to her.

She swallowed. "More."

He chuckled and smacked her behind again, a little stronger this time. It stung even more, like a slap of water when one jumped into a pond.

Exhilarating. And, even stronger now, she felt more beautiful sensations course down into her sex.

"More," she managed.

He fell into a rhythm, the light slap of his hand on her flesh bringing a waterfall of sensations, biting and burning, warm and wonderful, and delicious, and sweet. And she couldn't stop herself. She arched her back like a cat and gave him her behind, wanting more of his hand. More of his touch.

The need to feel these intense feelings was scratching at her nerves. She'd smiled her whole life, put on a mask, turning away from the discomfort of sadness, of anger, of confusion.

She moaned, feeling positively like a cat. He cursed again and began smacking her a little harder.

She was panting, overwhelmed by the delicious blend of ecstasy and warmth flooding her senses. Each mild stinging sensation was followed by a profound heat that radiated throughout her entire pelvis.

Now, she couldn't turn away from the darkness. The darkness came for her.

And, to her surprise, she didn't want to run. These slaps of skin against skin, the stinging and the throbbing was like opening a window into the night and taking a lungful of fresh, wet air.

She was in an intense heaven. And she was climbing somewhere, somewhere she didn't know and yet sinking even deeper into her own body.

And she wanted more. So much more.

She was also feeling something very, very long and hard pressing against her stomach.

And the more she squirmed on the duke's knees, the more that thing twitched and grew and poked at her. Then she was also hearing him moan, and growl, and curse.

"Did you have enough, love?" he asked, almost breathlessly, and she shook her head very distinctively no. "Then perhaps this should be your punishment."

He withdrew his hand, and she did give a sound of protest, but then his hand went between her legs, in the crease where her sex was, and his fingers cupped it.

She gasped, squirmed, and a different sort of pleasure shot through her, her sex clenching even harder with some sort of need, and something wet and slippery came out of her body.

"Oh God!" she whispered as she buried her face in her palms. "I'm sorry!"

He chuckled softly. "Don't worry, dear sweet girl, this is perfectly normal. This means you want me. Don't you?"

At that, his fingers went between her folds and played with her there, making her clench and ache with ever more intense need.

"So tight," he purred as he inserted a finger in her body—and it did feel tight to her, like he didn't have much space to move, and she loved the sensation of him entering her in that way. "So warm and so sleek," he murmured as he kept playing around her folds.

She began begging, unable to restrict herself. "Please..." and "Keep going..." and "Do not stop!"

And he didn't. His fingers found an interesting spot in her body, somewhere in the center of her folds, and she jerked with the unexpected intensity of pleasure.

He touched her there, played with that place, tugging, rubbing, pinching. It felt like the more she moaned and trembled, the more he did whatever felt best to her.

And it was when he leaned down and bit her bottom that something incredible happened to her body, and she reached a breathtaking peak.

She froze, uncertain what was happening, except for her bottom throbbing and pulsating and ecstasy consuming her. And she just hung there, experiencing this beautiful clenching, but in her entire pelvis.

After what felt like too soon, she fell apart, unable to stop her cries of bliss, her body shaking with uncontrollable tremors as he kept massaging that beautiful place inside her, milking every last drop of pleasure from her.

As she trembled in his arms, he gently stroked her back and her behind as though she was a cat. When she calmed down, feeling heavy and sated, the skin of her bottom still tingling, he pulled her on top of him as though she weighed nothing and stretched together with her along the bed.

He pulled the blanket over both of them, and she was wonderfully soft and warm in the embrace of his stone-hard muscular arms. The crease between his chest and his shoulder was a perfect place to lay her head.

She closed her eyes and released a long, satisfied sigh. Feeling his warm, solid presence gently holding her, her eyelids rolled down, and a sweet, heavy contentment filled her.

Oh, she was going to fall asleep. No noises, no scratches, no creaking of floorboards would touch her while he had his arms around her.

"Are you very hurt, sweet girl?" he whispered, his warm breath tickling her forehead.

"No," she murmured. "You're very welcome to punish me this way again."

Something more than physical had been released in this experience. He had satisfied a need she didn't know she had.

His chest moved sharply as he inhaled. "The only problem is, darling, I'd like to be much, much rougher with you."

Much, much rougher? She couldn't imagine him being rough with her at all, despite the lethal strength in the blows she'd seen during his boxing practice. And still, like some sort of masochist, her insides clenched with a sweet anticipation at the words.

She'd ask about her brother again tomorrow...or another day. And then he'd punish her again.

"We'll see," she murmured as she wriggled her head, finding even more comfort with him.

"You may plant your roses in the garden tomorrow," he murmured. Then he kissed the top of her head. "Now, sleep."

And sleep she did.

13

Dorian stood at the open window, his eyes transfixed on the delicate figure in the garden below. Patience knelt beside a withered rosebush, her slender fingers gently pulling the tangled branches apart. Sunlight was caught in her golden hair, under her white bonnet. She wore a simple dress, one of those she'd brought with her, and worked without any gloves.

When he'd put his ring on her finger, he noticed how calloused and rough the skin of her hands was. He'd assumed it was because she didn't have an easy life. Now that he knew the true reason, he was even more intrigued.

Beside her stood several small burlap sacks full of what must be soil, from which protruded rosebushes she must have brought from her family home. He wondered briefly where they'd been stored until now and if they had survived or if being uprooted like that and then held in burlap sacks without care had already killed them. He shouldn't have forbidden Patience working in the garden. If she had cared enough about her roses to defy her parents, it was clearly very important to her.

From here, he could hear her hum something, her voice high, like little bells, and so lovely his heart squeezed.

"O, where are you going?" "To Scarborough fair,"
Savoury, sage, rosemary, and thyme;
"Remember me to a lass who lives there,
For once she was a true love of mine.

He'd never liked folk songs, preferring Bach, Mozart, and Italian opera, but he closed his eyes, letting her voice seep into his psyche. He could listen to her sing anything for hours. Her gentle voice, her serene face, the way she tended to the roses with such care and devotion stirred something deep within Dorian.

His mind drifted to last night, the feel of her skin against his, the sound of her sighs in his ear. His heart quickened, and his breath caught in his throat. A tingling warmth spread through his chest and straight to his groin. His muscles tensed involuntarily, readying him for a closeness that was no longer there. But it was more than mere lust that moved him now.

He'd held her in his arms as she slept, her breath deep and even, tickling his skin. He'd guarded her as if she were a gentle otherworldly creature, fleeting and mercurial—one he was lucky enough to hold in his arms. Her presence soothed him, calmed his wrath, his inner demons. Something like peace had settled in his body, the strange sense that he was right where he was supposed to be, and he didn't need to run.

Getting a glimpse of the passion and tenderness he had denied himself for so long had opened a crack in his walls. And yet, even as he'd reveled in the pleasure of her responsiveness last night, a small voice had whispered that it was too good to be true.

She was a punishment sent to him by God. The forbidden fruit of happiness, so close its luscious scent tickled his nose.

And yet completely unreachable.

The memory of that dreadful night in Oxford twelve years ago slapped into his mind like a blast of fire, and his mangled hand ached and tingled in the leather glove.

Twenty-year-old Dorian had just got the news of his papa's death and marched out of the stuffy student pub The Bear, in urgent need of fresh air. Anything to relieve the strange mix of anger and loss he'd never felt before. *I regret to inform you that on 3 October your father, the Most High, Noble, and Potent Prince, His Grace Frederick Louis, Duke of Rath, passed away...* The words in the solicitor's letter rang in his head like a hammer striking iron. *As you are your father's heir, his title will be awarded to you—*

Lucien's footsteps hurried some distance behind him as Dorian shoved through the pub's back doors into the mews. The night air, cold and damp, clashed with the foul stench of pig manure. Despite the muck squelching under his shoes, Dorian relished the biting chill and the darkness that enveloped him, a stark contrast to the pub's noisy warmth filled with laughter and clinking mugs.

But the night wasn't silent. To his left, the distressing sounds of a struggle pierced the quiet—a woman's faint cries and a man's gruff grunts.

"Please, no..." the woman pleaded.

"Shut up. You'll like it," the man insisted.

Dorian turned, his heart hammering, and froze. Under the faint glow of a gas lamp, a man's back hunched over a figure pinned against a hay pile. The flicker of white under the lamp revealed a woman's skirt, female legs kicking on either side of the man. They were struggling, one arm of the man holding the woman down, the other fumbling at his breeches.

"You've been begging for this all night," grunted out the man.

It took only a moment to understand what was going on. Dorian needed an army of enemies to quench his rage and pain. But he didn't have an army.

He had only himself.

With fury shooting through him in a blast of fire, he launched himself at the man, his fists curling around the edge of his jacket, and pulled him back and away from the woman.

The man whirred around, freeing himself from Dorian's grasp. With yet another shock, Dorian saw that he recognized the man. It was Mr. John Rose shoving his shirt into his breeches.

The girl desperately pushed her skirts and her white apron down, tucked her hair under her bonnet, and ran away with her face flushed and her eyes big and teary. It was the maid, the daughter of the pub owner—Chloe... Catherine... Something starting with C... Christine, he remembered.

Mr. John Rose, a young gentleman with curly blond hair, bright blue eyes, high cheekbones, and full red lips stared at him. A vile expression twisted his angelic features, which now seemed as out of place as smudges of bright paint on a masterpiece.

Dorian didn't know the man except as someone who had tried several times to talk to him earlier this evening. He seemed to be one of those men who were desperate to know someone of importance to advance in life.

"Lord Perrin..." said Mr. Rose with no sign of regret. "I suggest you haven't seen anything."

Lucien finally caught up to Dorian, panting. Taking a look at both his friend and Mr. Rose, he shook his head. "Not another duel," Lucien said as he came to stand by Dorian.

"Don't challenge him to a duel, you oaf! The girl is no one to you! Give him a good smack in the face and let him go."

"Do maids not deserve to have their honor protected?" growled Dorian as the rage he felt inside crashed against his guts like a storm surge. It was not just about the maid's honor. "Who's going to step up for her?"

He needed someone to fight. He needed something to destroy. A pretty man like Mr. John Rose would just do the trick.

"Dorian—" There it was, the warning tone he'd heard from Lucien thousands of times.

Dorian... Just before he'd taken a cricket bat and smashed his papa's favorite colonial vases when he was eight, after Papa had killed his lamb, Bramble.

Dorian... Just before Dorian had smashed his fist into a pulp hitting the wall over and over after Papa had taken Mama away. He'd locked her in an estate up north because she was too soft with Dorian. Because she was undoing the effects of Papa's spartan education.

Dorian... Just before Dorian had taken the fencing sword and slashed Papa's favorite portrait commissioned by Sir Thomas Lawrence, a famous artist, into ribbons. That was after Papa had broken Chastity's microscope and forbidden her to even think about studying anatomy and reading medical books. She was supposed to be the perfect lady. A socialite, learning manners and the subtle ways of leading a social conversation.

"You bastard," growled Dorian, looking into John Rose's smug face. Not a sign of remorse in his eyes.

"Why, did I take your turn with her?" asked Rose. "I apologize. You should have said."

"You were assaulting her," Dorian growled. "I demand satisfaction!"

"What is going on?" asked yet another voice as someone else appeared in the mews.

Distantly, Dorian noticed it was Sir Bertram, who studied botany and was often seen together with Mr. Rose.

John Rose's face fell in surprise. "A duel? Because of a maid? It's not your honor I offended..." He frowned in confusion. "Did I?"

"You offended *her* honor," growled Dorian. "She has no one to defend her, so I will."

John Rose shook his head slowly. "Sir, I have to say, your reputation is true. No one has called more duels in the history of Oxford than you."

"Shut up," spat Dorian. "Do you accept?"

"What is going on?" asked the Duke of Pryde, who emerged from the door with a puzzled look and stood next to Sir Bertram.

Dorian knew Pryde, like most aristocratic sons knew each other, but had never liked him very much as the man seemed to be aloof, stuck-up, and rigid. Perhaps he reminded him of his father. Father would have loved Pryde as he would have been the perfect son.

"It appears I'm challenged to a duel," said Rose. "And I didn't even offend the man himself."

"Come on, Perrin," jeered Bertram, "let this go. You've already called five duels this autumn."

"Lord Perrin?" asked Pryde. "Is this true?"

"He offended the honor of a woman, and she has no way of defending herself. I must defend her honor."

Pryde winced, looking Rose over. By that time he didn't look ruffled, his shirt back in his breeches, his coat on his shoulders, the rosy blush on his cheeks.

"Mr. Rose is not a dishonorable man," said Pryde. "He

wouldn't assault a woman. You must be mistaken, Lord Perrin."

"Do you accept my challenge, or will you be a coward and dishonor yourself even further?" growled Dorian through gritted teeth.

Rose paled a little but straightened his neck and nodded. "I accept."

"I'll be your second," said Pryde.

Lucien sighed and shook his head. "I'll be yours, Dorian."

"First light in the morning. Shotover Park," threw Dorian. "Your choice of weapon."

The morning would come, but Mr. John Rose would never feel the warmth of the sun on his skin again.

With the memory still heavy in his chest, Dorian watched Mr. John Rose's sister—his wife—lost in her work, humming softly to herself.

He wondered what would have happened if John had lived. Would he have harmed more women? Would he have saved his family, like they had hoped? With better circumstances, would Miss Patience Rose be married to another man now?

Fear and jealousy clasped at his heart. Most men would have been better for her than him, no doubt.

Most men weren't her brother's murderer.

His right hand ached more and more under the heat of the glove. He needed to go to his physician again. Except, the man would say the same thing. He should remove the glove and let his skin breathe. His skin was suffocating, red and swollen, irritated and now aching all the time.

But he couldn't. He couldn't just openly show the world the physical evidence of that morning. Have people ask about it. Wonder about it.

Like his sin, it had to remain hidden.

Patience had already begun to chip away at his defenses

with every sweet smile and tender caress. With her surprising ability to be an excellent duchess. She had gotten through his barriers, which terrified him in a way that no duel ever had.

Dorian clenched his jaw, his heart racing as he watched her straighten, brushing the dirt from her hands. He knew he should turn away, put an end to this foolish infatuation before it consumed him entirely.

He'd need to show up with her to London's events: balls, soirées, dinners.

But even as the thought crossed his mind, she looked up, her blue eyes meeting his through the glass.

And he knew he no longer belonged to himself. And never would again.

But he had to keep his dark secret. No matter the cost to his soul and to his heart.

14

THE NEXT NIGHT, Patience came to him again. Honest to God, he tried to protest, alarmed at the desire in his body to feel her against him again, at how much he craved to have her under the same blanket, in the same bed.

She only brushed him off. And Titan was no help. By the scent of raw meat and the crunching of bones behind the door, he guessed she'd found a way to his loyal beast's heart, too.

Then, to Dorian's weak protests, she slid into the bed by his side, her small body warm and full and soft. And as she sighed and melted against him, he simply didn't have the heart to send her away. The scent of roses in his nostrils, her skin like silk, her hair like the sun... Who could resist?

But it was the feel of her plump behind against his groin that was his downfall.

While she calmed down and was falling asleep against him, he was becoming aroused, his cock hot and hard, pressing into her flesh, so close and so forbidden.

Forbidden by his own rules.

Stupid him and stupid rules.

The first night, she had slept while he lay barely breathing, watching her serene face, hard as a rock after making her come but feeling no release himself.

The torture of feeling her body against him had him groaning in helplessness.

The second night, she was more restless, and even after half an hour she kept wriggling in his arms and against his body. His iron-hard erection prodded into her soft curves.

"What is that?" she asked innocently. "The hard thing? Do you have a stick?"

Very...very slowly, he exhaled.

"Not a stick, sweet girl."

"What then?" she asked breathlessly.

Good Lord forgive him, was she as soaked down there as when he'd spanked her?

Her naivete made him even harder, his cock pressed against the cushion of her arse cheek feeling like the epicenter of his very being. What would he not give to thrust against her chemise-covered arse, just to feel the pleasure and relieve this tension.

Not to mention sinking into her...warm, tight, untouched by anyone...

Fully and completely his.

But he couldn't. He had set this rule, no one else. How weak would he be if he'd break it?

"Something you shouldn't bother yourself with," he said.

"But—"

"Sleep, Duchess," he murmured, one inch away from her ear, her silky hair tickling his lips. "If you want to come to my bed tomorrow, you will sleep now."

It was the third night that he gave in.

Like always, she lay pressed with her back against his front, his hard cock nudged against the focus of all his desires—her arse. His arms were wrapped around her, the sweet scent of roses in his nostrils, her breathing calm.

Then, like a little fish, she flipped around and faced him.

Suddenly, her face was right against his.

His breath halted, his lungs unable to function. Her breasts were now thrust against his chest, her leg thrown over his hip.

"Turn around," he commanded, his voice strangled and raspy.

"I...er...I wondered if it would be against your rules if I get to feel the same sort of...pleasure. Er...release...like when you spanked me. Do you always have to spank me for that?"

He ground his teeth, attempting to suppress a groan. God, give him strength not to throw himself on her. "No. Spanking is not required for...that."

"Oh. It's just..."

As she trailed off, he swallowed, his cock twitching.

She'd be his downfall, he knew it. An innocent, sweet creature like her was one thing that could completely destroy him. And she would never know.

"What?" he asked.

"I'm so restless... As wet as then...down there. And I want..."

His jaw clenched so hard he thought he'd break his own bones.

His hand was already moving up the curve of her hip of its own accord. "What do you want, sweet girl?"

Her hand tangled in his hair. "Why do you have this bit of white hair? You can't be that old...not older than John would have been, surely?"

He swallowed hard and shut his eyes tightly. "My life has not been easy. I am not in command of the color of my hair. That's the only explanation I can give you."

He opened his eyes and glared straight into hers.

But her hands were soft caresses in his hair, and he couldn't help but melt into her.

His hand was already moving down her stomach, and she hitched her breath, tilting her head backwards, her eyes in a sweet agony on him.

"Is this what you want?" he asked.

He should stop. This was torture. This was taking him in a direction he had vowed to avoid.

"Yes," she said, her hips moving in a wave towards him. "Yes."

"Where do you want it?" he asked, knowing exactly where but enjoying the game.

She bit her plump lower lip, and he practically growled. "There," she said as she took his left hand, surprising him, and guiding it down her stomach and right in between her thighs.

He could feel her through the fabric of her chemise, hot... drenched... This little minx was aroused, eager for him...for his touch.

If God had wanted to punish him, he was successful.

"Is it all right I want you to relieve this tension?" she asked. "It was wonderful last time."

Good Lord, if he had to suffer, she didn't need to. She was innocent. In some ways, it was his duty to make her happy...to bring her relief...and to abstain from it himself, no matter how much his cock was hurting wanting her and never being able to have her.

"It is all right," he murmured as his hand glided down her leg and hooked under her chemise and up her bare skin. "I will relieve it for you, sweet girl."

He must have been completely under her spell because he was not thinking at all. Had he been thinking, he'd stop. This was against everything he wanted this marriage to be. No sex. No intimacy. Pure coexistence to help her and her family.

To find redemption.

Instead, his hand had already found the wet, hot folds between her legs. She gasped at his touch, arching towards him. He played with her, completely lost in the face of her bliss. As he teased her folds, finding the already familiar hard nub, his own desire had his hips doing slight thrusts against her.

In this torture, he was lost. Watching her moan and hitch her breath, and cling to him, as he kept rubbing, circling, pulling at her clitoris, her wet arousal completely drenching his hand.

God, how he ached to plunge his cock into her, as she thrust her hips to meet his hand, to satisfy her desire. But, alas, that was one thing he would never do.

He wouldn't allow himself the gratification of her.

He could sense the exact moment she fell apart in his hands. He'd never forget these sweet cries of pleased distress, her fingers digging into his biceps, her breath on his neck.

As she cuddled into his embrace, face right against his heart, her breath and hair tickling his skin, he was still restless, aching, practically exploding with desire for her.

She was right in his arms.

But forever unreachable.

And so, indeed, she was his punishment.

Because he'd never stop wanting to bring her pleasure. Never stop wanting his own wife.

And yet, he could never truly have her.

Because once she knew the truth of what he had done, she'd never want to be in the same room with him again.

15

"Your garden has so much potential," Patience chirped as the carriage rattled. "Did you have a good gardener before?"

Dorian, looking incredibly dashing in his black tailored coat and his crimson waistcoat bearing the lions of Rath, turned his gaze from the small village passing by on their way to London to look at her. A tempest began brewing in the depths of his eyes, his stark face illuminated by the sunset from the window, the white patch of his hair ablaze with fiery sunlight.

He was breathtaking.

For the past three blissful days, she had been doing her botanical work! She'd found an excellent spot, removed the old, dried-up rosebushes, and transplanted her own roses into those locations. In the two weeks they'd stood like orphans in the mews of Rath Hall, next to the laundry building, she'd gone to check on them and at least water them.

They were suffering from the shock of being uprooted, transported, and transplanted into a new environment.

Just like her.

And the only one who had given her back her sleep and a feeling of home was him. The man with secrets. The man who had spanked her and then given her the most incredible experience of her life.

The man she ached to know, truly, soul to soul.

Her husband.

Dorian frowned fiercely. "The previous Duke of Rath had a good gardener. Yes."

"Do you mean your papa?"

A furious blink of his long eyelashes and his gaze grew darker. "I do."

"Right. I'm sure if the gardener had been allowed to keep working, the garden would be in its prime. Most of the plants seem to be fine, just wild and overgrown. I do understand why your roses died. It's not the neglect they had for what...a decade I would guess?"

"Twelve years," managed Dorian.

Twelve years? She frowned. That was how long ago John had died. A coincidence? Or was it yet another sign of the connection between her husband and her brother?

She'd asked Mrs. Knight two days ago if, to her knowledge, Mr. John Rose had been a friend or an acquaintance of the duke. Mrs. Knight had replied very sternly it was not her place to talk of her employer's social connections. The best person to ask was her husband or his friends and family.

To which Patience had blushed, embarrassed she had not thought of it herself. She might ask Lady Buchanan or one of Dorian's friends tonight if they were present.

"Well, the reason most of your garden is dried and those plants are dead is because of disease. I could see the signs of mildew, blight, and rust. Damask roses are very susceptible to those. So I suppose without a gardener who could fight the disease or perhaps uproot the unhealthy plants, these were left to fight for their lives or die. Some, I guess, couldn't survive without care."

Dorian rubbed his gloved hand, and when her gaze dropped to it, he hid it behind his back.

"The old gardener died soon after my papa," he explained. "And I never bothered to hire another one."

"Why not?"

He glared at her. Was he going to dismiss her again, or bark something about not asking questions?

But he surprised her when he said sadly, "I never liked that garden anyway."

She felt a smile tug at her lips. "Indeed, you shall find it far more to your liking once I have finished with it."

"No," he said. "Allow me to be clear. You may only plant your roses. You may not touch anything else."

She frowned. "Oh. What a shame. It could be so beautiful. And that glasshouse," she added dreamily.

A burst of warmth shot through her as she imagined the glory that glasshouse could be. A place where she could collect tropical plants, study their patterns, learn how to help them thrive, and make them stronger, and how she would draw them, paint them, document them. Perhaps she'd be able to make them flower and develop seeds. She could even find plants that would be useful for medicinal purposes.

Dorian's scowl deepened. "I don't want you to touch it. That is the rule. I did allow you to put in your roses, but it's only because you seemed so unhappy."

"Right."

He studied her, then his gaze softened. "Making you unhappy was never my intention," he added.

"Oh," she said, all words stolen.

She beamed at him then, and to her surprise, there was something like the shadow of a smile on his own lips. But it was gone so quickly, she thought it was surely her imagination.

"Well, I'm much less unhappy since I came to your room three nights ago," she said.

He nodded. "Good."

He cleared his throat and uncrossed his long legs, which looked especially firm and muscular in a pair of beige breeches, then crossed them again. "What could make you even happier?"

She studied him, blinking. "Are you trying to—"

"I do have my rules. But I'd like to know how to ease your discomfort in my…er…your new home."

And suddenly she knew…she was still lonely. She slept well in his arms and therefore felt better, but she spent her days alone. Her family had left after the wedding, so abruptly…

"If only I could see my family one more time…" she whispered. "To see that they are doing better. That our marriage… this sacrifice… has produced fruit, and they're well."

Dorian nodded without hesitation. "I'll write to your papa, inviting them to come and stay for a week. Would that be agreeable to you?"

Her chest felt light, her lips curving upward of their own accord. "Agreeable? Oh, that would be absolutely marvelous!"

At the same time, the carriage slowed, signaling their arrival. The Mayfair mansion was beautiful and grand. As if on wings, Patience put her arm through her husband's and ascended the stairs to the front entry. Then they walked into the ballroom accompanied by a very stern butler.

Patience was so blinded by glittering crystal chandeliers and the diamonds on the necks and clothes of the beautiful ladies and gentlemen, she had to squint. The new scratches and cuts under her silk gloves itched, and she ached to remove them.

This was her first ball in the London ton, and she couldn't feel any stranger as she walked into the grand room where dozens of mirrors lined the dove-blue paneled walls and hundreds of candles burned in ornate candelabras. Lady Buchanan's soirée a few days ago seemed cozy and familiar compared to the great ballroom and the sheer number of fashionably dressed and coifed guests.

If she didn't hold on to her husband's elbow, she might fall. Her tightly tied corset wasn't helping. Mademoiselle Antoinette had been ecstatic and outdone herself by dressing Patience into a gown of pale blue, finely embroidered, and with a layer of delicate tulle. The maid had also created a masterpiece with her hair, adding fabric roses of various shades of blue, from icy pale to the intense sky-blue color of her husband's eyes.

And her efforts had paid off. Looking into the mirror before walking out of her bedroom, Patience wouldn't have recognized herself. Dorian's intense gaze, feeling like he was going to scorch her skin, confirmed it.

His arm was solid under her hand, his fierce presence strangely reassuring in front of all these glittering strangers.

"Did I please you that first night?" she asked.

The muscles of his forearm tensed beneath her palm. "Excuse me, what?"

"Did I please you?" she repeated. "When you spanked me?"

"Why would you ask this now? There are dozens of people around."

"I want to know. It's a simple question. Yes or no?"

He grunted and walked forward, tugging her after him. Her heart beat strongly in her chest. Many pairs of eyes followed them, but instead of shrinking, Patience squared her shoulders.

Poor Dorian looked miserable. Despite his exterior of a grump, there was a haunted pain in his eyes.

"I've only been unhappy in Rath Hall for the past eighteen days," she said. "That is how long we've been married. But you look like you've been unhappy there your whole life. Please tell me if I pleased you?"

He inhaled sharply, and his arm grew as hard as granite.

"Very well," she said. "If you do not wish to reply, I will. *You* pleased me that night," she said quietly, watching that no one overheard them. "Did I please you...then and last night?"

When she craned her neck to look up at him, he appeared to be choking.

"You did," he coughed out.

She felt her lips stretch in a wide smile and it was not forced at all. Joy filled her heart.

"Good," she said. "I'd like to please you more. I'd like to bring you pleasure like you bring me."

He shook his head and lowered his mouth to her ear. "No, you wouldn't, dear girl." His warm breath tickled the edge of her ear. "No matter how much I want you to."

Before she could ask more about that, his aunt practically flew towards them. Lady Buchanan wore a striking red dress with a thin waist and a full skirt. She had a high white wig on, with a stunning arrangement of feathers and jewels.

"Ah, there you two are!" Her face brightened. "Goodness, Patience, you're even more beautiful today, if that is possible."

Patience smiled back. "How are you, Aunt? You look beautiful, too!"

"Would you serve us punch, Dorian, dearest?" asked Lady Buchanan.

"Of course, Aunt," said Dorian. They had reached a side table that held a huge crystal bowl of punch and glasses. He poured punch into a glass and handed it to her. It smelled like apples and oranges, and Patience realized she was quite thirsty. "How's Chastity? She's not here, is she?"

"No, of course not," said Lady Buchanan as she let go of Patience's hand and turned around to survey the guests. "You know her. Reading a new fascinating issue of the medical review magazine that was just delivered. She'll return to Rath Hall soon, after giving you two newlyweds your time to get acquainted."

"Of course," chuckled Dorian as he poured another glass and handed it to Patience. As she took the glass, their eyes locked, and their fingers brushed against each other, and even through her gloves she could feel a jolt of pleasure. "Chastity doesn't go to balls, soirées, dinners, or anything social."

Patience chuckled. "Right now, as delightful as this evening is, I am quite envious of that privilege."

Dorian sighed. "So am I."

Patience met his gaze in surprise. So powerful, so rich, so confident... She didn't take him for someone who tried to avoid society.

"Ah, stop, you two," said Dorian's aunt, who had taken a sip of punch and put her glass back on the table. "My dear new niece must be introduced into the larger society of London. Neither of you have the privilege of hiding from your social obligations. Soon, darling Patience, you will have to throw balls, soirées, dinners for peers, charity events—everything to uphold your husband's and the Perrin family's power and connections. Attending soirées and balls is just the first step, and I'm going to help you as much as you need me."

"Ah, Marquess of Huntingham," Lady Buchanan called.

The man came and bowed to her, and, recognizing Dorian, bowed to him, too. "Rath," he said with a cold face.

He was a man in his late twenties, Patience estimated, tall and pleasant looking, with high cheekbones and big brown eyes, a square jaw, and a mane of dark brown hair. But there was a barely hidden demeanor of arrogance under his polite expression.

Dorian greeted him with a cold grimace.

"And this is my new niece, the Duchess of Rath," said Lady Buchanan proudly.

The marquess nodded to her, and his dark, appraising eyes looked over her.

"So pleased to meet you, Marquess," Patience said.

As the marquess's gaze stopping briefly at her chest, she felt an onslaught of nerves. She wanted only one man to look at her like that…the one who stood by her side.

Like the Duke of Luhst, this man offered his hand for her to place into his. "The pleasure is mine."

Patience hesitated. She really didn't want to do this, but the alternative was embarrassing Dorian or Lady Buchanan with her bad manners. Reluctantly, she put her hand into his, and he placed a kiss on her knuckles.

He held her hand longer than she thought was necessary, and she had to almost tear it away.

"What occupies your time of late, Huntingham?" asked Dorian in a tone of clear annoyance.

"I heard you were looking for a wife?" asked Lady Buchanan.

The marquess nodded. "I still am. Though this season is quite dull. Until I met the new duchess, of course. Admittedly, if I could find a wife as pretty as yours, Duke, I would be the happiest man alive."

"Well, you will not," growled Dorian with a stronger tone than was socially acceptable—even Patience knew that as several heads turned into their direction. "She's already taken."

The marquess stepped back as his gaze fell on Dorian's clenched fists. "Clearly, Rath. I was just being friendly.

Welcome to London, Your Grace," he said as he turned around and disappeared into the crowd.

"Dorian!" hissed Lady Buchanan. "Where are your manners?"

Patience blinked, caught off guard by the edge in Dorian's voice. Did he truly fear the marquess's charm, or that she might find herself swayed by another?

The notion that Dorian might be concerned over such things sent a surprising warmth spreading through her.

Every gesture, every look, exuded a quiet authority that made her feel safe, cherished. In his presence, she felt a shield against the world's cruelties, his fierce protectiveness wrapping around her like an unspoken vow. She couldn't help but admire how he stood up for her, his strength reassuring her that she was never truly alone.

She longed to tell him, to show him that no one else could possibly catch her eye.

For better or worse, he was hers and she was his.

Lady Buchanan introduced her to more people. Lady Whitemouth, who was quite eager to learn about Patience's family and background and was rather scandalized to hear her father was only a small landowner in the north.

More ladies and gentlemen were introduced, and Patience found herself dancing from person to person. All she had to do was smile and ask them about their thoughts, opinions, and experiences. They all loved to talk about themselves, and she soon felt as if she had made many new friends.

Dorian kept barking at men who said anything pleasant to her. That did scare away several of the gentlemen, who preferred to retreat than deal with his temper.

Patience wondered if the men were afraid of the power and money that Dorian possessed? Or of losing a valuable connection with the Perrin family?

Or just of him?

Soon, Lady Buchanan was called to another corner of the room while some couples gathered in the center of the hall and began dancing.

A stunning woman in her late twenties, with lustrous dark brown hair, gracefully approached Dorian. Patience watched in awe, wondering how she could ever emulate such elegance. She moved with the poise of a true duchess—her back straight, her head high.

Her features were striking—brown eyes set above the high cheekbones of a perfectly sculpted face. Her skin was smooth and radiant, giving her complexion the appearance of pure silk. Yet, it was her intense, secretive gaze directed at Dorian that truly captivated, hinting at a private world shared between only them.

Like those they share in bedrooms, came a razor-sharp thought.

"Lady Hargrave," Dorian greeted her.

"Duke," she greeted him back, with a lazy, private smile, and a velvety voice.

She wore an elegant dress that didn't need to be revealing to show she had the most beautiful figure, with a thin waist and lush breasts and gorgeous feminine hips. She was taller than Patience, but most women were, and a much better fit for Dorian altogether.

"How wonderful to see you," said the woman.

She stood close to Dorian, so much closer than Patience would have liked.

"We are not often graced with your presence at social events in London anymore," she said. "Your absence has been noted."

Patience was going to explode. For the first time, she understood Dorian's barking and unnecessary explosions because that was how she felt, too. Hot and prickly inside, like she was a lidded cauldron about to burst and pour boiling anger all over Lady Hargrave.

But no. That wasn't her. Her parents had taught her she needed to give people grace. And perhaps this woman was not Dorian's lover at all. Perhaps it was just her manner.

She may be the kindest and most gentle woman and an excellent friend.

What did Patience know about Dorian's past, London's ton, and all the politics and relationships people had to have to succeed and progress with their interests?

"Allow me to introduce my wife," said Dorian, "The Duchess of Rath."

The woman's eyes landed on Patience, no surprise registering in them. She had likely read the papers. Perhaps she had followed them religiously to find out anything about Dorian.

"Oh, how wonderful to make your acquaintance, Your Grace," said Lady Hargrave. She did not appear to believe that it was wonderful at all. On the contrary, she looked quite displeased.

"And yours," said Patience with her usual bright smile, the smile that was her armor and not her weakness. "I see that you know my husband well?"

The woman gave her a fox-like smile. "We're old acquaintances."

Patience nodded politely. "And is your husband his acquaintance, as well?"

Lady Hargrave looked down at her like a parent speaking to a naive child. "He is. They're great friends."

Patience felt like a stone dropped in her gut. How could her own simple charms compare with Lady Hargrave's sophistication?

No. She wouldn't dwell on it. She needed to stay calm and

not to embarrass herself and Dorian. "Well then we must have you both at Rath Hall for dinner."

"Of course," said Lady Hargrave with forced enthusiasm.

The conversation continued, stilted, and Patience didn't bother to try and draw this woman out as she had the others. Nothing she could say would win Lady Hargrave over or make her give up her pursuit of Dorian.

Patience couldn't keep something that didn't belong to her anyway, she thought sadly. If Dorian wanted to find satisfaction elsewhere, he would.

As she looked to her right, she noticed the Duke of Pryde talking to someone a few steps away. She thought he might have just arrived and hadn't yet had an opportunity to say hello.

And she had wanted to talk to him.

Dorian had refused to tell her about the incident in Oxford with her brother. But she could ask Pryde directly and perhaps he'd tell her.

She excused herself from Dorian and Lady Hargrave, as much as it pained her to leave them alone. She knew she had to trust him, or this marriage was doomed.

He watched her with a puzzled gaze as she walked off but didn't follow her. He wanted to talk to Lady Hargrave privately, as well.

As Patience made her way through heavily perfumed ladies and gentlemen, Pryde saw her approaching, and gave her a nod and a polite smile. He introduced her to the gentleman to whom he was speaking. They chatted for a few minutes, and then, luckily, the gentleman was distracted by someone else.

"Sir, may I have a word?" she asked, quickly glancing around to see if anyone could hear them. "In private."

"I doubt Dorian will like that," said Pryde without looking at her.

He was right, of course.

"Please, this won't take long. It is about Dorian."

Pryde nodded. "Very well." He quickly led her towards a quiet corner where there were not many people gathered.

"How can I help?" he asked.

"I know you must be very disapproving of our marriage," said Patience, "and you're right. I am undeserving of the name of Rath. I wasn't born into an aristocratic family. I lack education, preparation, manners. But I fully intend to be a deserving wife to him. I know there's more to him than just those outbursts of rage."

Pryde was struck dumb for a few moments, staring at her. Finally, he said, "I must admit, I didn't expect you to say that."

"Oh. I suppose I have surprised Dorian quite a few times, as well." She smiled and found Pryde's gaze warming up.

"It's not you in particular I disapprove of," said Pryde finally, with a softer voice.

"What then?" she asked.

"I'm afraid I'm not at liberty to say."

"Is it something to do with my brother?" she asked, and knew she was right by the way he stood speechless again, defenselessness making his brown eyes soft and open. "That incident in Oxford you, Dorian, and Luhst discussed?"

His expression became shuttered, and he looked away. "Your brother was distressed."

"Distressed?" she asked, frowning. "I never saw him distressed in my life. What distressed him?"

"I don't know, Duchess. Look, it's hard to accept someone took his own life, but the sooner you come to terms with it, the better."

"So the Oxford incident is related to his suicide?" she said, undeterred. "How is my husband connected to it?"

Pryde sighed. "It's not me you should be asking, it's Dorian.

And because I do actually like you as a person, I feel obliged to inform you, I will tell him of your questions. I gave your husband my word, and it's nothing personal against you."

Patience straightened her shoulders. "Very well. You should do what you need to do. I thank you for your time, Duke."

With that, she left him, working her way back through the crowd. She was worried about Rath's reaction to her inquiries. Would he want to punish her again? Would he do something worse this time, something she truly wouldn't like?

Oh God, he wouldn't take away her roses, would he?

Still, she mustn't stop until she learned the truth.

If Pryde and Dorian didn't want to tell her anything, there was still one more person she could ask—even if that would make her husband more furious.

16

Seven days later, Patience's family arrived.

As Dorian and Patience stood by the entrance of Rath Hall to greet the Roses, they scattered out of the carriage he'd sent for them in a big, loud, cheerful bunch, all rosy-cheeked and curly-haired.

He really didn't want to see more of the Roses than he needed to. Pryde had been right. Now he must deal with not only the sister of his murder victim, but also his whole family. He hadn't considered families existed that loved each other and wanted to be a part of each other's lives.

But his trepidation and regret disappeared the moment he glanced at Patience. Her whole face transformed so fully that something sweet burst in his heart like a little firework.

An odd thought occurred... Was this happiness?

She ran into the arms of her parents and then hugged each of her sisters. The longest hug was with a young woman a little taller than she, and thinner—Anne, her favorite sister, about whom she had told him.

Watching Patience glow, blossom daily from good sleep and from her time in the garden gave him an interesting, warm feeling as though small wings fluttered in the middle of his chest...

Was it happiness?

It must be. To be happy, all he had to do was make *her* happy.

What a strange notion. He was thirty-two years old, and he had only just come to this realization. Had he made so few people happy in his life that he'd never noticed the connection until now?

During the past seven nights, Patience had continued to come into his bed. Happily, he obliged, spreading his arms wide, and having her put her head on his chest. It was some kind of pleasure of its own, to feel her sigh and melt into him, trusting and contented and finally about to find peace and let go in his arms.

Only, he'd never be able to make her truly happy. Because of the secret he held.

If she knew what he'd done, she'd never be able to forgive him.

The first day with her family passed in walking and, to his trepidation, talking. They walked through the garden, and Dorian noted the swelling buds of Patience's roses. He took her papa on a horse ride, and Mr. Rose floundered like a sack of potatoes, pleading for a halt just minutes into the ride.

The whole day, the family behaved like he was their savior. Telling him how they now could finally sleep better at night, and how Mr. Rose even had some ideas to improve the estate so that next year they could finally hire some servants.

Mrs. Rose and the sisters kept blushing tremendously every time a footman offered them a cup of tea or opened a door before them. They kept chirping about how beautiful Rath Hall was, how lucky Patience was, and how grateful they all were to have Dorian in their family.

Dorian simply clenched his teeth. This was torture. He should not have invited them. He didn't deserve their love, their gratitude, and their admiration.

Had they known what he'd done to their beloved son, they'd never have wanted anything to do with him.

Eventually, dinner arrived, and he was forced to share a meal with them.

The grand dining room was set to receive the guests of honor. A grand crystal chandelier hung from the ornate ceilings over the long, carved dining table, gilded mirrors reflecting the flickering light of many candles. The air was filled with the mouthwatering aroma of roasted meats, vegetables, and creamy sauces, mingling with the delicate scent of the floral centerpieces.

Footmen in crimson livery moved silently about the room, pouring wine and presenting each course with practiced precision while Popwell oversaw them.

Dorian glanced at the opposite end of the table where Patience sat, beautiful in her glittering pale pink dinner gown, her smile so bright it illuminated the room. It was the first time he had shared a dinner with his wife, and he was surprised by how much he liked it.

Normally so quiet and lonely, his dinner hour was now full of clanking forks and spoons, and inappropriately orchestrated conversation—too-loud bursts of laughter, interruptions, arguments—and it all felt like being a part of a family.

He wondered how it had been for Patience to grow up with Mr. Rose as her papa.

Had Dorian been born to the Rose family, would he have become spoiled and entitled like John, or would he be himself, except happier? Mr. Rose wouldn't have killed his son's pet, wouldn't have sent away Mrs. Rose so that he would raise a worthy heir. Mr. Rose wouldn't have made him duel every day and shamed his daughters for pursuing science. He wouldn't have locked Dorian in the glasshouse to starve and thirst, and finally break his way out and cut his arms so deeply that he almost died of blood loss.

But no matter now. All that was done.

It was strange, however, to imagine having a close-knit family who knew each other and who loved each other so much.

After dinner, they sat in the grand sitting room, drinking port.

"One thing I wish," said Mrs. Rose as she patted Patience's hand, "is that your brother was here to see you this happy. He would have been so proud of you."

Patience smiled warmly. "I'm certain he would be. I wish John was alive, too, Mama."

"He would be married now, too," said Mr. Rose. "I'm sure of it. Such a handsome boy. Was he not, Your Grace?"

All eyes fell on Dorian, and he froze, with his glass half raised to his mouth. The only sound was the crackling of coal in the grate standing in the fireplace.

"Did you know John, Duke?" asked Patience.

He'd told her not to ask questions, but she'd done so in front of her family, and now he was backed into the corner. The beast within him roared. He'd lash out, unable to control himself.

Damnation.

"Yes of course the duke knew him, Patience," said Mr. Rose. "He and the Duke of Pryde. When John wrote me, he wrote about all his friends. I was quite proud he had made friends in such high society. Is it not why you offered to marry Patience, Your Grace? Because you knew John?"

Dorian felt his shoulders and jaw tighten. How on Earth would he get out of this?

"Mhm," he mumbled.

"Were you as devastated as we were at the news of his death?" asked Mrs. Rose with tears in her eyes. "Goodness, of course you must have been. You were right there at that time, were you not? It was October, all courses and lectures in full swing."

"I still don't understand what could have made him kill himself," said Mr. Rose mournfully, his own eyes teary.

Dorian was in hell. He felt as heavy as granite, hot and sweaty. His mind drifted back to the morning at Shotover Park.

The woods around Oxford were quiet in the dim light of the rising sun. Dorian's breath pumped quickly in and out of his mouth, dissolving in the very fine rain that was like a heavy fog around him.

Black trees, shadows in the mist, were like cracks into a darker world. Only the cawing of hidden crows broke the silence. Cold water seeped through Dorian's shoes from the soggy grass.

Pryde, with his indigo coat and a pristine white shirt, held out the box with two dueling pistols. "Here are the pistols, gentlemen."

Dorian's face flushed hot with rage. He glared at Mr. John Rose, his opponent, who stood in front of him by Pryde's left shoulder. Fury was rolling through his body like waves of fire. He craved a war. Destruction. Enemies to obliterate. Anything to relieve the roaring energy that pulsed through his body like a chorus of battle drums.

"'Gentleman' is an extremely generous word for Mr. Rose," Dorian said through gritted teeth.

"Dorian—" Lucien's warning was tired.

Rose cocked one blond eyebrow as he crossed his arms over his chest. Dorian could see the weak seams of his coat, the thinning, faded fabric. Perhaps it had belonged to John's own papa; perhaps it had been given to him with love and blessings to go to Oxford University and make a life for himself, carefully mended by his mama as best as she could to make him look good among the sons of aristocrats and higher classes. Would they approve of their son's behavior last night? Would they believe their darling was capable of harming a woman?

Clearly, the man's manipulative charm worked on Pryde, who didn't believe Dorian had seen the angelic Mr. Rose assaulting the barmaid at The Bear.

"Would you inspect the pistols, Luhst?" asked Pryde. "After you do, I'll do the same, to ensure correctness and fairness. After that, we will load them."

Rose likely did not own pistols, so Pryde must have offered his own for the duel. Gleaming in the early light of day, the pistols were exquisite. Lucien inspected both, looking into each barrel.

Dorian's head was pounding, the same thoughts chasing through his mind since last night. His father was gone. He was gone. *Blasted!* He should be relieved. Finally, the despot, the man responsible for every bad thing in his life would no longer be able to hurt him or Chastity. But all he could feel was rage.

Lucien nodded and laid the pistols back in the case. A twig snapped twenty or so feet away from them, coming from the collection of bushes.

All four men's heads jerked in the direction of the sound. In the gap between barren trees, Dorian thought he saw a flicker of white.

Lucien threw a worried glance at him. "Goddamn it," he muttered. "No one can know about the duel."

Pryde put the case with the pistols on the stump of a tree, and Lucien and he sprinted over the wet ground towards the bushes. Dorian took a few steps in that direction, but stopped, not wanting to leave Mr. Rose alone with the weapons.

A few minutes later, Lucien and Pryde returned, walking briskly. There was no one there.

Feeling relieved, Dorian turned back to Mr. Rose…

But he caught a movement. Mr. Rose had leaned over the case with the pistols and was just straightening up, a fleeting expression of being caught in the wrong written across his face.

"What did you do?" demanded Dorian.

Mr. Rose blinked furiously, stepping away. "Nothing, I assure you, sir."

Dorian marched towards him. "You tampered with the pistols, didn't you?"

"What's going on?" asked Pryde as he and Lucien hurried towards them.

"Mr. Rose tampered with the pistols!" cried Dorian.

Pryde, looking abashed for the first time, frowned. He ran his hand though his thick brown hair. "Mr. Rose wouldn't do anything dishonorable. Would you, Mr. Rose?"

But doubt tinged Pryde's voice.

"Never," said Rose. "I was only admiring the metalwork, which is quite exquisite. I've never seen such beautiful weapons in my life."

"I thank you," said Pryde. "But—"

Rose lowered his eyes in regret. "I should not have gone near them. If you wish, Rath, we can meet tomorrow morning and take the weapons of your choice."

"I am not Rath yet!" growled Dorian. "My title was not yet officially awarded to me. Goddamn it to hell. I just want this done with."

Truth was, he needed this relief, this distraction of violence, after learning of his father's death.

"We will inspect the pistols carefully, of course," said Lucien.

"Of course," said Pryde.

Lucien and Pryde meticulously inspected each pistol, peering down the barrels and examining every mechanism. Dorian watched them like a hawk, ready to scrutinize any sign of foul play.

Finally, Pryde nodded to Lucien. "All seems in order."

They loaded the pistols carefully, ramming powder and ball down each muzzle. Pryde handed one to Rose, who had gone pale, his angelic façade cracking. Lucien passed the other to Dorian, who gripped it tightly, the pounding rage in his chest only growing.

Dorian and Mr. Rose took their positions, standing back-to-back.

"On my count," said Pryde solemnly. "Twenty paces on go. One...two...three..."

Dorian and Rose strode forward, puffs of breath visible in the cold morning air. At twenty paces, Pryde shouted, "Go!"

Whipping around, Dorian raised his pistol, adrenaline surging through his veins. Rose stood facing him, arm extended, face white with fear.

Dorian fired. A deafening crack split the air. Agonizing pain exploded in Dorian's hand. The pistol ruptured, metal and wood shredding his flesh. He howled, clutching his mangled hand. Blood poured over his fingers. Ringing filled his ears.

Through the smoke he saw Rose frozen. The bastard had sabotaged him after all. Rage wiped Dorian's mind clear of thought. Ignoring the maimed wreck of his hand, he charged Rose.

"Dorian!" cried Lucien, but he didn't heed the call this

time. He couldn't feel the pain anymore, just the warmth around his hand, just the red, scorching fury in his body, the all-consuming need to destroy the man.

"Stop!" cried Pryde. "Halt!"

He couldn't even if he tried. His father was dead. He was free and yet he would never be. And here was a dishonorable man in front of him, his quivering pistol pointed at Dorian, taking shaky steps back.

Rose should just fire and be done with it. Because Dorian was wrath itself, unstoppable, punishing, furiously cold.

Dorian reached him.

He didn't remember what he did. There was the pounding of fists. His blood smeared over John's face and clothes.

And then a blast of a gun, somehow in both their hands. But his finger was on the trigger...

Chest heaving, agony coursing through his ruined hand, and still furious, Dorian glared down at Rose's corpse.

He'd just killed a man. Taken a life. Dozens of duels, and this was the first time he had actually murdered someone.

He dropped the pistol on the ground with a quiet thud. Lucien and Pryde ran to stand on either side of him.

They looked at each other. Whatever happened next, their lives would never be the same.

"He did sabotage your pistol..." murmured Pryde in shock as he looked over the remnants of Dorian's pistol. "There's a stone in the barrel... How did I not notice it? He must have found the exact right size so that it didn't move...and before we loaded them."

Lucien sighed and shook his head. "How are we going to hide this?"

And now, twelve years later, Dorian was faced with John's grieving family. The hearts Dorian had broken because of his rage, because he couldn't stop himself from attacking the man who'd maimed his hand.

He had killed a man, and these were the consequences—not just John's life gone, but the lives of these people ruined. John's sisters could have each been married. His oldest sister was probably thirty, far too old now to find a good match.

He met Patience's gaze. She was eyeing him with an alert interest and attention.

She was onto him.

And they all were.

"No doubt you were as sad as we were?" asked Mrs. Rose again.

He clenched his jaws. "I did not know Mr. Rose at all."

"Well, he wrote that he did know you," said Mr. Rose. "I distinctively remember—I still have his letter..."

Unable to contain himself any longer, Dorian jumped to his feet, his chest heaving with barely contained fury. This had to end, this interrogation, this torture of his conscience. Had he not done enough for them? Marrying Patience, giving them money, and even promising them income?

"Enough!" he roared. "I beg of you."

They all jerked back.

"Your Grace..." whispered Mrs. Rose. "What is it that we said?"

"It's you who did not really know John," growled Dorian. "Do not talk of him as if he was a saint!"

"Ah, that is indeed enough," said Mrs. Rose with a tense chuckle. "You're quite right, Duke, of course John was not a saint. He had his quirks. We all forgave him them because he was our only son, our beautiful boy, our hope for a better life."

Dorian looked around the room. All of the girls looked at him with shock, Mr. Rose with a frown.

"Please forgive us, Your Grace," he said. "We did love our

John. You're just another connection to him, part of his life we wish we knew more about."

"Pray," said Mrs. Rose. "Let us not spoil such a nice day. Let's introduce the duke to a lovely tradition we have in our family."

"Indeed," said Mr. Rose as he plastered a broad smile on his face just like Patience often did. "Now, girls. How about our little game of basket?"

"Oh yes!" cried several of them in chorus, most of them putting broad smiles on their faces.

It was a little unnerving to see that, but Dorian could now understand where Patience had acquired this strange habit.

"I'll bring the basket!" Anne said and hurried out of the room.

Dorian had wanted to call after her suggesting that one of the footmen who stood at attention in the room could go and fetch it for her, but she was already gone.

Dorian sat back down in his chair, wishing for this evening to end and for this family to leave.

Not because he didn't like them.

On the contrary.

It was just that they were a constant reminder of his worst sin, and he worried he would lash out again. His nerves felt like the strings of a violin, and the presence of John's family did not make it better, especially since they kept singing his praises, and even forgave Dorian his very inappropriate and rude behavior.

Soon Anne returned with a simple square basket—one, Dorian imagined, that could be used to pick mushrooms or wild strawberries. Not that he had even done that himself.

He cleared his throat and watched Anne give the basket to her mother.

"We just go in a circle," said Mrs. Rose to Dorian. "And each of us tells what we experienced. Something good that happened. What we learned. And if we felt anything bad, we say it quickly and put that bad emotion in here and forget it. Pretend it doesn't exist. We lock it up, and it never bothers us again."

She gave him a smile that didn't touch her eyes. Dorian wondered how much of what she said was true.

His life was nothing but fury, frustration, regret, guilt, and doubt.

All he wanted was numbness.

Perhaps this basket would make him numb. Would this work? he wondered.

Again, he understood more of how Patience grew up—her joyfulness, which sometimes felt forced, and her attempts at putting on a brave and happy face.

He wondered if she had done this ritual by herself every night she'd been here. And if she was so unhappy here and had locked up all those unhappy thoughts every day in a mental basket, what would she have left?

Nothing.

"Today, I learned so much about my new son-in-law," said Mrs. Rose. "What a great host he is, that he is treating my daughter very well, and what a stately home he has. I was tired during the journey, so I'll put that here." She made a gesture like she had gathered the words in her hand and put them into the basket, closed the lid, and locked it with an invisible key. "I was also sad to talk about John, and very sad when the duke had such a strong reaction, so I'll put both of those experiences here." She mimed locking it again and gave a large, relieved smile. "That is it! Now it was a wonderful, perfect day."

The rest of the family smiled around her approvingly, and she passed the basket to her eldest daughter, who sat to her right.

Mrs. Rose did seem happier and more at ease afterward, and Dorian wondered if this odd method truly worked. Could he lock up his wrathful demon and the murder of John Rose and just live happily ever after?

Most of the girls said they were tired and surprised at Dorian's reaction but forgave him and understood he was going through some hard times and was probably tired, as well. Some of them said they felt envious of Patience, which made her blush deeply, and she nodded to them. Others had conflicts with each other and asked for forgiveness.

Dorian's mind reeled. How could a family be this way, so open and so vulnerable with each other? Sharing emotions?

His father's reaction would have been to lock each and every one of them in the glasshouse until they learned to be tough. Dorian had been too emotional, his papa had said. Emotions were for milksops, not for a duke worthy of his line. He couldn't show any softness in the House of Lords, or when pursuing his interests—plotting to take over better lands and gain more influence with the king or queen or making alliances with other dukes.

It was for his own good, his father had said. One day, Dorian would thank him.

His father had been wrong about that.

One after another, the Roses locked their fears, exhaustion, shame, envy, and anger into the basket—and every one of them looked fresher, their backs straighter and their smiles broader.

When the time came for Patience to speak, she looked at him. "I was so happy to see my family today," she said, and he knew she was talking to him directly.

A genuine smile crossed her face, and he melted all over again.

"I realize today, my perspective has changed. For the first

two weeks here, I wished I could leave. I didn't like it here." She put her hand around her mouth as though gathering those words and then put them into the basket. "But today, it's been over three weeks that I've been married to this man. I know that even if I'm still a little afraid in Rath Hall, I'm afraid less and less, and I wouldn't choose to leave even if I could."

She had wanted to leave? His heart lurched in desperation; he hadn't realized how much he hated that idea. But she didn't want to leave anymore. Relief washed over him.

Combined sighs and awws came from around the room.

Patience handed the basket to Dorian, and he took it with a feeling of dread.

"Er," he said, staring at it. "I don't think I'd be fit to—"

"Nonsense, Your Grace," said Mrs. Rose, smiling kindly. "Just say one thing you'd like to lock up and one thing you're grateful for. I know you high aristocrats do not like to talk about your emotions, but we're family now. It'll make you feel better, you'll see!"

He cleared his throat. Good God! What was he going to say? He needed to lock his whole self up in that basket. He didn't have any positive emotions.

Not until he saw Patience hugging her family, whispered a voice in his head.

"I really don't know—" He stood up to hand the basket to Mrs. Rose, but she shook her head very insistently.

"Just try," she said. "We're here to listen."

It was the family he'd wished for but never had.

This was so stupid.

"I'd like to lock up the anger," he said and quickly and awkwardly made the gesture of scooping up something around his mouth and putting it into the basket.

He hated this so much. What good was it going to do?

He didn't feel any less angry at all.

But these nice people didn't have to know that.

"And now what are you grateful for?" asked Mrs. Rose.

And that he didn't have to struggle with at all. His gaze fell on his beautiful wife—on her golden locks and her gorgeous face, so full of life. On her lush lips that begged to be kissed.

"Patience," he said simply, and there it was again, that warm, light feeling in the middle of his chest. The one he decided was called happiness. "I'm grateful for Patience."

17

THREE DAYS LATER, Patience waved goodbye to her family as she stood with Dorian in front of their home, a bittersweet tightening in her chest.

Having them here had lifted her spirits. Dorian seemed to enjoy their company, too, despite his grumpy and growly ways, and that brightened her mood further.

However, things had changed yesterday. Dorian had left for his usual gathering with six ducal friends and returned even more irritable. Last night, he hadn't allowed her to sleep in his arms, leaving her restless and anxious. So she'd crawled into Anne's bed. Although she fell asleep, it was not as restful as when she slept next to Dorian. Never in her life had she slept as well as she did in his arms.

This morning, he'd been scowling into his plate and his cup of coffee.

The Duke of Pryde must have informed Dorian of her inquiries.

But despite Dorian's claim that he hadn't known John at Oxford, she was sure something connected him to her brother.

Otherwise, why would John have mentioned Dorian in his letters to Papa? What other reason would Dorian, Luhst, and Pryde have for speaking of an incident involving her brother? Why would Dorian have paid off her family's debts and married her if not because of some connection with John?

Her life had been shadowed by the mystery of John's death, her emotions—grief, fear, confusion—stifled and unacknowledged.

She didn't understand why Dorian would be so furious about John. Perhaps her sisters would disagree—they'd been older when John died and could remember him better—but her few memories of her brother were fond ones. He had defended her from a group of older boys who were teasing her. He'd taught her how to skip stones across the pond near their home. He'd snuck her an extra slice of fruit cake on Christmas.

Dorian knew him, too, she was certain, despite his claim. But that didn't explain why he was lashing out, avoiding talking about John, and flinching with some strange emotions she couldn't decipher.

What mysterious incident was he reminded of every time he looked at her?

As Patience followed Dorian back inside the house, she stared at his broad, surly back. Even under layers of clothing and a tailored coat that accentuated his broad-shouldered silhouette, she could see his muscles subtly shifting with each movement.

After all, John had killed himself; Dorian had nothing to do with it.

But something had happened, and that something was big enough to haunt Dorian even twelve years afterward.

And she was living with this man, bound to him for the rest of her life. She didn't want to have secrets between them.

Whatever had happened with John was keeping Dorian from being able to let her in.

She had to know the truth if she wanted to get closer to her husband.

They entered the sitting room with its rich, deep green paneled walls, adorned with intricate gold leaf patterns that caught the light from the tall windows. Heavy velvet curtains in a complementary shade of emerald framed the windows, partially drawn to allow the warm afternoon sun to filter into the room. The floor was covered in a plush, intricately woven rug in hues of green, gold, and burgundy.

Dorian turned to her. "You asked Pryde," he said accusingly.

She could already see the storm forming in his eyes, thunder clouds rolling across a tumultuous sea.

"Yes," she said, her chin high. "I see your friend is bound to his word."

Dorian chuckled and shook his head once. "You have no idea."

"I might."

"Do not ask around about John!" he barked. "I told you not to. This is one thing I will not budge about. I gave you your roses. I gave you my bed. I will not be pushed on this one!"

She studied him and chuckled, her own anger rising in her chest. "He was my brother, Duke," she stated. "Don't you think I have the right to know?"

"No. I am your husband and I tell you, there's nothing to know."

She scoffed, trying to fight the anger down, and failing. The basket, she tried to remember. He must have his reasons to be this way. He was damaged and wounded, and he was miserable.

But it was hard to remember those things when he got like this.

"My husband! You haven't been my husband very much at all. You keep me at a distance, even when you let me sleep in your bed."

He shook his head and began pacing the room like a furious lion. "It's for your own good."

"What do you mean, for my own good?" she demanded, clasping her hands.

"For your own good means that you will stay safer and happier away from me," he barked out. "Have you not learned that?"

"No," she said. "I have not. I want to understand you better, understand my brother better. I know you're a good man despite your anger, and no matter how ill you think of yourself. Nothing will change that."

"Then you must be more daft than I thought you were."

His words stung like the lash of a whip. Daft?

Part of her told her to fight back, to scream something, to throw something at him.

But that was not her. She didn't scream or throw things; she had empathy.

And she was most certainly not daft. She had been complimented by Sir Smith and Mr. Essop for her botany studies—for her ideas, her execution, her patience, her observational skills, and even on her skills of illustration. Perhaps she hadn't lived as long as he had, but calling her daft was quite unfair.

He threw a furious glance at her, and his eyes softened for a moment.

"Ah, do not make those eyes at me!" he yelled as he stopped. "Just take your damn basket and throw your pain and hurt in there like you've done your whole life. That'll make you feel better, huh? Put your fake smile on your face and pretend like I didn't say anything."

He must mean well, she kept repeating to herself. He didn't truly mean to hurt her with those words. She had an urge to do something with her hands, so she walked to her needlework from yesterday, picked up the circle, and sat on the chair. She fought the tears, but her vision blurred. Her chest and throat hurt from spasms.

She tried to smile, but it came out all sad, with the corners of her lips pushing downwards instead of upwards. Oh God, how she wanted to cry. Just to let herself go and sob and wallow in this sad, bad emotion.

But that was not something she did. Look at the positive. What was she grateful for?

She picked up her needle, but her hands shook, and as she stabbed it through the fabric, a sharp pinch told her she'd pricked herself.

She cried out and put her finger into her mouth, smudging her needlework of a sunflower with a smear of blood.

No, no, no. She was actually going to cry, wasn't she?

"Great!" Dorian grumbled as he hurried towards her. "You can't even handle a needle."

She glared at him at that, and for perhaps the first time, she couldn't stop her harsh words.

"You can't handle a wife, sir!" she yelled. "Why can't you tell me of a simple memory with my brother? What is so horrible that happened in Oxford that you keep denying it, running away from it like a coward?"

"Like a coward?" he roared, his face going crimson.

"You are a good person. An angry person, but a good person. You can do better. If you just opened up and let me in—"

"A *good* person?" he spat out.

This was going badly. Very, very badly. She had never seen him this way.

In three great steps, he crossed the room towards the mantelpiece and grabbed a beautiful porcelain vase with freshly picked snow drops in it. With his eyes bulging and his mouth contorted into a fierce scowl, teeth bared, Dorian grasped the object and hurled it into the large mirror above the gilded mantelpiece. The mirror and vase shattered.

Patience shrieked. He was going to kill himself!

The spray of glass and porcelain went through the room like a storm. There were many flashes of light as the mirror broke into hundreds of sharp pieces, showering straight on him.

Patience covered herself instinctively, but the next moment, she was on her feet and dashing towards him.

Dorian stood in the pieces of glass with his back to her, breathing hard but not moving, and when he turned, she gasped in horror. There were several shallow cuts all over his face like a map of thin lines. But one was long, and a streak of blood rolled down from the cut. It was on the side of his face, from his temple down to his jawline, and a very small piece of glass was still stuck at the bottom of the cut.

"Dorian!" She couldn't stop the angry, terrified notes in her voice, and for the first time didn't want to retract it with an apology. "You could have killed yourself!"

"Step back, Patience," he said. "I don't want you to hurt yourself."

It was the first time he had addressed her by her name, and oh how she liked it, even in these terrible circumstances.

But she didn't step back. On the contrary, she walked through the carnage, with shards of porcelain and mirrored glass sparkling on the furniture, stuck in the upholstery of the chairs and the settee. Pieces crunched under her shoes as she made her way towards him.

"No, step back," he repeated.

Footsteps hurried towards the room, and Mrs. Knight and several footmen barged in.

"Duchess, please step away," said Mrs. Knight, who didn't show her distress with anything but a fleeting, terrified look, and was already on her determined way towards Dorian, lifting her skirts slightly.

"No," Patience said, surprised at the determination in her own voice, causing shocked glances from everyone. Perhaps she had spoken too harshly. "No," she said once again, softer. "I will not step away from my husband. Come, Duke, I'll take care of your cuts. Mrs. Knight, please call for a physician, I'm sure the duke has one?"

"Of course," said Mrs. Knight after a short pause and a questioning glance at Dorian. "The duke's medicinal basket is right here."

To Patience's surprise, the housekeeper went into one of the cabinets of the sideboard and retrieved a wooden box, which she handed to Patience.

"We keep one in every room of the house," said Mrs. Knight.

Patience held the basket in one hand and took Dorian under his elbow like a child.

"Come, Duke."

She ached to call him Dorian, like he'd called her Patience, but didn't dare.

He grumbled, "Do not fuss over me. And there's no need for a doctor, Mrs. Knight, I'm fine. I'm perfectly capable of tending to my own wounds, I've done this for most of my life."

Most of his life? Oh God, the image of the broken

glasshouse came to mind, and she imagined small Dorian trying to sew his own cuts.

"In every room?" Patience glanced at Mrs. Knight, who stood next to the footmen with a perfectly neutral face, though there was worry in her eyes.

"I'm afraid his grace is prone to...accidents."

*Accidents...*coming from outbursts of rage. Has he always been tending to himself? Did he never let anyone touch him?

Has he ever hurt others in one of his rages? she wondered with a slight chill down her back. Were the servants or his sister in any danger from him? Was she?

She remembered how safe she had felt in his arms even after he'd taught her the pleasures of being spanked, which was surely a barbaric thing to happen between two people. But even the way he had slapped her bottom was tender, in every single slap she didn't feel violence. She felt his desire to please her. To bring her pleasure and not pain.

"All right," said Patience. "Still, let us go and I'll take a look at you."

"That would be best, Your Grace," said Mrs. Knight, though she didn't meet Patience's eyes after Dorian opened his mouth to protest. "I'll make sure the sitting room is taken care of as soon as possible."

Dorian looked at the hundreds, maybe thousands, of shards around the floor and furniture and nodded.

They went upstairs and into Dorian's room. Quietly, Patience took a basin, poured in fresh water from the carafe standing by its side, and brought it to Dorian.

She had learned a little of tending wounds by watching her mama take care of her siblings and herself whenever anyone was injured. They didn't have money to spend on a real physician, so the mending of wounds and treatment of illnesses and such was in their own hands.

Dorian sat on his bed, propped by his pillows. Patience put the basin on the night table and opened the box. There were different instruments. Tweezers, a hooked needle, catgut thread, fresh and clean bandages, some salves, and bottles of what must have been used to clean wounds, as well.

"Are you certain you want to do this?" he asked. "I'm perfectly capable of doing it myself. I usually do. Mrs. Knight and the housekeeper in my London house, Mrs. MacAllister, only help in the worst cases, though both are trained to deliver urgent aid."

She looked at him, and there was a knot in her stomach again at the sight of his beautiful face, so wounded.

Because of her. He'd lashed out because of her.

"Of course I'm certain I want to take care of you. You could have seriously hurt yourself," she said as she picked up the tweezers.

"I don't care about that. I could have hurt you," he said. "And that, I couldn't bear."

She carefully picked the glass out of his skin. He didn't even flinch. The shard was small and came out all bloodied. A thin streak of blood oozed out when she removed it but thankfully only a small one.

"I was far enough away," she said softly. "I was scared for you."

His face went slack as he stared at her. "Scared for me?"

"Of course." She dipped a fresh cloth into the water and sat on the edge of the bed by his side. Softly, she patted the small scratches of blood over his forehead.

"You said you were scared," he chuckled. "That's a bad emotion. Wouldn't you like to lock it away?"

"I will," she said as she moved to the scratch on his nose. She was very aware of his big and vulnerable sky-blue eyes on her. He looked completely defenseless. "But you should know what effect your outbursts have on people."

He swallowed. "I have my suspicions."

"Then why do it? Aren't you a well-bred man? Aren't you supposed to be all cold and collected and not show any emotion at all?"

She cleaned the cloth in the water and wetted a fresh, untouched side of it and moved to the biggest scratch. He hissed slightly as she patted it.

"I am supposed to, yes," he said simply.

"Pray, what troubles you?"

Blood was still oozing from the cut, although not as much anymore. She didn't think he needed stitches, but it might leave a scar.

Another one.

"A great deal troubles me," he murmured. "I don't expect you to understand."

"But I'd like to," she whispered as her hand froze on the side of his face.

Their eyes locked. His anger was spent, his defenses down. And she could truly see him, all the pain and desperation that raged in his soul.

"I'd very much like to," she repeated.

"I—" he began and stopped. "I—I'm not worth it, Patience."

"What are you talking about?" she said and chuckled. "Of course you are."

He shook his head. "I'm really not."

But to her surprise, he leaned towards her across the few inches that separated them and very gently kissed her. The taste of his lips, the touch of his body against hers soothed an ache she hadn't known she had.

She moaned right into his face as she opened her lips and

let him in. He caressed her tongue, and she his. The kiss grew more desperate, needier. Heat coursed through her, her body aching, throbbing for his touch, yearning for him.

But he withdrew, his gaze wild and somewhat unhinged. He was panting as much as she was.

"Thank you, my dear girl," he rasped. "You cannot imagine how grateful I am. Your touch—" He cleared his throat. "Sometimes I wonder what I did in this life to deserve someone as wondrous as you treating me so well."

Patience blinked. As wondrous as she? Did he mean it?

She smiled, and this time there was nothing forced or fake in it.

18

The next morning, Dorian inhaled deeply of the damp earthy scents as Patience and he rattled along in the carriage through the countryside on the way to visit his tenants. Trees were dusted with new leaves. Primroses and daffodils dotted the low hedgerows. Birdsong filled the air.

He didn't remember the last time he'd actually looked at the spring landscape and enjoyed it, but next to Patience, everything felt beautiful and full of life. Even the slight pain from his cuts didn't bother him.

Patience's delicate fingertips traced the bud of a bluebell he'd picked for her before they got into the carriage.

Lucky bluebell.

"This will be the one task of a duchess that I will truly enjoy," she said with a tender smile as she stared dreamily at the countryside passing by. "Seeing the tenants, talking to them. Helping them."

Dorian thought with a pang of the very first rule she'd broken and how surprisingly well she took the punishment. Feeling her bare bottom, her growing wetness under his hand was an unsurpassed pleasure...until now. Seeing her overjoyed like this was even sweeter.

"That is one thing we can agree on," he said. "Papa never bothered with his duties to the tenants. Growing up, I always thought it was a shame. When I became duke, I did my best to make sure the steward was on top of repairs, solving problems, providing help whenever the tenants needed it. But I haven't visited them for months now. I should have, as should any good landlord."

She beamed at him, and he felt the urge to smile back. No one had made him feel like smiling in... God, he didn't remember how long. No one but her.

"Well, now you have me to help you," she said. "Do you usually organize the May Day?"

"No."

"That's what we should do! Would they enjoy it, do you think?"

"I'm sure they would."

"Marvelous!" Her eyes glimmered with excitement. "With the mild weather, wildflowers will be in bloom—perfect for weaving into garlands. And we can set up outdoor games and... Oh! Wouldn't it be great to have a maypole? Children would adore the ribbons!"

He watched sunlight play across her golden tresses. Such a generous spirit, so eager to bring joy to others.

I'd like to please you more.

Warmth swelled in his chest, cracking the ice encasing his heart.

He'd give her ten May Days if only it would bring a smile to her lips like that.

"Yes," he said. "Maypole. Ribbons. Children."

Yet dread clawed at his heart. Memories of Papa surged like a tidal wave—the sneer curling his lip as he berated a tenant short on rent, the whip cracking against a stable boy's back... Dorian gritted his teeth.

He had wanted Dorian to become a duke in his own image.

He refused to become that image, to let his father win.

And yet, the rage living within him every day of his life was Papa's creation.

Their carriage halted before a tumbledown cottage on the edge of the estate. An elderly woman, face lined and weathered, stepped out with two grandchildren ages roughly six and eight. Her eyes crinkled at the corners upon spotting them.

"Your Grace." She bobbed a curtsy. "What an unexpected delight."

"Mrs. Batten," said Dorian as he helped Patience get down. "This is my wife, the Duchess of Rath."

The Battens had always had a flock of sheep, and Bramble had been a lamb from one of their ewes.

The old lady looked at Patience with warmth in her face and curtsied again with a slight grimace of pain. "You are welcome, Your Grace," she said.

Patience went to the old woman and presented a basket of steaming blackberry pies, golden crusts glinting.

"This is for you. From his grace's kitchen."

Mrs. Batten clutched it close, eyes shining. Then she peered up at Dorian and smiled. "Bless you, Your Grace. You're a far kinder man than your father ever was. We're lucky to have you."

Dorian wrestled his features into a rigid smile even as nausea churned. *If only she knew the blood staining my hands. The life I took. The family I destroyed.* He clenched his fists behind his back until his knuckles ached.

As Patience knelt to exclaim over the giggling children, Mrs. Batten leaned in and said to Dorian, "You take good care of your duchess now, y'hear? You were a lovely little boy, and you can be a loving husband, not a brute like your papa was." Her gaze bore into him, unflinching.

Dorian swallowed against the bile rising in his throat. "Um," he managed hoarsely.

"Do you know what he did?" asked Mrs. Batten, addressing Patience. "As a boy, he found out I grew medicinal herbs and used them for remedies. Not a week after his papa's death he brings me books on herbs from the Mediterranean, and France, and even Constantinople, and pouches with seeds of rare herbs he bought at some apothecary in London."

Dorian felt his face heat. "It was the least I could do."

She leaned towards Patience. "Cinchona bark helped one of my other grandchildren as he had a fever. Your husband may have saved the boy."

The sight of tenderness and respect in Patience's face only made him crumble inside. God knew he didn't deserve it.

"I owed you much more than that," he croaked.

"You did not owe me anything," said Mrs. Batten with a soft smile. "You rescued that wee poor lamb. It was nae your fault what the old duke did. I hold no grudge, and I hope you could forgive yourself, too."

They said their goodbyes, and as the carriage trundled on, Dorian couldn't escape the old woman's words echoing in his mind. Patience, unlike half an hour ago, sat quietly beside him, her brow furrowed. The silence stretched between them, taut as a bowstring.

"Is everything all right?" Dorian finally asked.

Patience hesitated, twisting her gloved fingers in her lap. "Mrs. Batten mentioned... She said she was glad I have a kind husband. Unlike your father." Her azure eyes met his, searching. "What did she mean?"

His breath caught in his throat. Memories assailed him—his father's thunderous rage, his sister's muffled sobs. He gripped the carriage seat, the leather creaking beneath his fingers.

"My father," he began haltingly, "was a hard man. He disliked any hint of softness, of emotion. He wanted to mold me into a cold, unfeeling duke." His jaw clenched. "He was cruel, to me and to Chastity. I did my best to protect her, but..." His throat tightened and he shook his head. "Forgive me, I don't wish to speak of it further."

Patience laid a gentle hand on his arm, her touch soothing even through the layers of fabric. "That must have been hard for you," she murmured.

Dorian stared at her. Her compassion melted his heart. He ached to share with her, to tell her more. But he couldn't.

Tenderly, he took her small hand in both of his as a fierce protectiveness overwhelmed him, a desperate longing to shield her from any further pain. He could feel her gentle skin with the bare skin of his left hand. His right hand clad in the glove tingled, aching to feel her touch. There she was, surrounded by him, with his secrets hidden under thick leather, ugly and painful.

If only he could erase the hurts of her past, to cherish and protect her as she deserved...

"What happened to Mrs. Batten's lamb?" asked Patience softly. "If you wish to talk about that."

His usual response—closing up, getting angry before he could tear himself open and be vulnerable—made his throat ache. But the tenderness in her blue eyes pulled him past that painful guard.

"The Battens had sheep on their farm for generations," he said. "Mama disappeared from my life as Papa had sent her away to a distant estate and forbade any contact. I missed her. I was terrified of him. I didn't know what I was feeling—the hurt, the pain in my soul."

"You must have been grieving the loss of your mama," said Patience, and the truth of her words struck him with a devastating clarity. "She left, but you needed someone to love and to love you. Someone to protect you, to be on your side."

It was like she could see straight through into his soul, put words to the feelings that had ruled him for years. Explain things he couldn't.

Would she be able to explain the moment he had challenged her brother to a duel? Or the moment his finger had found the trigger and pulled?

"I suppose you're right," he said, his mangled fist tightening. "I found a lamb from one of their ewes. Somehow it had escaped and had fallen into a pit in the woods. I took it home, to my room, and named it Bramble. I cared for it until it recovered, which is when I went to Mrs. Batten to return it. Seeing my tears, she told me I could keep it. You've seen how kind she is. I wanted to keep Bramble more than anything in the entire world. It was the first time since Mama left that I felt better, when I held the little lamb. But even at my young age, I knew losing an animal was a great deal for tenants like the Battens, so I offered her a vase from Rath Hall as payment, but she refused and said I could keep the little thing as long as I kept it healthy and safe."

Patience's eyes watered. She squeezed his left hand and smiled. "Mrs. Batten is so good-hearted."

He nodded. "Unfortunately, Papa discovered my pet. It wasn't like I could hide Bramble in my room forever. I suppose our previous housekeeper got tired of having the maids clean sheep dung from the Aubusson rugs in my chamber. Papa was furious. A future duke nursing a pet lamb was completely laughable."

"What happened?"

"He killed it. Took my very own fencing sword and—"

His throat closed around the words once again, but it was her pale face that stopped him from telling of the gruesome scene, the horror of seeing yet another thing he loved taken away by his papa.

"No..." She shook her head, tears welling in her eyes. "I'm so sorry."

He nodded.

"Is that why you feel this rage...?" she wondered. "I suppose you must have felt quite helpless then."

He nodded once again. How could she see right through him? Yet again putting words to the explosion of feelings that had ruled him his whole life? Was it her basket exercise that had taught her this skill or simply her intuitive heart and incredible kindness? Lucien and Chastity had both seen what happened to Bramble, but he had never told either of them how he felt.

Strangely, naming the feelings took away their power, putting them outside of his body and allowing him to reclaim his strength.

Once again, he wondered what this was woman doing to him.

Was she healing him, when all he'd ever done was wound her...and her family?

"Yes," he said. "You're right, I felt helpless, and the one thing I could do was lash out. Destroy before I could be destroyed. I cut Papa's favorite portrait to ribbons."

He was lost in her eyes. No one had ever looked at him like she did then. He felt understood and accepted, known.

But would she understand every ugly thing he'd ever done...including what he did to John? He truly didn't deserve her.

"Lucien and Chastity witnessed everything," he said.

"Is that why you have such a strong bond with Lucien?" she asked.

"Yes. He stayed in Rath Hall for months while we were growing up. His parents, dare I say, have been as poisonous to him as my papa was to me and Chastity."

"How did you become friends with the rest? You seven dukes are quite a band."

The hint of a smile tugged at one corner of his lips at the thought of his brotherhood.

"I can't tell you everything. Above all, we keep each other's secrets. But what I can tell you is that Pryde became a friend after Oxford. Enveigh... Pryde was indebted to him, and Enveigh found himself in a bad situation because of another man's wife. We helped to save him from a duel and a scandal."

"Men and your code of honor," she chuckled. "What about the rest? Whatever you can say without betraying your secrets."

"Lucien knew Eccess from Elysium. Let's just say they both like to overindulge in their celebrations. Eccess once drove a carriage while very drunk, which led to a bad accident. It would have ruined him completely if Lucien hadn't asked us to help. Irevrence likes to make bad jokes and doesn't care about the consequences. After having told one in the wrong company, against the wrong high-ranking official, he would have landed in prison if we hadn't helped. And finally, Fortyne's acute business sense sometimes does not consider the legality of certain enterprises. He almost got caught. By then, there were six of us, and each of us helped using our own strengths."

"You have a strong bond with all of them," she said.

"We knew we had something special. Seven men as damaged as we are in our own ways... It was forever. No one would understand the extent of the way our souls are corrupted. Inside our group, everything is allowed. There's no judgment. But besides that, we started to help each other with investments, business, protecting each other's interests against threats. That was how the Seven Dukes of Sin was born."

Patience's gaze shimmered with curiosity. "Quite a group, I daresay."

"They're like the brothers I never had," he said. "Especially Lucien. I may not always see eye to eye with all of them, but I know we will never betray each other. Our loyalty runs deeper than personal conflicts or difference in interests. If anything happened to me, I know they would all protect and take care of Chastity…and, of course, you."

The carriage stopped too soon, and Dorian withdrew his hands from hers. They were at Cohen's house. The older man, whom Dorian had helped with a fence repair a month or so earlier, waited outside, his lined face brightening at the sight of Dorian.

After Patience presented him with the basket, he invited them inside. Over weak tea in chipped cups, the man turned to Patience, his eyes wet. "I can't thank ye enough, Yer Grace. After my Mary passed last winter, there are more things and less hands. My daughter has her hands full with the wee one. Ye're a right angel, ye are."

Patience ducked her head, color blooming in her cheeks. "It's not just me. It's the duke, too. And it's the least we can do, Cohen. Truly."

Cohen turned to Dorian, his gnarled fingers tightening around his cup. "We're right grateful to have a caring duke now, Yer Grace. After yer father's cruelty…'tis a blessed change, it is. And thank ye again for helping me repair the fence a few sennights ago. I couldna' have done it on my own."

Patience beamed at Dorian, her eyes alight with pride and

affection. But Dorian could muster only a weak twitch of his lips in return, nausea roiling in his gut like a living thing. If they knew the man he truly was, the sins he'd committed... they would recoil in horror and revulsion.

He didn't deserve their gratitude, their admiration. And he certainly didn't deserve Patience's nurturing and attention. Sooner or later, she would learn the truth...and he would lose her forever.

Outside the cottage, Patience chattered about the May Day festival with Cohen as they walked arm in arm down the sun-dappled path. "It was such joy! I was six, and my family was still welcome to participate in events like that. I remember the maypole, the dancing, the flowers... My sisters and I spun around that maypole. I think that must have been the happiest memory in my childhood. I can hardly wait to bring the same joy here!"

Dorian watched her animated face, the way her eyes sparkled with anticipation. Something twisted in his chest sharply. Her enthusiasm, her joy...it reminded him of all he had stolen from her when he'd killed her brother. The weight of his guilt pressed down on him.

He wanted to feel light and carefree, like her. He could feel the glimpses of that lightness in the surrounding landscape, in the flowers that peeked through fresh grass, in the blue sky. And he could feel it in the sparkle of her blue eyes every time she smiled at him.

An insane thought came. An impossible thought, and yet, so seductive.

What if he told her? What if she knew?

In that moment, Dorian allowed himself to believe. To hope, even if only for a heartbeat, that perhaps...perhaps there was still a chance for redemption. A chance to conquer the shadows that haunted him.

"...and I thought we could perhaps have a special tent set up for the children's games," Patience continued, oblivious to his inner turmoil. "What do you think?"

But deep in his heart, he knew the truth. She would never accept him if she knew the truth. And he was not courageous enough to risk losing her.

19

THE NEXT DAY, Patience knelt beside her roses, carefully examining their progress. She breathed in the earthy scent of the damp soil and the overgrown garden she had ached to put in order. Her spirits had been lifted since yesterday, one of the best days since her wedding.

She'd seen a side of Dorian she'd never expected. He was a kind man—a wounded man, but a kind one. She was worried about the cuts from the broken mirror, though they were now healing, and her heart was filled with the pain she'd seen in his eyes when he told her about his papa. And the connection that grew between the two of them was like an invisible but strong cord.

She looked at the tangle of weeds and grass, dotted with dandelions and brambles, that could become lawns with pretty flowering bushes. The garden was like him—abandoned, neglected, wild.

She longed to prune the ancient, gnarled trees with their branches like a canopy that swallowed the light, remove dried and diseased ones for firewood, and plant new trees. The paths that were now barely discernible amid the overgrowth could get fresh gravel and new, more pleasing shapes.

Dorian was everywhere, surrounding her, in the early April air—which held a chill despite the sun and the buzz of insects. Unseen creatures rustled in the undergrowth. Just like him, the garden was dark, and perhaps unwelcoming at first glance, but full of life if only one would care for it and allow it to thrive.

In the far corner was the glasshouse. She dreamed Dorian would allow her to use it one day. She could clean its glass panes, replace the broken ones, remove all the dead and rotting vegetation, and plant exotic species.

Oh, it could be such a joy to watch them grow, care for them, make observations and perhaps a new discovery.

Perhaps one day, she thought with a smile.

But there was one dark, ominous cloud in the clearing sky of their marriage.

The strange connection he had with her deceased brother. The "Oxford incident" he refused to acknowledge. His hand always hidden under the glove. These were secrets she ached to uncover.

He had opened up to her yesterday, and she now felt closer to him. She had more hope for her happiness with her husband than ever before. In time, he might feel comfortable enough with her that his walls would fall completely, and he'd tell her about John.

If not, she must do everything she could to learn the truth or there would always be a barrier between their hearts.

Amid all the untouched wilderness, the only place that showed signs of new life were the rosebushes she'd planted just two weeks ago. They seemed to be adapting well to their new environment. She could see tiny, bright green leaves and even more tiny red buds swelling.

She looked closely for any signs of disease—shriveling of

the buds or wilting of the leaves. She also looked for thrips, aphids, and other pests but could see only a ladybug and a bee, which were both beneficial.

She reached for her notebook, her fingers brushing against the supple leather cover. Inside, the pages were filled with meticulous notes and detailed sketches, years of observation and work. At least she didn't have to hide her notes and her roses here, nor report to anyone why she spent so much time staring at rosebushes instead of planting vegetables.

As she flipped to a blank page to happily record the progress of the roses and the lack of disease or pests, a shadow fell across the paper. Patience looked up, shielding her eyes against the sun, and found herself face-to-face with Chastity.

Dorian's sister wore a dark gray silk dress, which was plain despite the expensive material. Her sky-blue eyes, bright and kind behind her spectacles, resembled her brother's. Her hair was styled in a simple chignon with no curls, tendrils, or accessories to enhance her beauty. Patience, whom Mademoiselle Antoinette dressed with a fierce dedication to fashion, felt a pang of envy.

"Good morning, Duchess," Chastity said, her voice cool and measured, despite the curiosity glowing in her eyes. "Did Dorian allow you to plant these?"

Patience rose to her feet, brushing the dirt from her skirts. "Ah, Lady Chastity, welcome back. He did, can you imagine? Are you moving back in?"

"Yes, if that is agreeable? Did I give you and Dorian enough time to get acquainted after the wedding?"

"Of course!" said Patience, a little breathless. "I didn't mean to force you out of your own home. You were always welcome to stay."

"It's tradition, I think," said Chastity, a little shyly.

Her gaze dropped to the tiny leaves on the roses, such a

striking contrast with the rest of the dark and overgrown garden.

"Dorian hasn't let anyone touch the garden since he became duke twelve years ago," said Chastity with a slight wrinkle between her brows. "How did you manage to convince him?"

Patience chuckled. "He is a kind man deep down."

Chastity studied her with a puzzled look in her intelligent eyes. Patience decided not to elaborate on what it actually took to have Dorian agree to this…her bare buttocks, his hand, and oh dear God…

"Are you interested in roses?" Chastity asked.

"I am, indeed. It's been my project the past six years. I've been trying to create a new variety of roses that would be both beautiful and resistant to disease. I brought these with me from home."

Chastity's eyebrows rose. "Are you a botanist?"

"I suppose I am," said Patience with a shy smile.

"How marvelous! Never did I expect to have a new sister who's a fellow scientist. Tell me more." Chastity's eyes burned with enthusiasm, and a genuine smile lit up her face. It was the first time Patience had seen her smile.

Patience's own spirits soared. With her husband being such an enigma, she ached to have a true friend, like Anne. Chastity was her new sister. Like Dorian, she seemed aloof, cold, and distant, but maybe she had a good heart, too.

"Well," Patience began, excitement filling her with lightness, "I started by selecting two rose varieties—the gallica rose, known for its hardiness and disease resistance, and the damask rose, prized for its beautiful, fragrant blooms. I decided to artificially fertilize them."

Chastity clasped her hands. "Artificially fertilize them? How did you come up with that idea?"

Patience smiled, pleased to discuss her innovative technique. "I was inspired by a book my brother brought from Oxford. He brought several, to refresh our limited library, and there was one talking about the reproduction process of plants. From it, I wondered what would happen if I combined two varieties of roses by pollinating them before they pollinated themselves. I wondered if, like animals, the resulting plants might have the combined traits of both parents. A theory, of course, but I wanted to experiment and see what happened."

"Intriguing," Chastity murmured, her eyes alight. "All we know is that plants reproduce by pollination and that bees and other insects contribute to it. I suppose a person could do that themselves, though the results would be unknown. This is certainly a novel approach!"

"Yes, it is possible, but it took me several experiments to get it right. I found out it needed to be cold like in winter for them to germinate and grow. Not all of them took, but these did." She proudly gestured at her roses. "Bloomed two years ago for the first time."

"Remarkable," Chastity mused. "And have you been noting the performance of these hybrids?"

"Indeed I have," Patience said, her face glowing with pride. "I've been monitoring them since the very beginning. The results have been outstanding. They showed greater disease resistance than their parents, and the flowers are simply stunning."

Chastity leaned in, studying the meticulously recorded data. "This is impressive work, Patience. The level of detail in your observations, the innovative approach…it's quite brilliant."

Patience basked in the praise, feeling a surge of validation. "Thank you, Lady Chastity. That means a great deal. I must say, my sister Anne's eyes always glazed over when I talked to her about them, even though she's a mathematician herself. Talk to her about equations, the number pi, or number theory, and she lights up. It's the first time that I've spoken to someone who shares my enthusiasm."

Chastity chuckled. "I quite understand that. When I talk to Dorian about my medical experiments, I get a similar reaction."

An understanding of a shared passion ran between them, and a jolt of joy made Patience's stomach do a happy lurch. Medical experiments? Fascinating! She had just opened her mouth to ask about them when Chastity's expression grew serious.

"There's just one thing, Duchess. I may be wrong, but you haven't mentioned a control group. Have you been noting the performance of the original gallica and damask varieties alongside your hybrids in the same way?"

Patience's smile faltered, a sinking feeling settling in her stomach. "I...I have some data on them, but I haven't been as systematic. I was so focused on the hybrids..."

She trailed off, realizing the gravity of her mistake. Without a control group, how could she be certain that the improved disease resistance was due to intentional fertilization and not just natural variation?

Chastity sighed, not unkindly. "It's an understandable oversight for a beginning botanist. But for your findings to be truly meaningful, you need that baseline comparison. Without it, your conclusions could be just a coincidence."

Patience nodded, feeling a hot flush of shame wash over her. She had been so caught up in the excitement of her hybridization successes that she had neglected a fundamental aspect of scientific inquiry.

As Chastity continued to talk, Patience felt the weight of her shortcomings pressing down on her. The garden seemed to blur before her eyes, the once-vibrant roses now a mocking reminder of her own inadequacies. What was she hoping to publish? She'd be laughed at by the scientific community, especially being so young and a woman.

Mentally, she chastised herself for feeling this way. Positive thoughts! she told herself. It was good that she hadn't sent her paper yet. Perhaps she shouldn't do this at all.

She was just a beginning botanist, as Chastity had said.

"Thank you, Lady Chastity," said Patience, fighting to contain the pain of disappointment from spilling in tears. "You're very knowledgeable."

Chastity's blue eyes saddened behind her spectacles. "I must have disappointed you. I am sorry. It's not easy for me to make friends, but I do appreciate a fellow female scientist. There aren't many of us. Would you care for a walk?"

"Of course," said Patience and the two of them walked slowly towards Rath Hall, the sun warm on Patience's face.

"Did you have to work hard to educate yourself?" asked Chastity.

Patience smiled. "Yes. It was not easy, though I'm sure if we'd had money to buy food and a cook to prepare meals, my parents wouldn't have minded me growing roses, reading books, and making my notes. Instead, I had to grow what we ate, and my sisters prepared it."

Chastity nodded thoughtfully. "Our positions are not to be taken for granted. I hope you do have freedom now to pursue it?"

Patience smiled. "Your brother is very supportive."

"He is. He was for me, too."

Patience frowned. "How so?"

"My deceased papa disapproved of my scientific inclinations greatly."

Patience held her breath. That must have been what

Dorian had started to tell her in the carriage when they visited the tenants. He'd told her something about Chastity and his papa, but then interrupted himself.

Chastity continued, "He burned my books, forbade me access to the library, and even took away all paper and ink for a while. He called me vile names. No one in my life has hurt me as much as Papa did. My brother fought for my right to study science."

Chastity's gaze flickered shortly towards the glasshouse as her face grew somber and took on a haunted expression similar to Dorian's.

Patience's chest tightened with empathy, and her heart filled with tenderness towards Dorian. This was yet another side of her husband. He was a man who protected his sister's right to study what she wanted.

If only he would tell her about John... There was a mysterious, invisible thread that connected him and her, through her brother, and she wanted to know why.

"I'm so sorry to hear that, Chastity. My parents never burned my botanical books or took away my journals or ink. However, they told me to spend my time working in the kitchen garden rather than with my roses. For years, I had to carry out my research in secret. Thankfully, they couldn't see what I was doing from the house. My own rosebushes hid me."

Chastity smiled sadly as they came to the entrance into the house. "I suppose we have more in common than we both thought."

Patience smiled as she tried and failed to lock her disappointment and sadness in her emotion basket. Why was this not working? She had been doing it every night by herself, and most of the time, it made her feel better... Except...

What if it wasn't possible to run from these feelings? She'd never felt anything like what she felt towards Dorian before.

So...maybe she shouldn't lock away these feelings?

Could she ask Chastity? Was this too new of a friendship to ask about the one thing that had been bothering her from the moment at Lady Buchanan's soirée when she'd overheard Dorian speaking to Luhst and Pryde about John?

"Have you by any chance heard of Dorian's connection with my brother, Mr. John Rose?" asked Patience.

Chastity frowned and narrowed her eyes, looking at her. "No, I'm sorry. I've never heard of Mr. John Rose. Was he present at the wedding? I apologize if I forgot."

Disappointment fell through Patience's stomach like a stone. "You have not forgotten. My brother died twelve years ago, and I thought our brothers might have known each other."

She could have told Chastity about her worries. If they were real sisters now, she would have told her every worry she had and asked her for any tiny piece of information, any clue that could help her to discern this secret and get closer to her husband.

"Oh, I am so sorry, Patience," said Chastity, biting her lip. "I did not know."

"Please do not apologize," said Patience with a smile and a little relief Chastity didn't know about the suicide, that her opinion of Patience and her family wouldn't be destroyed. "You did nothing wrong. It's just...I've been always so surprised how your brother decided to marry me without ever meeting me."

"I was surprised by his sudden announcement of the wedding, too. All his adult life, he's resisted our aunt's insistence on him finding a wife and continuing the Rath line. Then from one day to the next, he announced he would marry. It was all very quick."

"Do you have any idea why it was so sudden?" asked Patience, her hands shaking a little as they walked.

"As far as I heard, he wanted to help your papa. Forgive me, but Mr. Rose was in a dire situation, was he not?"

"Indeed," said Patience, her stomach dropping with disappointment at the lack of new insight. "He was."

"Perhaps my brother is the best person to answer your questions," suggested Chastity. "I wish I could help, but I'm afraid I simply do not know."

Patience nodded, putting a smile on her face. It wasn't Lady Chastity's fault, but Patience's throat tightened, and she struggled to keep up a cheerful conversation with Chastity.

But, as always, she managed to cling to her happy smile.

20

"Good boy," Patience whispered to Titan, who raised his head and stood up as she closed Dorian's door behind her with as little sound as she could.

Titan's tall, shaggy body was a visible silhouette against the darkness of the room. She couldn't imagine what it would be like if every time she'd come here, Titan would have thrown himself at her the way he had that first night.

She'd managed to befriend the beast by bringing him treats and scraps from the kitchen each night she visited Dorian.

This time, she had a large piece of a boiled chicken breast that she had gone to the kitchen for herself. She could have, of course, asked her chambermaid or Mrs. Knight, but she still did not feel right asking servants to do tasks she could perform very easily.

She patted Titan's wiry head as he ate in large, satisfied bites. Goodness, she wouldn't have wanted to be that piece of chicken in his huge jaws. His giant tail thumped quickly and loudly from side to side, his ears pressed to his head. Both of his eyes, the black one and the white one, held an expression of utter worship as he chewed looking at her.

"Aw," she whispered with a grin. "I love you, too, Titan."

She opened the door so that he would walk out of the room. "And now, be a good boy and guard your master and me in the corridor, would you?"

Titan walked out of the room, for which she gave him another strategically saved treat and patted his head through the gap between the door and the frame before shutting it.

With Titan gone, Patience gave a long sigh and looked at Dorian's bed. In the moonlight falling through three large windows into the vast room, she could see him lying on his back with one arm flung over his head on the pillow. He looked so peaceful.

Without his habitual scowl, he was so handsome. He looked much younger, even with the patch of white hair at his temple.

Not wanting to wake him, she tiptoed her way towards her husband.

Her talk earlier today with Chastity had left her out of sorts. At first, she'd felt they could be friends, sisters like she and Anne. But Chastity's critique of Patience's method left her feeling misunderstood and discouraged. How could she have been so stupid and not thought of recording the progress of her original bushes more thoroughly? Chastity was older than her, and more experienced in scientific circles. She knew better what was required.

Patience had never needed Dorian's warm, strong, reassuring arms around her as much as she needed them now. She climbed under his warm blanket, relishing his heat. Like always, she slid along the length of his body and laid her head in the crease between his shoulder and his hard chest.

He smelled so good. Like quite a sinner, she pressed her

nose against his smooth skin and inhaled deeply several times. No one should ever know about this. If she could, she would wrap herself in his scent and wear it like a warm shawl on sad, cold days.

His scent melted something in her and made her think of bare parts of her body against bare parts of his body, and pleasure. So much pleasure.

She wriggled her head to find the best place, and sighed out when she did. His chest rose and fell evenly and deeply.

Finally, she could close her eyes. Much better. She didn't think of her failure over the last six years at all.

She was just drifting into sleep when she became aware of a disturbance. Muffled sounds of distress filled the air. Dorian's chest rose unevenly and rapidly.

She raised her head.

"No..." he mumbled, his eyes still closed. "No!" he repeated.

"Dorian?" she whispered.

His face in the moonlight was anguished, the crease of a frown marring his forehead. "No, let me go!"

Patience sat up, a cold rush of fear making her alert.

"No, Papa..." He thrashed, jerking his head to his left. "Let me out! Please!"

He was crying. His face was distorted in a terrible grimace. Chastity had told her that Dorian had protected her against his papa. Dorian, her damaged and wounded husband... Patience was desperate to help release him from this painful experience.

"Let me out, please!" Dorian kept thrashing.

Let him out of where?

She wrapped her arms around him. "You're safe, Dorian," she said gently, stroking his damp face. "It's all right."

He clutched her like she was his last salvation.

She kissed him on his misted forehead, and he opened his eyes and froze, staring at her blindly, confused.

"Patience," he mumbled, and wiped his face with both hands.

While her body was frozen in shock, quite strangely, part of her mind realized she'd just called him by his first name. For the first time.

And how right it felt on her lips, just as right as hearing her given name on his.

"Are you all right?" she asked, despite dozens of other questions rushing through her mind. "Did you have a nightmare?"

He sat up in his bed, leaning against the pillows. "I'm fine. I — What happened?" he asked, eyeing her carefully.

"You were dreaming. You called for your papa to let you out."

She saw the exact moment his defenses slammed down, like a portcullis forbidding her access.

"Damnation," he cursed quietly. "This is why I hadn't wanted you to sleep in my bed, share my quarters, or come anywhere near me. I should have never let you in."

All the things he'd said about his mama, about Bramble, the closeness they felt. The connection.

She felt like he'd just jerked that growing connection away. The words stung, and tears prickled her eyes. She nodded, defeated. Sometimes she felt like she was seeing more and more of him, glimpses of the man behind the fear, the pain, and the defenses. Other times, she felt like she'd never reach him. Never help him heal. Never be able to chase away the ghosts haunting him.

"I won't ask," she said.

That didn't mean she wouldn't try to find out more. But just for now, for his sake, she wouldn't push him.

"But I don't want to leave you alone in this state."

He studied her, and she saw his Adam's apple bob under

his chin. Then he nodded, and she nestled against him once again.

Her treacherous body felt like she'd arrived home as his arms closed around her and pressed her into his hard chest.

"If you have any more nightmares," she mumbled against his delicious skin as they both settled down into a lying position, "just give them to me. I won't be afraid."

21

THE FOLLOWING DAY, Dorian stood in the doorway of a room he hadn't set foot in for twelve years.

The outlines of furniture covered with white sheets were visible thanks to the sunlight peering through the narrow slits between the heavy curtains.

As Patience's delicate hands grasped the edge of a curtain, panic surged through him, his heart racing at the thought of the light that would soon flood the space. It was easy to hide the pain of losing his mother in the darkness. The light would expose everything, and something akin to terror clawed its way through him.

"What room was this?" she asked.

He took a few steps into the darkness. Surprisingly, the floor didn't open up under his feet. "Mama's sitting room," he croaked.

She shouldn't be touching anything here, roared the beast inside him. No one should touch anything of his mother's.

But this was the only room on the ground floor with a good

view of her precious roses. He'd foolishly blurted out this morning that perhaps she'd like to visit it.

"Your mama?" she asked and turned to him, her eyes big with understanding.

Good God, what was this woman doing to him? Rage licked the inside of his rib cage like a lion. How dare she enter this room, touch anything here?

How dare she make changes in his house…and in him?

"Yes," he said, marveling at the ease with which the word left his mouth.

One after another, he'd lowered his defenses and broken his rules just for the pleasure of seeing her brilliant smile, her sparkling eyes.

"And you haven't been here since…"

"Since the day I asked Mrs. Knight to close this room. It was the day of my papa's funeral. I had just got back from Oxford. Twelve years ago."

Twelve years ago… There was that number again. It was also twelve years ago that John had died, and he saw the significance of the date flicker in her eyes.

The room, once filled with light and the laughter his papa had disapproved of, had become a dungeon to Dorian's pain and anger.

On the day he returned home twelve years ago, all he knew was that he would never see the garden, never come to this room again. And so, the furniture had been covered, the curtains drawn together, and the doors locked.

Until today.

Patience shifted the curtain a little and peeked into the sunlight, her face immediately alight with enthusiasm—and he knew the view of her rosebushes was spectacular from here.

She turned to him, her eyes seeking his permission. "Are

you certain you won't be distressed by allowing me to use the room?"

Dorian found himself nodding, almost imperceptibly. There was something about her, a quiet strength and a gentle understanding, that made him want to trust her, to let her into the parts of himself he had long kept hidden.

With a deep breath, Patience pulled the curtains all the way open, and the room was instantly bathed in sunlight. She gasped in awe as she looked at the garden and around the room, and something shifted in Dorian, as though the very floor had careened.

Dust motes danced in the sunbeams. Dorian blinked, adjusting to the brightness. It was as if a weight had been lifted from his shoulders, the darkness that had shrouded him for so long suddenly dissipating in the face of Patience's radiance.

"This room is so pretty!"

As she walked about the room with its paneled walls painted in gentle pastel lavender, her fingers trailing over the furniture and the bookshelves, Dorian realized he would never have entered this room without her. She was like a breath of fresh air, a burst of sunshine in the gloom of his existence.

Patience pulled the drapes of the next window open and looked at the garden. "I love this room, Duke," she whispered. He ached to tell her to call him Dorian once again but said nothing. "Thank you for showing this to me. You're right, the view of my roses from here is superb. I have been working on them since I was just a girl."

Dorian moved to stand beside her. "Tell me about them," he said, his voice gentle.

She looked at him and chuckled softy. She was so pretty he couldn't breathe. "Are you certain you want to hear about cuttings, soil, artificial fertilization, and such?"

"There's nothing I'd like to hear more."

And so, bathed in the sunlight of the newly opened room, Patience told him of the long hours spent experimenting and tending to her roses, of the joy she felt as she watched them grow and thrive.

Like a fool, he had forbidden her to use the garden. Had he known on their wedding day that she'd brought plants with her and how important they were, he'd have said yes right away. He remembered the look of awe as she stood in the garden for the first time, and the look of complete devastation as he'd told her she couldn't even step inside it.

The longing gaze she cast at the glasshouse every time she saw it.

When she finished, Patience looked up at him, her eyes shining with hope, and her cheeks reddened a little. "I've been working on a paper to publish my findings," she said, her voice trembling slightly. "It's a secret. Anne and Chastity knew about the research. No one knows about my paper...except for the botanists I've been corresponding with."

His chest tightened. "It's safe with me."

"I suppose it is. You're an excellent keeper of secrets."

He swallowed hard as he expected this to be a jab, a criticism, but she smiled softly at him.

"You see," she continued, "there is not much research on artificial fertilization at all. And not many roses are both exquisitely beautiful and resistant to disease as mine. I think if I publish it, more botanists and even farmers will try this technique more deliberately, and I think it can help with a variety of plants, including crops. But...I'm just an eighteen-year-old woman who never had a governess or went to university. I've been too afraid to submit it. I don't know if it's good enough."

Dorian took her hand in his, his touch gentle and reassuring. "It is," he said, his voice firm with conviction. "You are quite brilliant… How did you learn botany? I can't imagine your papa could afford many books."

"No, he could not. And with our family being such a poor connection for the local community, the only library I had access to was the vicar Mr. Menon's. When I was ready to move beyond the book John had brought home, the vicar loaned me several books on botany. He also borrowed books from the Marchioness of Virtoux and other wealthy parishioners and passed them to me." She chuckled. "If those people only knew what a scandalous person read their books…"

She was determined…but he already knew that about her. Determined, intelligent, and tenacious. He was in awe of her.

"So you created a new rose hybrid on your own, starting from the time you were twelve? Your work must be out there for others to see. I will help. What do you need?"

She was seemingly at a loss for words, her eyes wide with surprise, her mouth open. "Duke…"

"Call me Dorian," he said.

Like last night, when he'd heard her gentle voice calling him Dorian, pulling him from the terrible nightmare, he didn't feel wrathful, didn't feel like smashing anything or exploding with rage. He wanted her to call him by his given name always.

She slammed into him, with her arms wrapped around his neck, and her flowery scent in his nose. It was his turn to be surprised. He pulled her closer, bathing his face in the silk of her golden hair. It tickled his skin so pleasantly, he didn't even feel the thin cuts on his skin.

"Both the garden and the glasshouse," he murmured before he could stop himself. "They're both yours. Use them for your research, for your experiments, or simply for your pleasure. Let it be a place of growth and discovery, just like your roses."

What are you doing, you fool? screamed the voice inside his head. *First you gave her your bed, then part of your garden, then your mama's room, and now...everything?*

Because she has my heart already.

Great. Are you going to tell her about John, too?

He jerked at the thought and, with regret, pulled out of her embrace as he imagined the pain, the fury on her face. The heartbreak in her eyes.

He couldn't bear it.

He'd rather break his own heart hundreds of times than break hers once.

And perhaps he was selfish, too, because all he could think about was that she'd never wrap her arms around him like that again. Never give him that brilliant smile that was sunshine itself.

Patience's eyes widened, her lips parting in surprise. "Truly?" she whispered, her voice filled with wonder.

Dorian nodded, his heart swelling with pure, unadulterated love for this woman who had brought light back into his life.

As they stood, bathed in the warmth of the sun, Dorian knew that something had irrevocably changed within him. She had opened the curtains, let the light back in. In doing so, she'd given him a glimpse of the happiness he could have with her.

But only if he could keep his secret from her forever.

22

"You have allowed me to use the garden and the glasshouse," Patience said gently. "May I ask what happened there? Why has it stood so abandoned? Why have you kept me away from it?"

He looked at the glasshouse, its triangular roof visible through the tree canopy, grime and algae making it almost impossible to see through. The angry beast within lashed at him. And he clenched his fists to stop it from lashing out at her.

But there was a new part of him that, to his great surprise, wanted to tell her the story.

He'd never told anyone before. Lucien and Chastity knew what had happened; they'd both been there to witness it. But she hadn't. And, just as she had shared with him about wanting to publish a paper, he ached to share with her, too.

"I was ten," he said. "A boy, really. It was right after Papa sent Mama away, and I rebelled against him."

His chest tightened, and he looked at the rest of the garden. His fists clenched while he battled the painful memories. He felt the weight of Patience's blue eyes, and the sympathy and understanding in them.

"My papa had taught me to fight. Every morning, in that very garden"—he pointed at the tangled overgrowth—"he'd have a fencing master fight me with real swords. He had fired three previous masters who had refused to train a ten-year-old boy with real steel. They preferred wooden swords at that tender age. But Mr. Beaumont didn't mind using real steel on me. I don't think he had any ability for empathy—just like my papa. He never injured me, though, not really. He was a true master who was skillful enough to make controlled movements without harming his opponent."

He cleared his throat.

"Chastity was six years old and grieving the sudden departure of our mama just as I was. It was a punishment, you see. I couldn't stop feeling all those emotions, crying because Papa had killed my lamb. A lamb was not a worthy pet for a future duke. If I'd decided to adopt a hunting hound, that would have been so much better. And Chastity was as bad. Already at that young age, she was reading books on the classification of species, microscopy, and classical mechanics, instead of playing the pianoforte, doing needlework, and learning to dance.

"And so Papa yelled and thundered at her, and she, even at six, told him she would rather have gone with Mama because Mama had thought she was too smart for her age and that giving her books on science was the only way to provide her mind enough challenge to develop."

Dorian cleared his throat again and met Patience's gaze. He wondered if she had experienced anything similar to Chastity, with her uncanny intelligence and talent for botany. Had John tried to defend her, as well, or would he have belittled her about her intelligence like Dorian's own papa had done with Chastity?

"But Papa got enraged and slapped her across the cheek. I couldn't just stand by. I picked up my sword and came between Papa and Chastity, shouting for Papa to back away and that he would not touch Chastity again.

"Chastity was crying, holding on to her cheek, and I was seeing red for the first time.

"Papa laughed and told the fencing master to fight me in a duel. The fencing master simply unarmed me. Papa always refused to fight his own battles, sending his servants to fight them for him.

"Then he threw me into the glasshouse and locked the door from the outside.

"It was summer. It was so incredibly hot. The humid air, barely any ventilation, the sun baking through the glass... I hid under the palms. They gave me some shade, but soon I was thirsty. Hungry. I spent two days there, drinking from the trough with dirty, slimy water that was kept inside to increase the humidity. I got sick and vomited. I'm ashamed to admit I was desperate enough for drink and for food and felt so bad that I knocked on the panes and cried for someone to let me out. It was on the third day that I saw Chastity coming to me, Lucien on her heels, crying that they were going to let me out.

"And Papa came behind them, screaming that he'd take a whip to Chastity if she took another step forward."

Dorian's beast screamed at him to not say another word. But he looked at Patience, who had the saddest eyes in the world, the eyes of someone who understood.

Who accepted him anyway.

"And it was that fear that turned the rest of my energy into rage. Fear of Papa doing something to Chastity again. I picked up one of the stone troughs and threw it into the glass panes.

"I had to get to her before Papa took out his whip. Glass shattered and flew just like the mirror the other day.

"I had to go through the hole to get to Chastity.

"I was just so enraged with Papa and so afraid for her. I think it's the fear that's always my downfall. I feel fear, and then I have to lash out. Have to rage. And attack. With words or with fists. Sometimes with weapons.

"Because if I'm not raging, then I'm afraid.

"Then I'm lonely.

"Then I'm so utterly unworthy that I just can't deal with the pain."

"Oh, Dorian," Patience whispered.

She reached out and took his wounded hand in both of hers. They were small and so tender he could almost choke.

"You are very worthy," she whispered. "You're perhaps the worthiest person I know. The worthiest and the most wounded."

He chuckled. He could hear and understand her words, but they didn't reach his heart; he couldn't accept them as the truth, even though hearing someone as brilliant and lovely and kind as her say them made his chest warm in response.

"I didn't realize how much I cut myself. My hand. I must have cut the vein on my wrist. I don't know. There were many cuts on my face, shoulders, and body as I pushed through the broken pane.

"Chastity screamed. Lucien screamed. I pushed Papa away from her, and his tailored coat was marred by smudges of blood from my palms."

Dorian didn't know how he was speaking so easily of this when the memories pounded in his head like a drum.

"Oh no, Dorian," Patience said, and when he looked at her, tears rolled down her cheeks.

Because of him.

"Darling, I don't deserve you," he whispered, his voice cracking.

He took her face in his hands and wiped her tears with his thumbs. Then when she didn't stop crying and new tears rolled down her pretty flushed cheeks, he kissed every one of them away, tasting salt.

"Don't cry," he whispered. "I'm alive. I'm fine. I lost consciousness, but the fencing master knew how to stop blood. Nature of his profession, I suppose. Papa called for a physician who tended to me properly. I did have a fever after as one of the cuts got infected, but I pulled through. See? I'm fine."

"Thank God," she croaked through a thick throat, and he couldn't stop being surprised.

How could someone be thanking God for his life?

If she knew what he had done to her brother, she'd be praying for his death instead.

"I'm so glad you pulled through," she said as she drew his hand towards her face.

She looked at his gloved hand and he swallowed hard. Over the past two weeks, he'd begun to notice the redness was spreading, and the ache had turned into true pain. The best thing for him would be to remove the glove.

But he just couldn't bring himself to do it.

"What happened to this hand?" she asked as she took it between her palms, and he could barely breathe. To his astonishment, she planted soft kisses right on the leather.

God, those lips. His mind was a complete wreck of confused emotions—the echoes of fear, wrath, and guilt...and love...and, to all demons, desire she'd started in the depths of his body with her full, pink lips.

He opened his mouth.

I challenged your brother to a duel, and he sabotaged my pistol, and it exploded in my hand. Enraged by his dishonorable act, I attacked him...and the pistol fired.

He didn't kill himself, Patience.

It was me.

I took his life.

I put your family through misery.

He imagined the pain in her eyes, the disappointment, the way she'd let go of his hand in disgust, and the way she'd never look at him again.

She'd never think of him as worthy.

He'd lose her.

And yet, he could have her for the rest of his life. She was his by right. All he had to do was to keep silent and hide what a monster he truly was.

That he was a murderer.

He closed his mouth.

"An accident," he whispered as he couldn't look away from the way her plush lips spread against the skin of his wrist now, above the glove.

And still, like a true scoundrel, thinking all those thoughts and feeling all those confused things, he was more and more aroused with every kiss she left on his body.

"Well." She let go of his hand, wrapped her arms around his neck, and looked straight into his eyes. "I hope I made it all better."

And then, like a little seductress, she kissed him.

23

Patience could feel the slight rasp of Dorian's stubble as she kissed him, and it sent a warm tingle through her entire body.

She didn't want to disturb the healing scabs of his cuts, and thought he might gently push her away, but his arms wrapped around her, locking her against him. His hard chest heaved in unison with hers. He deepened their kiss, tongues tangling, and her head swam with the pungent and sweet taste of him.

His mouth trailed scorching kisses along her neck, lower, lower, until his lips brushed the swell of her breasts peeking above her bodice. It felt like he was leaving places of sparking energy on her skin, and her breasts felt hot and heavy, too constricted in her corset. Her hands tangled in his dark hair, surprisingly silky, his lips hot on her skin.

She was a writhing creature of a strange, sweet need...and he was the only thing that could soothe it. She moaned and tilted her head back when his hand cupped her breast, his thumb stroking against her nipple, and even through the fabric of the corset, it tightened with a sharp, delicious ache. She shuddered and he cursed.

"Good God, Duchess..." he murmured. "If you're writhing like this when I touch you through clothes, how will you writhe when—"

He stopped abruptly and breathed into her neck, just holding her. She felt something hard and hot between his legs pressing against her stomach, the mysterious bulge she'd felt before.

"When...what?" she asked through hungry gasps of air, her body still swimming in the pleasure he'd just brought her.

"Nothing," he mumbled and let go of her, to her disappointment.

"Well, aren't I breaking rule number two?" she asked. "Something about no wifely duties? Shouldn't I be...um"—heat broke through her skin—"punished?"

He exhaled sharply, his dark gaze on her. He swallowed hard. "No wifely duties have been executed, dear girl. Not yet anyway."

"Oh..." She swallowed, too.

Heavens, how could she get him to do that to her again? How could she convince him to touch her as he had with the spanking...and that other night when he'd made her body soar. She wondered if she could do the same beautiful things to him as he did to her.

"What are wifely duties, exactly?" she asked.

He closed his eyes tight, breathing harder. His arm was pressed against the wall behind her, and he crushed the heavy curtain into his fist.

"Goddamn, woman, you're the biggest temptation I've ever had to resist."

She bit her lower lip. She was closer, perhaps? "Why?"

He opened his eyes. They were dark and penetrating, and

she felt pinned to the spot. "Because I've never wanted to break my own rules like I want to do now."

"Oh…" she murmured, feeling a satisfied smile spread on her lips. "So you do want me to perform the wifely duties?"

His glare intensified, his nostrils flaring as he breathed quicker. "There's nothing in this world I want more."

"Well… Why don't you let me, then?"

A pained expression crossed his face. "I'm hanging by a thread… And, believe me, my restraint is for your own good."

"I do not even know what wifely duties are," she said. "How would I know what not to do? Do you not think you ought to…teach me?"

"You know not what you ask," he ground out, voice raw. "I am not a gentle lover."

"And I'm not a flower," she said. "You're mistaken if you think I am."

She wasn't the naive girl who had come to this house. She wasn't yet someone like him, so decisive and certain in what he wanted. Perhaps she wasn't yet a true duchess. But she knew she wanted him, and she wanted this marriage.

He brushed his knuckles against her cheek, the pained expression intensifying. "You are most certainly a Rose."

She grinned. "Why, was that a jest, my lord?"

"You bring out the most surprising things in me, sweet girl. Branches I thought dried and broken off a long time ago."

"They didn't die," she said as she cupped his angled face with her palm, her calloused thumb brushing across his high cheekbone. "I can still see them. Let me revive them. I'm known to have a green thumb."

He groaned but stood still, just working his jaw as though in pain.

She needed to nudge him only a little. Just one tiny nudge, and he'd cave.

She didn't know what it might be but thought perhaps it was in the region of her breasts, which he'd seemed to enjoy kissing and touching just a moment ago.

Never breaking eye contact, she pulled the neckline of her dress down slightly, exposing more of her breasts to him. "Rest assured, whatever those forbidden wifely duties are…I want them as much as you do."

Just an inch or two of flesh was enough. His gaze dropped to her breasts, and a shudder passed through him. She watched his resolve snap like a twig.

"To hell with the rules," he growled, and the next moment he was on her.

Lips on her lips, he wrapped his arms around her, locking her to him in an unbreakable bond. He kissed her like he had been starving his whole life, with deep, hungry licks, lips brushing, gliding, and leaving her breathless. She responded with the same vigor, unable to breathe. All thoughts evaporated, and there was just an aching need in her whole body to be pressed against him, to have his fingers, his hands, his thighs, his stomach, his chest, and, God please, his lips on her…

She may have raised one of her legs to wrap it around his hips. She may have clutched his coat with her hands like she wanted to climb him.

"Are you certain?" he whispered against her lips.

"Yes. But you might need to tell me what to do," she breathed out. "How to be a good wife. How to please you."

Then she was airborne, and she realized he'd picked her up and was carrying her. The sheet from the sofa flew like a ghost across the room, and he laid her on the soft cushions, towering over her, even half crouching.

"First thing you need to do," he murmured, "is to give in to the sensations of your body. Everything you're feeling, everything you want to do is natural."

He kissed her in large strokes, the feel of his lips and tongue against hers wanton and wonderful. "Does this feel good?" he murmured as his mouth left hers and kissed her jaw. His hand traveled up and down her body, turning her into pliable, hot wax.

"Yes," she moaned, purring like a kitten. "Oh heavens, yes!"

Everything she wanted to do was natural... And she had always been a good student. Echoing his movements, she dragged her hands down his coat, his waistcoat, his shirt, aching to feel his naked chest and his stomach.

"Does this feel good to you?" she asked. "I'd like to please you. Show me how."

"Would you still like to?" he asked. "Even after everything ugly you learned about me?"

"Yes. More than you know."

Something dangerous flared in the depths of his eyes then, a hunger that sent a thrill racing down her spine. With a growl, he captured her mouth in a searing kiss that left her breathless and aching. His lips blazed a trail of fire down the column of her throat, his fingers deftly unfastening the buttons of her bodice to bare the creamy swells of her breasts.

"Exquisite," he breathed, his tongue darting out to taste her skin.

His mouth and hands mapped the contours of her body, igniting every nerve, and she was writhing, his body over her the only thing keeping her in place. She felt him push up the skirt of her gown and her chemise. And when his fingers delved into the slick heat at the apex of her thighs, she cried out, back arching off the sofa.

His fingers moved over her with expert strokes, coaxing her higher and higher.

She moaned and arched her back still further.

"That's it, my sweet," Dorian purred. "Surrender to the

pleasure. This is called your clitoris, right here." He rubbed the sensitive nub.

Clitoris...

He kept rubbing and teasing her, and soon, she was quivering on the edge of a precipice.

"Dorian, please..." she whimpered, nails digging into the sofa's upholstery.

He chuckled. "Yes, darling, your clit is a marvelous place..."

His finger traveled to her entrance.

"But your body is capable of so much more."

His fingers circled her entrance, inserting the tip of one into her, and she relaxed into his touch. He was pressing into something inside her, and she felt pressure, more and more intense. She wanted him deeper.

"What is it capable of?" she asked.

"To take me in. Inside you. Your pleasure will be even greater... In combination with your clit, and this beautiful spot... I can make you feel so good, love. Your body was designed to feel good."

"Designed to take your fingers inside?" she asked. "I liked that very much when you did it before."

"Not just my fingers, love. But there's a part of your body that stops the penetration because you're a virgin. It might hurt the first time. There might be blood. Or it might not. Every woman is different. However, it's likely there will be just a little pain the first time, and then after that, it will all be very, very good. I will make sure of it."

As his thumb found her clitoris again, and he resumed his teasing, the pressure passed.

"If at any moment you want me to stop, tell me, and I will. Do you understand?"

Stop? That was the last thing she wanted him to do at the moment, but it was nice to know she had the choice.

"I understand," she murmured, opening her legs wide. "Will it feel as good as what you're doing with your thumb and your mouth?"

He nodded, closed his eyes as though in pain, then rose and began undressing himself. Her sex clenched tighter as he opened one button after another of his coat.

Without looking away for a moment, his gaze always dark and intense on her, he dropped his black tailored coat to the floor. Her eyes widened as they lowered to the very large bulge between his legs, its shape clearly visible beneath his breeches, and a shock of fear ran through her.

He unbuttoned his scarlet waistcoat, and he was left in the breeches and his white shirt, the muscles of his broad shoulders rolling under the fabric. He tugged the shirt from his breeches and pulled it over his shoulders.

"Heavens..." she murmured, breathless.

He was so beautifully carved, he could be a Greek statue—broad shoulders, the hard outlines of biceps, and a very defined chest. He wasn't bulky but tall and lean, with ridges on his hard stomach that led into straight hips like a perfect triangle, pointing down towards the mysterious bulge.

"Do you like what you see, Duchess?" he purred.

"Yes...um...yes, very much."

His gaze dropped to her spread thighs. "So do I."

She chuckled, but the smile died on her face when he dropped his breeches and stepped out of his boots.

And she saw what the bulge was.

It was his member. Long, thick...it seemed enormous. And it was pointing straight at her. It was the size of a very large candlestick.

"This is what will go inside you, darling," he said as he palmed his impressive organ. "If you want to."

She couldn't speak and simply opened and closed her

mouth. Even a tip of his finger caused uncomfortable pressure. How would this ever fit?

And yet, a strange sort of heat rushed through her. Being taken by him that way, being connected body to body, soul to soul...

"Is this what you meant by wifely duties?" she asked.

"Yes, darling."

"And will it fit in?"

"It will. And you'll love it. I promise. And if not, I'll stop. So help me God."

She swallowed and nodded. "I just mean, it's so big, I don't know how it can ever not...hurt."

He leaned over her and stretched along her on the sofa. He was so tall, he couldn't fully extend his body, but he pressed against her, hot and hard and so pleasant.

He kissed her and took her hand in his, laying it on his naked chest. Her fingers caressed his smooth skin under the dusting of soft, dark hair. She was touching him for the first time, and her skin was ablaze with a prickly, beautiful energy. A tall, long, naked male lay next to her, warming her with his heat like he was a living and breathing furnace. She could see scars on his body, perhaps from his fencing lessons or his wild childhood days. He had only his right glove on.

She ran her hand down his hard muscles. "I love touching you," she whispered. "You're so solid, and big, and beautiful."

He chuckled. "Beautiful?"

"You are."

"It's you who's beautiful, love. The most beautiful thing I've ever seen."

Her throat clenched at the compliment, and then he led her fingers to pass the soft curls and then encircle his member... She gasped. Good Lord, it was hot and hard and yet silky.

"What do I do?" she asked.

"Caress me," he said hoarsely as his throat bobbed.

She began running the tips of her fingers up and down his length. A low growl escaped his throat, resonating deep in her belly, and her own sex clenched. He curled her palm around his thickness.

"Like so, love," he managed. "Up and down."

"Like so?" She did as he asked.

Her reward was his head falling back and him sucking in a sharp breath. "Yes, like so. Heaven help me..."

She kept doing that, biting her lip, and watching the veins on his neck thicken as she pumped her hand faster.

"This is how I will move inside you," he explained as he watched her from hooded eyes.

"So it will be good for you?" she asked.

"Very...very good. I don't expect it to get better for me anywhere else in the entire world, love."

She wanted to please him. The idea of pain, from his organ inside her, made her afraid. But what did she know? She had no true idea what wifely duties were or how to perform them. He was clearly so much more experienced. She just wished naive girls like her were better prepared and informed about these things.

He shuddered as she squeezed him a little tighter, and then he suddenly flipped himself and was on top of her, his weight like a pleasure on its own. He pinned her hands over her head and kissed her.

The kiss was contained hunger, deep and slow. A promise and a vow.

He kissed down her body, massaging her as he went, and then...quite shockingly, not just his fingers were on her sex, but...oh heavens—his mouth!

She gasped as the most velvety pleasure spilled through her.

"Oh, Duke!" she cried as he began sucking and licking at the center of her pleasure. "Oh my Lord!"

She was already burning and swollen, and it didn't take her long at all for her to near the peak she'd reached the first time when he'd spanked her and the second time when he'd relieved her tension in bed.

But before she could reach it, he withdrew and towered over her, nudging her thighs wider apart. She wanted him inside her.

He caressed her sex with his own, like he had with his fingers and his tongue just now, and she almost fell into shudders once again. She was sleek and wet, and his member glided easily all around her entrance. Every stroke brought her pleasure, and she wondered if he might be mistaken and it actually wouldn't hurt at all.

He positioned his member against her folds and looked at her. "If at any moment you want to stop, I will."

She nodded, and he began pressing into her. She widened her legs farther and welcomed the stretching, the intense pressure. There was a pinch and something broke and he was inside.

She cried in pain, and he froze, holding her but panting hard against her.

"I'm sorry, my darling," he murmured hotly, his eyes dark and shining with concern and tenderness. "Are you all right?"

She was so full. She never thought he'd fit, but he did, stretching her to impossible degrees, and yet she loved every minute of it. There was a burning and a tingling, but she craved more.

She nodded.

With infinite care, Dorian pushed forward in one smooth thrust. Patience gasped at the sharp twinge, her fingers digging into his shoulders. He stilled, his breath ragged against her throat.

He brushed tender kisses over her face as he began to move, slowly withdrawing before surging forward again. The discomfort quickly transmuted into a growing ache of pleasure that had Patience lifting her hips to meet his gentle thrusts.

"That's it, love. Take your pleasure from me," Dorian rasped. "I want to feel you come apart in my arms."

His words ignited a wildfire in her blood. Wanton moans spilled from her lips as she moved with him, chasing the bliss only he could provide. Dorian slid a hand between their straining bodies, finding her little clitoris at the apex of her thighs. He circled it over and over, and Patience could feel infinite pleasure, from both sides, and she was so incredibly full of Dorian, surrounded by him.

She was his. Completely his.

Her release crashed over her like nothing she'd ever felt before. She cried out, shuddering as the climax dragged her over the edge of ecstasy.

With a harsh groan, Dorian followed her over the edge, his big body shuddering as she felt a pulsing sensation deep inside, accompanied by a flood of warmth. For a long moment, they clung to each other, hearts pounding in unison as they breathed each other's air.

"It requires every ounce of my self-control not to flip you over and take you again, the way I'm aching to," Dorian confessed gruffly, his length still semihard within her. "Hard and rough and so deep you'll feel me for days."

With a possessive growl, Dorian captured her mouth again. Patience had never felt so cherished, so desired, so utterly alive. She was someone else now. Stronger. More vibrant. And she had hope for them. In his arms, she had found completion

—and she would spend eternity endeavoring to give him the same.

24

THERE WAS a knock at the door.

Dorian raised his head, not wanting to leave the sweet, soft heaven of his wife's body. She stirred under him to wrap her arms around his neck tighter and press herself to him.

Dorian breathed, inhaling her sweet scent.

This was heaven.

This could be his life. His beautiful wife, so willingly and lovingly giving herself to him. Happiness and love pulsing through his blood at the very sight of her. His future with her could be bright, soft. Wonderful.

The knock repeated. It was as though reality had finally come calling.

The door opened before he could react, and Mrs. Knight came in, her eyes falling on him covering Patience with his body, no doubt taking in Patience's legs wrapped around his bare arse. Like the perfect ducal housekeeper she was, she allowed herself only a moment of shock, surprise covering her usual neutral expression.

Then she averted her eyes towards the window.

Patience giggled into his neck, her hot breath tickling him.

"Your Grace and Your Grace," said Mrs. Knight. "I wondered if I should send the footmen to remove the sheets and the maids to clean the room after all these years... It was such a pretty room when Her Grace was alive... But perhaps it's best to do it later."

After all these years... Dorian's whole body chilled.

All these years that his mama was not here.

He remembered her, so pretty with her dark hair, drinking tea here, and looking at the garden through this window with an anxious sort of expression.

Good Lord, he'd make Patience look like that sooner or later. Because a beast of fury lived within him. He had fallen apart in her arms earlier, and he was already breaking every rule he'd set for her and for himself.

He felt his grip on his emotions loosening around her. Would he be able to control his beast and not hurt her like his papa had hurt his mama?

And what of the terrible secret that would surely break her heart?

He loved her. He never wanted to leave her sight.

"That would be best, Mrs. Knight," he said.

He could not feel his body.

The housekeeper nodded and retreated from the room.

Unwillingly, Dorian separated himself from Patience.

He needed to make sure he wouldn't fall apart again, wouldn't smash things around her from fear, wouldn't put her in harm's way... He didn't care about his own injuries, but he wouldn't be able to live with himself at all if he hurt Patience.

She straightened on the sofa, looking at him with sated hooded eyes as, to his regret, she pulled her skirts down her legs. He pulled on his shirt and tucked it into his waistband.

"Poor Mrs. Knight," giggled Patience, looking as satisfied and as happy as a cat with cream.

He didn't respond. He hated doing this, but he needed to remove himself from her before he'd hurt her.

He'd been a fool to fall apart like he had.

To fall in love with his wife.

Goodness gracious, he was *in love*. For the first time in his life, at the age of thirty-two, he loved a woman.

The last one in the world he should love.

His murder victim's sister.

Her smile fell as she looked into his face.

Good.

"Nothing she hasn't seen before, I'm sure," he said gruffly.

Her eyes widened. "With— Oh."

The look of hurt on her face made his own heart break a million times. He ached to calm her, to assure her he didn't mean him. It would be so much worse, though, if she ever found out the truth.

He didn't correct her. He never had women here, and he certainly never slept with any of the maids.

"I must go," he said, his stomach twisting.

He had to force his legs to move away from her, while what he wanted most in the world was to scoop her into his arms and stay with her here, in this sunlit room.

He ached to ask her if she was still in pain. If he hadn't hurt her too much. To reassure her that any discomfort would fade away in a few days and that he'd keep bringing her pleasure for the rest of their lives.

But he did none of those things.

Instead, fear chasing him, he walked out of the sunshine back into the dark hallway, and then he broke into a run.

He was terrified.

He loved a woman, and she responded to him. She could

love him, too. He had true happiness at his fingertips for the first time in his life…and he'd crush it all sooner or later. Hurt her like no one had hurt her before. He was sure of it.

He needed to hit something. Smash something.

Before he could break the love of his life's heart.

25

Patience sat at the rosewood desk in her sitting room, quill in hand as she pored over her botanical journal.

Her mind was divided. Part of it was focused on transcribing her data on the control group of roses, noting the progression of diseases like black spot and powdery mildew. After Chastity had pointed out to her that such data was missing from her research, Patience had gone through her journals and realized she actually might have enough data to represent the control group.

The other half of her mind wandered to Dorian.

A mere two days had passed since the best day of her life. When he had shared the deepest part of himself with her and they had become one. Truely husband and wife. When she had told him about her roses, and he had encouraged her to finish her botanical paper, and she had glowed from his belief in her.

He was the first person in her life who had supported her that way. Not even Anne had suggested she write the paper and submit it. Lady Chastity had found a flaw in it, even though that had turned out to be useful.

But he had said she should do it.

He had made her his, truly and irrevocably, and when they were connected in the deepest ways two people could, she had trusted him. And she'd been so, so happy.

In that blissful moment, entwined in his strong arms, she knew she loved him.

Which made it hurt even more when the next moment he had drawn back and become as cold as ice.

Since then, for two nights, he hadn't slept in his bed. And she, therefore, hadn't slept at all. Her eyes burned from the lack of sleep. Mrs. Knight told her Dorian was spending time in a little cottage he owned in Rathford Village.

Her hand holding her pen froze over her journal. Had she done something wrong? Was she not enough to hold his affection?

Tears pricked at her eyes, and she set down the quill, hands trembling. If she could just find out Dorian's secret. If she could just understand him, and reassure him there was nothing he could do to push her away... That she was ready to share his burden. That she would understand no matter what it was.

Whatever connected Dorian and John, she would understand like no one else. Uncovering the Oxford incident was the key to her marital happiness, she was sure.

If only she could break through to Dorian; if only he would stop running from her, pushing her away...

Her first impulse was to turn away from her sadness, her regret, her anger. Bad emotions belonged in the basket... Or did they?

The cheer she usually put on in situations such as these felt like a fragile mask. And, to her surprise, it didn't feel like it would help her with Dorian. Or even make her feel better.

Perhaps she should let herself feel her emotions?

The sound of approaching footsteps stirred Patience from her melancholy. Her pulse quickened and she sat up straighter, daring to hope it was Dorian seeking her out. Perhaps he had come to take her in his arms again and chase away the doubts plaguing her?

But it was not the duke who appeared in the doorway. Patience's heart sank as Lady Chastity stepped into the room, disappointment washing over her. She quickly fixed a smile on her face.

"Your Grace," Chastity greeted with a curtsy. "I hope I am not interrupting?"

"Not at all," Patience said as she turned to Chastity. Like last time, she was in a practical dark gown of excellent fabric and cut. Mademoiselle Antoinette would have had a fit and probably thrown such a gown away if Patience dared to wear something so plain. "And, please, do call me Patience. We're sisters now, after all."

Chastity cocked her head in acknowledgment, and her eyes behind her spectacles warmed. "Indeed, we are. You may call me Chastity. I never had a sister and am quite delighted."

Patience's smile widened, and there was nothing false about it at all. Chastity looked quite rigid and strict, and Patience wondered if it was mere shyness and lack of social confidence. Whatever the reason for her stiffness, Chastity was a brilliant woman, and Patience wanted to be friends with a fellow female scientist.

"Forgive me for enquiring, but are you all right?" asked Chastity.

Oh, Patience missed Anne. She missed Dorian, too. And having someone friendly ask her if she was all right lifted her spirits.

Patience nodded, putting on her smiling mask. "I'm perfectly fine. Thank you for asking. I was just working on my paper. After your suggestion, I did find notes that I recorded through the years on the growth, bloom quality, pests, and diseases of both the gallica rose and the damask rose. I think it's enough to represent the control group. I'm almost finished."

"That is good news." Chastity approached the desk, curiosity shining in her eyes. "May I take a closer look?"

With a nod, Patience slid the journal towards Chastity, swallowing back the lump in her throat. "Of course."

Chastity studied the pages intently, her brow furrowed in concentration. After a few moments, she looked up with a smile. "This is excellent work. Now your paper is so much more scientifically sound."

Patience felt a flush of pride at the compliment, which had no false notes at all. "Thank you! It was not easy to hear my paper may not be good enough after all these years… But you were right, and your feedback was exactly what I needed."

"I am glad." Chastity's eyes glimmered with enthusiasm. "We're stronger together, are we not?"

Patience's heart ached, and suddenly, she did not want to pretend. With Anne, she'd allow herself to cry for a minute or two because sometimes there was no other way to turn away from the sadness…and she'd tell her everything.

Chastity blurred before her eyes, a sob exploded through her chest, and she burst into tears.

"Patience…" Chastity mumbled, clearly in shock. "What— what did I say? I only meant we, as women, should stick together… Er—"

Patience covered her face with her hands and cried, nodding. "You did… It's not you…"

Chastity pulled another chair next to Patience and sat on it. Awkwardly, she put her arm around Patience's shoulders. "Oh, Patience, I—I don't know what to say… Please, calm down."

Instead of calming down, Patience turned towards her new sister and practically fell into Chastity's arms. Chastity wrapped her arms around Patience and patted her stiffly.

"Er...there, there?" Chastity said. "I...er...I'd never have said anything about control groups if I knew you'd cry like this. I only meant to help—"

"I know. It's not the control groups."

"What is it, then?"

"It's your wretched brother!"

Was the minute over? She didn't feel any better yet. She should be over her tears by now and ready to do the basket exercise.

"Dorian?" asked Chastity. "What did he do now?"

"He left me..."

"Left you?" demanded Chastity with outrage in her voice. Her arms wrapped tighter around Patience. "No, how could he?"

"I don't mean forever... I don't know. Maybe forever. He was so loving and so giving one moment... Then just after I gave myself to him, and hoped we'd be happy, he stood up and left. And I haven't seen him for two days!"

Chastity *tsk*ed, very much unlike a duke's sister, and it made Patience feel infinitely better. Anne would *tsk* on her behalf, too.

Chastity rubbed Patience's shoulder. "What an ungentlemanly thing to do!"

Patience suddenly grinned and looked up at Chastity. "Is that your way of saying 'what a scoundrel'?"

"Yes," said Chastity as she offered Patience a handkerchief. "It most certainly is."

As Patience wiped her tears and blew her nose, she realized she did feel better, and Chastity's eyes were full of sympathy. "I am sorry to hear my brother is making you so sad. Is there anything I can do to help?"

Patience sighed deeply, releasing the last of her anger and sadness. That was an excellent question. Not just because Chastity could actually help, but also because Patience could help herself. She could do something. Keep digging into the mystery that her husband hid from her.

The one that stood between them and their happiness.

"Perhaps..." said Patience thoughtfully. "You didn't know if Dorian knew my brother, but do you happen to know anything about the Oxford incident?"

Chastity frowned as she thought. "The Oxford incident? I'm sorry, is this some social concept I'm not familiar with? That would not be surprising."

"Oh, no, I believe it's something that happened in Oxford, involving your brother and mine. Twelve years ago."

"Oh," said Chastity. Her cool face, normally so collected and impartial, suddenly changed as ripples of fear and sadness passed through it. "Right. Yes. Twelve years ago, I remember Dorian coming back from Oxford for Papa's funeral. He was... um...in poor condition."

"What does that mean?" asked Patience.

"Well," said Chastity. "He was devastated. Distraught beyond what seemed reasonable."

"What seemed reasonable?" asked Patience as she looked at the rooftop of the glasshouse visible through the window. "Are you certain? Your papa died. I would suppose being quite distraught was to be expected."

"Yes." Chastity fingered the handle of her teacup. "You're right, of course. But I swear something else plagued him. It must have been his hand."

"His hand?" Patience asked, a chill running through her.

"Yes. He had some sort of an accident, and his hand was burned severely."

Patience swallowed. "Do you know what happened exactly?"

"He wouldn't say."

"Even to you?"

Chastity scoffed. "I'd be the last person he'd trouble with anything unpleasant or distressing. He's always been so protective of me. I know he loves me, but I sometimes wish he'd give me some credit."

Patience nodded. "I quite understand."

"But do you know who might know something about this incident?"

"Who?"

"Lucien. I am quite certain Lucien knows all Dorian's secrets. They've been best friends since they were boys."

Patience jumped to her feet, her chest lighting with hope. "Yes, I have been wanting to ask him but have not had an opportunity. Do you by any chance know where he lives, sister?"

Chastity followed her example and stood. "Yes, of course."

"Could you please take me there?"

Chastity nodded, enthusiasm shining through her eyes. "Of course. We will finish your paper after. I'll help you."

About one hour and a half later, their carriage was being parked in front of a grand three-story mansion in Mayfair, constructed of pristine Bath stone. Patience and Chastity passed through the wrought iron gates, imposing and black. They climbed broad marble steps leading to double doors. Cherry wood gleamed in the daylight, the brass knockers polished to a shine.

The butler opened the door and, to Patience's relief, said the duke was indeed at home and asked them to wait.

The entrance hall was grand, with black-and-white-checkered marble tiles under Patience's and Chastity's echoing footsteps. Exquisitely carved marble statues of the Greek pantheon stood on pedestals of polished granite. Proud and imposing portraits hung between them—likely the duke's ancestors. The air was cool against Patience's skin, the scent of fresh flowers from an ornate vase on a mahogany sideboard mingling with a hint of beeswax and turpentine polish.

Not a few minutes later, the man himself hurried down the red-carpeted staircase. He was as striking as ever. His blond hair was well-groomed and the violet color of his eyes contrasted brightly with the yellow silk of his waistcoat.

"Your Grace." He gave a small ceremonial bow by way of greeting. "Lady Chastity." He gave the same bow to Chastity. "What a surprise. A pleasant one," he said as he glanced at Chastity. "Please do come in." He gestured with his arm towards the doors where the butler stood waiting.

Patience and Chastity entered a beautiful sitting room with tall windows draped in velvet. A pianoforte stood in the sunlight. A gray stone fireplace with a shiny black grate dominated the long wall. Pale yellow panels hung with oil paintings lined the walls. An ornately carved sofa in the same dark color as the drapes stood in the center flanked by two similar armchairs. The room smelled fainty of tobacco and sandalwood. Patience could hear birdsong coming through the closed windows from the little park outside.

"Please, bring us tea," said Lucien as he followed them.

The butler nodded and retreated.

"Well," said Lucien, giving them a bright smile that Patience couldn't help but return.

"You look well," said Chastity as she took a seat in the chair opposite the sofa. "Did you not engage in any debauchery last night?"

Patience took a seat in the remaining armchair, next to Chastity, and Lucien grinned, his eyes glimmering with a special meaning. He leaned against the side of the sofa, his long, muscular legs showcased as the fabric of his dark pantaloons stretched over his thighs.

"You only wish," he said. "Perhaps your brother is lost to his marriage, and I just lost a great debauchery partner, but I still have five others willing to oblige. And you look well, as always," he said gallantly.

Chastity raised a single eyebrow.

Patience couldn't help but wonder if she was witnessing an exchange between two people who knew far too much about each other, like a brother and sister would, or if this was flirting.

"I'm very obliged by your visit," said Lucien while the butler came in with the tray laden with a teapot, cups, a milk jug, and some biscuits.

"I am here because I wanted to ask about the Oxford incident that involved my brother," said Patience.

Lucien lifted his cup of tea, which the butler had just poured. "Ah."

Patience and Chastity took their cups, as well. Lucien sat down on the sofa opposite them and leaned back, crossing one leg over the other. He took a long sip of his tea as he watched the butler bow and close the door behind him.

"I was afraid you would come to inquire," said Lucien. "Pryde told me you asked him."

"I did," said Patience. "But I'm no closer to discovering the truth. Will you help me understand? You don't seem to be as bothered by the question of honor as Pryde is."

Lucien chuckled as he put his cup on the saucer. "That is an excellent observation, Duchess. However, I will not betray my best friend's trust." His gaze lingered on Chastity...with longing? "Ever."

Disappointment churned in her gut. "I suppose I shouldn't have expected anything more."

"But you can tell us something," said Chastity. "Dorian is not just Patience's husband. He's my brother, too. You'd want to know in my place, right?"

Lucien sighed and looked at both of them, thinking.

"I can't say much. I know you were distraught yourself, Chastity, or you would have noticed the state of his health at that time. How angry he was before your father's death, how many duels he engaged in, that he didn't care what happened to his body. And how damaged he was when he returned home for the funeral. You're a smart woman, Chastity, and so are you, Duchess. I can't, however, tell you anything else. And I do suggest that you stop digging, even though I know it's difficult. He won't ever tell you. And you're going to ruin what little chance of happiness you have with him. I regret I will have to inform him of your enquiry."

Patience shook her head in frustration. "I wish your loyalty was to the truth, not to your brotherhood."

Lucien leaned back and sighed. "Impossible. We will always protect each other, to the death. That's what our parents made us. Each of us lacked true family. We found one in each other. All seven of us."

Patience and Chastity exchanged a long look.

"Well, then," said Patience, putting her teacup on the table and getting to her feet. "I suppose I have to find comfort knowing my husband has six loyal friends who would support him no matter what."

Chastity stood up, as well.

Lucien followed suit. "I am sorry I can't be of more help, Duchess."

As Chastity preceded Patience to the door, Luhst's gaze lingered on Chastity's back, and Patience heard him murmur, "How sweet is the fruit one can never taste."

26

Dorian marched through the hallway towards the back doors of Rath Hall. Three days he'd kept away from Patience, hanging on to sanity by a thread.

He finally came home—*to this?*

"Dorian—" Lucien's warning voice sounded after him. "Goddamn it, don't do anything you'll—"

"Shut up, Lucien!" Dorian roared over his shoulder. "Stay out of this!"

However, Lucien's hurried footsteps followed Dorian.

She'd gone to Lucien! She had asked Chastity for help! Would Chastity find out, too, that her brother was a murderer?

Fear and hurt worse than he'd ever known split his heart in half. She hadn't promised him she'd stop digging, so why did her going to Lucien feel like a betrayal?

And yet, that secret would destroy her, too. Destroy their happiness.

There was not much to destroy, his demon reminded him.

He had been avoiding her like a coward for three days since

he'd taken her virginity, even though it killed him to think of how she'd probably failed to sleep during that time.

She must think you just used her for your own pleasure. She must be so confused.

That was of no consequence. He covered the length of the hallway quickly, and pushed the back doors open so forcefully they crashed against the outer walls with a loud bang, almost falling off their hinges.

He saw her working in the garden, her back bent as she used the shovel. She had a simple straw bonnet on to protect herself from the sun, and her sleeves were up to her elbows. As usual, she wasn't wearing gloves, and her hands would be so blistered and painful later.

She looked up at the sound of the crash, and her face changed from being deeply satisfied with her work to alert. The footmen and gardeners who had been working all around the garden looked up, as well, pausing.

He didn't care. He didn't even stop to notice that after only a few days the garden he had hated so much had changed significantly. With the overgrown branches now gone, sunlight flooded the space, transforming it into a place of light and warmth. A few dried and sick tree limbs and a thick trunk lay on the ground in the farthest corner of the vast garden. The sounds of a hand saw and axes being wielded resounded as the tree's dark gnarly branches trembled.

"Duchess," he hissed as he stopped before her, remarking distantly how strangely pale she looked.

Was that because she couldn't sleep without him? Guilt gnawed at him like that hand saw at the tree.

"You're back," she said, and he could hear a longing in her voice that made a pleasant shiver rush through him.

He'd slept in the cottage on the other side of the estate as he'd decided to see the tenants there. Normally, his demon would have had him hurry to Elysium and take Lilith or run himself into a grave by boxing and fencing. But his visit to the Battens and Cohen and the other tenants nearby with Patience had reminded him he could be useful. And so he'd spent the past three days channeling his fury, his pain, into mending roofs, doors, animal pens, and making lists of more repairs that were beyond his personal ability but would need to be seen to.

It was deeply satisfying work.

But he couldn't tell her that. Not now anyway. Now he had to stop her.

"Dorian!" called Lucien again, striding up to stand next to him. Patience's gaze flickered to Luhst and then back to Dorian. "Don't make me regret I told you." Then he added, looking at Patience, "I'm sorry."

Patience nodded gracefully, but her smile didn't reach her eyes. "Of course. What can I do for you, Your Grace?" she asked Dorian.

Her formal address hit him like a slap.

Around them, the footmen and gardeners resumed their duties, maintaining a deliberate silence. A tense atmosphere enveloped the garden.

"You must stop, Patience," Dorian growled as low as he could.

Fury had him ready to snap, and he couldn't take in enough air. Patience was also taking shallow, light breaths, the ovals of her breasts moving fast while her stomach—no doubt tied with a corset—did not. The spring day was warm and sweat glistened on her forehead. He didn't like that she looked so pale.

"Have you slept at all?" he asked, worry for her well-being suddenly much more important than any anger he felt.

"No," she said. "Not since you left."

Goddamn it. He felt his hands clench into fists.

"I'd best be off," said Lucien, gravel crunching under his feet as he slowly backed away. "I'll see if Lady Chastity might have a minute for tea. Dorian, behave."

Dorian didn't give Lucien another glance as he heard his best friend retreat into the house. He could barely contain himself from yanking the shovel out of Patience's hands and demanding that she take a rest.

He felt sorry he had left her. Sorry she wasn't sleeping without him. Truth was, he hadn't got much sleep without her, either.

"You should get out of the sun," he said more gruffly than he intended. "And you should stop digging into Oxford. I can't tell you what you want to know, Patience."

"Can't or won't?" she demanded.

Even her voice sounded weak. He really did not like how fast she breathed. She seemed almost breathless.

"Won't," he said.

"You have been secretive," she said, and for the first time he could hear notes of anger, hear her actually raising her voice. "You have been avoiding me. There's something about my brother that you're hiding. You left me no choice."

"You have a choice. You can stop asking questions and trust me."

She scoffed. "Trust you? I thought I could, but then you left me alone after the most incredible experience of my life! You made me feel so isolated just when I thought we had connected more deeply than I ever have with anyone!" Her voice faltered, she swayed slightly, and her eyelids drooped. "How can I trust—"

Alarm surged through Dorian like a war horn.

She staggered to the side, her movement unsteady, and her foot caught on the stump of a fallen tree. She began to fall sideways, shockingly silent, not even extending her arms to break her descent.

She was about to hit the ground...

Nothing mattered more than preventing her fall.

He lunged forward and caught her before she could collide with the earth, his knees hitting the soil. She yelped in pain. He cradled her in his arms, her eyes blinking slowly as she looked up at him. Fear for her sent a jolt through him, his body both limp and prickling with adrenaline. Calls of concern rose, and he noticed footmen and gardeners hurrying over to form a circle around them.

Dorian lifted her into his arms and rose. "Go and find Mrs. Knight," he barked at one of the footmen. "Have her bring water to my bedchamber. Find Popwell and send someone for the physician."

"Yes, Your Grace," replied the footman.

"My ankle..." she whispered.

He glanced at her ankle. There was blood trickling down her shoe.

As Dorian carried her into the house, he felt like he was cradling the most precious thing in the entire world and he had almost lost her.

He shoved the raging beast inside him deep down. For her, he'd do anything.

Almost anything.

He still couldn't tell her about the duel.

He marveled at how calm he could be, while one part of him was furious with her and another was so terrified he felt cold.

"Have you had anything to drink today?" he asked as the blessed coolness of the house's interior wrapped around them.

"A cup of tea," she replied. "At breakfast."

"It's almost five o'clock," he growled. "You must have lost a lot of fluid, working in the sun all day."

"And my corset," she breathed out. "It's my own fault. I let Mademoiselle Antoinette lace it so tightly. She said that's how duchesses are supposed to wear them. I should have told her I wasn't a duchess today but a mere gardener."

"You should have," he agreed as he took the steps upstairs.

Having her cradled in his arms felt like the rightest thing in the world.

As he laid her on the bed, Mrs. Knight hurried in with a tray bearing a carafe of water, a teapot, and biscuits. Behind his housekeeper's usual cool and collected face, he could see traces of worry.

"Here you go, Your Grace," she said to Patience.

Dorian had already taken out his medical emergency basket. For the first time ever, it was going to be used for someone other than him. While Mrs. Knight poured water and added sugar, he looked at the cut on Patience's ankle.

It was not deep, thankfully, and had already started to clot at the sides. That was a relief.

He was not going to let anything else happen to her.

Chastity had told him about one of her medical experiments, which involved cleansing wounds to avoid infection. She assured him that wounds should be cleaned with spirits, or if that was not available, soap and water or vinegar. And she'd said that it was important to boil water before treating wounds with it. She insisted that every medical basket he had included a small bottle of spirits. As Chastity had showed him, he poured a small amount of the spirits on a clean cloth.

Patience took a few sips of water and put the glass on the night table.

"This is going to sting," he warned her.

"Oh."

With his right hand holding her ankle in place, he gently rubbed the cloth down her cut with his left hand. She yelped. The sight of her hurt made his gut twist. It was his fault, too. If he had stayed, she'd have slept in his bed and wouldn't be so tired.

"Sorry, love," he said.

The cut was long, extending from the bone at the juncture of the foot and ankle to the middle of her ankle, but thankfully, it didn't look deep.

"Can I do anything else?" asked Mrs. Knight.

"You can untie my corset," complained Patience, who was removing her bonnet.

"I'll do that," said Dorian.

It came out more gruffly than he liked, but the thought of anyone else touching Patience was unbearable. Knowing in theory that her lady's maid helped her dress and undress was one thing; witnessing it was quite another.

It was possessive of him, he knew, but he wanted to be the only one who saw his wife in such moments.

"Of course, Your Grace," said Mrs. Knight. "May I suggest asking the cook to prepare some chicken soup for Your Grace? Perhaps I'm speaking out of place, but my mother always said chicken soup will cure anything."

"That would be lovely," said Patience. "Thank you."

As Mrs. Knight retreated from the room, Dorian secured a fresh, clean bandage to Patience's ankle.

"Now the corset?" asked Patience. "Please do unlace it. You were completely right. I couldn't breathe right all day long working in the garden, and I should have drunk more water. It was a surprisingly warm day."

"Of course."

He helped her sit upright. When she turned her back to him, he unlaced her dress. The act was simple, and he didn't even see much of her skin, and yet, touching her, even through the fabric, had his cock standing at attention. As he unlaced her corset, his resolve to distance himself from her evaporated.

"You will sleep here tonight," he said.

She turned to him, and her blue eyes sparkled as they locked with his. The smile that spread on her lips made a needle of joy pierce his heart.

"Yes," she said, and his chest filled with lightness and warmth, like a hot air balloon.

And then there was something strange happening to his face. He felt a tug at the corners of his lips, and her eyes dropped to his mouth, her grin widening.

She gently touched his lips with her fingertips, her expression akin to the awe one might feel when seeing a rare animal up close. "You're smiling," she whispered. "Heavens, you're smiling, Dorian. You're breathtaking when you smile."

She had done this. She had opened the curtains inside his chest and let the sunshine straight into his dark heart.

He was a fool. He couldn't distance himself from her no matter how much he tried.

This woman felt like his salvation.

But one day she very well may also be his damnation.

27

Patience cuddled into her husband's hard chest and heard the fast *thurump-thurump* of his heart. His bedchamber around them was dark, the mattress and the sheets were soft, and Dorian was as hot as a furnace.

He was back.

And he had smiled! The most gorgeous, precious smile she'd ever seen. It was like she had broken through the hard shell of Dorian, the Duke of Rath, and through that crack in the shell, she'd glimpsed the Dorian who had existed before the glasshouse...before his mama had been sent away...before he'd had to protect Chastity...before the glove.

And she loved him.

She forcibly pushed away the thoughts that had plagued her ever since she'd talked to Lucien. Dorian had been dueling in Oxford. Did that have anything to do with John? Could John have somehow dishonored himself and then killed himself in shame? Did John's death have anything to do with Dorian at all, or were these things unrelated...?

This was not the time to ask him. She did not want to break the peace between them. She'd just got him back.

She pressed her nose against his bare skin and inhaled a lungful of his scent: the intoxicating mixture of musk, bergamot, and something spicy, like pepper. His smell always did this to her—made her nipples harden and ache for his touch… made her skin tingle and set her body on fire.

"So, the wifely duties," she murmured as she planted a kiss on his warm, smooth skin, feeling the muscle tense under her and his heartbeat speed up. "They were quite lovely."

His arm wrapped around her and pulled her closer. "Patience…" he rumbled. "You need rest."

Such a pleasant rumble of his voice, resonating through his ribs and against her ear.

"I've been resting all afternoon and night," she said as she ran her hand down his naked chest. She planted another soft kiss on his side, right between two ribs. "I've drunk, I've eaten. Your physician checked and rebandaged my ankle. Chastity fussed about clean instruments. The cook sent up dinner, and you fed it to me as if I were a child."

She felt quite brave, quite empowered, feeling him freeze under her, his heart beating even faster. It was all her doing, was it not? She could make this gorgeous, powerful, strong man's heart beat like that, with just a touch…and a kiss…

What else could she do to him?

"All right," she chuckled. "If you're worried about my ankle, is there a way for me to perform my wifely duties and not bother the ankle much?"

He growled, and in one motion, flipped her from her side onto her back, pinning her arms high above her head. She felt spread out for him, all his, every inch of her at his disposal as he towered over her, his face dangerous in the semidarkness of the room, his sky-blue eyes like pools of night, staring at her with intensity.

"For one so inexperienced, you're remarkably skilled at bringing a man to his knees."

Patience bit her lip to stop a satisfied smile.

"Are you certain your ankle doesn't hurt?"

"Very certain."

"God knows, I should be staying away from you," he said. "Should be leaving you alone. But it's the most difficult thing I've ever had to do in my life. And I simply can't. So I won't."

He lowered his delicious weight onto her, crushing her into the mattress.

"I'll be gentle," he whispered against her lips.

She was about to protest, to say she didn't want him to be... didn't need him to be. But he covered her lips with his and kissed her, wiping all thoughts from her head. Delicious swipes of his lips against hers, his tongue playing with hers, made her writhe under him with impatience. Her skin felt hot and suddenly so sensitive she could feel every crease of her chemise, the fabric rubbing against her nipples as she breathed quickly.

His right arm pinned her hands over her head and his left hand went under her chemise, caressing her legs, her thighs, and then higher. He moved to her breasts and cupped one with his hand. They felt heavier, nipples aching with sweet pain as he rolled one nipple and tugged on it.

She arched towards him, the simultaneous stimulation of his touch and his kiss making her head dizzy. His hard member was already pressing into her stomach through his breeches, and she opened her legs, wrapping them around his hips.

Moving his hips so that his erection was pressing into her sex, he murmured a male sound of pleasure and impatience into her mouth.

"Don't be..." she managed as she tore away from his lips.

"Pardon me?" he asked, blinking. "Am I hurting you?"

"No. Don't be gentle," she said.

His eyes met hers, and she saw his Adam's apple rise and fall. "You don't know what you're asking," he said.

She cupped his face, and her fingers found the white lock of his hair, brushing it back. "I'd like to know. I'm asking you to show me what you truly want."

A visible shiver ran through his body as his gaze swept over her, from head to toe, as though he was taking inventory of a new and unexpected treasure he'd secretly wanted his entire life. He exhaled audibly as he closed his eyes for a few moments.

"You'll be the end of me, sweet girl," he murmured as he opened his eyes. "You're a gift... A gift I will never deserve."

A thrill ran through her. She? A gift? Surely he didn't mean it. She didn't do anything—

Her thoughts were interrupted when he kissed her, hungrier this time, then withdrew again.

"If at any moment you wish me to stop, just say one word, and I will. Promise me, love."

She nodded eagerly, her chest heaving as she sucked in air, feeling nervous. "I promise."

Then he was kissing her again, all gentleness gone. Instead, these were hungry brushes of his lips and possessive strokes of his tongue that resonated deep in her sex.

He dragged her chemise over her head, and she was naked under him, her skin feeling as if it were extended to the borders of his body, feeling every movement of air acutely.

He removed his breeches and kneeled over her, the glove on his right hand his only clothing. Her breath caught at the sight of him, towering above her, moonlight falling on the smooth hills and valleys of the defined muscles of his chest, his narrow waist and hips, the rippling muscles of his stomach, his thick, muscular thighs...

And his gorgeous cock, long and thick, surrounded by dark curly hair. The sight of it had her sex clench in anticipation, in the memory of the intense pleasure it had brought her last time. His gaze swept over her, igniting her skin.

"You're the most beautiful thing I've ever seen in my life," he murmured as his eyes lingered on her breasts, her waist, her full hips. "And until the day I die, you will be the most beautiful thing."

As she struggled to try to believe what he said, he lowered himself to her, his glorious body completely naked against hers. She could feel every hair, every rib, every indent.

And the one thing that still separated them, its smooth leather cool on her skin.

"Would you remove your glove?" she asked. "I'd like to see you bare...as you see me."

His face froze, all intensity gone, and pure fear overtook his features. She should have never asked. "No," he said. "You will never see it."

She ached for the closeness, the intimacy between them to return and for him to forget whatever was hiding beneath that glove. "Of course," she said. "I just want to be close to you."

"You already are, darling," he murmured. "You are closer to me than anyone has ever been. Can this be enough?"

She nodded.

He kissed her—hard, fervent, almost hurried—as his hands resumed their glorious torture.

And she loved every second of it.

He was exploring her body, learning where she liked a firmer touch and where she liked gentle caresses. Until he could play her body like an instrument, and all she could do was moan, cry out, and writhe under him, despite the slight pain in her ankle.

He rose over her again, like a God, his gaze so intense she felt she was burning. "Patience," he said, his voice like a command, sending a thrill down her spine. "Spread your legs for me."

Like a good, obedient girl, she did. Her legs parted wide, revealing her throbbing, wet sex to him. His head fell back, the sinews of his neck thick, his pulse beating in his veins.

He palmed his erection, and she bit her lip. He lowered himself to her and entered her in one swift motion. There was no more pain. He filled her completely, stretching her to the limit, and she took him in whole. If she could, she wanted him to be even deeper.

He locked his eyes with hers, dark and intense.

Like a king conquering a new land, his gaze told her she would be his and nothing would stand between them.

And then he began to move, pounding into her, quickly and relentlessly.

She arched her back as intense pleasure spread through her, as he was hitting some sort of beautiful spot inside her. Every slap of flesh against hers told her whom she belonged to—him.

He angled his hips and even more pleasure spilled through her. She cried out, her fingers wrapping around the blanket, her fists clenching.

Good God, Good God, Good God...

This was intense, powerful, all encompassing. He demanded complete submission, and all she could do was to give it. The hard slaps of his flesh, the way his cock took possession of her sex, and the unyielding onslaught that took her higher and higher.

And then he took her even higher when she felt his gloved

hand wrap around her throat. He didn't press hard, but she could feel the leather, cool against her overheated skin.

She opened her eyes in surprise, but all she could see was his intense focus on her, the limitless desire in his black eyes, and the strange way she could feel the danger wrapping around her neck. She could say *no* now, could say *stop*.

But she didn't want to.

She only wished that, no matter what was under that glove, he'd remove it, and she could feel his skin on her skin.

This was him having control over her; this was her submitting to him.

She was acutely aware of every inch of her body, each nerve ending alight with longing. Her lips parted on a soft gasp, her breathing growing shallow as her heart raced in her chest. The ache between her thighs intensified, a pulsing need that demanded satisfaction.

"Take it, sweet girl," he murmured. "Feel the intensity. What does your body want you to do?"

It wanted her to let go. To give in and just feel this.

The moment she did, her climax slammed into her hard. Her muscles clenched tightly around him. Her whole pelvis felt like it radiated ecstasy. Dorian grunted and pounded into her with an animalistic speed. His own release had him buck for several seconds, and then he collapsed onto her as they both breathed hard and in unison.

Like one being.

Except for his gloved hand. The forbidden clue to the mystery that lay between them...and according to him, always would.

28

"Patience, no," growled Dorian three days later when he spotted her passing his study doors in her gardening bonnet, her gait lively and unencumbered by a corset. Her breasts bounced freely as she moved out of his view.

Titan, who lay by his feet as he wrote, raised his head, his tail wagging when he saw Patience. Dorian sprang to his feet, flinging his quill aside, unconcerned that it left a large ink blot across the letter he had been writing. Fuming, Dorian followed her, noting the wooden box in her hands. Titan trotted after him. When he caught up to her, he saw the box was filled with brown bulbs.

Titan whimpered happily and did a little greeting dance around Patience, his tail moving quickly from side to side. She cooed to him, unable to pet him with both of her hands holding the crate.

"Patience, your ankle!" he said. "You're not well enough! You almost fainted not three days ago!"

She beamed at him, her smile full of sunshine. "And you made it all better. Who knew you had such a nurturing side?"

"Goddamn it!" he growled. "It's even warmer today."

"I already asked Mrs. Knight to bring plenty of water. You have nothing to worry about. I also have no corset to constrict me."

"I saw that. What are you thinking, going out without a corset, for any man to see...?"

Her gorgeous, full, tender breasts were his alone to enjoy.

"The footmen and the gardeners have a free day today," she chirped, and as they both stepped out through the back doors and into the garden, she stopped and took a lungful of air, closing her eyes. "What a perfect day for gardening."

She eyed him critically, from head to toe, before passing him the box she was carrying. "How about you help me today and protect my uncorseted breasts from anyone trying to take an unsolicited peek? Anyone such as a bee...a bird...an unscrupulous caterpillar?"

He swallowed as he stared at the garden, which looked nothing like it had before she'd moved in.

They'd spent the last three days in each other's arms and he hadn't let her take a single step out of his bedchamber. He nursed her, rebandaged her ankle every day, had Chastity inspect the cut and approve the positive effect of her antiseptic, which she also written down in her papers. They didn't talk about Lucien or Patience's persistent digging, even though every time he thought about it, his blood chilled.

She hadn't promised him she'd stop searching, and helplessness made him want to lash out, hit something, destroy something, like before.

But he didn't. Because she was more important. Their happiness was more important.

He fucked her every night, free from his former restraint. And he was happy, seeing her fall apart in his arms, seeing her seemingly enjoy the rough way he liked to couple as much as he did. Perhaps that was what had helped to dull his fury.

Or perhaps it was simply her. She was stronger than the beast of wrath inside him. But the day of reckoning would still come, he knew, no matter how happy he was now, no matter how much he was turning away from his fury.

However, during the past three days, he had smiled more often than he had in all thirty-two years of his life.

So, to hell with the angry, wrathful beast inside.

The garden that had brought so much pain to him, that had twisted his very soul, was unrecognizable. She had transformed it. And to his amazement, he quite liked the idea of helping Patience tend it.

And keeping an eye on her, of course, ensuring she drank plenty of water and didn't get overheated.

He allowed his mouth to stretch into a smile, and his chest filled with the most agreeable, light feeling. "Yes," he said as he took the wooden box from her hands. "I would quite like that."

Her smile was bright enough to blind him.

And he loved it.

When they reached a well-raked patch of dirt bordered by gray stones along the curvy garden path, Patience peered into the box of bulbs he was holding.

"Would you mind helping me plant these hyacinths?" she asked, her eyes sparkling with enthusiasm. "I know it's a not the ideal time to plant them, but I couldn't resist their lovely colors and fragrances. We'll need to dig holes about six inches deep and space them about six inches apart. It's a bit of an experiment—they might not bloom fully this season, but we can hope for at least some flowers, and they'll certainly be beautiful next spring."

Dorian put the box on the ground and rolled up his sleeves. "Just show me where to begin."

Patience knelt to the black earth and demonstrated how to use a trowel to dig a hole, carefully placing a bulb inside and covering it with soil. Dorian watched intently, then selected a bulb from the basket and knelt down to try his hand at planting.

As he worked the trowel into the earth, Dorian marveled at the unfamiliar sensations—the cool, damp soil beneath the fingers of his left hand, the earthy scent that filled his nostrils, the satisfying resistance of the ground as he dug. He had never imagined that such simple manual labor could be so fulfilling, but with Patience by his side, he found himself thoroughly enjoying the task.

And he did not at all let himself become distracted by any other sort of bulb...two gorgeous, delicious bulbs that were hanging and bouncing so loosely in his wife's dress as she worked by his side.

His chest filled with lightness, sweet tension.

Happiness, he thought, and grinned to himself. The sun on his skin, the dirt under his fingernails, the woman he loved by his side.

This was true happiness.

He never imagined he would feel this emotion in the garden that had been the source of so much misery.

It was all her.

Together, they worked their way down the row, planting each bulb with care and precision. As he covered a bulb with soil, Dorian sat back on his heels, surveying their work with a sense of accomplishment. The bed looked no different than it had before, but in a matter of weeks, the bulbs would sprout and grow, their green shoots pushing up through the earth to unfurl into a glorious display of color.

As they worked, Titan trotted over to investigate their

activities. He sniffed curiously at the freshly dug earth, his wet nose leaving imprints in the soil.

Patience laughed and gently pushed his muzzle away, saying, "No, Titan, these bulbs are not for you to dig up!"

Titan tilted his head, as if considering her words, then flopped down beside them, content to watch their progress with his intelligent eyes.

"I cannot wait to see them bloom," Dorian said, standing and turning to Patience with a smile. "To think that we have played a part in bringing such beauty into the world—it is a wonderful feeling, is it not?"

She beamed at him once again and wrapped her dirty arms around his neck. She kissed him lightly, with just a hint of passion, but he was already aflame.

"I love it that you understand what I feel when I work with plants," she murmured. "Today…now…is my favorite day ever. I've said this to myself several times recently, and yet each succeeding day surpasses its predecessor."

His throat contracted and he wrapped his arms around her, bringing her tighter to him. "I find myself thinking exactly the same."

They kissed, standing in the sun, surrounded by sprouting life and the new garden, which was quite barren still, but filled with happiness. When they broke apart, afraid that they would need to hurry back into the house to satisfy their growing ache for each other, Patience looked at several gardening tools, which were leaning against the brick half wall.

"Would you mind helping me rake the next garden patch?"

"Not at all," he said.

He picked up the rake, and a quick burst of laugh escaped her lips, then another.

"Well, well, well. The notorious rake of London, now

raking leaves in our humble garden. How the mighty have fallen!" Patience teased, her eyes sparkling with mirth.

He grinned and looked at the tool in his hand. "Only for you, love."

While they were raking, Titan spotted a red squirrel darting along the brick half wall. With an excited bark, he bounded after the tiny creature, his large paws clumsily attempting to navigate the narrow surface. The squirrel, quick and agile, easily evaded Titan, pausing atop the wall to look victoriously at the massive hound. Titan wagged his tail and panted, as if this was a delightful game. Dorian and Patience exchanged amused glances, chuckling.

Dorian had forgotten the last time he'd tried to jest, but he wanted Patience to keep laughing. It was such a glorious sound that resonated in his chest like a bell chiming.

"How are your roses doing, Patience?" he asked.

"No disease. Growing well."

"I heard somewhere that talking to plants helps them grow," he said. "Do you think it would help if I recited Shakespeare's sonnets to the roses?"

Patience stopped raking and burst out laughing. "Dorian, are you trying to make a jest, darling?"

He straightened and leaned on the rake, enjoying the sight of her beautiful face as she laughed. "I am."

The same sort of infectious laughter was born right in his chest, and he chuckled as he looked at his dirty hands. "Look, love, I may not be able to grow a single flower, but I seem to have a real talent for growing the dirt under my fingernails."

Patience laughed even harder. Wiping the corners of her eyes with her sleeve, she managed, "Please stop. I love your attempts, but seeing you try to make a humorous remark is funnier than your jests themselves."

He grinned. Good God, when was the last time he had tried

to make someone laugh? He must have been six. His papa was away, and he was dancing around in front of Chastity and Mama, making very comical faces. It was a relief Papa had left the estate for a day or two, and the three of them felt like they were free.

His pathetic mind came up with another thing: "You're right, love. I used to think my only talent was to direct my valet to tie a cravat perfectly. But now, I've discovered a new skill—the ability to make a complete fool of myself in front of you."

Patience giggled and came to him, giving him a soft kiss on the cheek. "You're not. I lo—" She cut herself off abruptly, and all humor fell from him.

Lo—loved him?

The ground careened under his feet.

She glanced over her shoulder at the pond where he swam every morning. Then she looked back at him with mischief in her eyes.

"Shall we wash out all that grime from your ducal fingernails, Your Grace?"

He grinned. He did feel warm; the sun was hot today. He had allowed her into the garden, the glasshouse...why not let her into the pond where he usually swam to numb himself?

Because there was not much he wanted to be numb from anymore.

"Excellent suggestion, Your Grace," he chuckled, then scooped her into his arms.

Behind him, Titan barked. As Dorian ran towards the pond with Patience in his arms, Titan bounded alongside them, his long legs easily keeping pace. When they reached the water's edge, Titan didn't hesitate to plunge in after them, sending up a great splash that drenched them all. He paddled around the couple, his head held high above the water, his tail acting as a rudder. Every so often, he would swim close to Patience, gently nudging her with his nose as if to make sure she was safe and happy. Patience reached out to stroke his wet fur, marveling at the dog's unwavering loyalty and love for his humans.

Dorian and Patience kissed, and she wrapped her legs around his waist and clung to him while he swam around with her as his passenger.

As the water glistened with reflections of the sun and he felt weightless, he was never as sure as he was then that he loved her.

And that one day he'd ruin everything.

Which scared him to death.

29

THE NEXT EVENING, Patience knocked softly on the door of Dorian's study, the light of the candle in her hands trembling from her breath. It was late and Rath Hall was quiet, with all the servants having retired for the day.

"Come in," came his voice from behind the polished mahogany, and she entered, her heart beating in her throat.

His study was dark, save for candelabras standing on the fireplace and on his desk, illuminating his serious face. Her stomach fluttered as she saw him studying a document, his gloved hand on his chin, deep in thought.

"Are you coming to bed?" she asked, and his face jerked up, surprised.

And terrified…?

"Patience…" he murmured as he snatched up the paper he had been studying and pushed it under the stack of books. "I thought it was Mrs. Knight."

She frowned. Did he just hide something from her?

She approached him. The scent of his study was an extension of him—bergamot, pepper, and something musky, like leather. The scent that made her think of pure bliss, skin gliding against skin, lips brushing.

"No, it's just me. All of the servants have retired."

"Oh." He licked his lips.

She cocked her head. "I came to fetch you to bed. You must rest before your long stay in London. All those business things you must do…"

He looked so lonely, sitting in the dark room with just a few candles illuminating his kingdom—the books, the stacks of paper, the quills and ink jars, the portraits of the previous dukes staring down at him with judgmental eyes.

"Are you certain you don't want to come with me?" he asked. "Will you be able to sleep by yourself?"

She sighed and nodded. "I will try. I don't want to leave the garden while there are still a few last weeks of spring to prune and to plant seeds."

He nodded. "And I have business that I have been putting off for far too long."

"Are you worried about something?" she asked. "Something in London?"

His gaze darkened as he rubbed his hand under the leather glove.

She put her candle on the sideboard next to the other candelabra, walked over to the desk, and leaned against its side. "Come to bed with me?" she asked. "You're leaving for London tomorrow, and I'll miss you."

He stretched his hand out to her, his gaze softening. She laid her left hand in his, allowing skin-to-skin contact, and tingles danced through her blood.

"It's me," he purred as he pulled her to him. "It's me who'll miss you, sweet girl."

He spread his thighs and placed her between them, her arse leaning against the edge of the desktop. His hands ran up her thighs and towards her waist. She was already changed for bed, her hair falling freely over her shoulders. As he undid the belt of her dressing gown, its sides fell open, revealing her chemise. She shuddered and arched her back as he began kissing her stomach, waking up her body, her flesh responding to him with an aching desire.

"Did you come to ask me to bed?" he murmured, his lips brushing against her skin through her chemise. "Or to seduce me in my study?"

As he pulled her chemise up, revealing her naked thighs, her head fell back. Before she could respond to him, her gaze grazed over one particular portrait, and she froze.

Good Lord...the man strongly resembled Dorian... Except he wore a white wig and had harsher, more angular features. He was also larger, with more flesh around his stomach.

She sat straight up. "Is that your papa?"

His head shot to the portrait. "Yes."

She looked at him, his gaze haunted as he stared at the image. Then he met her eyes.

"Do not allow him to interrupt us," he murmured as he reached for her lips, resolve in his face. "You chase away the darkness that he's cast over me my entire life."

Her heart squeezed tightly. "And you're the strength I thought I'd never have," she replied.

She glanced down at his glove. Her body wanted him. Her spirit did, too.

And yet, the glimpses into the happiness they could share for the rest of their lives were just that...glimpses. Dreams. That's what their true happiness would always be as long as there were secrets between them.

She cupped his face. "What would it be like, to trust you as I trust Anne? To know everything I feel and think...you can understand? And for you, to be able to tell me every little thing that crosses your mind...?"

She took his gloved hand and looked straight into his face. His gaze was haunted. "For you to tell me what's hiding here? And whatever it is that you can never tell me about Oxford?"

He was frozen in place, completely terrified.

She ached to tell him she loved him. That she would understand, whatever his secret was. She'd accept him.

He rose to his feet and left her proximity, walking behind his desk. "Leave it be."

She jumped to her feet. "Wait... Dorian." She reached out to him.

In her hurry, her hand knocked the stack of books and papers that was at the edge of his desk, and they fell, scattering around the floor, papers flying.

She dropped to her heels next to him to help him pick them up. Book by book, she gathered them and put them onto the desk.

When she went to pick up the aged sheet of paper with ruffled edges and old ink, blurry with time, she didn't at first register anything. She'd almost put it on top of the desk when her eyes grazed over the date.

October 8, 1802.

And then the place.

Oxford.

She froze, the paper trembling in her hands. Dorian was still picking up the books and the letters, and her gaze flicked over the writing, at times unclear. Unfamiliar.

Severe burns... she managed to read.

Metallic fragments in the sinew...

...likely from a great burst, like a gun or a bomb...
...likely will never have full control of the fingers...
...might lose the hand...
Services in the amount of £10.
Dr. Long, Oxford.

Shock pulsed through her like slashing blades against her skin. Slowly, she raised her gaze to meet his.

"Is that what's hiding under your glove?" she asked, her voice trembling. "Burns...lacerations...?"

The words caught in her throat. Chastity had mentioned burns, but this... this was far worse than she had imagined. The severity of the injury, the implication of violence—it all crashed over her in a rush.

He froze, his gorgeous face distorted in a grimace of terrible fear. He could be a cornered animal.

"From what?" she demanded.

He swallowed hard. "An accident. I told you."

She stood up and approached him. Clearly, he was distressed. Traumatized, perhaps, from whatever had happened back then.

"Yes, you told me. But here it says from a gun or a bomb."

"Patience—" he said, stepping back from her. "Stop."

As though she was going to hurt him.

"I'd never hurt you, Dorian," she said, her voice trembling, her hand stretching out to give him back the doctor's bill. "Don't you know that?"

He snatched it, almost tearing it apart. "Just leave this alone," he grumbled. "Please. It's just ghosts."

Ghosts that were still haunting both of them. Their marriage.

And his soul.

Dr. Long, Oxford.

The idea formed in her head. He'd be in London for at least five days. Enough time for her to sneak in a trip to Oxford.

She nodded. "Very well. I'm sorry I've inquired about something you're not ready to share. Let me just tell you, whenever you're ready, I want to see all of you. The good. The bad. And whatever you're hiding under your glove."

30

Two days later, Patience's steps echoed softly on the cobblestone streets of Oxford, the ancient stones worn smooth. The air was crisp, carrying the scent of April—a mix of damp earth and the faint, sweet bloom of the clusters of daffodils planted in a few squares along her way. She wrapped her shawl tighter around her shoulders, the cool breeze teasing loose strands of her hair from under her bonnet.

She looked over her shoulder. A footman had accompanied her and Mademoiselle Antoinette to Oxford. Should she have brought him with her on her errand today? No. She'd told them both she would meet with Sir James Edward Smith, a renowned botanist—which was an outright lie.

She'd sent a footman from Rath Hall to tell Dorian she was going to Oxford to meet Sir Smith, as well. How betrayed would he feel if he found out the true reason for her excursion?

Sir Smith didn't live in Oxford.

And she felt like a fraud.

But she had been compelled to come here and learn what she could of the secret that haunted her marriage.

As she wandered, the muffled sounds of the town enveloped her—the distant clop of horse hooves, the soft chatter of townsfolk, and the occasional burst of laughter from students spilling out of doorways. She passed by towering spires and grand, ivy-clad façades. The sunlight filtered through the budding trees, casting dappled shadows on her path, and for a moment, she could almost feel the presence of her brother, John, in the laughter and footfalls that surrounded her.

This was the place where Dorian, Luhst, Pryde, and John had all somehow become intertwined in an incident that had been kept secret the past twelve years.

An incident that had required a physician—Dr. Long.

And that was the interesting thing.

The girl she'd been when she'd married Dorian wouldn't have dreamed of going against her husband's wishes and finding a way to continue her investigation. Because she would have been afraid to displease him. Afraid to cast a shadow on their peace.

And especially afraid to face her family's dark past.

She'd always wondered why John had killed himself when he'd been such an enthusiastic and charming man who seemed to never stop smiling.

Looking at those dark ideas and thoughts was not the Rose way. Did not correspond well with folding the negative emotions neatly up and putting them into a basket.

And yet, here she was. Facing them straight on.

She hadn't done the basket exercise since she'd found the doctor's bill two days ago. And, surprisingly, it felt right.

Patience found herself in front of a house in the center of Oxford. Dr. Long's office was supposedly on the first floor. However, she soon learned that the doctor had died five years earlier, and it was now the office of a solicitor. Disappointment ran through her.

She'd come to Oxford to speak with the physician who'd treated Dorian's burns and lacerations on the same day her brother had died, to ask him if he thought there could be any connection between the two events. But now she'd never know.

On the ground floor was the student pub, its wooden sign, with a bear against a red background, creaking gently in the wind.

The Bear, she read.

It sounded familiar. John had mentioned this pub before, she was sure. As a six-year-old, she had wondered if there was a real bear inside.

The door stood ajar, inviting her into a world her brother had once known. It was early afternoon, and she heard no signs of one of the loud, drunken debaucheries her brother had mentioned. As a child, she'd wondered if such a reckless crowd of people would have bothered a real bear... If there had been one.

Needles prickled her skin as she stood watching the pub, the stained-glass windows dark. It was half-timbered, with a wooden frame, white plaster filling the spaces between the beams. She wondered if this was one of the last places John may have been in his life. And if Dorian had frequented the pub, too.

A woman in her early thirties came out of the pub and began slapping out some wet cloths. She was dressed like a servant, with a grayish cap and an apron. She had beautiful red hair under her cap and a tired face with more wrinkles than she should have at her age.

Patience stepped back so that the wind wouldn't blow

crumbs and dust on her, and the woman stopped, looking at her.

"Oh, I am so sorry, my lady," she said with a genuine expression of regret. "I thought you were just passing by. Ladies don't come here, so I didn't think you were waiting..."

"Oh," said Patience, suddenly feeling out of place since someone called her "my lady."

She should be used to this by now. And yet...

"No, I can't walk in anyway," she said with a thankful smile. "I was just thinking of my brother."

"Your brother, my lady?" asked the woman. "Does he study here?"

"He used to. A long time ago. And he talked about The Bear many times."

"Ah, I see. Yes, well, most students do come here for some ale and some trouble."

Patience chuckled. "Some trouble. That was what John was after, no doubt."

"John?" she asked and frowned, thinking. "Mayhap I know him, even from a long time ago. I've been working here my entire life. My father owned this public house, and I've always been the maid here. I'm now the owner. Never married, you see."

Patience smiled sadly and shook her head. "I doubt it. It was twelve years ago."

The woman nodded. "My name is Christine, by the way. And you are?"

"I'm Lady... Ahem, forgive me, I still can't get used to my title. I'm the Duchess of Rath."

"Oh, Your Grace," said Christine and curtsied. "We do have some dukes and their sort visiting, but never a duchess. Twelve years ago, you say... Yes, I was the maid here then. Where's your brother now? Is he a solicitor? That's what most young men become when they graduate. Or perhaps a vicar?"

Patience's chest ached painfully. "He would have been a solicitor. He died twelve years ago."

Christine's face changed, a shadow of alerted concern crossing it. "What was the name of your brother, did you say?"

"I doubt you knew him. There must have been so many students passing through your public house. His name was John Rose."

All color drained from the woman's face. She stood in complete silence, looking like a statue made of human flesh.

"Mr. John Rose?" she asked, her voice barely a whisper.

Patience took a step forward, afraid Christine might fall. "The very same. Did you know him?"

The woman's hand still clutched her wet linen, which moved weakly in the slight breeze blowing through the street. "Oh, I knew him. And you're...the Duchess of Rath? Why does that sound so familiar?"

Patience's senses tightened and sharpened at the same time. As though a crack ran through her very existence. There had been the part of her life before the crack. And there would be the part after. Would Christine's next words split apart her life completely?

Patience swallowed hard. "Did you know my husband, too?" she asked, her voice croaking through the tension in her throat.

Christine took a few steps towards her and clutched the wet cloth to her chest, her eyes wide and strangely unseeing. "I did," said Christine, her blue eyes framed by reddish eyelashes glancing over Patience. "John looked like you...back then. Pretty. Golden curls. Blue eyes. The face of an angel."

Patience licked her lips nervously. She may have come

closer to the truth than ever before. She chuckled softly. "Yes, all Roses look alike."

Christine's gaze shifted, distant and unfocused, as if peering through Patience to something unsettling just beyond. A tremor passed through her. "John attacked me," she said. "I know I should not speak ill of the dead. But..."

Attacked her?

John?

Patience shook her head in disbelief.

On that quiet Oxford street with daffodils in bloom and geraniums on the windowsills, under a blue sky, her world was shattering.

No. It was as though Patience was hearing about a completely different person. The John she knew had taught her how to do country dances, had helped her climb a tree to rescue a kitten, had brought her a bouquet of wildflowers every time he went out for a walk.

"He forced himself on me," said the woman shakily. "And Lord Perrin, he found us. He protected me against John. He threw him off me, and he saved me from utter disgrace..."

Lord Perrin... Dorian! Dorian had been Lord Perrin while his papa was alive.

He had protected this maid...from John?

John had forced himself on Christine? No, surely not John... Could she believe this woman she'd only just met? A stranger? Yet, somehow, she did. Christine's gaze, so full of fear and desperation and helplessness, could not lie.

But what did that mean? Was this the Oxford incident Dorian had been hiding from her? Could she be wrong about John? Was it possible that John was a terrible man and Dorian simply didn't want to destroy her opinion of her brother...? Despite her confusion and sadness over John's actions, her chest filled with warmth. Dorian had been broken by his father, but he was honorable and kind. He rescued women in peril—and rescued her family from financial ruin. That was the man she knew and loved.

Christine's gaze fell on something behind Patience's shoulder and her eyes widened. "Oh, no," she whispered, dropping the cloth from splayed fingers. For a moment she contemplated picking it up, then turned and rushed back through the dark door of The Bear.

"Christine!" cried Patience as she picked up the damp cloth.

She was set to run after her despite the social rules forbidding an unchaperoned woman of good standing from entering such an establishment.

"Patience."

She'd know that voice among hundreds, thousands, a million others.

The only voice that made her entire being reverberate like a tuning fork and stand at attention with the joy of being alive.

Her husband.

31

Patience turned slowly to look at him.

Dorian had just witnessed her talking to the maid he'd saved from John Rose all those years ago, and he couldn't move. For the first time, even his beast felt helpless.

It raged and spat and threw things like the horrible demon it was.

But he was numb.

Perhaps, he realized, part of him wanted Patience to find out, even while most of him did not.

Stop the barmaid! his wrath roared. *Shut her up!*

Perhaps, he distractedly thought as he heard Christine ask for Patience's brother's name, she wouldn't remember.

Perhaps, thought his heart as it shattered, his wife had met this woman by chance.

While he was in London, she had sent him a note with a footman that she was going to go to Oxford to meet Sir James Edward Smith, one of the botanists she had corresponded with. The notion of Patience in Oxford made a heavy feeling churn in his gut. Especially after she'd seen the bill for the treatment of his burns.

However, he wanted to believe her, that she was indeed going to meet Sir Smith.

Patience wouldn't have lied to him like that, surely.

Not Patience.

It was just by chance that she passed by The Bear, and at exact that moment, Christine had walked out.

He had a strange sensation of being at the theater or an opera. That he was a spectator watching the tragedy of his life unfold. Him killing a terrible man, a man who was a rapist, a man who had no honor and had sabotaged his opponent's pistol. And just like in a Greek or Roman tragedy, or an Italian opera, destiny punishing him by having him foolishly try to redeem himself by marrying his victim's sister... Good Lord, he thought, feeling as though he were watching himself from a distance as he stood gaping at his wife on street in Oxford.

He was on the verge of a complete downfall, he knew. No religion in the world would leave him unpunished.

"Patience," he said when Christine ran away.

He was caught between two versions of himself.

The first was the man he had been before his life shattered around him—the demon within, the tyrant driven by rage, who lashed out when overwhelmed by love, loss, and pain.

The second was the man he became after—the man who had learned to love, who truly knew Patience, who wanted to kneel down and bare his soul.

He stood at the very spot where it had all unraveled, where he had read the cursed letter announcing his father's death, witnessed Mr. Rose's assault on Christine, and challenged him to a duel. Here, the better version of himself, forged through Patience's love, could prevail. All he needed was to vanquish the inner demon urging him to wrath and destruction.

But he was not that man.

As guilt shifted across her face, something within him was triggered. In an instant, like the snap of fingers, his darker side won. The fire within him roared to life.

"Dorian," she said softly as she hurried towards him, and he retreated.

"You lied," he snarled before he could stop himself.

"I—" she said, and her face betrayed everything. "I'm sorry."

Damnation.

Why was she not denying everything?

Her apology was disarming, stripping him to the last of his defenses.

"Damn it, Patience. I had plans in the House of Lords, but silly me. I missed you. Couldn't stand a few days without you. So I followed."

Also, he was concerned about her visiting Oxford, learning the truth and hating him...

"Oh, Dorian..." she murmured, all guilty looking.

He showed her the book he'd been holding, *Flora Londinensis* by William Curtis, and she looked at it longingly. It had roses on it; he had bet she'd love them.

"Oh no..." she whispered.

"I found it earlier this morning in London, thought you'd enjoy immensely identifying local flora. I couldn't think of anything but giving it to you," he whispered. "I couldn't stay away so I canceled my plans and came straight to Oxford. Mademoiselle Antoinette said you were having a meeting with Sir Smith in the town center, so here I am."

"Dorian..."

"I wanted to take you to the botanical garden you'd dreamed of going to, the one that belongs to the Earl of Chans, who's a good friend of Pryde. I was also hoping to spend a few days with you alone at Briarstone Park, my estate near Oxford. I seldom visit, but it has hills and brooks and a beautiful house kept up by the staff. I imagined how much you would love it. Perhaps you might want to live there once your year is up." The idea that she would choose to live apart from him at the end of the year tore his insides to pieces, but he would honor his word and his contract, even if it meant dying of loneliness without her.

She went utterly still.

The wind tugged at her golden locks under her elaborate bonnet, decorated with what looked like a bird on top and peacock feathers.

It looked as wrong on her as a palm in the middle of a snowstorm.

"I'm sorry," she repeated. "I lied to you."

"Goddamn it. Patience, I came to bring you all of the things you ever desired, but you deceived me."

She nodded, her cheeks reddening even more. "I did. But I also finally found out the truth."

He went rigid, as stiff as a board. "You did?"

He couldn't breathe; his lungs felt like they were full of water. He stared at her face, watching for any sign of anger, hurt, disgust, but her big blue eyes were full of regret and guilt, her plush pink mouth with that gorgeous Cupid's bow slightly open as though in surprise.

"So then why are you apologizing? And you're not appalled?" he asked carefully.

"I am appalled with John," she said, her cheeks gaining color. "I'm sorry I thought there was something sinister that you were hiding. But you were merely trying to protect my family and me from the knowledge that my brother had forced himself on a woman."

Dorian stood, blinking. This was his chance to correct her, to tell her the whole truth. And yet, his mouth was not moving.

"That was the Oxford incident," she said as she stepped closer to him, her eyes shining, a sweet smile on her lips.

No... No!

She couldn't look at him like at a hero, like she adored him, loved him.

He should say something. Contradict her.

"But you protected Christine. You had nothing to hide from me, Dorian. All this time, you were protecting my memory of John. He must have killed himself because he was caught in a dishonorable act."

How had she come to this conclusion? He gaped, unable to muster the words to contradict her, to tell her how worthless he was. That he was no hero. That he was the villain who had taken her brother's life.

And yet, a cowardly thought came, it would resolve everything if he let her believe this...

She took his hand in hers, the one in the glove. He winced a little from the pain.

"We can let go of it now," she whispered. "It's over. There are no more secrets between us. And now, please take me to the estate, show me the book, and when are we going to visit the botanical gardens you talked about?"

Dorian swallowed a hard knot. "You will not be searching anymore?"

"No, I found everything I wanted. I'm married to a wonderful, honorable man, and I could not be happier."

Dorian's heart shattered. He could never truly be the man she believed him to be.

32

Dorian sat on the chair in the chamber of the inn where Patience was staying, a decanter of brandy glinting in the candlelight on the table by his side. Slowly, he rotated a glass of the amber liquid between his fingers.

He watched Patience walk around the room as she got ready for bed. Mademoiselle Antoinette had already undressed her, and she'd had her bath, and now that they were alone. Patience brushed her long, golden hair as she hummed to herself, catching his gaze occasionally and smiling.

He didn't deserve her. She had too high a regard for him, especially after Christine's words earlier today.

He deserved to be punished.

Even though, it seemed, the problem of her ever finding out about her brother's murder was resolved, and he could now simply let go and enjoy their life together, he had never felt worse.

"Patience," he said.

Her name on his lips was enough to stop her. Wide blue

eyes, guileless and pure, gazed back at him. Pink lips parted on a hitched breath.

Desire pulsed through his veins as he looked her over. He stood and stripped his shirt and breeches off. The cool air of the room caressed his skin, raising goosebumps along his arms.

"Undress for me," he commanded huskily. "Slowly."

She bit her lip as she untied the belt of her dressing gown. Her small hands shook as she untied the ribbons at her bosom. The thin white fabric of her chemise slipped from her smooth shoulders, revealing the tantalizing curves of her breasts, tipped with tender nipples. Lower it fell, catching on the flare of her hips before floating to the floor.

Dorian's lungs refused to take in any air. She was perfection—flawless limbs and soft femininity. He walked to her. Reaching out a calloused palm, he cupped the warm weight of her breast, brushing a thumb over the peak. She gasped, arching into his touch.

He gathered her close, crushing her soft curves against the hard planes of his chest. One hand fisted in her hair, the one in the glove splaying across her lower back. Dipping his head, he captured her mouth in a searing kiss, all tongue and teeth and desperate hunger.

As she melted into him, pliant and responsive, something fractured inside Dorian yet again. She was softening his resolve, making him believe, if only for a moment, that he was worth her love and affection...capable of a deep connection.

Something he craved like air and yet feared.

He deepened the kiss, his tongue hungry for hers. It was more than base lust. More than fleeting pleasure or carnal satisfaction. In her guileless embrace, her sweet responsiveness, he found...home. Acceptance. Love. Everything his life had lacked.

And yet, he didn't deserve her.

Cradling her face, he pulled back to meet her dazed eyes, his thumb stroking her kiss-swollen lips. "My darling Patience..." His voice broke on her name. "What are you doing to me?"

Dorian gazed down at his wife, his heart swelling with emotions he dared not name. Her eyes, dark with desire, also shimmered with a tender vulnerability that made his breath catch. Slowly, almost shyly, she trailed her fingertips down his chest, mapping the contours of his flesh.

"Let me love you...all of you," she whispered. "Let me show you how I feel."

Her words made a shudder run through him, collapsing his restraint.

All of him...

With a groan, Dorian captured her wandering hand and brought it to his lips, pressing a fervent kiss to her palm.

"Then have me, sweet girl. I am yours."

Patience pushed him back onto the bed. His back hit the mattress, and he watched how she walked to him leisurely, her small, curvy body making his cock stand harder. Those round hips with gorgeous dimples, her thin waist and soft belly, the amazing, heavy breasts, and those rosebud nipples...

She was going to take control.

Alarm filled him. Never in his life had he wanted to give up control. It was terrifying. And fear would spark his fury.

And yet...with her he felt safe.

"Show me what you need," he murmured. "Take the lead, darling."

Her eyes widened. His chest heaved in hungry gulps of air as she straddled his hips, the wet heat of her core pressing against his straining erection. Dorian's hands flew to her waist, but she caught them and took his gloved hand into both of hers.

"This is what I need," she said softly. "Let me see. Let me in, Dorian."

His heart slammed so hard against his rib cage it might break through his bones. Panic seized his limbs, stole his breath, made him as rigid as a statue.

"No one has seen it for twelve years but my physician," he murmured. "It is a terrible sight, sweet girl."

"You know me by now. Terrible sights will not discourage me."

He could feel his stomach heaving, his usual reaction to helplessness, to closeness rising within him like a tidal wave. The beast inside wished to throw her off him, yell at her, and escape.

Before she would see how truly ugly and unworthy he was.

Before she'd see the physical manifestation of her brother's death—a scar on his body to match the scar on his soul.

Before she'd make the connection by some miracle.

And leave him.

Because there was nothing he was more afraid now than Patience abandoning him.

And yet, part of him ached to show her, to have another human being in his life who knew his pain. To give up control and just be...him.

He said nothing, only nodded, his chest tightening as though a slab of granite was laid on top of him.

Slowly, she pulled the glove off, and his skin under the leather ached, irritated and yet craving air. He'd worn the glove for twelve years, removing it only when he was alone. He almost snatched his hand away, almost yelled at her for daring this. But he didn't. He watched her face, anticipating revulsion, knowing she'd jump to her feet and retreat from him and never look at him the same way.

But when she threw the glove to the floor, she looked at his hand with tenderness and with sympathy.

Gently, she took his hand into hers, the cool touch of her tender fingers like a healing balm. He didn't know how much he had longed for someone to touch him there, to love and accept the ugliest part of him.

She surprised him again when she leaned towards his hand and planted a tender kiss on his skin. He jerked as tingles spread through his hand. His skin was like the bark of an old, gnarled tree, twisted, raw in places, with thick scars covering it. The reddening of his skin was worse than ever before, as was the pain, which he ignored. He was used to it by now.

"What happened?" she asked. "Can you tell me?"

What could he tell her? He hated himself for still hiding, for covering things up, but he could say some of the truth. "A pistol burst right in my hand," he said.

She nodded. "Was it on the same day as John's death? Is that why the doctor's bill has the same date?"

"Yes."

She looked at him, gently stroking his hand, waiting for him to keep talking, but he didn't say another word. Finally, she nodded and smiled tenderly.

"Thank you for sharing this with me," she said. "I'm sorry that happened to you. Such a terrible accident."

Patience's gentle touch on his scarred hand sent a shiver through Dorian's body. Her acceptance and tenderness were unraveling him, layer by layer, exposing his very soul to her. With trembling fingers, she guided his hands to the headboard, her eyes seeking permission. He nodded, surrendering himself to her completely.

She took the belt of his dressing gown from the bedside

table and bound his wrists to the headboard, her movements slow and deliberate. Dorian's heart raced, his body and soul laid bare before her. Patience trailed feather-light kisses along his jaw, his neck, his chest, each touch like a healing caress.

As she positioned herself above him, Dorian drank in the generous curves of her breasts, the swell of her hips, the glistening evidence of her arousal. She rubbed her sex against his hard length until he thought he might go mad with desire.

She smiled, a wicked gleam in her eye, and slowly sank down upon him. They both moaned as her tight heat surrounded him, clasping him like a glove. She began to move, rolling her hips in a sensual rhythm that had him seeing stars. Dorian strained against his bonds, desperate to touch her, to hold her, but she placed her hands on his chest, keeping him pinned beneath her.

That was what she must have felt like, bound and helpless, trusting him.

Like he trusted her.

"Let me love you," she whispered. "Let me show you how much you mean to me."

Love him...

If only she knew how much he didn't deserve a drop of her love, and yet would spend the rest of his life trying to deserve it. Serving her needs. She was all that mattered. Perhaps that was what God intended for him, a twisted way fate could work.

She rode him, her hips moving, her breasts bouncing, her head thrown back in ecstasy.

"That's right," Dorian rasped. "Take what you need. Take all the pleasure."

She was all his. Her pleasure, her joy, her happiness.

He gave all of himself to her. With his wrists bound, and his mangled hand at her full disposal, he felt raw and vulnerable.

And, somehow, that was healing.

Each rise and fall of her hips drove him closer to the edge, his body wound tight with impending release.

But it was the love in her eyes, the pure devotion and acceptance, that truly undid him. As she cried out his name, her inner walls spasming around him, Dorian let go, surrendering to the bliss she brought him. He shattered beneath her, his release pulsing deep within her womb, his heart laid bare in the afterglow.

Patience collapsed onto his chest, her body warm and soft against his. Dorian ached to hold her, to wrap his arms around her and never let go. She seemed to sense his need, and with gentle hands, she untied his wrists, bringing them to her lips for a tender kiss.

"I love you, Dorian," she whispered against his skin. "You make me so happy."

Dorian pulled her close, burying his face in her hair as he fought back the emotions threatening to overwhelm him. In her arms, he found acceptance, redemption, and a love he'd never thought possible.

He loved her, but the words were stuck in his throat. What was the point of telling her that while she loved an illusion of him, he loved the person she truly was?

Dared he hope for a happy future?

Somehow he knew he'd never be able to unless he could cast light onto the shadows of his past. Only by exposing them could chase them away.

But that might chase her away, too.

33

"Well, knock me down with a feather," said Lady Buchanan two weeks later as she gaped at the garden of Rath Hall. "The garden has never looked better."

Patience exchanged an amused glance with Dorian, who grinned back at her. Happy butterflies danced in her stomach, as they had every day for the past two weeks. She and Dorian woke up in the hazy light of dawn each day, their limbs entwined. Every night was a blur of passion and pleasure, their bodies joining again and again.

"Two months ago, I wouldn't have believed it myself," said Chastity, who stood next to Patience while the butler and the footmen were arranging tea on the terrace overlooking the garden.

Lady Buchanan looked at Dorian and her eyebrows rose to her high and elaborate hairstyle that was more suited for the court of Louis XVI than the garden terrace. "Are you…smiling, Dorian?" asked his aunt, her own lips stretching.

Dorian cleared his throat and wiped the smile off his face, frowning. "Er… No."

Lady Buchanan's eyes practically glimmered with mirth. "You have been smiling! Goodness, I have not seen a smile on your face since... Oh, Lord, since your wretched papa sent my dear sister away from you!"

Chastity nodded. "He has been doing that recently, yes."

Patience's heart felt so full of love, even as an undercurrent of unease rippled through her. The past two weeks, she'd been happier than ever before. She loved her husband, and he showed every sign he loved her, too, even though he never said it. The only thing casting a shadow over their happiness was that he was going through his horrible, exhausting morning routine with more vigor than ever, and she had no idea why... The shadows in the depths of his sky-blue eyes had darkened. Had she not resolved the great mystery that had kept them apart?

It took her a long time to get accustomed to the idea that the brother she had known as a child was not the man he truly was. Very carefully, she wrote a letter to Mama asking if John had ever been capricious, mean, or selfish. Mama's reply was as positive as ever—however, she did say John had different sides to him. That he thought he had the right to have whatever he wanted, since he was the oldest child and the only boy. Papa's heir. That sometimes he took it too far, but he always apologized and tried to do better.

Patience didn't remember these sides of her brother. Then again, she was the youngest, and her childish memories had no doubt been influenced by the innocence and simplicity of youth, missing the complexities of the man John had become.

"Well, my darling," said Lady Buchanan, squeezing Patience's hand, "I was right about you."

Patience grinned back at her. "Your nephew makes me very happy," she said, and Dorian's eyes melted again with warmth as he looked at her.

The tea was ready, and they were invited to take their places at the round table. Patience served tea while a slight breeze brought the scents of awakening flowers in bloom from the garden. Over the weeks, it had become lush and beautifully manicured. Her work and the work of Dorian, who helped her occasionally, as well that of the footmen and gardeners, had paid off. Life bloomed where there had once been only decay.

She loved it. She loved that she didn't have to hide her interest in botany, that she could sit on a bench and enjoy watching her plants grow. She could take a stroll with Dorian down the narrow, meandering path of white gravel, now flanked by perennial bushes.

To their left, her roses were thriving. She could see their glossy leaves, their buds just beginning to unfurl. Next to them was the striking yellow yarrow. The plumed seed heads of tall grasses nodded gently in the breeze, and she enjoyed the sight of them next to the roses and the yarrow. An oak tree, an ash, and a chestnut tree had replaced the diseased trees, and their green branches swayed in the wind. Ahead, on the right, lavender plants had bees buzzing around them. Interspersed with the lavender were the yellow umbel-shaped flowers of fennel, which would be not just pretty but also useful. Beyond the stone path and past the bursts of lavender and goldenrod, there was a glimpse of the soft blues of periwinkle, which gave a nice splash of cooler color.

And the glasshouse... It was not yet complete, as she had ordered some plants and was waiting for their delivery. But it was clean. It was repaired. It had humidity, windows that opened for ventilation, and a working oven to provide warmth in winter.

She had done this. Her work, her passions—they mattered. She mattered.

Lady Buchanan took a sip of tea and replaced her cup with

the tiniest, slyest smile. "Well, the garden has come to fruition. Clearly, the fertility here is abundant."

Patience's smile died as the older lady's gaze dropped to Patience's stomach.

"That is a good sign, I would say," Lady Buchanan said softly.

Patience felt Dorian go rigid, and mortification struck her. Her hand clutched around the fabric of her gown. A baby... Dorian didn't want one...did he? She looked at him, and his gaze was haunted, looking somewhere into space, with a blank and yet terrified expression.

"Grandbabies," said Lady Buchanan dreamily.

Chastity sighed as she bit into a biscuit and chewed delicately. "Aunt says grandbabies but what she really means are grandnieces or -nephews. She was as close to being our mama as we would ever have, after Papa died, of course. She was not allowed to visit before, but both Dorian and I wrote secret correspondence with her. She even snuck us a couple letters from Mama before our mother died."

Patience nodded, amazed at yet another layer to this broken family. She ached to hug all three of them and make them feel as loved as she felt with her parents. But they were all together now, and she couldn't feel more accepted and appreciated by them.

"Forgive me," said Popwell as he appeared with a tray in his hand. "There is a letter for the duchess."

Patience took the envelope with her name written in an elegant script on the front. With eager fingers, she broke the seal and unfolded the letter, her eyes scanning the contents. With a trembling voice, she read aloud:

Her Grace, Duchess of Rath,
Rath Hall,

. . .

Most Noble Duchess,

It is with great pleasure that we inform you of the acceptance of your paper, "Creation of a Hybrid English Rose," for publication in the Linnean Society of London's quarterly journal. Your work shows exceptional insight and scientific rigor, and we believe it will make a significant contribution to the field.

We cordially invite you to attend a soirée at the Society's headquarters in Burlington House in London on the 8 of May, where your paper will be discussed among our esteemed members. It would be an honor to have you present your findings to our community.

I have the honor to be, Madam,
    Your most obedient and humble servant,
    Sir James Edward Smith
    President, Linnean Society of London

Patience looked up, and her gaze locked with Dorian's. His eyes were big and shone with pride and happiness.

Her stomach lurched with joy at such wonderful news... But as she pictured the room full of well-educated men, listening to her present her paper, she could just imagine their scorn. How dared she—a woman, whose highest goal should be embroidering a perfect rose—dare to create a new hybrid with a method no one had considered previously? Surely they would look at her with judgment, destroy her with questions...

"You must go, Patience," Dorian said. "This is everything you worked so hard for."

It was as though he read her mind. She opened and closed her mouth. She wanted to say yes. She should go. Did the acceptance of her paper not prove that her mind was worthy of recognition, that she needn't shrink herself to fit society's suffocating mold for women?

And yet, she was an eighteen-year-old girl who had never gone to university, who had hidden her true passion for years. Should she not hide it now?

"Oh, darling," said Lady Buchanan. "You must!"

"I see it in your eyes, Patience," said Chastity, squeezing her hand under the table. "Go for both of us... In fact, I'll come, too."

"And I!" declared Lady Buchanan. "I do have a dinner at the Marchioness of Virtoux's, but I'd rather go and see the faces of all those old farts as you rub their noses in it with your brilliant work."

Dorian sat straighter, his expression inscrutable. "You must go, sweet girl," he murmured as he took her hand in his and kissed it. "And I'll make sure they give you the respect you deserve."

The purr of his velvety voice made resolve rise up in her. Perhaps it was his doing, the positive side of his wrathfulness, but she felt a vigorous anger stir in her stomach. She squared her shoulders. Her previous self would have cowered and hidden, afraid of conflict.

Not anymore. She was not afraid.

"You're all correct," she said. "All the more reason for me to go. To show them that a woman's intellect is a force to be reckoned with." Her chin lifted with determination. "I will not be cowed by their prejudice."

A slow smile curved Dorian's sensual mouth. "That's my fearless Patience. You're right—we'll go to London. Let them tremble before you."

"Hear, hear!" toasted Lady Buchanan, and the four of them clinked their teacups together.

Pride suffused Patience's being as Dorian rose to embrace her. She sank into his arms, fortified by his belief in her.

If only he would trust her with whatever demons still plagued him...

34

THE NEXT DAY, Dorian struck the punching bag of a London boxing gym with furious force, each blow landing with a satisfying thud. His muscles were coiled and tense, his bare chest misted with sweat, his mind consumed by the chaos of emotion churning within him.

"You seem agitated," Luhst remarked, leaning against the wall, his expression one of cool amusement. "Did your duchess throw you out of her bed?"

Dorian grunted, not breaking his rhythm. "Shut up, Lucien."

Lucien smirked.

Eccess drank from a flask and punched another bag. "If she did throw you out, I can't say I blame her. With that scowl on your face, you'd scare off even the most determined of women."

Dorian glared at him but kept pummeling the punching bag with relentless intensity.

Irevrence chuckled from his lounging position a nearby

bench. "Perhaps he has lost his touch. Marriage has made him soft in more ways than one."

The other dukes guffawed at the crude joke.

Dorian paused, his chest heaving, and fixed Irevrence with a steely gaze. "I assure you, Sylvester, my 'touch' is as potent as ever. And there's nothing soft about me."

Pryde, who was boxing with Enveigh, scoffed as he paused and gave Dorian a look full of rare mischief. "Is that so?" he asked. "Then why are you here, beating your frustrations into a leather sack instead of satisfying your wife?"

Dorian clenched his teeth. He'd never thought he would fall into this trap. But he loved Patience. And he could glimpse true happiness for the first time in his life. He could sense it, so close it was almost within his reach.

But it was also as far away as ever.

Because he was living a lie. He was in love with his wife, but she was in love with a false version of him. Not with who he really was.

There was only one way out.

"I feel compelled to reveal the truth of her brother's death," he said.

The rhythmic thumps and grunts of the men boxing died away, and it was only Dorian's own fists that were hitting the bag.

Dorian stopped, too, looking at his friends' shocked faces.

Pryde shook his head, his brown hair misted and clinging to his forehead, his chestnut eyes dark and serious on Dorian. "I told you. You should have never married her."

"You're going to risk all of our futures," said Lucien, taking one step forward. Dorian didn't remember last time Lucien looked so serious. "We helped you cover it up!"

"I know," Dorian said, though doubt colored his tone. "But it's all I keep thinking about. Honesty."

Another fierce jab sent the bag swinging. Honesty was what he kept thinking about as he intensified his morning routines. He was split between the desire to keep everything as it was, to continue lying to the woman he loved...

And the need to confess.

When he'd opened up to her, showed her his hand, and then let her take control in their lovemaking... It was one of the best moments of his life.

What would it feel like if he didn't need to pretend anymore, if he could just lay out everything as it was, tell her what had truly happened to her brother?

Relief. Acceptance. Peace. God, how he craved it all.

Eccess stumbled over, cheeks ruddy from overindulgence. "Honesty? Pah! Save that for the pulpit, I say. A man must have his secrets."

The temptation to unleash his wrath upon his so-called friends grew with each glib remark, and he jabbed the bag again.

Enveigh sighed, his gaze distant. "We all bear our crosses, Dorian. Some truths are better left buried, lest they poison what happiness we have found."

The words hung heavy in the air, each man reflecting on his own sins and shortcomings. For Dorian, the weight of his past pressed upon him like a physical burden.

He stepped back from the punching bag, chest heaving. The fear of losing Patience warred with the gnawing guilt that ate at his soul. How could their love flourish when built upon a foundation of deceit?

Yet the thought of witnessing the light fade from her eyes, of seeing her recoil from him in horror and revulsion, was a fate more terrible than he could bear.

Dorian turned to his companions, jaw set in grim determination. "I shall keep my own counsel on this matter. But mark my words, gentlemen. Our sins have a way of finding us out, no matter how deep we bury them."

With that, he strode from the room, leaving behind an uneasy silence and the echoes of his own troubled heart.

35

One week later, Patience walked into the soirée hall of Burlington House in Mayfair. Her hand was hooked through Dorian's bent arm, and her breath caught like she was on fire. Chastity walked right next to her. Lady Buchanan was on Dorian's other side.

Patience couldn't feel the floor under her feet and appreciated Dorian's strong arm supporting her.

The room before her was alight with candles, their reflections sparkling from gilded frames and mirrors. High ceilings were decorated with intricate frescoes, and glittering chandeliers cast a warm glow over the assembled crowd. There were at least fifty men there, with only one or two women. Some scientists were older, distinguished-looking gentlemen with graying hair and neatly trimmed beards while others were younger, with eager, bright-eyed faces.

"I am so proud of you, darling," murmured Lady Buchanan. "Goodness knows, this kind of recognition for a woman was simply impossible in my time."

Patience exhaled shakily. "I think I'm dreaming. And your

support means so much to me. Dorian, Chastity, and you, Aunt, are my new family."

Chastity's hand squeezed around Patience's. "You deserve everything, sister."

Dorian leaned over and murmured, "Enjoy this, sweet girl."

The master of ceremonies announced, "The Duke and Duchess of Rath. Lady Buchanan. Lady Chastity Perrin."

A man in his fifties in a white powdered wig hurried towards them and gave a polite bow to Dorian, then to Patience, and to Chastity and Lady Buchanan.

Applause exploded through the crowd of men, and Patience felt like she was flying. To receive so much recognition and appreciation from the society that had very rarely accepted female contributions and had no female members at all, at her age... She simply couldn't believe this was real. A warm glow suffused her chest. She was seen, respected, appreciated.

Was this really her life? A man she loved was her husband. Her passion in life, her work, was being honored by real scientists. Would she at any moment wake up back in Rose Cottage?

"You're so very welcome, Duchess!" he exclaimed. "Duke, Lady Buchanan, and Lady Chastity, as well, of course! Sir James Edward Smith, at your service." He looked at Patience with great enthusiasm shining through his gray eyes. "I believe I had the honor of corresponding with you, Duchess."

"Pleased to meet you," said Patience, breathless, giving Sir Smith her biggest smile. "I'm very honored my paper was accepted and I'm very honored by this soirée."

"We all are eager to discuss your paper!" Sir Smith assured her. "Please, do come in."

As the three of them walked farther into the room, Dorian leaned to her and whispered, "I couldn't be more proud, love."

The glow in her heart got warmer. "Pinch me, Dorian," she whispered back. "I can't believe this is real."

"It is." He squeezed her hand, and his reassurance allowed her to feel the ground under her feet again.

Sir Smith introduced her to several scientists, including Mr. Jay Essop, the other scientist with whom she had corresponded.

"And this is Sir Bertram," said Sir Smith, nodding to a man in his early thirties with a red face, who stared at Patience and at Dorian with a strangely burning gaze. "Sir Bertram was especially eager to meet you, given he knew your brother... Do I remember that right, Sir Bertram?"

A jolt shot through Patience. Why was he staring at her in that way, as if with some special meaning? Good God, did he by any chance know of John's assault on the barmaid and any other sins her brother had committed?

Dorian became as rigid as a log by her side. He rubbed his gloved hand so hard Patience ached to put her hand into his to calm him down. But she couldn't do so openly in public.

"Indeed. You were Miss Patience Rose, am I right?"

"I was," she said.

Dorian was breathing hard now. She could see color flush his cheeks. Oh goodness, was his wrath about to burst free? A bad premonition settled in her stomach like a heavy stone. Whatever was the matter, she needed to remove Dorian from Sir Bertram.

"Mr. Essop told me about your correspondence. It was I who gifted John the botanical illustrations book back in the day."

"Did you?" Patience chuckled nervously. "In a way, it was you, then, who inspired me to study botany."

He chuckled and reddened even more. "Perhaps. After what happened to John, I never expected the Duchess of Rath to be you, out of all women."

What did that mean? His dark, drunken gaze full of

contempt landed on Dorian, whose teeth were bared. Patience's heart slammed. Something was very, very wrong. Chastity and Lady Buchanan both exchanged puzzled glances.

"Enough," Dorian growled.

Sir Smith and Mr. Essop both looked at each other uncomfortably.

"It is time to talk about your paper, Duchess," said Sir Smith as he gestured towards the fireplace, where there was an empty space.

Still puzzled, and her pulse racing, Patience followed him to stand in front of everyone for a scientific discussion. She clutched her shaking hands together.

Whatever Sir Bertram had referred to, she couldn't think of it now. While Dorian retreated into the shadows at the back of the room, she locked her eyes with Chastity, who smiled and nodded at her reassuringly, which gave Patience strength. She looked at the men around her, who didn't just tinker with roses in their gardens but did botanical and horticultural work for a living, working in universities and botanical gardens.

Just focus on your roses.

"Your discoveries will revolutionize the cultivation of species, Duchess," remarked Dr. Bellamy, a renowned botanist. "Truly remarkable work for anyone, let alone a woman. You must be immensely proud."

"You are too kind, sir," Patience replied, dipping her head modestly even as a bright smile lit her face. "I am gratified my humble studies may advance our understanding in some small way. Botany is my greatest passion."

As Patience basked in the praise and admiration of her colleagues, she forced her mind to turn away from the questions about John that kept running through her head.

A man with salt-and-pepper hair and a keen, appraising look stepped forward. "Your Grace," he began, his voice rich with curiosity, "your work on artificial fertilization of roses to produce a new hybrid is very impressive. I suppose we had not yet thought that creatures other than bees could do that. Could you explain the inheritance of specific traits from each parent variety?"

She could do this. She knew her method like no one. "Of course. From my readings and observations, it appears that certain characteristics from parent plants are more likely to manifest in their progeny under specific conditions. I employed Lamarck's theory of 'the inheritance of acquired characteristics,' but he talks mostly about animals. I applied the same theory to plants—in particular, to the gallica rose and the damask rose."

Another botanist, a younger man, said, "Fascinating! How did you ensure that the artificial fertilization was successful?"

Patience nodded, her smile widening. "Meticulous manual approach. I realized they would pollinate themselves if their stamens were allowed to stay, so I had to remove the stamens before each flower opened."

As the botanists continued to pepper Patience with questions, Lady Buchanan and Lady Chastity stood a mere three steps away from her, their eyes alight with pride and support.

She tried to forget about the incident with Sir Bertram, but her gaze kept returning to Dorian. Why, oh why did she have such a bad feeling now? Like she had missed something vital. Why was Sir Bertram so condescending towards Dorian? And why had Dorian reacted with such fierce nervousness? She could sense his anxiety, and the wrath that he barely managed to contain.

He remained at the edge of the room, his eyes fixed on her. His tall, broad-shouldered frame was tense, his handsome face a brooding mask. There it was, the shadow in his eyes she'd observed in the past three weeks. The other guests gave him a wide berth, intimidated by his formidable presence.

A tangle of emotions rose within her as their eyes met—affection, worry, curiosity at what thoughts churned behind those dark hooded eyes.

Head high, Patience turned back to accept the botanists' accolades, trying to regain her genuine joy. This night was about her. She couldn't let some doubts spoil it.

As the discussion continued, she became more and more relaxed. It was her right to be here, she knew. She deserved every ounce of this. Of course, she wouldn't be here without Chastity's feedback and Dorian's support. But she shouldn't feel shy or guilty or that this might be a mistake. It wasn't. It had been earned through hard work and dedication.

Dorian's eyes remained on her face, but there was movement in the group of people where he stood, and Patience caught sight of Sir Bertram walking towards him.

She kept replying to the scientists' questions, her focus on her work, even though her stomach chilled with the certainty that something bad was about to happen.

In the middle of her reply to the next question, she became aware of raised voices. She trailed off when she saw Dorian looking wrathful, his jaw clenched and eyes flashing, facing off against Sir Bertram. The man jabbed an accusing finger at the duke.

"You have some nerve showing your face here, Rath," the man spat, slurring his words. "After what you did to poor John Rose."

Patience's hand clutched at her neck as her head spun a little. A puzzled murmur ran through the people. She felt Chastity's hand clutch hers. Lady Buchanan stood on her other side.

The feeling of impending doom grew inside her like a

storm. Like she was seconds away from a disaster and could not do a single thing to stop it, only stand and watch the worst thing imaginable unfold.

"Sir Bertram, do calm down," snapped Dorian. "Our having been acquainted in Oxford does not give you the right to speak to me this way."

"What are you going to do? Challenge me to a duel like you do with anyone who angers you? Kill me?"

A collective gasp ran through the crowd. Dorian's eyes blazed in fury.

A chilling realization hit Patience in that moment: Dorian could actually kill a man.

Sir Smith hurried towards Sir Bertram, begging him to come outside and take some fresh air. But the drunk man only waved his hand dismissively.

"I suppose if you can't win fairly," mumbled Bertram, "there's always another convenient suicide to be arranged, isn't there?"

Patience's heart stumbled, her breath catching in her throat. The room seemed to tilt around her as the pieces fell into place with sickening clarity.

John assaulting Christine and Dorian protecting her. The mysterious Oxford incident. The treatment of Dorian's hand for a pistol wound on the day of John's death. Dorian's guilt-ridden eyes...

The truth was at her fingertips, but her mind refused to look at it too closely, refused to put the final piece in the puzzle.

"You go too far, sir," Dorian growled, his voice low and dangerous. "I demand satisfaction. Name your second."

An agitated murmur ran through the soirée. Patience had the sensation of falling into an abyss.

Sir Bertram scoffed. "Of course you do. Heaven forbid anyone speak the truth about the great Duke of Rath."

Dropping Chastity's hand, Patience walked through the crowd, feeling as if she were watching herself from above. She went to stand by Dorian's side. Her voice trembling, she said, "Dorian, what is he talking about? What does he mean about John?"

Dorian whirled to face her, his expression a mix of anger and anguish. "Patience, not here."

"It's never the right place or the right time, Dorian, is it? You can never tell me about what truly happened at Oxford. Can never explain to me..." she said, tears blurring her vision. "That you... That my brother... Oh God."

The full understanding of what must have happened hit her like a slap. Dorian was an angry man.

He used to challenge many men to duels.

But not after Oxford. Not after the Oxford incident involving him and John.

The puzzle pieces moved together in her mind, and this time she was unable to look away, to not see the image that formed.

John assaulted Christine and Dorian stopped him.

His hand was burned, pieces of metal needing to be removed from his flesh...because of a pistol explosion.

On the same day as John's death.

From a gunshot.

Convenient suicide to be arranged...

Her blood chilled and goose bumps rose on her flesh as she acknowledged the truth.

Dorian was not a hero who had protected Christine and walked away.

Dorian had challenged John to a duel. He killed her brother. Then he made it look like a suicide.

She pressed a hand to her mouth, fighting back a sob.

The hall erupted in whispers, curious eyes fixed on the unfolding drama.

Dorian reached for her, his voice urgent. "Patience, please, you don't understand. I never meant for any of this to happen."

She flinched away from his touch, her heart shattering. "Don't. Just...don't."

"What is happening, my darling?" asked Lady Buchanan from just behind Patience, her voice quavering.

"Sister, what is it?" Chastity asked, finally reaching her side after making her way through the crowd.

Gathering her skirts, Patience fled the hall, tears streaming down her face. The cool night air hit her like a wall as she burst through the doors, gulping in desperate breaths.

She heard quick, heavy steps after her and a hand caught her elbow and whirled her around. The courtyard of Burlington House was empty save for several carriages visible in the flickering lights of the gas lamps hanging from them.

It was Dorian. His gaze was haunted. He looked shrunken in on himself, like a cornered animal. "Patience, I— Please don't run away. I wanted to spare you the pain—"

She tore her arm out of his grasp, tears escaping her eyes to run down her cheeks. "Do not dare to ever touch me again!" she cried. "You killed him, didn't you? You fought him in a duel and killed him and arranged it to look like a suicide?"

He closed his eyes tight, as though waiting to be struck, and hung his head between his shoulders. "Yes."

"And you lied to me! You let me believe you were an honorable man... You monster!" she yelled and shoved against his chest. "You selfish bastard! You couldn't control your anger, could you? That's why John is dead."

"Yes."

"And then you married me. Touched me with your hands.

Oh God... Oh God... You made me fall in love with you! My brother's murderer!"

A chasm was opening in her chest, a ragged, bleeding wound.

His head snapped back up and he looked at her with a pained intensity.

"You have lied for years," she growled. "You have lied to me since our wedding day. You should have never married me! What is this, you've been using me to what...make yourself feel better? To atone by giving my family charity for the life you took from us?"

He was breathing so fast she thought he might be having an apoplexy. His eyes filled with tears. To her utter amazement, he dropped to his knees in front of her, grasped her hips, and pressed his head into her stomach.

"I am sorry," he muttered. "Do not leave me. Please, forgive me. My darling..."

"Forgive you?" she spat out.

Fury and pain she never thought she was capable of mixed in her chest like fire and oil. This rage was what he must have felt for years, his whole life.

"You were right, Dorian," she said as she stepped back. "Your father did create a monster. But what your father did to you doesn't excuse what you did to John! To my family! You could have atoned so many times before now! You took a man's life—my brother's! And then you lied to us. Do you understand how long my parents have wondered why he took his own life?"

He was silent. Tears fell from his eyes as he stared up at her, kneeling, his head hung low, as though ready for a final blow. For an executioner's blade. Her heart cracked all over. He stretched one arm out for her, but she stepped back, out of his reach.

"Do not try to find me," she said. "Do not write. Do not look for me. Do not talk to me. As far as I'm concerned, you're no longer my husband and I'm no longer your wife. I know the law won't let us separate, but in every other way, I do not belong to you. I wish I had never met you."

She whirled and ran towards their carriage.

Behind her, Dorian's anguished call of her name echoed in the darkness, but she couldn't bear to look back. The weight of the truth crashed over her, drowning out all else.

There would be no more hiding, no more pretending. Only the stark, painful truth, and the long road ahead to find her way through the darkness.

She was married to a murderer.

36

She was gone.

Dorian's fists clenched and his chest felt like it was quivering in helpless convulsions as he stood in the door frame of her bedchamber—it was the first time he'd ever been there.

He could still smell her here...roses.

Her desk had papers scattered on top of it. Potted plants brought a personal charm to the orderly chaos of the room.

He felt her absence like a giant, sucking hole in his soul.

He'd had her, the wondrous being that was Patience. And she'd fled from him. A monster, she'd called him. And she was right.

He could still see the incredible heartbreak in her eyes, the moment it all fell into place in her mind.

The moment she knew what he had done.

"What a fool I am," he said to the room where his wife couldn't sleep alone.

His stomach burned, and he couldn't stop his hands from shaking. He felt like every muscle in his body was as hard as wood. The need to smash something, to destroy, was coursing through him like poison.

He didn't dare to step inside this room as helpless tears of rage filled his eyes. He should have come to her every night that she had chosen to be with him. He should have come to her and made sure she could sleep, that she slept as deeply as she possibly could. He should have made her feel safe and loved.

Because he loved her more than life itself. And he'd never even told her.

Tension in his chest built to the point where he thought his rib cage would burst.

Unable to look at the empty room any longer, he marched back down the hallway into his bedchamber.

His sister was staying with his aunt in London. Save for servants, he was truly alone.

He picked up the prettiest vase he could lay his eyes on and smashed it against the floor. Shards spilled onto his shoes, onto his breeches. He felt one fly by his face. That didn't make him feel any better at all.

Pryde was right. This was always going to end in disaster.

He didn't deserve her. Didn't deserve to be loved. Didn't deserve to be happy.

He was a murderer.

A lying monster.

He deserved to be punished this way. To touch the divine for a few miraculous weeks, only to have it be snatched out of his hands so cruelly.

He hooked his hands around the edge of the night table and threw it across the room. The crash exploded in his ears, the sound of wood breaking both satisfying and yet not enough to ease the pain.

More... demanded the beast inside him.

More.

He took two large steps towards the chair by his desk and lifted it, throwing it through the window.

Glass and wooden panes shattered. Pain stung him as shards cut his face and ears, stuck in his hair and the creases of his cravat, his shirt, his tailored coat.

The sound of a crashing wood from outside, somewhere below, was much too satisfying.

Good God, came a terrifying thought through the haze of fury, *what if someone had walked by?* He rushed to the window, but thankfully there was no one below, just the splinters and the ruined chair. He wanted his entire world to be in splinters.

He wanted to burn this house to the ground.

Because that what his life would be without Patience.

Pure hell.

One week later, Rath Hall looked like the aftermath of a war.

He'd broken every vase, every cup, and torn apart every painting apart. He'd smashed the mirrors, the sofas, the tables. He was covered in bandages, but only for the worst of his cuts. His knuckles were encrusted in caked blood. He'd destroyed every single thing in the house except for those that Patience had touched, slept on, commented on, or admired.

He slept in minute increments huddled on the sofa where he'd deflowered her, with the curtains pulled closed, in darkness.

I could force her to return, came a selfish, pathetic thought. *She broke the terms of our marriage and left me before the year was over.*

Mrs. Knight had told him she was back at her parents' home. He could go and fetch her and threaten her with the terms of their agreement. Either she would come back, or he wouldn't give her parents the estate and the income he'd promised.

But no. He'd taken so much from her already. He wouldn't take her freedom to choose. She had every right to leave him. She should have done it long ago.

He couldn't bear looking at the garden. And her roses, which were now in full bloom, looking more and more beautiful every day. Resilient and breathtaking, their pink petals reminded him, so painfully, of Patience's lips, the color of her nipples, and of her sweet sex.

Lucien and the dukes came to visit and were appalled at the state of him. They tried to convince him to come to Elysium. Perhaps now he would find solace in Lilith's arms. Or, if not, drinking and playing cards would take his mind off of things. He threw a chair at them.

Mrs. Knight and the footmen watched everything with their usual cold observation.

Not a word of judgment was spoken.

They quietly cleaned and tidied the mess he left behind him. A carpenter came to take measurements for the new window in his bedchamber.

The only rooms in the house that still had furniture were Patience's rooms and his mama's sitting room. He hadn't bathed. He didn't remember if he'd eaten anything. If he drank anything, it was brandy.

Now, he lay curled on the sofa, his body aching inside and out, covered in cuts and bruises.

Not bothering to knock, Mrs. Knight strode into the sitting room. She put a tray bearing toast, butter, and coffee on the tea table.

His eyes burned when she went to the windows and mercilessly shoved the curtains apart.

The sunshine, just like on that day when Patience had

changed him forever, flooded the room, and he covered his face with his hands.

"Perhaps a walk outside," she said. "If you'll forgive my impertinence."

Through the window, he stared at the roses. Vibrant. Glorious. Resilient.

Patience's triumph.

His weakness.

God, what would he do to have her back? She'd return for her roses, would she not? But not for him, surely? Of course not. Not for her brother's murderer.

"No," he said.

His head was exploding.

"There's no more furniture or things to break in the house, Your Grace," said Mrs. Knight. "Perhaps a ride on Erebus, then. He hasn't been ridden for over a week now."

He couldn't imagine allowing himself any pleasure. He had to be punished for what he'd done, and riding, swimming, being in the fresh air would bring him pleasure.

"Leave me," he growled. "Take the food away. Bring more brandy."

Mrs. Knight stiffened, her eyes full of concern. "Your Grace, I'm speaking out of place, but—"

"You are." He shot to his feet. He didn't deserve anyone's concern, let alone this woman's who had been looking after him and his family for years. "Leave."

"But—"

"I will not repeat myself!" he roared, hating himself for raising his voice to her. She didn't deserve this. But he didn't know how else to send her away. "One more word and you will be sacked!"

Mrs. Knight's eyes clouded with hurt and she left him, picking up the tray on her way out.

He put his hands on the curtains to shut them when his eyes fell on the garden again.

The glasshouse.

Goddamn it, he wanted to see it burn. Wanted to cut the new trees with an ax and see the petals of roses flying through the wind.

The last thing that reminded him of her. Of his pain.

Of the wonderful days she'd gifted him.

Yes. He just needed an ax, oil, a candle, and a tinderbox.

He found a tinderbox and candle on the fireplace mantel in the sitting room. Now he needed an ax and the oil. Oil for lamps would do perfectly well. Whale oil, too. He walked through the hallway where the footman stood at attention the moment he saw Dorian, and Dorian suspected he might have been listening through the door.

He barged through the door into the servants' area.

Several of them sat around a large table in the servants' hall, talking about him in quiet, sad voices. Mrs. Knight was there, as well as the cook and her undercooks, the butler, and the footmen. They all sprang to their feet, faces drawn, eyes wide.

"Your Grace," said Mrs. Knight. "Is the servant bell not working? Can I help you?"

"Yes," he barked, his hand clutching the striking steel shaking. "An ax and a bucket of oil. No, five buckets."

The servants looked at each other.

"May I ask what for?" said Popwell carefully.

"No, you may not. Do I have to find them myself?"

"Your Grace, clearly, you're out of sorts," said Mrs. Knight pleadingly.

Mrs. Knight never pleaded. She was the perfect image of a housekeeper, especially since she always closed her eyes on his insanities.

"You are on very thin ice," he growled at her. "Will someone help me or not? I will find them one way or the other."

"Very well, Your Grace," said the butler, hiding his concerned expression under the mask of a respectful servant. "They are in the backyard. Please follow me."

He fetched the ax and a bucket of foul-smelling whale oil. Dorian inspected them and then marched towards the garden, his guts burning with an insane frenzy.

He stopped at the entrance to the garden, feeling the servants' worried eyes on his back. He turned to look over his shoulder. They were lined up outside, three dozen of them, all staring at him. The footmen, no doubt, at the ready to fight whatever fire he might set.

He looked back at the garden. It was not just the fruit of Patience's hard labor. But that of many of these footmen. Every stone laid out lovingly and with care, every tree planted with intent, and her roses... Her goddamn, gorgeous roses.

Angry tears burned his eyes like acid, his chest bursting like it had been set aflame.

No. He couldn't do this to the garden. No matter how much he wanted to hurt himself or her. But he could destroy the place that had made him the monster he was. The place his father had used to forge his son into a blade of wrath.

The place that had made him into a killer.

"Go back into the house!" he roared towards the servants. "Under no circumstances are you to try to save me or come near. Do you understand?"

They didn't move.

"Otherwise you're all sacked! I am not jesting!"

Slowly, they turned around and, one by one, disappeared into the house.

He marched along the beautiful, meandering path, white

gravel crunching under his feet. Bees flew from tree to tree, flower to flower.

He wouldn't touch them.

If he had just destroyed the glasshouse like he had intended many years ago...

He'd feel better. More sane.

Maybe destroying it would heal him, make him a normal man. A man who didn't burst into angry flames, who didn't hit walls and furniture, who didn't yell at people who cared about him.

A man who didn't kill.

Twelve years... he thought as he stood before the door to the glasshouse. He hadn't been inside for twelve years. Even during Patience's work to restore the glasshouse, he had never been inside, the sight of it still unbearable.

He swallowed hard, and his hands ached as he remembered the cuts and the blood. His father's cold indifference.

The glasshouse stood tall and intact, glass panes clean and transparent, held by a freshly painted iron frame. Within the walls, he could see plants. Droplets of condensation clung to the glass, catching the sun and casting playful specks of light.

He lifted the iron bar latch and opened the door. He stepped in.

Behind him, the door shut more forcefully than he expected, and he heard the soft sound of metal knocking against metal.

His heart pounded hard. It smelled just like all those years ago. Wet and grassy, like water and damp earth. He could feel the humid air on his lips. The central aisle of the glasshouse stretched out before him, flanked by citrus trees, palms, ferns, and figs, their leaves almost brushing against each other overhead, creating a tunnel of greenery.

Just like then, he felt small, insignificant, powerless. His only way to deal with his deep emotions, his passionate nature, was to rage.

As his father wanted.

Rage was acceptable—tears and tenderness and laughter were not.

That was what Papa had taught him. To be powerful and successful as a man and as a duke, the only emotion he could have was wrath.

To hell with him, Dorian thought as he poured whale oil over the lemon tree, the ficus, and a palm.

He wanted a strong son? He'd have him.

He poured oil on the ferns and on the flowers he didn't even know the name of to his left. He was shaking. He was not actually sure this would work given the dampness in the air and the foliage. He struck the flint and steel over the tinderbox, and once a spark caught, he used it to light the candle.

He touched the flame to the plants glistening with oil. The oil began burning, and then the dry strands of a palm tree. Slowly, fire began blackening and consuming green parts of grasses and plants. Black smoke rose from the palm tree and the plants. The stench of smoke was acrid and sharp in his nostrils, tickling his throat.

He then threw the still-burning candle to the other side of the glasshouse. That side was a little harder to light because there weren't many dry parts, but the oil did its work. The ferns had some dry tips, and those caught fire quickly, then the thin leaves.

He began coughing. Smoke could escape slowly through a few panes that were open for ventilation, but most of it was trapped in the glasshouse. Despite the humid air, the fire was winning. It was a wet fire, with plenty of smoke.

Dorian watched the fire burning, waiting for the raging

pain to subside, for the anger and resentment against the tyrant who'd dictated his entire life to die away.

He waited for the healing to come.

It didn't.

Instead, his lungs were filling with smoke, and soon it was hard to see. His eyes burned, and he was coughing in rough, dry heaves.

More and more plants down the aisle were consumed by fire. It became very hot, and he was sweating.

What was he doing? Chasing a ghost from his past? Trying to kill himself?

He didn't want to die. He wanted the wrathful part of him to die, the part that had gotten him into so much trouble in the first place. So that he would become worthy of the one person who mattered the most to him.

His wife.

He loved Patience. He wanted to live for her.

And to be worthy of her.

He needed to get out.

He hurried to the door and pushed it.

It didn't move.

Dorian's mind began to go black. It was just like when he was a child, and he felt as helpless and as small and as sinful and as worthless as he had then. He pushed with his shoulder. It was the damned latch! The sound he'd heard before—metal clicking against metal—it was the latch falling into the lock.

Panic made his heart beat faster. He kept pushing, but nothing happened. Goddamn it, he'd left the ax right there; he could see it leaning against the outside wall on the other side of the glass.

He looked around frantically, falling into another coughing fit. There was no trough, nothing except the bucket he'd brought the whale oil in, which was now also consumed in flames. Perhaps in the farthest corner of the glasshouse, which was not yet aflame, he could find a potted palm and use that to break through the glass. But he'd need to get past the wall of fire rising from the oil bucket and the plants that fell onto the path.

He felt faint. His head and his eyes hurt. He could barely breathe. He moved towards the wall of fire, hoping to somehow get past it, but he staggered. Good Lord, he was going to fall right into the fire.

He was going to die, wasn't he?

He swayed and fell to the floor. Panic took over at first as his chest burned, and he exploded in a fit of coughing. His mind was numbing.

These were going to be his last moments. He could feel death present, the strange sense of time slowing, stretching like melting glass.

But he wasn't afraid.

If these were his last moments in his life, he'd spend them well. He'd go feeling love. He'd go thinking of one person who mattered.

Patience...

Love for her filled his whole being. He was full of her gentle touch, the spark of light in her eyes, her lips stretching in a smile that was like his personal sunlight.

He should have told her how much he loved her. He didn't need to rage anymore, throw things out of the window, challenge anyone to a duel. What a waste of time.

As everything began to fade into black, he thought he could smell a whiff of fresh air, and feel someone holding him.

"You goddamn fool! What the hell did you do?"

Lucien.

It was Lucien's voice. Dorian opened his eyes to a blue sky

and white, dreamy clouds and a rising column of black and gray smoke.

Smoke was still billowing from the glasshouse. Footmen and maids were passing buckets of water in a line and throwing it into the building.

He was being held by someone, but not Lucien because Lucien towered over him, his face distorted with rage and concern.

"What if Chastity were here?" Lucien roared. "Have you thought about your sister at all? Your poor aunt? Patience, for God's sake?"

Dorian's throat hurt so much it felt like there was an actual fire inside.

Lucien was right. He hadn't thought of his sister or his aunt.

"I was a selfish arse," he confessed.

"You were," said the voice directly above him.

He looked up and saw Spencer Seaton, a deep frown furrowing his dark eyebrows on his angular face.

He was pressed against Spencer, who was crouching and holding him half upright.

"What are you doing here?" Dorian croaked, his voice like sand against glass.

"I asked him to come," exclaimed Lucien.

Dorian rarely saw Lucien serious. Even more rarely did he see his friend terrified and pacing, like he was now.

"You clearly didn't want to hear from me, or the rest of the seven. Lord Seaton is the only friend of yours I know who is actually...well..."

"Happily married," chuckled Spencer. "But who had been a selfish arse and almost lost everything important to revenge?"

"Well..." Lucien gestured with many circles of his hands. "Yes. Exactly."

"You once saved the woman I love," said Spencer as he looked at Dorian, who actually felt glad to see him. And, although he'd never say it out loud, he agreed with Lucien. He wouldn't listen to his six friends because they were all... corrupted. Some even worse than him.

But Spencer wasn't. He had gotten his life back together.

Dorian sat straighter. Mrs. Knight, who appeared out of nowhere, handed him a glass of water.

"One of the few items of glassware that are left in the house," she said.

He drank the water without protesting, enjoying the cool, soothing comfort that it brought to his sore flesh.

"Explain to me," said Spencer as he moved from crouching to sitting on the white gravel. "What were you thinking?"

"I didn't think," Dorian said. "Well, I did think. I wanted to destroy the glasshouse. My rage started there."

Lucien stood with his arms crossed over his chest. "When he was a child, his father trapped him in there for days. He finally broke through the glass, cutting his wrists and suffering much blood loss in the process."

"Good Lord," said Spencer.

Dorian breathed through his ragged, scratchy throat. He looked around. He was so glad he hadn't destroyed Patience's garden.

Or the glasshouse, which still stood intact, even though her plants had been burned.

He'd buy her new ones. A jungle of new plants if that was what she wished.

Though he didn't expect her to forgive him.

"I—" he said with a coughing breath. "I was a fool."

"You can't go on like this," said Spencer softly. "Take it from another fool. You and I...we're similar. I, too, was consumed by rage, by thoughts of vengeance against the man who had me press-ganged. I, too, lost the woman I loved when I chose revenge and destruction over my love for her. You were there, you know. It was only by surrendering and deciding to change my stupid ways, to be a better man, to forever abandon my rage and my pride and my destruction that I was able to be good enough for her. To be happy."

Dorian stared at him. Yes, he had been there when Spencer had fought with his enemy, had achieved his goal. Only to give it up completely for Joanna, the woman he loved.

He'd witnessed Spencer fall apart and be saved by love, and knew he was now a happy man.

"You're right," he said. "I know I must become better for her. But I—I don't deserve her. I never will. I—" He swallowed hard and leaned closer to Spencer. "I killed her brother in a duel."

This wasn't exactly the full truth, but it would seem too dramatic to say he murdered her brother, and this wasn't the time to explain the details to his friend.

Shock froze Spencer's face for a few moments. He nodded and looked at Lucien, whose raised eyebrows and grim expression said, *I know. It's bad.*

Then he stared into the distance. "But you love her?"

"I do," Dorian croaked out. "I love her more than anything."

He should have spent precious moments with her, telling her how much he loved her, making her smile brighter, making her the happiest woman alive. He should have confessed to her about John, told her the whole truth, dropped his defenses, and surrendered. How silly it all seemed now that his life had almost ended.

Him fighting against himself. His love for her. Running away from her.

When all along he should have run towards her. It was her love that showed him he could be better.

"You have to decide if your love is stronger than your wrath," said Spencer.

Dorian looked at the glasshouse, which now emanated only a weak, dark stream of smoke. The footmen and the maids were taking a well-deserved rest by the house, wiping their foreheads. He wondered distantly why his beast was not raging, why he did not want to take the ax and destroy the rest of the glasshouse.

Perhaps, he thought, he had died in some way in that glasshouse after all. There was no more fear, guilt, or any need to control others or protect himself with wrath.

And instead of wrath, what he felt inside his chest...was love. Wide, deep, all-encompassing, accepting, and forgiving love.

Love that gave him the strength of acceptance and redemption. The power to kneel and ask forgiveness of John's family.

And then he needed to give himself to the authorities. He was a murderer. And even if he was a duke, he needed to be punished for what he had done, take responsibility, and face the consequences.

Even if the punishment for murder was hanging.

Even for a duke.

He looked at Lucien. "I won't say a word about you or Pryde."

Lucien's face fell, but he nodded solemnly. Slowly, he stood up.

"Where's my valet?" Dorian asked. "I have a trip to make."

37

The wind howled through the garden, whipping Patience's skirts about her ankles as she knelt amid the rosebushes. Thorns pricked at her hands through the thin gloves as she carefully snipped away diseased leaves, her shears trembling slightly. The overcast sky hung heavy and gray above, promising a storm.

Patience gazed at the drooping buds of the damask rose, already succumbing to the relentless assault of black spot, a common fungal disease that weakened roses before they could even bloom.

How fitting that they should mirror the state of her own heart, she thought bitterly. The man she loved, the man who had awakened feelings in her she never knew she was capable of, was the same man who had killed her brother.

And yet, like the pretty damask rose, she lacked the strength of the hardy gallica rose.

She also lacked Dorian.

Hot tears stung her eyes, and a strangled sob escaped her throat. She squeezed her eyes shut, willing the tears not to fall.

Her family had been quite distressed to see her return. Everybody knew she had broken Dorian's condition that she couldn't leave him for one year. Things had finally started to improve for them; with the debts paid, some of her papa's meager income went to buy the food that Patience no longer grew. However, the biggest improvement in their position would come after one year, so they still couldn't afford to hire servants or do the larger repairs that Rose Cottage sorely needed. Still, their spirits had lifted significantly.

What would happen now with Dorian? she wondered. Would he punish her family for her disobedience?

Even now, thinking of the way he punished her brought a shudder of desire. Despite her pain at his betrayal, and her broken heart, she still wanted him.

Still loved him.

"Patience?"

Anne's gentle voice broke through her thoughts. Her sister approached, her golden locks teased by the wind, her kind blue-gray eyes filled with concern. Just like the day Papa had brought the news of Patience's engagement, Anne knelt beside her on the damp earth. She laid a comforting hand on Patience's shoulder.

"Some things never change," she chuckled. "Even as a duchess, Patience still takes care of her roses."

Patience chuckled softly as she cut off yet another diseased leaf. "Have you been working on another mathematical treatise?" she asked.

"Of course," said Anne. "With Papa's debts cleared, I do have more time and peace of mind."

Patience smiled sadly.

"Cheer up, darling," said Anne. "Remember the basket? The lock?"

Patience frowned. She hadn't done the basket exercise for a

few weeks now. Every day with Dorian, she had felt less and less need to turn away from her sadness, despair, or fear. And she'd started to listen to what those feelings were telling her.

"I don't want to," said Patience.

Anne raised her eyebrows. "No? What are you talking about? You were always the first one to suggest doing it."

"I haven't done it for weeks."

Anne nodded. "That's why you came back so sad."

Anger roiled in Patience's gut. Her first instinct was to shove it down, like she had done her entire life.

But living with Dorian taught her not to.

And she didn't chase it away. Didn't turn away from it or lock it in a basket. She was angry. She had every right to be.

"No," Patience whispered, her voice cracking. "That is not why I came back sad. I came back sad and angry because the man I love betrayed me."

Anne swallowed and looked around. "Patience, darling, are you sure you want to say this all out loud?"

But around them were just the trees and bushes swaying violently in the wind, pieces of leaves and branches flying in the air.

Mama, Papa, and her other sisters were inside. Perhaps she and Anne should be, as well.

"I am very sure," said Patience with more strength than she had ever heard in her voice. "He lied to me. He let me believe he was a man of honor when he had hidden the worst possible secret, let me believe what I wanted to believe. How could the man to whom I gave my heart treat me so? I feel so foolish, so naive to have trusted him."

Patience could feel the handle of her garden scissors pinch painfully into her palms.

She hadn't told any of her family about the truth of John's death. She still felt loyal to Dorian, silly her. She didn't know if she could tell her family their son- and brother-in-law—the man who had saved them from debt—had murdered John.

"Oh, darling," Anne said as she gently pried the sharp scissors from Patience's hand and laid them behind her, as far away from Patience as she could. "It's not your fault."

Patience shook her head vehemently, a swell of anger rising in her chest. "I should have seen it. I sensed the darkness in him, the barely restrained rage and cynicism. Yet I pushed it aside, choosing to see only the good, only what I wanted to believe." She looked at Anne imploringly, desperate for answers. "Was I wrong to love him, despite the signs? Does it make me wicked to still yearn for his touch, even as I despise what he's done?"

"Oh, Patience." Anne pulled her into an embrace as the sobs overtook her. "It's not wrong to have loved, to have seen the best in someone. Never apologize for the desires of your heart. It's just perhaps you should do the basket—"

"I love you, sister, but please stop talking about the basket!" Patience said and pulled back. "And you should stop using the basket, too, darling. Allow yourself to feel the pain and anger and talk about it. Keeping it inside will only poison you." Patience drew a shuddering breath and met her sister's sympathetic gaze.

"You have changed," said Anne as she eyed Patience. "I thought you had but now I know. You're like...like a true duchess now."

Patience chuckled and turned her face to the wind, letting it dry her tears. "I've spent so long trying to be the perfect daughter. The mask of an innocent girl untouched by life's cruelties felt safe. But I see now that true strength lies in acknowledging the shadows within myself and others. I cannot go back to the girl I was."

She stood, looking out over the wind-tossed garden with

new eyes. The storm clouds on the horizon no longer seemed so menacing. Like pruning dead leaves from the roses, she could shed the beliefs and practices that were holding her back and put her energy into growing stronger and more vibrant. She could let go of her past self and emerge anew.

Patience squared her shoulders, a sense of purpose infusing her. She may have fallen in love with a man with terrible secrets, but she would not let him drag her into darkness and despair. No, she would find the strength to confront him and the uncomfortable truths his presence in her life had revealed. She was now a recognized scientist, a duchess in her own right, unafraid to face the realities of life and death, pain and joy. The naive girl who had once frolicked amid the roses was gone. In her place stood a woman armored with wisdom and resilience, ready to fight for her own happiness.

"I must speak with him," she declared, turning to Anne with fire in her eyes. "I'm not yet ready to forgive, but I will hear his explanation and judge for myself the man he truly is. And I will no longer shy away from my own anger and heartache. It's time I seized control of my own life."

Anne smiled and rose to join her, tucking a stray curl behind Patience's ear with sisterly affection. "There she is. There's the strong, unstoppable woman I always knew was inside you. You will weather this storm and come out the other side even more radiant."

Patience nodded, a ghost of a smile on her lips as she gazed out at the windswept garden. She linked arms with Anne and strode determinedly back to the house, the wind at her back propelling her forward into an uncertain but uncompromising future. The Patience of old was gone, buried in the garden with the ghosts of the past. In her place walked a duchess, ready to fight for her own happiness.

38

The carriage jolted to a halt outside Rose Cottage and Dorian descended.

He stopped and stared at the house where Patience had grown up. Where John had grown up. His heart squeezed. It was so small, old, and crumbling. He wished he had not only paid off Mr. Rose's debts but given him money to do much-needed repairs.

The garden behind the house was quite large, and he imagined Patience working there for hours like she had worked in Rath Hall. Weeds sprouted here and there, vines of ivy wrapped around a tree, and the leaves of some plants had large holes, perhaps eaten by slugs. Knowing Patience, Dorian was sure this wouldn't have happened had she lived here the past months. And even though she'd now been back for over a dozen days, the unkempt garden suggested she was too sad or tired to properly care for it.

His fault.

He swallowed and reached into the carriage and picked up a leather folder that held important papers. He tucked it under his arm and proceeded down the gravel path towards the cottage.

It was time to pay for his sin. To atone. To surrender. To take responsibility.

He knocked, the hollow sound echoing the emptiness in his heart.

The door creaked open, and Patience stood before him, her golden hair framing a face etched with worry and sorrow. Even so, she was a divine, feminine vision that pierced his blackened soul.

Seeing her was like gulping down pure water after years of drought. He drank in her features, searching for any signs of distress. She was paler, thinner, with dark circles under her eyes, and he didn't like that at all. She was dressed in one of the gowns that had been made for her while she was in Rath Hall. It was the color of lilacs, with delicate embroidery of purple leaves and white roses, which suited her clear complexion and highlighted her natural blush.

"Your Grace," she murmured.

"I know you told me not to look for you," he said, unable to tear his gaze away from her. "I will not take much of your time. I promise you, I didn't come to take you back." He gestured at his leather folder. "I must discuss this with you...my will...and then I'm off to London."

Her eyebrows drew together, and her eyes widened in worry. "Your will?"

"Yes. If you allow me to come in and take a few moments of your and your family's time, I will explain everything."

She nodded. "Please, come in."

He followed her inside, noting the simple furnishings with scratches, tears, and signs of wear. The walls had cracks in the plaster, and the embroidery hangings were yellowed and had moth holes. Yellow stains marred the ceiling, the result of a leaking roof. Everything was in stark contrast to the opulent grandeur of Rath Hall.

She led him into the sitting room, which looked more like a workroom where clothes were sewn, laundry was hung, and preserves were made. It smelled faintly of vinegar.

As Patience turned to face him, Dorian felt the weight of his sins pressing upon his shoulders.

Somewhere down the hall, perhaps in the actual kitchen, several female voices chattered, and occasionally laughed. And he guessed that Mrs. Rose and her daughters were in there, preparing supper or cooking something judging by the clanking of cutlery and dishes.

But Patience didn't belong here anymore, he thought, and was even more satisfied with the contents of the folder he had brought.

"Is your papa at home?" he asked. "Your mama and your sisters?"

She stood so far away from him, like a stranger, and he fought an impulse to stretch his arm out to her and beckon her to come closer.

"They are," she said.

So distant. When she'd left him, darkness had engulfed him. But he couldn't rely on her to always bring him light. He must find it on his own.

And this was the start.

"By the cheerful sounds, am I correct in assuming you have not told them about John?"

She shook her head. "I have not."

He nodded. He thought she wouldn't. He hoped deep down she still had some loyalty to him. But he knew he had never earned that loyalty. "Might they join us here?"

She searched his face, then nodded and left the room. When she returned with her whole family, the Roses gasped and called out cheerful greetings he didn't deserve. The small sitting room was soon crowded.

"What brings you here, Duke?" asked Mr. Rose with a smile from ear to ear. "Have you come to take our Patience back home?"

Dorian fiddled with the folder in his hands. It was quite a freeing sensation to realize the wrathful anger had no more power over him. Surrender and acceptance were both the hardest and easiest things he'd ever had to do. "I'm afraid not, sir. I have come to make a full confession, Patience, both to you and your esteemed family. The burden of my past weighs heavily, and I can no longer allow it to cast a shadow upon our...connection."

His voice caught on the final word. He had no right to hope. And still, he did.

Never mind. There wouldn't be any hope left after he returned to London.

"Whatever could this be?" asked Mrs. Rose as she and the girls took their places on the sofa and the free chairs. Patience remained standing. Was she nervous?

"Please, Your Grace, speak your truth," she said.

Dorian's burned hand ached under the glove. He clenched and unclenched his fist, massaged it with his healthy hand. He had finally gone to his physician, who had treated his skin with salves. Dorian had been removing the glove whenever he was alone and when he slept, and the pain and swelling were getting much better.

He had resolved to make this confession—he was ready—and yet, the words he was about to say burned his throat like acid. Slowly, he took a lungful of air, commanding the tremor in his body to calm. When the words finally came, he didn't cower. Didn't hide. He had to take this straight on, and he looked directly into each of the Roses' eyes. He deserved to have to look into the eyes of these people, from whom he robbed a son and a brother, and receive the full strength of their wrath and pain.

And then he let the ax fall.

"I ended John's life."

Silence fell over the room as Patience sucked in air.

"John...who?" asked Mrs. Rose in confusion, looking around at her family for help.

"Your son, Mrs. Rose," he said softly, and her eyes grew into two saucers. "I was with him in Oxford. One night, I was a witness to him committing a grievous offense against a young woman. I intervened to defend her honor. It got very heated, and I challenged him to a duel. Sir Bertram witnessed that challenge. That's why he was so surprised I married you, Patience."

Mr. Rose jumped to his feet, his face paling at first, then reddening to beetroot.

"My John? An offense against a woman? He'd never—"

"Of course he'd never—" began Patience's mama.

"Papa, Mama," said Beatrice—the second oldest sister, Dorian remembered. "You knew John wasn't all goodness and honor. We all knew it, didn't we, sisters?"

Her sisters all exchanged glances, looking sheepish.

"It's true," said Emily, the oldest. "I knew him best. He could be...quite petty. And vengeful, about small things. If I didn't give him what he asked, he would break my doll...and he broke your bottle of French brandy, Papa, and said it was Beatrice."

"No..." mumbled Mrs. Rose. "He didn't mean it, surely."

"It's just that you closed your eyes to his misgivings," said Clarice, who Dorian remembered was the third eldest sister.

"Locking them in the basket, perhaps?" suggested Patience.

Anne's eyes shimmered with unshed tears, her porcelain features a mask of conflicting emotions. "I...I had suspicions of John's cruelty, although I did not remember him doing anything to me. But to hear it confirmed..." She drew a shuddering breath, her slender frame trembling.

Silence fell on the room as Mrs. Rose and Mr. Rose stared at the worn, moth-eaten carpet.

"What happened during the duel, Duke?" asked Patience softly.

"While our seconds and I were distracted, I noticed John doing something to my pistol," he said. "I was sure of it. But his second assured us of Mr. Rose's honor, and then both seconds inspected the pistols and found no fault. However, when I fired...it burst right in my hand."

Slowly, he removed his glove. He winced when leather scratched over the aching flesh. Heat flushed through him. Even if he had allowed Patience to see it, letting others see it was another matter. But he had to take all of the pain on, all of the discomfort, and accept his punishment. Slowly, he stretched it out for everyone to see, the burn scars like the landscape of an uninhabited world.

He cleared his throat as the memories of that morning clawed into him. "Wrath completely took me over. Had I been a normal human, a balanced man, or someone who has your ability, Mr. Rose, to turn away from dark emotions, your son would still be alive."

Mrs. Rose released a shuddering breath, her eyes filled with tears. "I don't want to know. Please, stop. We should not talk about this."

Patience watched him with the stoic expression of a queen. "I want to know about my brother's last minutes. And you all need to know, too. What happened, Duke?"

He swallowed hard. The horror and pain in their eyes—he

needed to bear it and finish his story, tell them what was in the folder, and leave. He owed them that much. "Overcome with rage, I strode to him. I did not know what I was doing. All I could see was red. I attacked him. We struggled. He had his charged pistol in his hands. It fired with my finger on the trigger. He died in my arms."

Silence fell on the room, and then a pained sob broke it as Mrs. Rose turned to Anne and buried her face in her daughter's shoulder, her body shaking in tremors. Mr. Rose stood stoically, breathing hard, his mouth crooked as he attempted to hide his grief but was unable to do so.

"And then you arranged it to look like suicide," finished Mr. Rose.

Dorian nodded. "I was a coward. An angry, despicable coward. I made it look like a suicide, and then I left for Rath Hall."

Patience frowned. "For your papa's funeral?" she asked. "Chastity said you came back with an injured hand and that you were not yourself..."

"Just prior to John's assault on the barmaid, I received a letter informing me of my papa's death," he said.

Patience's breath shuddered. "It is little wonder you lashed out as you did. You would not have been yourself after such a letter... That must have been quite a shock for you. He was your papa...even if he was a monster."

How did she do this? He was telling her exactly how he'd killed her brother, and she still found a way to feel compassionate towards him.

Mr. Rose lost the battle to contain his emotions, and his face contorted with rage as he pointed an accusing finger at Dorian. "You murdered my son! I don't care what he did. You had no right to take the law into your own hands!"

Dorian flinched at the accusation, the weight of his guilt

pressing down on his shoulders. It was the simple truth—he had no right to play judge, jury, and executioner. And yet he had.

Mrs. Rose, her eyes red and swollen from crying, glared at Dorian with a mixture of grief and fury. "How dare you come into our home and tell us this now? After all these years, you finally have the decency to confess? You robbed me of my son, and now you expect us to understand?"

Each word felt like a dagger to Dorian's heart. He could feel the pain and anger radiating from Mrs. Rose, and he knew that no amount of apologies could ever erase the harm he had caused.

Emily jumped to her feet, her fists clenched at her sides. "You killed our brother and then had the audacity to marry our sister? Was this all some sick game to you?"

Beatrice, usually the most level-headed of the siblings according to Patience, couldn't contain her anger. "I know John had his faults, but he was our brother! You had no right to take his life, no matter what he did!"

Clarice's and Frances's faces were flushed with anger. Clarice declared, "We trusted you, Your Grace. We welcomed you into our family, and all this time, you were hiding the truth about our brother's death!"

Anne, tears streaming down her face, looked at Dorian with a mixture of disbelief and betrayal. "I looked up to you, Your Grace. I thought you were a man of honor. But now I see that you're nothing more than a liar and a murderer!"

The accusation hit Dorian like a physical blow. The guilt was overwhelming, threatening to crush him under its weight.

Patience stood in the middle of the room, her face torn in a helpless expression. "Please, everyone, let's try to remain calm. I know this is a lot to process, but we must try to understand—"

Mr. Rose cut her off, his voice shaking with fury. "Understand? What is there to understand, Patience? This man killed your brother and then married you! How can you defend him?"

Mrs. Rose, her voice hoarse from crying, turned her anger towards Patience. "And you! How long have you known about this? How could you keep such a secret from us, from your own family?"

The room descended into chaos, with the Rose family hurling accusations and insults at both Dorian and Patience. The air was thick with tension and raw emotion, as years of grief and betrayal came pouring out in a torrent of angry words. They could no longer stuff their negative feelings in a basket and pretend that all was well. And it seemed as if everything they'd been tamping down for more than a decade was bursting forth.

Dorian stood silently in the middle of the room, his head bowed, accepting the fury of the Rose family. He knew he deserved their anger, their hatred. He had taken the life of their son and brother, and no amount of explanation or justification could ever erase that fact.

A few minutes later, the angry, pained shouts calmed down, and Dorian opened his leather folder. "I do not deserve your forgiveness. And I'm not daring to ask for it. All I wanted to do was to tell you the truth. I do, however, want to tell you that I would give anything, *everything* to go back and to stop myself in that moment. To take control of my anger and to have compassion, like all of you have. I'd do anything to keep your son alive, Mr. and Mrs. Rose."

Some of Mr. Rose's anger fell from his face, and the man nodded solemnly. "I...er...I appreciate you saying so, Duke."

Dorian exhaled sharply, expecting for the man to do something, but he only stared at him with great sadness and tears in his eyes. "Sir, if you would like to beat me, I will not fight back," said Dorian.

Mr. Rose exhaled a long breath and stared at him for a while. Dorian stood, waiting for the man's reaction, hoping he would take a swing at him.

"That is not needed, Sir," said Mr. Rose. "I have no wish to beat you."

Dorian nodded and shook his head. He did not deserve these people. He didn't deserve Patience.

But he wouldn't stop trying.

He retrieved a document he'd had his solicitors compose yesterday. "This is my will. Patience, you will get everything I own, and should you be pregnant...should there be an heir, he will inherit my title. An heiress will have a substantial inheritance and a dowry, which no one can touch but her when she is grown enough to decide to marry."

"Dorian..." began Patience, but he didn't let her finish.

He had to go through this and leave to face his destiny.

"However, in the event that my title is stripped from me in a few weeks or months, this document"—he raised another paper—"transfers everything, all assets except Rath Hall, which remains tied to the title, to your name, Patience. The state cannot touch it or take it from you, even if you're no longer the duchess."

Everyone opened their mouths to ask something, and Patience took a step towards him, worry on her face. But he wasn't finished, and he raised the third document, which he laid on the tea table in the small space between stacks of books and a heap of fabric.

"And this document, Mr. Rose, is for you. I hereby free you of the clause of our marriage contract whereby Patience must spend one year with me. As of today, you are granted an estate nearby and an income of two thousand pounds, which, I believe, will be enough to repair your home and help you restore your tenant properties, as well as provide you a good income and a worthy dowry for your daughters should any of them wish to marry. Money will never return John to you, but I hope it will give you some relief in your circumstances."

He handed the leather folder to Patience, who watched him with an open mouth.

He locked eyes with her amid the shocked stares of her family as the room fell into complete silence. He drank in her features for the last time. The softness of her pink lips, the delicate curve of her cheekbones, and the way her golden hair framed her beautiful face like a halo. Her blue eyes, usually so warm and inviting, were now filled with a mixture of pain, confusion, and love. It was a sight that would be forever etched into his memory, a bittersweet reminder of all that he had lost.

"Goodbye, the light of my life," he said softly. "I will love you till my last breath."

Patience's eyelashes trembled as her eyes filled with tears. She swayed towards him but didn't take a step. He nodded to the Roses and walked out of the room, through the corridor, and through the door and into the open air.

The sun had begun to set, painting the sky in shades of orange and pink. It seemed almost mocking, the beauty of the world when his own was crumbling to dust. He strode towards the carriage, his vision blurring with the tears he fought back.

He got into the carriage and it pulled away from the house, the horses' hooves drumming. He closed his eyes and leaned back against the seat. His mind still reeled with the pain and accusations the Roses had thrown at him. His life was over. His heart was shattered. God knew, he had earned every last piece of that pain.

And together with the guilt, a blessed sense of peace began to seep into him. There was no more anguish, no more wrath to torment him. No more demons to escape. Because he had finally done the right thing. He'd leave this life with peace and a clear conscience. He'd still be in hell, but at least he'd spend the last days, weeks, or months of his life in peace.

He looked down at his hands. He realized he'd forgotten to put on the glove, and his mangled hand was free. Strangely, he had no more desire to hide it. On the contrary, it was a relief to feel the air on his scarred flesh.

Everything was in the open now. He was surely going to his death, but his soul felt lighter.

"Dorian, wait!" a voice called out, clear and strong. A dear, familiar voice.

He froze for a moment, scarcely daring to breathe. Then he turned and looked out of the window. Patience ran after the carriage.

His heart slamming hard, he knocked on the opposite wall to signal the driver to stop. The carriage came to a halt, and he descended.

"Where are you going?" she demanded as she stopped before him, breathing hard.

"To London," he rasped. "To give myself to the authorities."

Her face slackened in shock. "To... But you will hang."

He nodded. "I will accept whatever punishment is suited."

She shook her head. "That's why the will...all these documents..."

"Yes. My affairs are in order. You will be protected, secure, free to do whatever you wish for the rest of your life. Just—" He had to catch a breath before saying the next part. "Just don't marry anyone you don't love. Don't give your freedom away for anything else."

She gasped. "No, this is ridiculous. Mama and Papa are not pressing charges."

"They should. You should. I deserve it."

He turned to climb back into the carriage, but she stopped him. "I will never do that. Neither will Papa and Mama. I'm sure they've already forgiven you."

Forgiven him? "How could they?" he asked.

She swallowed hard and laid her hand on his cheek. "I know I have."

His heart cracked open, unfurled like a rose in the first rays of spring, her words a balm to his soul. He leaned into her touch, savoring the warmth of her palm against his cheek, the tender caress a lifeline in the tempest of his emotions.

"Patience," he whispered, his voice ragged with longing. "I don't deserve your forgiveness. I don't deserve you."

She shook her head, her eyes shimmering with unshed tears. "But you have it, Dorian. You have my forgiveness, my love, my everything. I cannot bear the thought of losing you."

He closed his eyes, a single tear escaping to trail down his cheek. "I am a broken man, Patience. A murderer. How can you still want me, knowing the blood that stains my hands?"

Her thumb brushed away the tear, her touch infinitely gentle. "Because I see the man beneath the scars, the beautiful soul that has been battered but not broken. You are more than your worst mistake. You are the man I love, the man I choose, now and always."

A shuddering breath escaped him, the weight of her words settling into his very bones. He reached up to cradle her face in his hands, his gaze searching hers for any hint of hesitation or doubt. There was none, only a love so fierce and pure it stole the breath from his lungs.

"I don't know what I did to deserve you," he murmured, resting his forehead against hers. "But I swear, I will spend the rest of my days making you happy."

She smiled then, the smile that always flooded his heart with sunlight. "You already are, my love. You already are."

And then she was kissing him, her lips soft and insistent against his own. He surrendered to her, pouring all the love and gratitude into the slide of his mouth over hers, the gentle nip of his teeth, the sweep of his tongue.

When they finally parted, breathless and flushed, he knew he could never let her go. She was his salvation, his guiding light, the beacon that would lead him out of the darkness and into a future brighter than he'd ever dared to dream.

And in that moment, he knew he was home.

Patience squeezed his hand, her eyes shining with happiness and love. "I love you, Dorian."

Dorian felt the last vestiges of his old, bitter self fall away.

For with Patience by his side, he could do anything, be anything. She was his redemption, his salvation, his everything.

"It is me who loves you, sweet girl," he murmured. "I'll spend the rest of my days proving myself worthy of the precious gift of you."

39

Two weeks later...

Patience hurried up the stairs of Chastity's round turret in the east wing of Rath Hall, her heart pounding. Just a moment ago, she had heard a loud explosion coming from the tower and feared for her sister-in-law's safety.

As she burst through the door, she stopped. Shattered glassware littered the floor, and a thin layer of smoke hung in the air. Chastity stood in the middle of the room, her hair disheveled and her face smudged with soot.

"Chastity! Are you all right?" Patience rushed to her side, checking for any signs of injury.

Chastity coughed and waved away the smoke. "I'm fine, sister. Just a small mishap with my latest experiment."

Patience looked around the sunlight-filled laboratory, taking in the damage. The large tables in front of the diamond-pane, leaded windows were covered in broken beakers, flasks, and test tubes. The air smelled faintly of burnt alcohol.

The two women opened the windows to let out the smoke and fumes, then made their way to the adjacent room, a cozy space filled with bookshelves and comfortable armchairs. The same diamond-pane windows let in great light for reading here. Patience rang the bellpull for tea as Chastity sat in an armchair. Patience couldn't help but notice how her hands shook slightly.

"What happened?" Patience asked, helping Chastity to a nearby chair.

Chastity sighed. "I was heating spirits of wine with quicklime, trying to increase the concentration of ethanol. I must have added too much quicklime, and the vapors ignited."

Patience shook her head, relief washing over her. "Thank goodness you're not hurt."

Chastity nodded but said nothing.

"Are you sure you wouldn't like to lie down, Chastity?" Patience asked gently. "Shall I send for a physician?"

Chastity shook her head, a determined look in her eye. "I'm fine, sister. It's just frustrating, you know? I'm so close to a breakthrough, but it feels like the world is against me."

Patience reached out and squeezed her hand. "I understand completely. It's not easy being a woman in science. But you're not alone, Chastity. We have each other."

Mrs. Knight knocked and brought in a tray bearing a teapot, teacups, and a plate of biscuits. When she retreated, Chastity poured, the teapot shaking in her hand, and the tea spilled on the saucer.

"Oh, I'm sorry," said Chastity as she picked up a snow-white linen to wipe up the brown drops. "I've never had a visitor here before. Mrs. Knight and the maids don't count. And I'm afraid my social manners are the weakest quality I have."

Patience smiled kindly at her. "Please, sister, do not worry. I'm not a visitor. We're family."

Chastity nodded, her sky-blue eyes wide and beautiful behind her spectacles. "We are. Never did I think I'd have a sister who's a scientist, as well."

"Neither did I," said Patience, beaming as she picked up her teacup and sipped.

"Would you like a biscuit?" asked Chastity, picking up a plate of cinnamon biscuits. Patience swallowed an onslaught of nausea.

"Oh, no, thank you. Those make me queasy."

"Right..." Gingerly, she placed the plate as far away from Patience as she could—so far that it balanced precariously on the edge of the table. "I'm sorry, sister. I didn't mean to do anything that made you uncomfortable. In your condition, especially."

Patience shook her head and sipped more tea. "Don't worry, you couldn't know they would disturb me. And you can always learn social manners if you wish. Though I would argue you have much more important qualities. Like a brilliant mind many would envy."

Chastity picked up her own cup and sipped. "Don't most ladies and gentlemen value beauty over brains?"

Patience cocked her head. "I'd take brains any day. I hope my child is as brilliant as you are."

Chastity's normally serious expression brightened as a small smile curved her lips. "Thank you, sister. I hope the baby will be the perfect blend of you and Dorian—beautiful, strong, and fiercely intelligent." Before Patience could respond, she continued, "It's fascinating the changes in a female body during pregnancy. I hope you will allow me to document the progress of your condition."

Patience sprayed a little of her tea with a chuckle, her own social manners flagging. "Oh, darling, of course! Are you conducting new research on pregnancy?"

"No," said Chastity. "But I do not come across pregnant women often—especially not those that are willing to answer questions from time to time. You never know what I might observe or what use I might find for the data in the future. Wouldn't it be useful to know how to help pregnant women with nausea, for instance?"

Patience beamed. "It would. And since we're already slipping into the meat of the discussion, allow me to officially call the first meeting of the Misses with Microscopes Club to order!" Only a few days earlier, they had decided to create a club for themselves and any other women who wanted to study science and support each other in a society where they had to fight to be heard.

Chastity grinned and straightened her back. "Indeed!"

"What are you working on?" asked Patience. "And can I be of help?"

"I have a theory that infection, often called 'blood poisoning' or 'sepsis,' occurs when wounds are not handled with clean instruments or hands. I believe some impurities enter, so small we cannot see them. I am working on a disinfectant that will, I hope, kill any impurities that may enter a wound."

"Fascinating!" said Patience as she set her cup on the table. "That is what you put in Dorian's medical baskets! You must need some real people to try out your solutions on."

"Well," Chastity said and sighed. "Yes. Indeed, I do. But I don't have patients here."

"Of course not. Then how do you experiment and learn?"

Chastity pursed her lips. "All right. This is a secret club, isn't it? Nothing we say here can be shared with anyone."

"Of course not. Not unless specifically allowed."

"Even if you might think it's in my best interests to inform say...my brother?"

Patience frowned. "Goodness, what in the world are you talking about?"

"You must promise you won't say anything to Dorian. That's what I'm trying to say."

"I won't."

"Even if you think it's dangerous?"

"Even if I think it's dangerous."

Chastity seemed to relax a little. "Good. It's Lady Seaton, Jane. Do you remember her?"

"Of course. She's Lord Richard Seaton's wife."

"Exactly. She…um. Did you know her half-brother is Thorne Blackmore?"

Patience's eyebrows drew together. "The owner of Elysium?"

Chastity chuckled. "Yes. Did Dorian tell you about him?"

"He did. He told me about the monthly meetings he used to join, the ones Lucien and the rest of the dukes go to."

Chastity licked her bottom lip at the mention of Lucien and raised an eyebrow in an angry contemplation. "Yes. That one. Anyway, when I told her about my project, she made an interesting suggestion."

"Oh?" asked Patience.

"Mr. Blackmore has an associate…or rather a close friend. The same way the seven dukes are close, that's how Mr. Blackmore is close to that man. His name is Brace Sterling, and he's a doctor in Whitechapel… Well, he's not officially licensed. He spent some years in Oxford, but he never graduated. He runs a free clinic and a hospital for the inhabitants of Whitechapel."

Patience blinked, her mind putting all the pieces together. "Oh. And so you…?"

"I volunteer there. No official hospital in London wanted to recognize my work, my research, or support my medical claims," she said, her voice breaking but her back straight.

She may not know the perfect manners of a socialite, but she was every bit a duke's sister—proud and stoic.

Patience shook her head. "Why?"

"Because I'm a woman," she said. "I swear, Patience, had I had any other passion suitable for a woman—embroidery, painting, music, anything at all—I'd be so happy. Had I had a male organ, my research would have been accepted with open arms. I'd have received funding. I'd have earned respect. But all I got was rejection and pitiful glances. As if wearing a skirt means I do not have the brains or courage to do medical research and help people."

Patience sighed. "I hate that this is so for you. That's why we have created our club. And that's why it's secret."

"And that's why I had to go and ask Mr. Sterling if he would consider using my methods on selected patients and allowing me to observe them while also caring for them as a nurse."

Patience nodded. "And he agreed?"

"He was the only one who agreed. I suppose, in the underworld of London, the social rules and standards of the ton don't matter. In the slums, women can do science and run their own businesses. And bastards can be kings."

Patience gave a sigh and couldn't stop a chuckle. "Bastards and women of science. That's quite a team."

Chastity giggled, and Patience joined her. Together, they laughed, spilling tea and not caring.

"If he needs a botanist, I'm happy to help," said Patience as she wiped away tears of laughter. "But are you quite safe in Whitechapel?"

"Of course," Chastity said and hesitated. "I mean, besides being alone with a single man... And walking among thieves and criminals..."

Patience's eyes widened. "Goodness. Are you sure—?"

"It's Jane's brother's area. Thorne Blackmore is the king of Whitechapel. Nothing happens without him knowing. I'm perfectly safe."

"Is Mr. Sterling a gentleman?"

Chastity's cheeks flushed. "Oh, please. There's no danger of any man trying anything with me. No man would see a woman in me, or anyone they might be interested in!"

Patience blinked. "Forgive me for such harsh words, but that is nonsense!"

Chastity chuckled bitterly. "Oh, it is not. Not that I'm interested in marriage in any event."

"Truly?" asked Patience. "Have you never fancied anyone?"

To Patience's great surprise, Chastity's cheeks flushed. "Well...I wouldn't say that."

Patience grinned. "I knew it. Who was it?"

Chastity scoffed and reddened even more. It was quite fascinating to see this smart, confident, brilliant woman blush like a little girl. "I...er..."

"You know I will never tell anyone. You're my sister and my friend, and a fellow Miss with a Microscope!"

Chastity looked at her hands. "Um..."

"Come on, Chastity, it feels good to open up. Have you never talked about this with anyone?"

"No. I suppose there's no harm in it. It's in the past anyway, and nothing will ever be possible. Nor do I want it to be."

"Well, never say never... Who is it?"

Chastity sighed and put her teacup down with resolve. "It is...it *was*...Lucien."

Patience raised her eyebrows. "Lucien? I suppose I shouldn't be surprised. He does favor you. I just didn't realize you favored him, too."

"You're mistaken. He does not favor me, nor did he ever. In my silly adolescent years—and only because we practically grew up together—I had thought I loved him. And we were close, so I thought he might love me back... But there is nothing like seeing the boy you fancy kiss a maid to clear such silly notions."

"And Dorian would kill him," said Patience, nodding. "There's no man in England who has had more liaisons than the Duke of Luhst."

Chastity nodded. "Precisely. We could not be more different. His way is passion. My way is science. Not Lucien. Not marriage. And I never want children. So you see, it is quite liberating that I'm not attractive to men. Truly."

Patience shook her head. "I cannot fathom why a beautiful and smart woman would ever think of herself that way! You are a diamond of the first water. Any man would be lucky to have a drop of your attention. But...you both are attending Pryde's upcoming month-long house party. Will you manage?"

Chastity scoffed. "Of course I'll manage. It's a mere inconvenience with my research. Nothing more." She cleared her throat and put on a strict face. "Anyway, I would appreciate it greatly if you would read my findings so far and give your feedback." She pointed at a stack of handwritten papers lying on the tea table.

Patience agreed eagerly and then asked Chastity's opinion about her next hybridization project, the challenges and opportunities.

The two women spent the next hour discussing their projects and excitedly planning their new club, Chastity's earlier mishap all but forgotten. They were deep in discussion, giggling like schoolgirls, when a knock sounded at the door.

"Who is it?" Chastity called out, trying to stifle her laughter.

"It's Dorian," came the muffled reply. "Is everything all

right in there? I heard a loud noise earlier, and there is a strange odor in the hall."

Patience and Chastity exchanged a conspiratorial look. "Everything's fine, brother," Chastity called back. "Just a small accident in the lab. Nothing to worry about."

"Are you sure?" Dorian's voice was laced with concern. "I could come in and help clean up."

"No!" both women exclaimed in unison, dissolving into another fit of giggles.

"We have the situation under control, Dorian," Patience managed between laughs. "We are discussing women's matters. We'll see you at dinner."

There was a pause, then a sigh of resignation from the other side of the door. "You know it's not polite sending your husband away like this."

Patience's smile tugged at her lips. "Perhaps said husband may need to discipline such a rude wife…later?"

"I'm afraid measures must be taken," he said, and Patience's skin heated.

Chastity frowned. "She wasn't really rude, Dorian! Don't you dare hurt your pregnant wife."

Patience felt her cheeks flush as she turned to Chastity. "Oh, no, dearest, we've been just jesting. Right, Dorian?" she called.

"Of course," he called back, his muffled voice amused. "Sister, you know I'd never really— Er…all right, ladies. I'll leave you to it."

As Dorian's footsteps receded down the corridor, Patience and Chastity grinned at each other, their hearts light with the promise of their new adventure. The world may not always understand or appreciate their passion for science, but together, they would face any challenge that came their way.

For they were Misses with Microscopes, and nothing could stand in the way of their quest for knowledge and discovery.

EPILOGUE

Four months later...

Dorian inhaled the lungful of humid, warm air and didn't flinch. His fists didn't clench, and his stomach wasn't burning with the desire to destroy everything. He was in the glasshouse with the love of his life, the sun falling on his face through the leaves of a palm tree that almost reached the glass ceiling.

The door was closed.

Fig, lemon, and orange trees, bushes of hibiscus and other plants surrounded him, and he didn't feel trapped.

He felt at peace. And in love. He wrapped his arm around Patience's shoulders.

She wrapped her arm around his waist and leaned with her head against his shoulder as they walked down the aisle.

"Are you all right, love?" asked Patience. "Your palms aren't twitching to burn everything to the ground?"

He chuckled and kissed the top of her head.

"No," he said. "I have no need for that anymore. I have you."

She chuckled. "And you have someone who will very much need you in maybe three months."

He laid his hand on her growing stomach and a feeling like pure sunlight shot straight through him. A little foot or an elbow nudged against his palm and his face split in a grin. Patience gasped slightly and both of them laughed; he was swimming in the beauty of her blue eyes.

"It's the first time the baby kicked!" Patience exclaimed, putting her hand over her mouth. "Oh...what a wonderful, strange feeling!"

Dorian exhaled and kissed her lightly on her lips. "I quite agree."

They walked out of the glasshouse. The door gave in easily as there was no latch on it anymore. No one would ever have to fear being trapped inside again.

They walked into the garden she had transformed, just as she had allowed him to find the strength to transform himself into a man deserving the love of this beautiful woman. The woman he loved with every fiber of his being.

He chuckled as they walked down the white gravel path. Flowers bloomed around them, and the air smelled of roses, greenery, and nature. Bees buzzed about and butterflies flapped their colorful wings. Fruit trees as well as the young ash and chestnut and oak grew taller with every day. Dorian looked around and inhaled deeply, letting his body take in the beauty and relax.

He hadn't done his punishing morning routine for months now, and his body was recovering.

He had gained a little weight, the scabs on his hands had healed, and even though there were scars, his skin looked much healthier. He still rode Erebus with Titan trotting by their side, but only for pleasure. He would no longer exhaust himself or the animal. But he wanted to keep his physical strength and muscle tone, which he liked...

Especially given how much sexual prowess he needed to satisfy his and his wife's appetites.

He still did boxing, too, but he went out to London to box with Spencer, who needed a patient partner. Dorian enjoyed seeing his friend more regularly, especially now that they had even more in common.

"Come, let's sit by your roses," he suggested.

He led Patience towards the meadow in the very heart of the garden where her gorgeous roses were blooming, the color of blush against dark foliage.

"I love sitting here," he said. "This is my favorite place in the garden."

Patience rewarded him with one of her brightest smiles.

"Is it now, Duke?" she asked cheerfully.

He sat on the bench and placed her on his lap, one of his palms conveniently nestled under her plush, gorgeous arse.

She giggled. "Dorian..."

"No, there's no one here, darling," he whispered, his cock already waking up at the feel of her lush thighs touching him, at the feel of her round flesh under his palm. Her breasts were now right next to his mouth, and they were even bigger now that she was pregnant, and swelled so seductively above the neckline of the red gown she wore.

He leaned closer to the two lush orbs, opened his mouth, and licked one of them with his full tongue, then the other. She shuddered and he grinned.

Perhaps he didn't need to punish himself and his body anymore, didn't need to destroy and crash and thunder. But he needed her. He'd always need her.

And her breasts. And her arse. And her sex.

But, most of all, he'd always need her heart.

She was as bright as the sun, as colorful as this garden she'd created. As cheerful as spring.

And as resilient as a true queen.

"I love you, Patience," he murmured as he looked up into her face, searching her eyes. "I'm yours. Body and soul."

"And I'm yours," she whispered, her eyes suddenly serious. "And I love you," she said and kissed him.

God in heaven, how he loved it when she kissed him, when she took the initiative. He, who'd wanted control in every aspect of his life, found their lovemaking the most satisfying when she was the one deciding how, and when, and how intense. He loved sometimes just being a vessel for her pleasure. Seeing her fall apart—shake and shudder and mutter the naughtiest words from that angelic mouth—was one of his biggest pleasures these days.

He smiled as they kissed, and she leaned back, gently brushing her thumb over his smiling lips. "This sight is my favorite thing in the world," she said. "Your smile. Any particular reason you're smiling?"

"I was just thinking how far we've come," he said. "You came to me shy, obedient, so naive, so innocent. But now, you're so strong. A true duchess. A queen of your own kingdom. I'm so proud of you. Darkness doesn't scare you. You stopped running away from it and turned to face it."

"I was afraid of it, yes. I was afraid it would swallow me whole. But you were the darkness, and I fell in love with you. You showed me I could face it. You showed me by turning to it, it could became my strength."

He chuckled. "And you showed me I could turn to the light, too. I have been all about control. Controlling my rage. My beast. Exhausting myself. Punishing myself." He kissed her. "But I wanted to change for you. Because I fell in love with you, and I knew I didn't deserve you. Didn't deserve your love. Not just because of my rage but because of John. Because of what I did to him. And, strangely enough, the way to become the man you needed me to be wasn't to maintain control. It was to surrender."

She brushed her knuckles against his cheekbone, and he felt a shudder run through him. The wicked woman could make even such a gentle and innocent gesture sensual, calling forth his desire for her.

"I will be the proudest mother to your child, Dorian," she said softly, "because he or she will have the most amazing father."

He felt his heart swell with love, like a sea sponge filling with water, bigger and bigger, and bigger still. There was no limit to the love he had for his wife and would have for his child. "I don't know if I can be a good father," he said. "God knows, I never had a good example."

"That is exactly why you will be," she said, taking his face in both of her hands. "Because you're different from him in every single way."

His chest ached with some pain he didn't know, perhaps grief for the family he'd wished for but never had. Or for his own ruined childhood. "You're right, love," he said, placing soft kisses along her neckline. "I will make sure my son or daughter has everything. But most of all, that they have their mother. If they have you, they will have all they need."

"And you, darling," she whispered and kissed his lips. "Both of us. Darkness and light. You think I'm the soft one, but I'm sure the child will weave a rope around you!"

He wrapped his arms around her and held her tight, her and the life she was carrying inside. Part him, part her, a wonderful new person they would both love and cherish their entire lives.

"You're right, I would never do anything but try to make them happy. Just like you. I will never stop trying to make you happy."

"Oh, darling," she whispered. "You already have. All you need to do is just be yourself."

And as they kissed in the sunlight, next to her roses that were both strong and beautiful, he knew that she was right.

She was his center. His love. His breath. His spring.

His queen.

And all she needed to do to make him happy was just be herself.

***

Thanks for reading **DUKE OF RATH**. If you enjoyed Dorian and Patience's story, make sure to get your exclusive bonus epilogue here:

https://mariahstone.com/rath-bonus/

Don't stop here! To find out how our story continues, keep reading book 2 of our SEVEN DUKES OF SIN series: **DUKE OF LUHST**!

The rake who can charm any debutante finds himself captivated by the one scholarly spinster he can never have.

Read DUKE OF LUHST now >

More Beauty and the Beast Regency Romances?

If you love regency romances with a beauty and the beast vibe and haven't read Prestons and Penelope's story yet, be sure to pick up **ALL DUKE AND BOTHERED,** book 1 of my **DUKES AND SECRETS** Series.

Brooding Duke. Notorious rake. Driven by grief. Forcing his enemy's daughter into marriage for revenge. About to lose his heart...

★★★★★ *"Such a fascinating, well-written, well-paced and passionate enemies-to-lovers stories. Absolutely loved it!"*

Read ALL DUKE AND BOTHERED now >

Or stay with our loyal brotherhood of the Seven Dukes of Sin, and keep reading **DUKE OF LUHST** now.

ACKNOWLEDGMENTS

This book… this whole series was a great labor of love, and not just mine. Thank you to all my beta readers who generously read the roughest, unedited version of this book — Alexandra, Gloria, Fedy, Dezi — and gave their honest opinion on how to make it better. Thank you to my incredible team of editors — Laura Barth, Beth Attwood, and Leigh Teetzel. Thank you for your unwavering dedication, your advice, and your hard work. Laura is always with me on every step of the way of creating this series, and while writing is a lonely business, our brainstorming sessions where we often laugh and bounce ideas off each other are so precious to me. This series wouldn't be here without Skye Warren, my mentor and coach who encouraged, supported, and helped me develop this series. I still hear your words in my head… "You think there's a tiger in the room… There's no tiger." Finally, thank you to my husband, Michael, who keeps believing in me, supporting me, and inspiring me! Thank you for having the vision.

Thank you. I would never be here without you.

GET A FREE MARIAH STONE BOOK!

Join Mariah's mailing list to be the first to know of new releases, free books, special prices, and other author giveaways.

freehistoricalromancebooks.com

ALSO BY MARIAH STONE

MARIAH'S TIME TRAVEL ROMANCE SERIES

- Called by a Highlander
- Called by a Viking
- Called by a Pirate
- Fated

MARIAH'S REGENCY ROMANCE SERIES

- Dukes and Secrets
- Seven Dukes of Sin

VIEW ALL OF MARIAH'S BOOKS IN READING ORDER

Scan the QR code for all ebooks, paperbacks, and audiobooks.

ENJOY THE BOOK? YOU CAN MAKE A DIFFERENCE!

Please, leave your honest review for the book.
As much as I'd love to, I don't have financial capacity like New York publishers to run ads in the newspaper or put posters in subway.

But I have something much, much more powerful!

Committed and loyal readers

If you enjoyed the book, I'd be so grateful if you could spend five minutes leaving a review on the book's sales page.

Thank you very much!

ABOUT MARIAH STONE

Mariah Stone is a bestselling author of historical romance novels, including her popular Regency series Dukes and Secrets, her historical romance series Called by a Highlander and her hot Viking, Pirate, and Regency novels. With nearly one million books sold, Mariah writes about strong women falling in love with their soulmates across time. Her books are available worldwide in multiple languages in e-book, print, and audio.

Subscribe to Mariah's newsletter for a free historical romance book today at mariahstone.com/signup!

facebook.com/mariahstoneauthor
instagram.com/mariahstoneauthor
bookbub.com/authors/mariah-stone
pinterest.com/mariahstoneauthor
amazon.com/Mariah-Stone/e/B07JVW28PJ

Printed in Germany
by Amazon Distribution
GmbH, Leipzig